THE REDEMPTION OF GEORGE BAXTER HENRY

ACKNOWLEDGEMENTS:

I would like to express my gratitude and appreciation to the following people who all helped me in some way in the writing of this book: John Trainor, Rita Considine, Mary Kirwan, Sarah Moorehead, Mal & Sarah-Lyn McKenna, Siobhán Gaffney, Alan Dodd, Lilian Bell, David (at Elvis Presley Music Australia), Ray Lynn, Seamus Brett, Brendan Flynn, Cormac Kinsella, Susan Waine, Ronnie Robins, Hubert McDermott, Richard A. Lyng and all of the staff at Graceland. Thanks to Sylvia, Hannah, Charlie, Ruth and Zoe for their support and belief. Special thanks is due to Sharon O' Malley; who listened as the book was being hand-written. Finally I would like to thank Mary Honan, who has had an enormous role in bringing George Baxter Henry to life. Without you Mary; George might not even exist. Lots of love CB.

The Redemption of George Baxter Henry

CONOR BOWMAN

CLOCKWORK

PRESS

Published in 2008 by
CLOCKWORK PRESS,
AT 8-10 COKE LANE, SMITHFIELD, DUBLIN 7

www. clockworkpress.com

ISBN: 978-0-9548403-1-0
(The Redemption of George Baxter Henry & The Last Estate)

A catalogue record for this book is available from The British Library.

10 9 8 7 6 5 4 3 2 1

'Power of My Love'; Recorded by Elvis Presley in February 1969
at American Studios Memphis
Words and Music: Giant/Baum/Kaye
Lyric Reprint; by kind permission of Elvis Presley Music Publishing

ISKA FRIDGE NOTES: Written by Hannah Bowman

SOURCEBOOKS: The Book of Apples by Morgan & Richards 1993
The Book of the Apple By H. H. Thomas 1902

TYPESET BY: Linden Publishing Services in 11.5 on 15 point Quadraat
DESIGNED BY: Susan Waine
PRINTED IN IRELAND BY: Betaprint Limited, Dublin

For George N. Allen (1925-2007)
to whom I am related by ink.

Hey Dad

Adam's Pearmain;

Indispensible to every collection;

Fairly large, brisk flavor.
A good keeping variety.

Iska Appleby

Chapter One

THIS WHOLE FUCKING THING starts at twenty-five thousand feet over the Azores, or some place, with my seventeen-year-old son's head down the toilet. Don't believe me? You better batten down the latches (or whatever the fuck the phrase is) and listen up because every word is absolutely true. This story begins in a john on a 747. The noise was absolutely mind-blowing. People shouting and screaming and stewards and stewardesses (sometimes there's little enough difference) shooping past each other in the aisles trying to formulate some plan to extricate Billy's head from the toilet bowl.

My son Billy (*our* son, sorry Honey) is a genius. At least that's what he keeps telling us. He plays drums in a college band called East Pole and, in between writing suicidal lyrics and hammering the shit out of his drum kit, he flunks history exams in a two-bit college for social welfare veterans (and other categories of unwanted citizens) in Lancing, Idaho. This should *never* be confused with the Michigan State capital of the same name. This place is an afterthought belonging to a backwater in the middle of absolutely nowhere you'd ever want to intentionally go or stay. This is the sort of place the word 'remote' was invented for. Anyway, with report cards saying 'could do better' and straight 'A's in absenteeism and disinterest, Billy and his prospects were already heading for the toilet even before we caught the plane at JFK. Billy had to be dragged into school on his first day at the age of five and he's still running from education. Like a giant rabbit, who's supposed to like lettuce and carrots but actually prefers cocktails and steak, our son has been kicking against his genes since he was old enough to vomit deliberately. He got into this pathetic repository for educationally challenged drifters because of his scholarship-winning entrance exam. (This *scholarship* consisted of rooms on campus on a first-come first-served basis at a 10% reduction. Whoopee!)

The other factor which clinched his place on the course (Bolivian History, 1811-1814) was a fifty-thousand-dollar donation from guess-fucking-who? (You've guessed it). The other benefit for yours truly was a brass plate with my name on a bench in the colonnades outside the college library. The George Baxter Henry seat; rest your ass on that! In a hundred years they'll still be sitting on me, shifting their lard-filled rear ends from side to side and coughing loudly to mask their flatulence. Great! Before you get ahead of yourself and start thinking you're the first to notice it, yes I am in fact a lawyer and, yes, my initials *are* GBH! In Europe they find it funny, like in England with the crime of Grievous Bodily Harm and a TV series with the acronym as its title. When you're fifty-one, and have haemorrhoids the size of golf balls every August, your initials are way down the list of priorities, believe you me.

Anyway, Billy had two main problems in the summer of 1999. His band had come to the attention of a major label in New York called Carnivore Records. Sounds great, but there's a snag. Billy was only seventeen and the label wanted his signature so he needed the consent of his parents. What father could stand in the way of a multi-album deal which might secure his child's financial future? You're looking at him. The second problem Billy had was a little less negotiable than securing my signature; he was a coke addict. Now while most rock stars only go off the rails and burn themselves out *after* a couple of hits, Billy managed to do all this in

8

advance of even getting the deal. What a trooper! He'd seen the path to riches and was actively practicing one of its primary constituent elements. Who could thwart the path of such a genius? Once more, look here. On the way to the airport, he was kicking up again about having to come to Europe with us.

'Why can't I stay here and rehearse with the band?'

'What's to rehearse?' I said. 'I thought you made it up as you went along?'

'In your dreams, Dad. Look, Hairy and Joe are renting this room in New York, like, a rehearsal studio. The label are paying for the whole thing. It's, like, a development deal where we just jam for a couple of hours a day and then when we go in to record the album, they use the tapes as, like, a template for the songs.'

'The Beatles used to record a whole album in about forty minutes. They didn't need to blow someone else's budget or rent rehearsal studios in New York."

'That was different, Dad. They had so little time. I mean, studios were hardly invented then. It was rush, rush, rush.'

'They had talent Billy. Don't tell me Sergeant Pepper's was simply the product of lucky studio engineering.'

'I bet they didn't have parents who were blocking their paths on the road to stardom.'

'I bet their parents didn't have children who snorted more coke than the whole of San Francisco in their first year in college.'

'Do we have to go over all of this again, Dad? I told you I've quit, I'm clean.'

'You could tell me you're Superman's shrink and I'd believe you sooner.'

'You think I'm lying?' His flat nose twitched and I knew he was lying. 'You'd never get that story past a jury,' I said.

'How would you know? You haven't fought a trial for thirty years.' That was my mother-in-law, Muriel, beside Billy in the back of the limo. We'll get to her later.

'Four weeks of clean urine or no signature, that's the deal. Take it or leave it, Billy.'

'I hate France,' Billy retorted.

'No, you don't. You hate yourself, you hate mowing the lawn, you hate goat's milk, but you don't hate France. You've never even been there, you know nothing about it.'

'I know that I'm gonna hate it. They weren't even in the Vietnam war.' I didn't reply; I was tempted to say something derogatory about Bolivia.

'I *am* clean,' said Billy, folding his arms across a t-shirt that said, "Vote No to Democracy."

'Four weeks, Billy, that's what's required.' I closed the subject.

Billy may have been clean in the limo but by the time *we* hit twenty four thousand feet over the Azores, *he* was at about fifty thousand feet himself. He tried to escape from the plane via the toilet or something. Anyway, he made the steward's day when he presented a denim rear view to the main aisle of the 747. After he'd been rescued from the john, by three of the crew, he was given a sedative and slept for the rest of the journey.

'Has your son taken any non-prescription medication?' a smiling hostess in a horrible red uniform asked politely.

'Oh no, of course not,' I replied. 'He inhaled the lot from humming an Eric Clapton song by accident. What do you think?'

At best, the four clean weeks would have to start when we landed in Nice. There were a thousand toilets between now and our return flight at the end of September.

The US is a pretty fucked up place. Everybody knows that. It's a given; like tax return audits and the curse of Hello magazine. We have the greatest country in the world; so we're the biggest and the best at everything. We have enormous buildings, the most trailer parks per capita, the craziest TV shows, the most expensive military, and, of course, when it comes to being fucked up we're way out front too. Don't get me wrong, I love my country, I'm just smart enough to realize it doesn't love me back. This whole music thing with Billy has brought it home to me more than ever. I mean ever since his damn band attracted the mitts of one of the biggest record companies in the world, the phones at Schwartz, McNaghten, Stamp and Henry just hadn't given it a rest. A couple of days before we left for vacation two of their "Executive Vice-Presidents" came to Boston to plead with me for my signature. Oh yeah, I forgot to tell you. The record company don't know squat about the white stuff; they just think Billy has a permanent flu. Figure that out from the country that gave us "Gesundheit" (or was that Peru?).

Anyhow, these two morons land in my office on a Wednesday afternoon of all days (I'll tell you about that later too). They looked like two Mormon evangelizers; Elder Smarter and Elder Younger. They stood on the carpet shifting their glances from each other back to me before I decided to break the ice.

'Talk to me, Fellas. I got a plane to catch on Saturday.'

'Mr Henry.' The older guy took up the chase.

'Yes?'

'Carnivore are one of the biggest record companies in the world.'

'In the *whole world*,' echoed his partner.

'Now that scares a lot of people.'

'Do I look worried?' I grinned. They looked at each other and then back to me. The younger guy caught the pass and kept running.

'We don't mean that *you* are scared. What we are saying is that we know you have concerns, and, no matter what those concerns are, we're here to take care of them.'

'Yes, to address them.' Jeff followed Mutt. They looked like two guys who had managed to hit the potty first time. A satisfied pall settled over them.

'Great,' I said. 'How are you on environmental planning-code violations?' They had to figure out, through a series of exchanged shrugs and glances, that this was a joke. They smiled together. I could see that they *couldn't* see they were getting nowhere. I sent out a few hints.

'Don't miss your train to Logan.' They still didn't register.

'Mr Henry,' the now-fatigued older Mormon tried to re-open the conversation, 'I suppose you're curious about how a corporation as large as ours can still offer to give every band-'

'-And band member,' Dopey helped.

'Yes, of course, and each band member, individual attention and care so as to maximize their longevity as an act and their integrity as an artist?'

The old "integrity as an artist" line. I was ready to puke. Who the hell did they think would buy baloney in such quantities? Not old GBH, I don't mind telling you.

'Nope, I have no interest in any of that. The whole George Michael thing cleared up all the fuzz around those particular concerns for me. There's nothing I want to ask you, no concerns, no paternal worries about how 'integrity' and 'artist' come to be mixed up in one single phrase you feel like peddling to me in my own office.'

'But, surely, you've discussed with Billy how his choice, and of course *your* choice, may affect the band. Timing is everything in the music industry, I mean what's in vogue today may not even get regional play next week, Mr Henry.' Elder Smarter tried to come the heavy. He was woofing up the wrong tree.

'Would you say that the US is ahead of Europe as far as music is concerned?' I asked the question in a tone I usually reserved for waitresses who'd got the order wrong.

'Sure, yeah, definitely.'

'Ab-so-lutely.' Dopey found his echo voice on repeat-sentiment-but-vary-text mode.

'Weeks ahead?'

'Oh sure, I mean, like months, you know?'

'I didn't know that but I'm delighted to hear it, Gentlemen.

Because it seems as if East Pole should still be a 'hot ticket', I believe the phrase is, when we meet EMI in Paris on Monday, even if they've already gone out of fashion in New York by then.'

I stood up, dismissing them with an extension of my hand for a warm shake. They both bore the 'oh fuck' expression common to their species when out-flanked, and reached for their cell phones simultaneously as they exited the room. I was sure we'd upped the ante on whatever deal they would now offer. Billy would never appreciate my actions, even if I could get him to stop lashing his drumskins long enough to think about it.

I called my secretary, Judy, on the intercom.

'Yes, Mr Henry? I *have* checked the library for that LA Times article in 1930. I've copied it and put one in the safe and the other in your red folder.'

'Great, Judy, I'll read it on the plane. But there's something else I need you to do. Get on to Rex Verdmin in London. Ask him to put a call through to Carnivore Records' legal department in New York. Tell him to ask for a copy of East Pole's development deal contract.'

'You got it, Mr Henry.'

A bit of interest from London would have them pooping in their Lexus.

Same old same old. You know, I hate it when people talk bullshit and pretend it doesn't stink. I overheard some jerk in a restaurant lately talking about how great Chicago was and how the all-seater stadium was standing room only for the home games. Work that out! Of course, the place is empty for the fucking away games! Duh.

'We have a little joke, like a special thing we say in Chicago. You know, when we're not going to be at the office. We say, "Oh, I have an appointment with the *doctor* today," (he winks) "Doctor Wrigley." He laughs and his companion throws him a look that says either, "Take me home and bonk me rigid" or, "What?" He sniggers again and lowers his voice. 'You see Wrigley is the name of the park and so when you say *doctor*, I have an appointment at the "Doctor Wrigley," (wink, wink) *Everybody* knows what you mean.'

I wonder what people in Chicago say when they're sick and going to see a real doctor? Maybe, "Hey, I got a game to play this afternoon, I'm shortstop down at the hospital." Or some stupid thing like that.

Those two morons from the label ought to meet *that* prick and they could all go to Dr. Wrigley's together and bore each other instead of me. You got these guys back from the Gulf War, and suddenly their asthma charts make a more interesting topic of conversation than these twits from Chicago, twittering on about the "doctor".

Billy discovered cocaine around the time most teenage boys are swapping Palmelo Hand for a real grope. Some kid from the other side of the river brought a couple of lines in his knapsack to summer camp and there you go. While other people's children were being busted for taking their old man's car out without a license, Billy was doing lines of coke on top of the dashboard while his contemporaries were exchanging pieces of ass in the back seat. It got so his nose was red all the time and that's what tipped us off. I mean the blank stares, the glazed eyes, the lethargy and the frequent uncontrollable fits of laughing or diarrhoea had all been part of Billy's repertoire since third grade, so how were we to know it was drugs? Apparently, half of the stuff is cut with Italian laxatives to give you a run for your money. There's a little piece of Colombia that should have a plaque to Billy Stanisulaus Henry, saying, "I'm dreaming of a white Christmas, and Easter and Thanksgiving and Halloween." God bless the cartels and General Noriega.

I suppose I should reveal a little of myself here and say that, on a social level and from the point of view of family aesthetics, I would prefer my kids to do cocaine rather than crack or heroin. At least we were able to give Billy the opportunities we never had ourselves. There were no syringes and shared needles. Out-of-date credit cards and a flat surface was all it took to send Billy on his way. Our family doctor, Dr. Volt of the Cantronelli Medical Centre, put our minds at ease about Billy's addiction. 'He's unlikely to contract AIDS with this habit.' This was an enormous consolation to me as a parent. My wife, Pearl, however, was alarmed by the mention of the 'A' word.

'AIDS? I thought only homosexual-intravenous-drug-taking Africans could get that.' She was as alarmed as a cat that hears of a slump in the value of mouse shares.

'Well, to a degree, you're correct in your analysis, Mrs Henry.' (There was no way he was going to risk losing a twenty-thousand-a-year insurance-plan family like ours). 'Many of the categories of person you've described are indeed in the high risk bracket but what I'm saying is that Billy is in that particular grouping of...'

'Drug addicts?' I helped.

'Yes, yes. Billy is in a grouping who have a high likelihood of non-contraction.'

A "high likelihood of non-contraction," What the hell is that for a social category? It sounds like an anti-pregnancy lobby. I thought of Iska, our daughter, named after the Apache word for water, because of the associated complications her home birth might have brought. Pearl was pressurized by her mother to try the 'natural method' with our second child, but declined, thank Christ. The 'natural method' is too horrific to go into; but, by way of analogy, it's a bit like inviting your local butcher to slaughter his herd in your front room just so you can have a piece of beef for your Sunday lunch. Ever wondered why there's no such thing as natural dentistry? Anyhow, I digress, back to old Doctor Volt; he, of course, had the perfect solution to Billy's problem.

'There's a clinic in Lebanon, PA, Mr and Mrs. Henry. It houses a facility called the Youth Outreach Realignment Scheme. Billy would be met at the airport by an addiction marshal who would provide one-on – one buddy contact for the eight-week program which –'

'How much?' I asked, cutting across him.

'How much success? Well in percentile terms the recidivism rate compares...'

'I meant how much does the fucking treatment cost? I don't need to hear how other people's children got on,' I snapped.

'Oh.' He appeared, for the first time in his life, embarrassed to talk about money. 'Thirty-five thousand dollars,' he whispered and then, remembering the best thing of all about it. 'That *does* include meals.'

Let me tell you, I've had it up to fucking here with doctors. The *only* guarantee every patient of every doctor has, is that sooner or later they're gonna die. If every car was definitely gonna crash who'd ever buy one? I didn't swallow old Voltometer's pitch for that over-reaching reassignment thing in Pennsylvania. Let's get it straight; there's very little in my book that medical science can ever hope to achieve with thirty-five thousand bucks, that the average parent can't match with some bulk-bought Tylenol and a little creativity around the house.

When we landed in Nice, the heat rushed up at us from the tarred runways and seeped into the airport through inch-thick glass as we headed for the baggage carousel. Billy was still half-asleep, but we managed to sit him on top of the luggage trolley as we headed for the customs post. I saw a policeman with a German Shepherd nosing around a couple of people's bags. I immediately panicked and thought of Billy's suitcase. God only knew what he'd packed. I imagined for a moment that the suitcase would be opened to reveal a mountain of white powder which would cover the dog from head to paw as it toppled over under the weight of its one hundred-percent Columbian coat. The dog, I reckoned, was an addict too. He looked at Billy and woofed and then hung his tongue out to lick Billy's hand. Billy stood there with his own tongue hanging out, and they looked strangely kindred for a few intimate seconds before the tranquillity of the airport hum was shattered by the clatter of dozens of silver spoons cascading out of a holdall belonging to a passenger going through the green channel.

'It's not the France I remember," my mother-in-law criticized, as two backpackers edged through her rather than around her.

'Of course it's not,' I assisted. 'They've got cars now and the Revolution is over.' My wife, Pearl, who had not spoken to me for nearly two weeks, suddenly broke her vigil.

'Mother is ninety-one, you know, George. I wish you'd try to show some respect for at least *one* of the girls in this family every once in a while.'

'Don't cry, Dear,' Muriel auto-suggested her daughter into floods of wailing in the most public place you could imagine. 'George doesn't mean to be nasty and unfaithful, it's just his way.' She smiled a grin which tempted me to spit at her but I was afraid I might miss.

'C'mon, Dad.' My daughter tugged at my arm. 'Billy's just been sick on the trousers of the metal detector man. I think we should catch up.'

'I'm trying,' I said, at the coal-face of weariness and still ever vigilant that the goons from the record label might have followed us. I looked around; no sign. My mother-in-law was in top form now, smiling inanely at people like she thought they recognized her from the big screen. My ass they did. Pearl, meanwhile, gave me a look which said 'Get the luggage' and 'Why did we ever marry?' in one fell swoop.

When you plan your own retirement, make sure it doesn't include your family. Half of them will bleed you dry in a second and embarrass you from toilet to arrivals lounge, in any fucking language you care to try, while the other half subject you to the silent treatment for the slightest perceived transgression. At least we'd arrived and were all in one piece. Just as long as Billy's nose stayed attached to his face.

Dad,

Found a great book about
cidar apples

'The Mystery of Husbandry
Discovered and layd open'.
(from 1675)

Love from gska

Chapter Two

W E WERE PRETTY LATE starting a family. I don't deny that. You can't ever be too late starting because, to be honest, children are the cosmic method of reminding you of the frailty of human existence and the inadequacy of man's earning potential. You can lose the run of yourself with a credit card or a check book every once in a while, but it's all controllable ultimately; you nip and tuck next month's earnings to compensate and you learn from the experience when there's just you. With children (and a wife who has an equity share in your law firm) it's completely different. It's like having an army of robbers out there with unlimited access to your private finances and absolutely no way of slowing them down. It's like wearing a sign around your neck that says, "my Personal Identification Number is 543210 and, by the way, I'm not home right now, so why don't you call round and trash the fucking house as well." It's actually worse than that, because every night the thieves come home to your house and have their own rooms and enjoy unlimited access to your fridge as well. You know the Catholic kick about never saying you can't afford more children? It's bullshit. Children are the single greatest drain on the world's finances after global warming and oil-slick clean-up costs. The most blatant lawyer/client rip-off is only in the shadows when compared to the financial fraud visited on parents by their children.

Thankfully, Pearl has her limits in the spend department. She's as prone to a crazy bout of retail therapy as the next woman, but she's pretty sensible about it. She knows that if she kicks the golden goose in the balls, eventually the goose may cough up blood instead of dollars. With children, there's no endgame, no realization that the supply is finite. As far as they're concerned, it's win, win, win. They didn't ask to be born so you pay for that. You want the best for them, so you pay for that, and, best of all, they hate you and you want them to love you, so you pay for that too. Stick a dunce hat on me and call me Chase Manhattan! Jeez.

Let me tell you about Iska. She's fourteen and the doctors told us she'd always be a 'little slow'. What's the big deal with that? I mean traffic from Brooklyn to Central Park is often a 'little slow' but it gets there in the end. I never could figure out what they meant by that phrase. Were we to start believing that something was wrong and, if it was *how* wrong would that be? Iska was an identical twin and the other girl died about a day after they were born. We were told that if we'd gone the home-birth route we'd almost certainly have lost Iska as well. Iska weighed two and half pounds and was eight weeks early. Doesn't sound slow to me. It was like she couldn't get here fast enough. Do you know who I think was a 'little slow'? The fucking gynaecologist. I mean he told us that it was a single pregnancy. I interpreted the scan and said, "hey, it looks like two in there." He gave me a look that said, "fuck you *and* I know you're a lawyer," but he changed his tune when the assistant, who was, like, only printing out the damn thing, put him right. How big of a moron would someone have to be before *you'd* let him poke his hands up your wife? What do most of them have, besides a med-school certificate and an office the size of Las Vegas? Very little if you ask me.

Like I said before, (I hope), I hate doctors, they're worse than lawyers. At least we don't drop the hand on our clients and then pretend it's all part of the service. Doctors are probably the most depraved bunch of qualified people anywhere. They have the power over life and death. It's just shades of incompetence which decide the details. "A little slow," my joystick.

I do want to make the subtle distinction here between medical negligence and medical negligence lawsuits. One is a reprehensible side-effect of an inadequate medical care system, and the other is the legitimate pursuit of constitutional rights by perhaps the last of the truly caring professions. There, I've got that off my chest.

Anyhow, Iska arrived safe and sound and continues to confound the text-book fucking doom and gloom prophesies that surrounded her entry into our world. In kindergarten, she outshone all of her competitors in that cosseted world of the rules and philosophy of Maria Mussolini, with novel learning-methods and endless games of point-out-the-plastic-fruit.

For the last two years or so, Iska's been researching for a book she intends writing about apples. Every couple of days, she leaves me notes about her latest discovery pinned to the refrigerator by magnets. She signs them 'Iska Applebee,' so I know who they're from. It's just a thing she does. I mean, half the time I don't understand the notes but I *do* read them and, yeah, I hang onto them for God-knows why. I guess Freud, or even Dr Volt, would make a connection between those notes and some basic disfunction in our own household. Find me a family devoid of disfunction and I'll show you bunch of lying medics living together in some parallel universe.

Anyway, we land in Nice and, in about thirty seconds, my temperature is higher than Mount fucking Rushmore. The city is bang in the middle of the biggest taxi strike the world has ever seen. There's lines of the bastards sitting in their air-conditioned rip-off-mobiles with their engaged signs on and nobody's getting a ride anywhere. I have to say that they're the same the world over these guys; insidious money-grabbing-know-all-road-ragers in every city or town you visit. Why is it that only people with criminal records and brain damage (that lethal cocktail) are allowed to drive cabs?

'I thought you'd organized a car, George.' Mother-in-law kicks the situation closer to the sewer.

'I tried, but they were all out of hearses.' I smile.

Pearl gives me the cold shoulder again in the heat. Iska's left us baking on the sidewalk and she returns a minute later with a smart-looking man in a blue uniform.

'This is Philippe,' she says. 'He's going to drive us to the place.'

'Who is this guy?' Billy wakes up for the first time in about two months.

'He's a driver from one of the hotels in Monte Carlo. He's just finished for the weekend and he'd love a bit of private work.' Iska smiles at the cute guy from Monte Carlo and then talks in some strange language. (It has to be French). We all hit the sidewalk with our jaws and then he starts loading the bags back onto a trolley and indicates for to us to follow him. About fifty yards down behind the Neanderthal cab-strike he's got a mini-bus and packs the trunk with our collective junk and opens the door of the bus for us. Cool manufactured air whacks us and Billy looks like he's just done a line.

'This is worse than LA,' the ninety-one year-old witch remarks as we are stuck in traffic just outside the airport. This is a swipe at me because I'm from LA. Nobody ever admits to being from LA (except me). Everyone is either from Jersey and just passing through, or they're from San Jose or they're waitressing their way to an Oscar. Me? I'm from LA and proud of it.

We edge out of the traffic and across some motorway junction and suddenly we're in the country with scorched grass and signs for Antibes. We're heading north and away from the sea. Maybe this is a good time to tell you a few things about LA and our family.

My mother-in-law, Muriel Hale, was a movie star in the twenties and thirties. She was nominated for an Oscar as Best Supporting Actress in 1930 but, thank Christ (and the Academy), she didn't win. The film was called "Turn Left at Brooklyn Bridge" and was a box-office flop. Muriel starred opposite some poor unfortunate called William Craw who was never heard of again. God only knows how she got the nomination, but, anyway, she never stops telling us about it. Born plain old Muriel Meek, she changed her name to copper-fasten her star status. I never heard of anyone so inappropriately maiden-named as Muriel Meek. She's about as goddamned meek as a Panzer Division. When those bible people said the meek would take over the world, I bet most people thought they were kidding. To get a clear picture of my precious mother-in-law in your head, think Godzilla meets Margaret Thatcher and they have a child! I bet the whole movie industry got shivers up its ass when she was nominated for an Oscar. Muriel wears so much make-up now she'd be a shoo-in for an award for special effects.

So the thing about LA is that she lived there for movie star reasons. But I'm *from* there, so she looks down on me. The stuck-up cricket, who does she think she is? So, anytime she can she puts LA down and, with it, yours truly.

'Elvis had a house in LA,' I remark, as a comeback to her comment at the airport half an hour earlier. 'Family is family.' She doesn't take the bait but looks at Pearl and shakes her head to convey thirty years of mother-in-law-ship disappointment. The driver picks up on the Elvis reference and asks Iska if she likes Elvis Presley. She grins a 'yes' back and he touches the button on the CD player; 'Suspicious Minds'. Absolutely fantastic. I sing along.

Muriel's husband, Louie, who died in 1970, was a third cousin twice-removed of Elvis's father's (Vernon) second wife: Dee Stanley. It was about as far removed as you could be, but it absolutely infuriated Pearl's mother because it meant that there was a rival genetic line to greatness in the family.

Muriel detested mention of the singer and became particularly irate at any reference to the family connection. None of us had ever met Elvis, but Pearl and I saw him in concert in Indianapolis in 1977. I told Muriel once that I'd sent a note to Elvis, via the concert promoter, telling him some relatives were in the audience and mentioning her name just to press home the advantage. Elvis died shortly afterwards and I often told Muriel not to blame herself.

'He probably just couldn't live with the fact that there was another huge star in the family,' I said one Christmas Day, helping things along in the seasonal spirit.

'Don't patronize me, George,' she retorted. 'He was never nominated for an Oscar was he?'

'No, but he probably got paid a lot more for each movie than you made in an entire career spanning, what would it be, eighty years?'

'Twenty years. I gave up the screen because I wanted to concentrate on my family.'

'Perhaps you should have ignored them a little more, Muriel. Maybe they'd have turned out normal.'

'Normal? What is normal, George? A man who spends years qualifying as a lawyer and then develops trial-phobia? Is that normal, George?'

Of course I'd never sent a note to the King at the concert at all but, from time to time, I'd reverse-revive the story and start blaming myself for his death. That drove her bananas. We had a dog for about ten years whose real name was Chirpy but whom I insisted on calling Old Shep. It drove Muriel crazy to be reminded of the Elvis 'connection' so you can take it that I never missed an opportunity to do just that. One year I rang every Elvis Fan-Club I could find through a business name search and asked them to mail a membership form to Muriel. It got so she began to rip up her mail without even opening it and destroyed at least one check from her retirement policy. We don't really get on.

I have one brother called Paul Cezanne Henry and he lives in Detroit where he runs an auto-repairs dealership. The thing is my mom saw a painting by Van Gogh which she hated in some bridal magazine and set about trying to find a name for her new arrival which would be a statement against Van Gogh! What was that all about? Van Gogh probably wasn't even alive in the 1950's. If it had been a girl it was going to be Marnie Renoir Henry so that the other option wouldn't be extinguished in case of future offspring. Go figure. Dad died in 1956 of old age at thirty-eight. (That's what they told me, and it was never revised up or out). I never knew him really. My mom got a heart attack and died in the Cedar Sinai Hospital while visiting a neighbour who subsequently made a full recovery. For obvious reasons, our family never entered flower shows or crossword competitions. At my mom's funeral some horrible priest, who didn't know her at all, gave a sermon in which he kept referring to her as "Karen" (her name was Katherine). So there's a fair quantity of death in our families but very little of it in the zones I'd hoped for. Muriel looks like living another couple of hundred years. In a way, I couldn't care less if she outlived me. At least I'd have a couple of quiet years before she joined me in Hell.

Pearl. Well, where do I start? We met at High School in Malibu and dated for a while then broke up and didn't meet for ten or twelve years. We married when we were both on the rebound, so you can imagine the combined velocity there. She'd been to college in Wyoming and had majored in sewing or something. Maybe that's unfair, it was domestic economics with a final year thesis on the role of knitting in Government Defense budgeting. We met up again in a bar in Los Angeles when she was escaping from accompanying her mother to an Oscar Ceremony, where everyone who'd made Schlock-buster failures in the previous two hundred years was invited for cocktails and a chance to see some real talent pick up their awards.

We got married in Palm Springs and Lucille Ball was the only real celebrity at the wedding besides Muriel. Gregory Peck was supposed to come, but he was at a film festival somewhere in Europe promoting "The Omen". Maybe he could have worked his exorcizing skills on Muriel. We'll never know now. We moved to Boston in '79 and I became a partner in Schwartz, McNaghten &

Stamp in 1982, the year that Billy was born. When Iska arrived in 1985 she was a bit of a surprise, but then what pregnancy isn't a surprise. Plus, we were lucky to have her at all, with the twin stuff I mentioned earlier. Pearl and I got on well for most of the time and when I needed money to outbid Herby Dykeman, for partner, Muriel advanced her daughter most of her inheritance in exchange for a cash payola of a sum equal to 60% of my share in the firm, on top of alimony, if we ever got divorced (Muriel's idea). It sounded like a good deal for me at the time. I was young and in debt, you know what I mean?

I've heard people say that the reason a bride smiles walking down the aisle is because she knows she'll never have to give another blow-job in her entire life. I can't agree with that, but I will say that Pearl grinned broadly on the return flight from our honeymoon in Hawaii and I'm now re-evaluating the genesis of her contentment. What can I say? You marry in good faith, you gel in good times, and every now and then, when the cracks appear, you paper them over with a mixture of realism and regret and get fucking on with it. At least that's the theory. We've been through a lot together and we're twenty-three years married last April. We have two cars and a summerhouse in Martha's Vineyard. Some bastard reintroduced skunks to the island some time ago and now you walk around on tip-toe waiting for the fucking stink to appear and you have to bathe your dog in tomato juice to get rid of the smell when they've been sprayed, or whatever method it is skunks employ to make their mark.

Anyway, skunks aside, we usually make the best of our stay on MV, spending a little time together. Usually it works, but, over the years the fireworks have taken a bit longer each summer to dry out and stoke up if you know what I mean? Three years ago we reached breaking point when Billy threw an axe at a skunk from the upstairs window and missed, but killed the Labrador next door. Now the neighbour's place is up for sale and the emotional distress of their kids is the subject of litigation. That's what I call an abuse of the legal system. Why didn't they just have the funeral and then buy another mutt? Some people, all they want is to extend their own grief and wallow in it by flashback for as long as they fucking can. Needless to say, their over-reaction impinged on our stay as well and suddenly it's the freeze-out from them and Pearl and I find myself having to justify Billy to everybody, including himself.

'Dad, do you think dogs go to heaven?' (This was *before* he discovered cocaine, if you can credit it).

'You mean what will happen to Grandma when she dies?'

'No, the dog next door.'

'The lady whose mutt you beheaded?'

'No, no Dad, I mean the fucking Labrador.'

'Don't use language like that when your grandmother's not around. I told you once, I've told you a million times, Billy.'

What I'm really saying about Pearl is that, well, frankly, we stopped having sex about five years ago. There have been a couple of incidents of congress since; but usually we fly solo and sleep soundly. I don't think she misses it at all and, as each year passed, I was kinda forgetting what it all looked or felt like myself too. People say marriage isn't all roses but I'd go further and say it's mostly bills and parent/teacher meetings with a little pasta and misunderstanding thrown in. What keeps people together? What drives them apart? Damned if I know.

This family trip to France was planned at short notice. The catalyst was really a single incident about a month earlier when Pearl found out that I was having an affair, every Wednesday afternoon, with one of the girls in the translation service on the ninth floor of the building where Schwartz, McNaghten, Stamp and Henry bill clients by the hour. Now, I know a lot of people run the stock excuses about extra-marital sex (or in my case just sex) when they're caught, like, "she means nothing to me" or, "I'm sorry, Honey, it's not that there's something wrong with you; this is about me." Take it from me; that's wholesale bullshit at a knockdown price. As far as I'm concerned, I went elsewhere to get something that had dried up at home. It was either that or sleazy cinemas and hookers. So I chose the hump-kitten from the translation service on the ninth floor.

If I'm so goddamn frank about the reasons for my infidelity, why didn't I have the balls (don't even go there) to tell Pearl about it before she found out? The oldest reason in the world; the fear of having a divorce-court trigger the post-nuptial equity sale bargain struck when I became partner. (Well, maybe not verbatim the oldest reason in the world, but close). Was I putting her feelings first and hoping that what she didn't know wouldn't bother her? Absolutely not. If it weren't for the money thing, I'd have walked out on Pearl after the Ark docked. Naw, scratch that. Sure, I had feelings for her, but maybe sometimes people just drift apart and, by the time you notice it, they're outta sight. Who knows?

How did Pearl find out about the affair? Take a guess. Old prehistoric Miss Marple suspected something was going on and, to protect her daughter's honour, hired a P.I. to sneak around behind my back and do the dirty on me. How low is that? So she takes a couple of snapshots and next thing an envelope appears at breakfast and Pearl and Muriel sit at the other end of the table, one crying, the other gloating (you figure who's who). I open the flap and a shot of my own ass greets me, poking away at Gloria who is fluent in Greek and Urdhu. It's not the most flattering image of me available in the known world, but it did the trick. I turn the photo upside down and feign confusion as long as I think I can get away with it.

'Pearl wants a divorce, George.' Muriel smirks.

'No I don't,' Pearl said, sobbing.

'Shut up, Pearl. She wants a divorce.'

It's clear who's in the driver's seat here. I don't even dare try the, "I-can-explain-routine". What's to explain? My ass is in the air and in pretty good focus.

'Now, George.' Muriel sniffs the air to convey measured disappointment rather than anger. 'You have two choices. One; you can move out today and nominate a firm to handle the divorce for you and sort out Pearl's sixty percent share of your partnership holding, plus alimony and child support and leave the family home or...two; you ditch the twenty-year-old tongue queen and attend counseling with a mediator to save your marriage.'

'What was option one again?' I ask. Pearl shifts the sobbing into fifth gear and her mom puts an arm around her shoulders in a gesture that says, "I won't let the rabid dog near you". So, we do counseling.

The prick attempting to superglue our relationship back together looks like a Chinese version of Bill Gates. From the get-go, I sense that he may be an even bigger prick than he looks.

'Have either of you ever used sex toys? Or "sex aids" as they're known in the trade.'

'Which trade?' I ask. 'The sex toy industry or counseling?' Pearl is embarrassed. It's hard to gauge why exactly, but old mediator-counselor-accuser is not about to give in.

'No one enjoys a joke more than myself, George. But unless we are all focused on goals here, I won't be able to help you and Earl get through your problems.'

'Pearl,' I corrected.

'Excuse me?'

'Her name is Pearl, not Earl. It's like the oyster thing. Okay?' He ignored my admonition and we were right back in jargonsville with vibrators and blow-up dolls. He continued in the intrusive question vein and eventually, when we'd established that neither of us had used them, David (Yong) produced some samples from a drawer and ran through each by description, like he was telling us how to assemble an inhaler or giving the safety speech on an aircraft.

'This is a multi-speed vibrator,' he said, as he picked up a gold-coloured slim model which looked like a cigar holder. He switched it on and it sat there on the table buzzing like a wasp and twitching slowly like an uncertain compass. We saw all the various shapes and sizes and contraptions and equipment with enough straps and buckles to fit out a herd of greyhounds. By the end of the first half hour, the table was barely visible under the weight of buzzing vibrators and fur-lined handcuffs. Whatever happened to good old straight sex? I was exhausted looking at the stuff and, instead of seeing ideas to spice up our lives back home and getting turned on in any way, I began to wonder if in fact the whole collection actually belonged to Mr Yong for his own gratification.

We discussed my infidelity and I was encouraged to "own" my behaviour.

'Of course I *own* it,' I replied. 'I'm talking about my own infidelity. How can that not be mine?' Ownership apparently was a couple of steps ahead of that place.

'We can have something belong to us and yet not *own* it,' David, the prick, said patronizingly, with a smile which revealed expensive dental care.

'Oh I see, like listening but not hearing,' I threw out the line. He grabbed it and sent it racing up his ass with the buzzers and twitches.

'Ex-act-ly, George. That is ex-act-ly what I mean.'

'Like looking but not seeing.' I pushed the boat right out into the rapids. David Yong leaned forwards towards us and, resting his elbows on the table between some handcuffs and double headed dildos, tapped his fingertips and said.

'We are all in the same zone now. Let's move forward together shall we? Stepping carefully to avoid the traps and hazards we *can* push through to the other side.'

'Ouch,' I thought, looking at the armory on the table.

Two weeks of daily sessions with that pervert and I was ready to "own" Mount-fucking-Everest. He stiffed us (me) for eight thousand bucks and sent us on our way with a mock-up diploma each which read:

"I'm making the grade in listening but I need a distinction in hearing to continue to graduate in my relationship."

Our final task was to promise to take a holiday together immediately. "No cell phones," were the prick's last words of advice and it was about the only thing he'd said in two weeks which made sense to me. (Altho' hardly eight thousand dollars' worth.) Pearl insisted on Europe (to get away from, "that woman in the translation service"). Muriel insisted on coming to protect her daughter but dressed it up as some doctor's advice to spend more time with her family. How much more time with us did she need? I mean, she fucking lives with us. I imagined her playing the martyr and offering to stay at home on her own except for some recent sharp pains in her chest and a desire to help save our marriage. Such a thought gave me about as much comfort as I would have derived from finding Himmler in our garage reading the gas meter.

We couldn't let Billy out of our sight for more than twenty minutes in case he overdosed, so he came as well. Iska was too young to leave in Boston on her own, plus she was probably the only one who'd talk to me, so I was happy to have her along. A friend of mine in a travel agency in Harvard Square found the ideal venue. It was a small chateau, or manor house, in Provence with a six-week all-in deal (including a housekeeper and all our meals) with an option to purchase at the end of our stay. We didn't speak French, but then that's not a problem for Americans, all we do is shout (or overthrow the local regime) in order to get understood whenever we're abroad.

'Here it is,' Iska yelled, as we drove in a haze of dust past some olive groves and fields of vines. Red-tiled roofs and white, or off-white, walls gleamed in the afternoon sun. I put my hand in my pocket to feel for the slip of paper with the key-pad combination on it. Instead, I found a fax which had arrived in my office as I was leaving. I'd have to put that in the red folder before I forgot.

Someone in the bus laid a silent one which gave the air-conditioning a good run for its money!

Get This,

The best spot to grow fruit
is on a south-faceing
gentle slope, open to the sun
shelterd from wind and where
the frost does not gather

but filters down
and
away.

Jsky

Chapter Three

I DON'T KNOW how long the French lasted against the Germans in the Second World War. Maybe six days, but it's not clear whether that included a weekend. They've some fucking unbelievable country, you know. They blocked our troops from using their air space during the Gulf War and, at the same time, expected us to continue buying goat's cheese. What the hell was that all about? I tell you, they were glad to see us twice in the last hundred years, when the Germans kicked their asses, but they don't want to see us at all when we're saving someone else in the Middle or Central East, or whatever, and preserving the price of oil. Last time I bought goat's cheese, it was in a jar full of fucking oil! Figure that out. They're a country founded on the twin pillars of petulant shrugs and incomprehensible cinema techniques. No wonder they don't have the stomach for war.

So, we arrive in the village, Gigondas (you *do* pronounce the "ass" at the end), and there's the house we're renting for six weeks to save our marriage (thanks to Mr Vibrator). It's about a thousand years old and made of stone (like Hilary Clinton) and it's perched at the edge of a tiny village (no shopping malls) and overshadowed by a set of mountains which look like false teeth. It's hot, it's dry, it's dusty and it's August. But it's also kinda pretty, in that sparse

European way. We haven't seen a McDonalds since Nice and, in a way, that's comforting. It means that France can survive in the kitchen on its own if it puts a little thought into it. Don't get me wrong, I know they're famous for their chefs and all that, but, to be fair, most of it is just hype; like the "Avenue Du Roi" in Boston near the wharves. You gotta book three months in advance and binge eat for about the same length, given the microscopic fucking portions they serve. They leave the microscope in the kitchen when they make up the bill though; you can see that from about two hundred yards. They even leave a space for tips, like they do in France. I remember once, a couple of months after I was made partner, we went there and Ivel Schwartz wrote, "thanks a bunch" in the space. That may seem pretty tame to you as far as outrage goes, but, let me tell you, it's pretty extreme from a guy whose response to Watergate was, "Well, well, well." You have to refinance your mortgage at the door just to be allowed in to eat their tiny portions of lettuce and mint bay-leaf roulade or whatever. You wouldn't want to arrive there hungry. That's all I can say.

The village hadn't changed in years, I'd bet. There was a small square with a few wine shops and a tourist advice center that always seemed to be closed. There was a pair of churches, one small hotel, a couple of cafes, some winding streets and that's about it. Everywhere, there was the scent of perfume; like they had litres of lavender oil and sprayed it on the fields. Hell, they probably even grow the stuff, altho' I didn't see any oil derricks. There were lots of vineyards, all gathered around the outside of the village. The houses were mostly roofed in red tiles. A mountain range, looking like decayed teeth, loomed behind the village. I'll say this for the place tho', it was awfully quiet. There was a tranquillity to the place that even Dan Quayle couldn't misunderstand.

The holiday house was absolutely magical. It had a charm that superimposed itself on you even if you were determined to be miserable. I wasn't miserable, but I did kinda hope that some rotting beams might collapse the laundry room on Pearl's mother. But, of course, nothing like that happened. Muriel grabbed the largest bedroom, while Pearl and I had two rooms with a linking door in case we got back together. Iska had a single which had a huge oak windowsill with the initials CA carved in faint ridges near the left inside window sash. Billy's room was downstairs in a converted back kitchen. I'd phoned ahead some days earlier and got Gloria to put her limited French to good use by giving a couple of customizing tips to the agent handling the rental. He'd said that the house had been attached to a vineyard at some stage, but the fields nearest to it now were just dirt and dust. Gloria's final act of separation was to apply lipstick to her adventurous mouth in the aftermath of our last Wednesday ration of passion, three days before I boarded the plane for France. It was going to be tough on her, having me so far away from her for a month and a half, and I told her so.

'Don't go crazy on the credit card, okay, Gloria? The limit is right down to four thousand a month while I'm away.'

'George, you make me feel like a hooker; talking about money like that. It's as if my bank account only goes up with your pecker.'

'Inflation is a curse, Gloria. You need a little lull every now and then to remind you how good it is to be taken care of. How could you think of yourself as a hooker? I'm absolutely shocked to think you only want my body because I'm paying for you to have sex with me. Haven't you any feelings for me at all?'

'Of course I have, George. It's just that sometimes I feel cheap about this arrangement.'

'Cheap? Are you fucking joking? If I shelled out this kind of money on real hookers, I'd own half of Thailand by now. Whatever you are, Honey, "cheap" aint it.'

I don't mean to be down on Gloria (apart from in the sexual sense), but any commercial deal has to be two-way. Sure, if it develops into something more, I'm open to that. Let's face it, I'm no oil painting. But a bunch of real estate and cash on-hand is better than a few pastels when you're fifty-one. The sex with Gloria was great. I mean, really great. People often talk about true love and fulfilment and happiness, and all that shit, but take it from me, money *can* buy it all. If you want me to say that every Wednesday I came away from Gloria's apartment feeling empty and lonely, you're completely wrong. What could be better than a girl who's thirty-and-dirty making you feel twenty-with-plenty when you're fifty and shifty? It don't grow on trees and they don't have it at Walmart. So where you gotta go is where it is. All you ever have to pay is the asking price. They got salamis in France that would make you think twice about your personal hygiene. The fridge was full when we got to the house and a cross-eyed housekeeper in an apron greeted us at the door. Iska continued her conversation with the driver as he unloaded our cases. I began to wonder if she was suddenly becoming a woman without my having noticed. If so, it was another episode in her life when she was anything but, "a little slow".

It struck me that, apart from her notes, I had little communication with my daughter. I didn't even know who her favourite actor was, or whether she still ate cheeseburgers. That shows you how little I really knew about her life. Pearl smiled at me over coffee in the kitchen, while Billy disappeared and Iska spoke away merrily in French to the housekeeper,

'Dad, her name is Olivia,' Iska enlightened me.

Pearl spoke her first words of kindness to me in years, as Iska and the housekeeper appeared through the window in the courtyard, beside some old rusted machine which looked like a giant mangle.

'I think this could be a good holiday, George. Thanks for agreeing to come.' I *was* touched by her kindness and I knew that this was a moment to savor, as it might provide some encouragement for her not to divorce me if I responded appropriately.

'Don't mention it, Pearl. You know, I think it might be a good time for us here in this house, as a family.' Her eyes lit up and she smiled again just as the silence was broken by Norma-fucking-Desmond.

'Family? What would you know about family? Your son is a cocaine addict, your daughter hardly knows you and your wife wants a divorce. Family? Don't make me laugh'.

'George and I are having a private conversation, Mom. Can you leave us alone for a few minutes?' I don't think I'd ever heard Pearl even hintingly rebuke her mother before that.

'I know when I'm not wanted,' Muriel said, turning her head and marching towards the front of the house. She paused at the door and turned round, smirking, and said 'Heard from your little tramp, Goldilocks, since you arrived, George?'

'It's, Gloria,' I snapped back before I'd had a chance to think. Pearl's eyes filled with hurt and she retreated from where she'd been moments earlier.

'Glory be to Gloria,' Muriel said as she left the room. Oh Fuck.

'Billy's on top of the roof with his drumsticks,' Iska announced, as she poked her head round the door from the courtyard. Pearl looked at me like it was all my fault. Maybe it was. I arose wearily from an ancient chair and made my way out into the sunlight.

'Hurry, Dad. He says he's going to jump.'

Now one thing I'll say in Billy's favor is that he is decisive. I know it doesn't tip the balance completely perhaps, when weighed against drug addiction and serial stupidity, but it's something. Ever since I can remember, Billy has had at least a half a mind of his own. He's threatened to kill other people in the past. He's actually only managed to murder that dog on MV. But, to be fair, this was the first time he'd ever threatened to do away with himself.

The sun beat down on the courtyard and as I got outside I heard the clattery tapping of Billy's drumsticks on the roof tiles. He was clearly not himself, but he was muttering the words to some inane song and it sounded like he was chanting,

"Eiderdown any rings tooth decay"

and repeating it almost in time to his drumming. He was straddling the top of the roof so only one leg was visible. He was drumming away, shaking his head from side to side in a kind of stupor and, of course, chanting loudly about bedcovers and bad teeth. Oh, and he was naked. The housekeeper was straining to get a glimpse of Billy's slowly bouncing genitalia.

'There's a ladder in the large shed, Dad,' Iska said helpfully.

It wasn't readily apparent how Billy had got up there, but that was not my immediate concern. I carried this huge double aluminium ladder out into the sunshine and start to shove it up the wall at the gable end of the house.

'This is all George's fault,' Muriel's voice sailed out the kitchen door ahead of her. She was clearly still miles ahead in the bitching stakes because of the kitchen exchange.

'It's nobody's *fault*, Mom,' Pearl countered. 'Why do you always have to talk about everything like it was a car accident and you're handing out liability?'

'Do you think Billy would be sitting on top of the house naked with his drumsticks if his father had managed to remain faithful to you, Pearl?' Muriel moved up a gear and courted a response.

'I don't know, Mom,' Pearl answered tiredly.

'Elvis used to shoot light bulbs in his swimming pool,' I said jauntily. 'Maybe this kind of behaviour is just genetic on your side, Muriel?'

'When I lived in Los Angeles, George, marriage was for life.' She tossed her head as I pushed the ladder to its fullest extent.

'Tell that to Elizabeth Taylor and Rock Hudson.'

'*They* were not contemporaries of *mine*.' Muriel sucked in warm air and was short of breath for a moment.

'Oh yes, I forgot. You were a movie star back in the 20's before they invented sound. Ten years earlier and you'd have been a movie star before they invented movies.'

'Don't come up here,' Billy warned, holding his sticks above his head in a momentary interval in the song. 'I'm gonna jump, Dad. I really am.'

'It's okay, Billy.' I segued into calm-rescuing-parent mode. 'I'm only coming up to talk to you.' As I spoke, I caught my left foot under a tile which then came loose and slid down the roof, falling thirty feet onto the courtyard where it smashed, unfortunately some distance from Muriel's head. Pearl and Iska stood together, holding hands and looking up at the sky.

'I mean it, Dad.' Billy started to move the one leg I could see back up towards the apex of the roof. I was about fifteen feet from him, and had visions of him standing on the round tile seam at the top then falling to his demise. I inched forward using the inside part of my right shoe for a grip against the grainy surface.

'If you want to talk, then talk from there,' Billy menaced as best he could.

'I want to talk to you, Billy, about what you are doing.' I tried a bit of reason but I could see by now that his eyes were like blue marbles rolling freely around inside ice cubes.

'What's all this about bedclothes and dentists?' I asked.

'What?' I had his attention.

'You were singing about eiderdowns and tooth decay,' I said. 'What is that all about, Billy?'

'I was singing the chorus from one of our songs, Dad. "I disown anything you say, I disown anything you say"'.

'Oh, I thought it was about bedclothes. I thought you said "eiderdown".'

'What the fuck is this, Dad? A sudden interest in my lyrics? You're the one who's blocking my career. You won't give your fucking consent to let me follow my dream. What about that? What about that?' He was shouting now and I was getting a pain in my ear, as well as my ass, with the whole scenario.

Over Billy's left shoulder I could see out beyond the swimming pool and down into the village. There seemed to be a small gathering of people in the square, all shading their eyes and gazing in our direction. On one level I can appreciate that type of attention in a small place where very little happens. But, the last thing I wanted for this outdoor Henry family confrontation was an audience.

'I'm gonna jump, Dad.' Billy's voice assumed a higher register quality, which probably didn't suit most of his lyrics. All I could think of was, Jesus, if he jumps forward, maybe he'll kill *me* as well.

'Billy? Billy!' I really wanted his attention now. He leaned forward and flicked both drumsticks over my head into the courtyard like a true rockstar. I contemplated the situation with my eyes level with his nipples.

'Don't come any closer, I'm fucking warning you, Dad.' I was so close to his doped head now that I began to feel a couple of percent Colombian myself.

'I'm not against this rock band thing, Billy. In fact, I'm all for it. You think I really want to stop you from succeeding?'

'You don't even like our music.'

'I do,' I lied, lyingly.

'Okay then, what's your favorite song?'

'"Everybody's Got to Learn Sometime," by The Korgis,' I replied.

'I mean *our* songs, the band; East Pole. Do you even *know* any of our songs?'

I became aware of Pearl waving up at me from just under the eave of the gable end. She had heard Billy's question and was trying to prompt me. I watched as she made gestures indicating whiskers on herself, and then put both of her hands on her head, mimicking ears. The final motion of using her hand as a tail gave me the hint I required.

'The one about cats,' I announced. 'I like that one.' Billy's face assumed an air of almost reasonableness and he smiled wryly.

'"The Pussy Farm"? You like *that* song best?'

'Well I know I never told you before but, yeah, that's the one I

40

like best.' (Trust me to choose the fucking stupidest song in their repertoire).

'But, that's filthy. Grandma says those lyrics are the musical equivalent of Satan's poetry. I can't believe you like that song.' He shook his head to emphasize incredulity. I shook my own head in response.

'Well there you go. Maybe it's the melody which mostly attracts me to it.'

If Muriel hated the song; at least that was something in its favor. I had no idea my son was capable of writing lyrics that could piss off the old bitch. Maybe Billy *was* a genius after all. I couldn't believe Pearl had really meant to prompt me *that* song, though. I mean she's pretty straight.

'Why don't you sing a bit of it; if it's your favorite song by the band?' Billy was emboldened now by this apparent show of knowledge on my part. I knew that it must have been less a desire to have me sing his appalling lyrics, on top of a house in France in 90° of heat, which heartened him at that moment, than a suspicion that I did not know the song and would therefore be exposed as a liar on the first day of our holidays.

'Who am I? The fiddler on the fucking roof, Billy? You sing it and I'll join in, but only if you promise to come down first. Okay'

'No deal, Dad. You sing the chorus and *then* I'll come down.'

'You're coming down, Billy?' I heard his grandmother's rasping voice interrupt my rescue efforts. 'That's great. I knew your dad would sign the contract'.

'No I'm not,' he shouted back at her, suddenly remembering that my signature held the key to his dreams. 'I'm not coming down until you give your written consent, Dad, nothing less than that'.

The rancid cow, she'd blown any chance of talking him down now and I'd really felt that I was making progress. Time for plan B.

'I've got the contract here,' I said, tapping my closed shirt pocket. 'I'll sign it now if you want.'

'Show me,' Billy demanded. I unbuttoned the pocket and took out the folded document and inched towards him, proffering the paper. Billy leaned forward and took it in his right hand. I figured he'd have to use both hands to unfold it. I was right. He opened the first flap of the paper cautiously and, round about the time he realized it was a list of telephone numbers and e-mail addresses from my office, I punched my only son as hard as I could in the face with my right fist. BANG. Billy dropped the paper and then righted himself with an involuntary movement of his torso which made him seem virtually still conscious. I waited for the kick or the jump which would signal his intention to kill me, but nothing came. Instead, a gust of wind slapped the paper flat against his chest and, as I had vaguely anticipated with my punch, Billy fell backwards and began to roll down the other side of the roof. I clambered up and grabbed hold of his left ankle as it threatened to disappear from view. I was unable to stop him falling but I did kinda slow his progress and in the end his descent from the roof into the kidney-shaped swimming pool was awkward and comical rather than dangerous. We fished him out pretty much immediately, or rather Iska and Pearl did. He lay, panting, on the pool surround, coughing up water and occasionally trying to cover his private parts with his hands in odd moments of self-conscious lucidity. Wrapped in a towel some minutes later, he announced that he had a headache and wished to lie down. I helped him to his feet and walked him to the downstairs bedroom. Once in bed, I saw him glance quizzically at the bars on the windows and blink to try and refocus. I closed the door behind me then bolted and padlocked it. There was a vent near the floor through which food and water could be provided if and when required. First up, though, was a double helping of cold turkey.

CHAPTER FOUR

'HELLO?' The line crackled as I held the receiver to my ear.

'Hi, can I speak to Billy Henry?' The suave voice on the other end was already on my nerve-endings. I wondered if this might be Billy's dealer.

'Who's this?'

'Who's that?'

'Never mind who's *that*? Who's *this*? Tell me or I hang up.'

'It's Gooch Witherspoon from Carnivore Records.'

'The meat storage company?' I jerked the jerk's chain.

"No, the *record* company. I'm looking for Billy Henry. I need to speak with him.'

'I'm afraid Billy's not available right now.'

'Do you know when he'll be back?'

'About 2047,' I almost replied, but instead said: 'Well he's got some meeting in Paris tomorrow.'

'Who's he meeting? Is it another record company?' Old Gooch was toilet-skid material at this point so I hooshed his confidence along.

'I don't know, but it's down here in the diary. A girl called Emmy or something.'

'Oh, okay, so he's meeting friends, right?' The relief hustled its way down the phone at me for a moment.

'Yes, I guess so. Emmy London her name is, like the city I guess. I'll spell her first name E-M-I.'

'E.M.I. London? Jesus!'

'Do you know her?' I smiled but he couldn't tell that through his ear.

'No, no I don't. Just. Well. I wonder if you could get him to call me as soon as he gets back. Could you do that?'

'Sure,' I said. 'Gimme your number.' (But I had his number already, oh yeah).

As I put down the phone I could hear Billy hammering on the door of his room.

'Let me out of this fucking room, Dad. Do you hear me?' I tried to ignore the screaming and the hammering by going out into the garden, but I did hear him and it broke my heart.

The village itself, Gigondas, is a quiet place where there is generally absolutely nothing to do except eat or sleep. Sure, the mountains provide a picturesque backdrop to the quaint red roofs, and the sun oversees the scene like a benign nurse, blah-di-fucking blah and all that, but once you've seen it, you've seen it, if you know what I mean. I gotta say, tho', that it's as pretty as a picture. The tiny winding streets are all peppered with sunshine and shade and, here and there, the gurgling of water fountains sounds like pensioners clearing their throats while waiting in line to get served. Anyone I met in the streets stared at me for a moment, like they'd never seen a lawyer before. But they seemed friendly enough too, despite this morbid curiosity.

After the first four or five days we settled into a non-contentious morning routine; I had breakfast with Iska on the terrace about eight thirty, and Pearl and Muriel usually came down about nine just as we finished our coffee and croissants. Olivia kept stacking pyramids of those small jars of jam on the table each morning. I kinda liked the strawberry one, but the small pictures on the labels looked so similar I kept choosing the raspberry one, which I hated;

so I stopped. Life is too short to have to eat raspberry jam when what you really want is strawberry. Analyse that if you want but it's just me talking.

'Dad, did you know that in Ireland they've got eleven strains of apple that don't grow anywhere else in the world?'

'No, Honey. I didn't know that.'

'Well, one day maybe we can go there and see. Just to help me write my book, can we, Dad?'

'Sure, sure we can,' I replied. But what I really meant was, 'Probably not, isn't there a war on there?'

Iska is the person in the family to whom I feel closest. Sure, she's my daughter. But, beyond that, out in the fucking prairie of life where marriage is a cactus, a daughter is the oasis put there to allow fathers to drink something worthwhile in the heat. Iska never makes demands beyond asking me to sign the renewal slip for her library card. That, and costing a fortune in clothes and telephone bills. I got a bill once for her cell phone that was so high I almost slit my throat with the letter-opener after reading it.

'What did you do to rack this up, phone the speaking clock on the moon and not hang up?' I roared at her.

'I just phoned some friends,' she replied calmly.

'Well, next time, why don't you just fly them all to Africa for lunch? It would be cheaper.'

Two hours later a fax arrived at the house from an airline company giving a quote for chartering a plane to take sixteen children to Casablanca. I never queried her phone bills again.

I decided that each day after breakfast I'd take a walk in the village. At least part of my motivation was to avoid having to listen to the drone of Muriel's voice echo through the old house like a chainsaw. 'When Hedy Lamarr finished filming "Experiment Perilous" with George Brent, she threw this huge blow-out in Palm Springs. I was dating Trevor Howard's brother at the time and we just......'

Sometimes I wanted to grab the old biddy by the throat and shake her till she shut up. But, considering the way things were between Pearl and me, a stroll seemed the more sensible course of action.

Days two and three of the cold turkey were the toughest for me. Hearing Billy screaming his lungs out for more drugs, and promising the fucking earth to anyone who'd help him, cut me in two, but I tried to ignore it and went out for more walks. Right in the middle of the village, up a small laneway, was a tiny square with just a fountain and a stone bench. I'd often walk through the main square and up around by the graveyard. Usually I'd just sit on the stone bench near an old wash house in the shade before making my way back for lunch. The fountain attracted me 'cos I've always had this thing about running water. I find the sound of it so relaxing that it nearly puts me to sleep. I'd read the week-old Herald Tribune they sold in the small tobacco shop, and get the results of ballgames I'd attended before we left the U.S. The other thing about running water, when you're over fifty, is sometimes the sound makes you have to pee more often that you'd normally be comfortable with. "Swings and roundabouts," as someone I know in the law business says.

All the thoughts of peeing made me recall the findings of an autopsy, which was read into the record at an inquest I attended in my first week as a qualified lawyer (twenty five years ago). The deceased had been shot in a fight over a parking space in an underground garage beneath a department store. The victim had pulled a knife to make his point, but the rival for the car space had a magnum forty-five and blew the knife-thrower's face off. Anyway, the thing is I attended the inquest on behalf of the owners of the garage. They were afraid of being sued for not making the spaces small enough so that both parties could have had a parking space each! (Don't believe me? see Commonwealth of Mass -v- Gardner, 1976). When the autopsy report was read into the record it

46

contained the phrase, "penis and testicles unremarkable". Talk about kicking someone in the nuts when they can't fight back. So it made me wonder one day at the fountain whether my own equipment would be deemed, "unremarkable", when I died. I suppose the alternative verdicts would be, "Noteworthy" or maybe even – in exceptional circumstances – "Impressive" or "Oh, my God!!" (See what paranoia one is cursed with when spare time and middle age intersect?)

'Billy's been sick again,' Pearl said, when I got back for lunch on the Thursday after we'd arrived. This was day five of the cold turkey.

'He'll be fine,' I responded, sitting down in an armchair in the front room from where I could see Muriel and Iska in bathing suits on their way around the corner to the pool.

'I mean *really* sick, George. Mom says he's been coughing blood and asked her to call a doctor.'

'He's faking it, Pearl. Drugs make liars out of ordinary people.'

'Billy's not just an ordinary person, George. He's our son.' She picked up a magazine from the coffee table and threw it back down. It had Saddam Hussein on the cover with half his head stained by espresso.

'Look, Pearl. I know things haven't been easy, but just trust me on this, okay? This is best for Billy.'

'Trust you 'cos you're a lawyer?' Pearl half-smiled, recalling a standing joke between us.

'Something like that.' I smiled back.

Screams brought us running from the front room. Billy was yelling like a madman inside the door as we arrived.

'She's an animal. The fucking bitch, she's an animal.'

As Olivia pushed a tray of food through the flap, Billy had grabbed her hand and tried to break her wrist.

'I am sorry, Mr and Mrs Henry, he grabbed my hand, so I bit his finger.' Iska dripped water onto the stone flag floor as she interpreted the housekeeper's apology. Billy kept slamming at the door with his fists and demanding to be let out. Muriel stood accusingly in the kitchen with her hands on her hips and her sagging skin falling around her like melting ice cream. Here and there, the hint of tan peeked out between the folds. Even though her expression said it all, she felt compelled to augment that statement with the use of her vocal chords.

'This is all your fault, George Baxter Henry. Pearl should never have married you. I was against it from the start.' She folded her arms in a defiant full stop to this disclosure.

'I wasn't a million percent in favour of it myself,' I said. 'A mixture of ignorance and good faith made me think that by marrying Pearl I'd rescue her from you and a lifetime of Clarke-fucking-Gable anecdotes. Plus, I'd fallen in love with her and thought that any obstacles you could put in our way would be surmountable with a cocktail of affection and wishful thinking.'

'You've never thought about anyone but yourself, George,' Muriel responded. 'If you thought you'd get away with it, you'd sell your own children if there was a profit in it. Look at you, fifty-something with a cocaine addict for a son and a two-week counselling course for a marriage. Even Iska doesn't understand what's going on around her. Maybe if she knew you were humping some slut on the ninth floor instead of caring for her mother, things would be clearer for her.'

'Leave Iska out of this, Mom,' Pearl intervened. 'My marital problems are my own business, not yours or Iska's.'

'If you'd listened to me all those years ago, you'd have married somebody suitable instead of scraping the barrel for an engagement ring and a time-share in George's pecker.'

'Suitable? Like who? Like that bald pervert whose father made his fortune in pool-cleaning solutions? Or maybe the lazy son of some film star who could drink champagne all day then come home every night and punch my lights out?'

'Like someone who had a little class, Pearl. Your mother was a famous actress. She was respected and adored. What possessed you to marry the son of an olive-oil salesman? Your mother did everything she could to give you opportunities, and all you could do was throw them back in her face! How dare you!'

'Grandma? Grandma?' Billy's voice rang out plaintively from the other side of the door. We all stopped to listen.

'Yes, Billy dear?' Muriel pulled a towel around her shoulders like a cape, and shrugged to emphasise that she was the only one capable of eliciting sensible talk from Billy.

'Stop talking about yourself in the third person! And what's with the past tense thing? It makes you sound like you're dead. You'll only get Dad's hopes up,' Billy said. There was a maniacal snigger after this from him and then complete silence. Iska started to laugh and even Pearl grinned a little. Muriel turned on her bare heels and went back out to the pool.

I don't want to go into too much detail about the attempt to detox Billy but, suffice to say, it's a good thing the room had a bathroom attached to it. The only things within the reach of my junkie son were; a mattress, a toilet bowl, toilet paper, a faucet and a basin. In almost a week now he hadn't even eaten but he had been able to drink plenty of water and shit the stuff out of his system. Someone once told me that the Italian for suppository is innuendo. Suicide is the biggest risk to people in cold turkey, as far as I've read. Billy had no belt, no shoelaces, and nothing to stand on or hang from. The need for all of this had been clearly spelled out to the realtor when we booked the place. At home in Boston this kind of treatment would have been much more difficult to organise; with dealers and fellow coke-heads only a local call away. I know that there was nothing scientific about the method I'd chosen to clear Billy's system, but it was the best I could come up with. I have to confess that, apart from a few discreet enquiries to Karl, a former psychiatric nurse who now sells newspapers, the treatment was pretty much my own recipe.

'Just don't leave him anything he could hang himself with,' Karl had said.

'What about medication to ease him off the stuff?' I'd asked innocently.

'You'll need the medication, George. Just keep the door locked and your ears closed.'

We could have got Billy into the Betty Ford Clinic, but who wants to spend two hundred thousand dollars to find out that their son is incurable? Not me. Not even Dr Volt's suggestion about detox marshals appealed to me for even a second. Sometimes you gotta do the parenting yourself. I looked in at Billy that night and he was asleep like a baby on the mattress, with a plastic cup of water on the floor beside him. If things didn't get any worse, maybe they'd get better.

Let me say that what I really wanted to happen at that time was for Billy to get better and for Pearl not to divorce me. I also wanted good things for Iska and, of course, bad things for Muriel. That was about the height of it in early August 1999 in Gigondas, that cute village which survived quite well despite the absence of fast food outlets or an organized sex industry.

One day early on in the "holiday", maybe on a Monday or something, I saw a group of four or five men, mostly in their seventies I guessed, playing a game in the shade of some trees in the main square. The trees were old and sort of grey on their trunks with huge warts like some branches had never got going. The tops of the trees were an awkward shape as they spread out in thick short branches with clumps of leaves at the end of each, like a yellow-haired man after chemotherapy. The men each had a set of three metal balls like slightly reduced baseballs. The trick seemed to be to get closest to a small wooden ball they threw ten or fifteen yards ahead before each game. The terrain was sandy gravel, and the trees threw enough shade to allow them play without being oppressed by the heat. I watched them that day and was mesmerized by the calm which seemed to shroud their competition. The oldest of them appeared the best player, a man in a blue suit with a white tie and a flat cap. After that first morning I sought them out each day and, you know, the one time they weren't there I felt sad. They spoke to each other in low voices, and from time to time looked over at me and then back at each other and spoke again. On the first few occasions, they'd barely acknowledged my presence as I watched them. But, over a week or so, they gradually came to nod hello in my direction when I came into view around the corner. In the afternoon, sometimes, I saw them gathered at a table outside the small hotel in the square, drinking Pernod, reviving their drinks with water which made the glasses cloudy.

One day as I entered the phone booth, one of them raised his glass to me in a salute. I put coins in the slot and dialed.

'Hello?'

'Hi, is that Gloria?'

'Yeah, who's that?'

'George.'

'George?' The voice became muffled as though she'd put her hand over the receiver.

'Hello, Gloria? Are you still there?'

'Sure, sure. Where are you, George? Are you back in Boston?'

'No, I'm still in France, we're in this small village. It's very hot.'

'I'm very hot too, George,' she said slowly. I could picture her there in her short skirt with her tits pushed high and frontal in some tight t-shirt.

'I got your message on my answering machine last night but I couldn't call you from the house because of-'

'I know, I know, your wife Priscilla.'

'Pearl,' I corrected.

'Oh yeah, Pearl. I forgot, Priscilla is someone else.'

'Elvis's wife,'

'Who?'

'Elvis Presley's wife was called Priscilla.'

'You *know* Priscilla Presley? George you're amazing.' I didn't even reply to try and sort that one out. I saw the fucking telephone meter thing flashing so I put in a few more coins.

'What's up, Gloria? You sounded concerned on the answering machine.'

'Yeah, George. I know you said I was only to call in an emergency, but this *is* an emergency.'

My heart leaped into my fucking mouth and started to bounce my face all over the phone booth. Pregnant. It had to be.

'Okay,' I said calmly. 'Tell me what's wrong.' I closed my eyes and awaited the inevitable.

'I need a new car, George.'

'What? You need a new car? You fucking telephone me to where I'm not, when I'm away, to have me call you from five hours ahead just to tell me that?'

'Don't get mad, George.'

'Oh, I'm not mad,' I shouted. 'I'm absolutely fucking livid.'

'George, George,' she calmed me from five and a half thousand miles. 'Listen'.

'Yes?'

'Do you love me, George?'

'What?' I couldn't believe this shit.

'Do-you-love-me-George?'

'Of course I do, of course I do. Why do you think I bang you every Wednesday and pay your credit card? Out of some sense of animosity, is that what you think?'

'Oh, George, I don't know. You're miles away and I need to be with you. Maybe if you could buy me a new car, I could drive to see you in France.'

'James fucking Bond couldn't drive from Boston to France,' I said. I heard something, or someone, as she started sobbing, like as if it was someone saying 'Don't worry, Baby.'

'Are you alone, Gloria?'

'Of course, why are you asking that, George?'

'I thought I heard someone there with you.'

'No, no of course not, George. It's eight o'clock in the morning.' A door slammed behind her somewhere.

'What the fuck was that?'

'The plumber,' she said. 'He was just looking at my boiler.' Her tone of voice is worried now. I decide not to come the heavy.

'A plumber, at eight in the morning?'

'He was just passing by and remembered I'd called him out about a week ago.'

'Just passing by? In what? A fucking helicopter? You live on the seventeenth floor.'

'Are you going to divorce her, George? I need some stability in my life.' She sobbed down the phone as time clicked away.

'Divorce? You know we're talking about that, Gloria. We're actually talking about that at the moment. But it's difficult to find time to discuss it properly what with Billy and all. Look, I'm out of coins here.'

'What about the new car?' She sounded remarkably coherent and sob-free now.

'I'll sort out the limit on the card, okay? Try Chaney Philips down at Faneuil, he's got those new Mazdas. Okay?'

'Okay, George. Bye, take care, I'll be-' The coins ran out. I got some more change in the hotel and rang my secretary.

'Yes, Mr Henry? How are things in France?'

'Pretty good, Judy,' I lied. 'Any calls since yesterday?'

'That Mr Witherspoon called and asked me for your address. He says your number in France is always busy.'

'It's off the hook. Don't give him the address.'

'Okay. Anything else I can do?'

'Yes, Judy. You know that credit card I got for that lady in Global Translating?'

'Yes?'

'Call the bank and talk to Arnie Bollster. Tell him to change the limit to fifty.'

'Fifty thousand?'

'No, fifty bucks. Old Gloria has found another sponsor from what I can tell. Some plumber's looking at her pipes.'

'Hot and cold, Mr Henry?' she said, as she laughed.

'Absol-fucking-lutely, Judy.' Click. I don't mind infidelity but I can't tolerate breach of contract.

Back in the house, I heard voices. Iska was sitting on the floor outside Billy's room, reading to him.

'In Devonshire, that's in England, they used to do this thing on Twelfth Night back in the 1800s. It was called *wassailing* and it means thanking the God of Apples so they'd get good cider that year. Will I keep reading?' There was silence from the drug tank.

'Okay, Billy, I'm going to stop now if you're tired of hearing me read.' Iska closed the book with a slam but I saw she'd marked the page.

'Don't go, Iska. Tell me more about the goddamn apples,' Billy said. I could hear my own voice in my son's. Iska looked up at me and winked as I passed by her. I kissed my index finger and hunched down to transfer the kiss to the tip of her nose.

Night eight in the cell and Billy's asked for some milk and cookies. No meat yet, but maybe Carnivore's dream is gonna come true.

CHAPTER FIVE

"The Clever Boy is tall and young,
Well educated; speaks many tongues
The Clever Girl stays a step ahead;
She does all her sleeping in her own bed.
Drink yourself insensible, life has passed you by
Miss Galore says she wants more; but you can't even try.

(AND THEN THE CHORUS)
You can come, you can come, but you'll come to no harm; down on
the Pussy Farm.
(REPEAT CHORUS)."

'D GONE THROUGH Billy's suitcase, looking for clean clothes to throw under the door to him, and a folder full of lyrics had tumbled out. Some of the titles were of the predictable suicidal-teenager variety like that nut Kurt Cockburn wrote (from whatever the band was called, Valhalla or something). Of course, I was curious to find the words to the song I'd pretended to like up on the roof two weeks earlier. To be honest, I was impressed at the kid's ability not only to string sentences together, but to rhyme them too. Despite the subject matter, I was pretty proud of old Billy. Not only the lyrics, but the coke thing as well; he was now eleven days without the stuff and eating almost normally. He was still in the room, but a letter had arrived for him so I'd opened it and read it to him through the door.

'They want you in New York on the sixteenth to start recording, Billy.'

'That's in five days time, Dad'

'I can count.'

'So what's gonna happen, Dad?'

'About what?' (As if I didn't know)

'About the contract, the band, are you going to give your consent or what?'

'We said four weeks of clean urine samples, Billy. Remember?'

'That was two weeks ago, Dad.'

'Eleven days ago, Billy, a week and a half.'

'So I'm clean eleven days. That's not bad.'

'Eleven days in a room in France with a reinforced door and bars on the windows, I'd hardly call it, "voluntary detox".'

'It's a start, Dad. It's a start. So, I needed a helping hand. And I'm eating.'

'You were eating a week ago, Billy. Only it was the house-keeper's hand you wanted for lunch.'

'I'm sorry 'bout that, Dad.'

'I know, Billy, so is she.'

There was silence. I took the key out of my pocket and opened the door. Billy stood in the middle of the room wearing a Bart Simpson t-shirt and khaki shorts. His feet were bare and the stink from the bathroom brought me back to my diaper-changing days.

'You wanna come out, Billy?'

'Sure, Dad.' He began to walk towards me.

'Here's the deal, Billy,' I said. 'You stay clean until the night of the fifteenth and I'll put you on the plane with the contract signed.'

'And after that?'

'After that you're on your own, Billy, you can do what you like with whatever it is you got coming.'

'You mean that, Dad?' He was incredulous.

'Sure. We all gotta make our own way, Billy, and you're old enough to make up your own mind about things. We all gotta cut loose someday and make our own mistakes.'

'That's it, Dad? Stay clean for five days and I'm home clear?' His eyes were brighter now than they'd been in months.

'Yep. Just one small thing.'

'Name it.'

I produced a bound deed and handed it to him. He walked to the kitchen reading it. Once there, he sat at the table and flipped over to the second page. His eyes widened as he read down to the end.

'A million dollars? I have to pay you a million dollars?'

'Read the conditions Billy, only if you test positive for any illegal substances in blood or urine in the next five years. I can turn up anywhere, any when, with a doctor, and you consent to giving him a blood or urine sample.'

'And in return for this?'

'In return, you get my signature, along with your mom's, to let you get on the plane in five day's time.'

'And I have to give a blood sample here to the local doctor before we leave for the airport?'

'You got it. Take it or leave it, Billy.'

'How much time have I got to consider this proposal?'

'All the time you need, say by three this afternoon.' (It was two-thirty now).

'What about independent legal advice?'

'You're lookin' at it.' I grinned.

'So what's your independent legal advice then, Dad?'

'Don't sign, you're not mentally up to keeping your part of the bargain.'

'You're telling me not to sign and yet at the same time you're the person who drafted the agreement for me to sign in the first place! What's that about?'

'Can't get more independent than that, Billy.'

'Suppose I can't pay you the million bucks, what happens then?'

'Then you'll have to file for bankruptcy, which you'll see, from the new contract Carnivore sent, allows them to treat your contract as being at an end and to terminate it with a declaration that you owe them two million for breach of clause 11.4.'

'So it's win-win for everyone except me?' Billy smiled.

'You got it, Billy. What's it gonna be?'

'Gimme that pen, Dad.'

By the time Billy got around to getting legal advice, on the enforceability of our deal, he would either be on his way to crack-cocaine heaven or so clean or rich he wouldn't give a fuck either way. I folded the deed and pocketed it.

'What's the pool like, Dad?' Billy began to take off his t-shirt.

'Don't you remember? No of course not, last time you swam there you were asleep.'

Making Carnivore nervous, about a rival company's interest, had really paid dividends. Their new contract offered twice the money the first one had, and the royalties from Billy's lyrics would no longer be carrying the financial can if the album flopped. Cross-collateralization, my swizzle stick!

'Would you like to play, Monsieur?' It was almost the end of our second week in France and the ice was finally broken with the old guys and their game of boules. One of them offered me a spare set of metal balls.

'Sure,' I said, shifting my ass off the wall and walking over to where the three old guys stood in the long shadow cast by a plane tree. (That's what the guide-book calls them) One of the regulars hadn't turned up and I got my big chance.

'American?' one of the other two asked. I nodded and shrugged my shoulders in a gesture I hoped would disarm them of their prejudice.

'John Wayne, George Bush, Jane Fonda.' The third guy smiled

as he intoned the names of our national heroes.

'Charles de Gaulle, Cezanne, Pinochet.' I did my best to reciprocate. All three men laughed and one after another extended their hands and introduced themselves.

'De Gaulle.'

'Cezanne.'

'Pinochet,' the expert with the white tie said. 'And you?'

'George,' I replied. They all cracked up laughing and one of them said, 'Mesteer Bush,' and we were off.

We played in pairs and I was fucking awful for the first few games but got the hang of it near lunchtime. We adjourned for a drink and as I finished mine, I made a knife and fork gesture and pretended to gobble food. They understood.

'Tomorrow?' The oldest guy made throwing signs with his hand curled towards him, indicating play.

'Wee, wee,' I said, using, the only French word I knew.

On the way back to the house I took a different route and passed by an old schoolhouse. There was a war memorial on the roadside nearby. I read down through the list and my eye was caught by a name which seemed familiar. "Eugene Aragon". I knew what it was that made me look twice. Some of the old wine bottles in the kitchen over the cooker had candles in them and the name Aragon appeared on the labels. I don't know if there was a connection between the house and this guy Eugene, but anyhow it sorta surprised me that I noticed something that was French and had at least made the connection in my mind, if you know what I mean. The twenty-fifth of February 1916 was the day he'd died. I'd never really thought about the First World War much; because nobody I knew had been caught up in it. My old man had been in the next one, though. There was a photograph, somewhere at home, of him in his uniform with one of his comrades lying on a sand dune in Normandy with the sun in his eyes.

I traced some of the names on the memorial with a finger and became aware of someone watching me. I looked around, and this gorgeous broad was standing with a bicycle on the other side of the road. Her bicycle faced towards the village but she was pointed the other way, staring back up the road in my direction. At first, I thought that perhaps she was related to someone listed on the memorial and was concerned that a stranger was poking at their name with a foreign finger. She didn't seem unhappy, though. She was very pretty, with long legs which were nearly up to her ears. She wore a sky blue blouse with the sleeves rolled, or pushed back up her arms, like she was ready for some hard work. Her skirt was a sort of apron, all white and tied around her waist like a hug. We stared at each other for a few moments then she asked, in pretty good English.

'You are staying at the Montmirail house?' She pointed towards our holiday home.

'Yes,' I answered, somewhat short of breath because of the effect she was having on my "unremarkable" equipment beneath the shallow cover of my cotton slacks. I wondered if my excitement was visible to her. She seemed to give me the once-over look before hopping on her bicycle and freewheeling the short trip down to the village square. She was some honey bunch, I don't mind telling you. Old Gloria Dinerman wouldn't be fit to unclip her bra (I'd reserve that onerous task to myself). Being a non-trial lawyer, it had to have been a while since I'd filed an affidavit, but I wouldn't mind filing one in *her* courtroom office. What a bitch Gloria was, trying to pull the fast one on me when I was thousands of miles away, rebuilding my marriage. Jesus, she had some nerve. I thought, as I watched one of the cutest asses I'd ever seen freewheel out of view.

Iska had found a new strain of Peruvian apple on the internet and she told me all about it at breakfast.

'You know, Dad, they tie square glass jars on the buds with a string and the apples grow square. Can you believe that?'

'Unbelievable,' I said, with my mouth full of croissant and strawberry (No, fuck, raspberry) jam. God, I hate raspberries. Iska seemed in pretty good form. 'Billy's talking to Hairy and Joe by e-mail, Dad. They're so excited about recording the single next week. Hairy says that they've got this producer lined up who worked with Eye Twitch and Stainmaster.'

'Wow!' I tried to sound impressed.

'I think it's all noise,' Muriel said, sneaking behind me and grabbing the pot of coffee. 'When I made films, they used orchestras. They had to play live, too, when they recorded the music. Now it's all computers and electric bells.'

'I think Billy's a good lyricist,' I pitched in.

'A good lyricist? Are you out of your mind, George? Billy is a very sick boy who writes evil lyrics. He's a Satanist at heart.'

'At least he has a heart, Muriel.' I came to Billy's defence. 'I understand you were scheduled for a heart transplant once, but they couldn't find enough granite.'

Pearl came out onto the veranda in her dressing gown. For the first time I noticed that she'd lost a little weight and looked tanned.

'Your husband is being his usual nasty snide self,' Muriel addressed Pearl.

'I'm sure you're well able to handle it, Mom.' Pearl flicked her lack of concern at her mother with a glance and a sway of her hips as she came round to my side of the table and sat in a deck chair near me.

'Billy's doing really well, George,' Pearl said, as she put her rolled up towel on her lap and leaned in to pour herself some coffee.

'He's still got a long way to go, Pearl,' I warned.

'Yeah, Billy's gonna be a superstar.' Iska laughed, clapping her hands together. 'He's gonna be a millionaire.'

'It'd be great to have a real superstar in the family,' I said, biting into a dry piece of bread, hoping it would counteract the taste of raspberries. I could feel Muriel's eyes boring into the top of my head as I looked down at the rolled-up towel and imagined Pearl unravelling it at the edge of the pool and then lying on it and.....

'I was a star of the silver screen.' Muriel interrupted my coarse thoughts about her daughter.

'Oh, yeah, I forgot,' I said, grinning, '"Turn Right at the Golden Gate Bridge."'

' "Turn *Left* at the *Brooklyn* Bridge",' she corrected. 'You *know* the name of the film I got my nomination for, George. Don't try and pretend you don't. I caught you watching it six months ago on a rental video. So don't deny it.'

'Of course I don't deny it, Muriel. But I have to confess I watched it with ulterior motives.'

'Ulterior motives?' She seemed surprised.

'Yeah,' I said casually. 'I wanted to see if there were any other elements in the film, besides your own Oscar-nominated performance, which would explain its complete commercial failure.'

'Art is not about money, George. Of course, I wouldn't expect a soulless commercial lawyer to understand that.'

'Why do you two have to argue all the time?' Iska intervened, looking up from her square-apples print-out.

'Because your grandmother is a former silent screen star who just can't shut the fuck up.' I tried "owning" my feelings out loud.

'George!' Pearl snapped. 'Not in front of the children, please. I don't want that kind of language in this family.'

'Or that kind of husband.' Muriel threw a final punch.

'Tell us about Clarke Gable and Humphrey Bogart.' Iska invited her grandmother to press the "rewind" and "play" buttons simultaneously.

'Well, Honey. It was the week after Carole Lombard and I returned from vacation in Miami. We had just started shooting "Mr and Mrs. Smith" and then...'

I wandered off to try and find some paint drying I could watch instead.

Billy was out in the courtyard behind the house. He was wearing his disc-man while drumming along on an old wine cask that looked even more tired than I felt. I stood at a distance watching him, with his eyes closed and his drumsticks tapping rhythm on wood which was probably a hundred years old. I'd seen him do this before at home, when I'd stopped him from using the full drum kit in the basement to allow the neighborhood a couple of hours sleep. As I watched, I tried to remember what Billy had been like as a child and the times we'd had together. But, you know, when I thought back, it seemed like I was always either shouting at him or he was beheading neighbours' pets.

'The Happy Boy treats his lady right;,
Up on time and stays up all night.
The Happy Girl cannot be denied;
Purrs like a-'

'What, Dad? Did you say something?' Billy unplugged his earpieces and switched off the disc-man.

'I was just recalling the lyrics of one of your songs.'

'One of our songs? You mean East Pole?'

'Yeah.'

'Which one?'

'The one about the cats, "The Pussy Farm".' I felt myself blush for the first time in about thirty years.

'Go on then, let's hear it, Dad.' Billy stood opposite me and, for the first time ever, I noticed he was taller than me.

'The Happy Girl cannot be denied,' I recited. Billy joined in,

'Purrs like a kitten when she's satisfied.'
Call me a perfectionist; it's just the way I am.
No more six feet tall with one inch small, I need a man.'

We finished verse two and laughed together like a pair of drains for the first time since God-knows when.

A few days later, I was on my morning walk when I did a double- take. I retraced a couple of paces and saw a scene I'd never imagined having to deal with. Iska was sitting on the steps of a narrow tall house holding hands with a tanned boy who seemed about the same age. As I watched, they kissed lightly and looked into each other's eyes. She didn't notice me, and I doubt that she would have even if I'd been standing between them. My instinct as a father was, of course, to skewer the little French runt with a flag-pole and beat him to a pulp for taking advantage of my daughter. But I didn't. They both seemed to be equally culpable. Who the fuck was I to stomp on her dreams? She's the only one in the family who really keeps me sane.

The first time I ever kissed a girl, it was this pig-tailed broad called Julie Miller. I remember it was on the corner of the street where she lived. I chanced a kiss outta view of her house; only her dad was passing by in his rusty Buick and he got out and told Julie to get into the car. Then he smacked me so hard in the teeth I nearly landed in next year's school photograph. Ah, memories, memories.......

I continued my walk and made a detour from my normal route, and arrived out onto a small track above the village which leads up into the mountains. Half a mile up, the track turns right and, on the left is an old ruined cottage in the shadow of a clump of cypress trees. From there, a wonderful view of the village is the reward for the trek. It's like a small oasis in the desert. The houses huddle around the square and the sun drops by for company. Jeez, I'm beginning to sound like a fucking tourist brochure. I sat for a while in the shade of a tree and the sun fell all around me like a blanket. The humidity was something else and the only way to ultimately get any relief was to take off my shirt and fan myself with it. I kept thinking about that girl on the bicycle near the war memorial, and the recollection of her raised much more than a tremor. I could tell you about how I managed with great self-restraint to ignore my unexpected erection but I'd be lying. Invigorated by my morning jaunt, I jogged back down the track and paddled in a stream above the graveyard, before joining Pinochet and the others for our daily game.

"Spend your days just watching and your nights just learning how;
Doggie does it from behind. Pussy says 'Meow'"

It was less than twenty-four hours before the flight to New York when I got Olivia to phone the local doctor to come and test Billy. After six days of recording, East Pole would have a day full of press interviews and then Billy would fly back to join us for the last two weeks of our holiday. The album would be completed in September. True to their word, the record company wired two hundred and fifty thousand dollars into my account in trust for Billy. It was an advance against lyric royalties for the music publishing end of things. I honestly couldn't fucking believe it, but I tried hard to.

That night, there was a knock on the partition door. I slid the bolt back and Pearl was there in her dressing gown, wearing the red underwear I'd got her in Vegas three years earlier.

'Can I come in, George?'

'Sure, Honey.' We got into bed together for the first time in months.

'I'm so proud of the way you dealt with Billy,' she whispered, snuggling up so close to me that I could smell the toothpaste from her breath.

'Trust me, I'm a lawyer,' I said, as her hand found the back of my neck and pulled me in for a kiss.

'You can come, you can come but you'll come to no harm....'
(Repeat Chorus).

CHAPTER SIX

'I HOPE you're not back sleeping with him, Pearl.'

Muriel's voice was clear as a bell through the open window of the landing on the first floor. I was sitting on the window seat, out of the heat of the Provencal sun, reading. Pearl and Muriel were lying on sunbeds beside the pool.

'Of course not, Mom. It's far too early into this whole process for anything like that.'

'I knew it, I knew it. You *are* sleeping with him, aren't you?'

'I told you, Mom, I'm not.'

'I don't believe you. I always know when you're fibbing, Pearl. Remember the time you let that Landers boy see your tootie? I knew you were fibbing then.'

'For Christ's sake, Mom, that was forty years ago. I was ten.'

'So you *are* back sleeping with George?'

'Mom, let it go please.'

'You've got to divorce him, Pearl. There's no other way. He's worth more to you in a divorce settlement than he is dead. You get sixty percent of his share of the law firm *and* alimony and child support. When I struck that deal for you there were three other partners. Now there's only George and Ivel Schwartz. How much is that gonna be? Three, four, five million, ten million? He'll have to borrow if he wants to stop the firm from being liquidated. Maybe Ivel would buy him out?'

'Mom,' Pearl shrieked. 'I-do-not-want-a-divorce.'

'Then you want your head examined. Look, I told you before we even came here, all you have to do is keep away from him for six weeks. Then file for divorce and say you tried reconciliation but it didn't work. A couple of well-placed sobs in court, plus the photographs of George's ass in the air while he's giving Gloria some, and who knows, you might even take him for seventy five percent of everything.'

'Mom, will you please shut up. George and I will work our way through this. I know he's going to change. It's a mid-life crisis and we'll get past it. Okay? So just butt out.'

'You want to be worrying about who he's with or what he's doing when you're my age, huh? Is that what you want? Get out now and take him for as much as you can. That's my advice.'

'I don't want to grow old alone, Mom,' Pearl said.

'You mean like me? Is that what you mean? Your father and I were faithful to each other. Don't you think you could find someone else who *would* be faithful if you had all that money?'

'You mean pay someone to be my husband?'

'Don't be ridiculous, Pearl. You know what I mean.'

'No, I don't.'

'Live a little, Pearl. You deserve a second chance. George is not going to suddenly change his spots and only want to sleep in his wife's bed.'

'He hasn't been there for a long time, Mom. Maybe I haven't been paying him enough attention. Maybe that's why he went somewhere else.'

I could sense from her voice that Pearl was close to tears.

'He went somewhere else because he's a rat, Pearl. He has serial middle-age infidelity, it's a condition brought on by a combination of the presence of younger women and the absence of prostate cancer. Face it, Pearl, you've got to get rid of him. Find someone else if you're afraid of being lonely.'

'I don't want anyone else, Mom. That's why I married him. Now this conversation is at an end or I'm going swimming.'

'All I'm saying is......'

SPLASH.

In actual fact, Pearl wasn't lying when she'd said she wasn't back sleeping with me. When she'd come into my room the previous night we'd had a couple of preliminary smooches and gropes, only Pearl had pulled back from any further intimacy just as I had been all fired up and ready to go.

'I can't, George. I'm sorry.' She rolled away from me and began to get out of bed.

'What? What is it, Pearl? Are you ill or something?' (I'd tactfully avoided the phrase "time of the month" because to the best of my recollection that particular ailment had abandoned Pearl in the 1980's.)

'No George, I'm not ill.' She stood up. 'It's just that it's too soon, that's all.'

'Too soon? We've been here two weeks, for God's sake.'

'I don't mean that, George. I mean it's too soon after the shock of your....' She searched for the word. 'Your connection with that woman.'

'My, "connection"?'

'Yes, George. It's too soon after that. I need time to let my feelings readjust to the man you've become.'

'What do you mean? You think I've changed, that I'm not the same old George you've always known?'

'No, George, you're not. You've slept with someone else and I need time to come to terms with that. I thought I would be ready now for, well- you know. But I'm not. I'm sorry, George, but I need some more time.'

She kissed me on the lips as a sort of disallowed appetizer and then went back to her own room. This divorce thing might be harder to head off at the pass than I'd thought. The conversation I'd overheard, however, led me to believe that Pearl was genuine in her efforts to save our marriage; but I really had to be wary of Muriel's influence. Why didn't the old cow just up and die? I'd have poisoned her; only you just can't buy hemlock in that kind of quantity without a license. The thing about the deal that Muriel had brokered was that, if we divorced, then the law firm would be liquidated and the partnership dissolved. Sixty percent of my net worth at that point was somewhere in the region of seven million dollars, as the partnership had acquired quite a bit of real-estate along the way. We were a commercial law firm and I could expect to treble or quadruple my stake between now and sixty-five, if things continued at the same pace. Even borrowing that kind of money in a divorce scenario, to avoid losing the firm, would be cripplingly hard to do. If that happened, the repayments would catch up on me before the Green Reaper did. No, it was clear to me what had to be done; my marriage had to be saved at all costs. Muriel was absolutely correct in her assessment of Pearl's bargaining power in a divorce court. The lethal combination of my infidelity and Pearl's vulnerability, might result in even bigger damage than I was reckoning on. I had to face up to my responsibilities as a husband and a father. Marriage is always cheaper in the long run. A couple of months of lawyers' letters and a two-day hearing, with Muriel and the P.I. swearing up, would ruin me. I might still be able to retire to the Bahamas, but I'd be mixing the cocktails myself and that wasn't what I wanted.

'What's the weather like in New York?' I asked Billy when he phoned a few days later.

'Hot as Hell, Dad, but we're really enjoying the studio. You'll never guess who dropped in to see us yesterday and just hang out?'

'Who?'

'E.L.B.L. the rapper from Iowa.'

'Wow-wee, that's fantastic, Billy.' (I had no idea who the fuck this BLT guy was but, whatever).

'Looks like your favorite song's gonna be the single, Dad.'
Billy's voice echoed across the Atlantic.
'The one about the cats?'
'That's the one, Dad.'
'So are you on a break now or what, Billy?'
'Yeah, we've got the afternoon off and then it's back to the grind till Friday when the publicity begins. Rolling Stone are sending a photographer over and we're gonna do the shots for the album cover, too. Looks like we'll have half the songs in the can by then.'
'You're still coming back to join us for the last two weeks?'
'Sure am. I can't wait to take you all out to dinner and spend some of this dough.'
'I talked to Ivel and he's got some good ideas about investments. You should think about buying a house, bricks and-'
'Bricks and mortar. I know, I know. When we all get back to Boston I'm gonna organize a trip for the whole lot of us, to guess where?'
'The moon? Who am I, the fucking memory man?'
'Memphis, Dad. To see the spiritual home of the Henry family.'
He laughed and so did I.
'Absolutely great, Billy. Grandma will love that,' I said, as she passed by me in the hall on her way out to annoy the brains of the Mistral. She gave me a look that would have squeezed an all-male Golf Club out of the Vagina Monologues.
'I gotta go now, Dad. I'll phone before I get the flight on Tuesday, okay? Just to let you know when I'll be back.'
'Okay, Billy'
'Okay, Dad'
'Hey, Billy?' I said before he hung up.
'Yeah, Dad?'
'You're keeping your nose clean, right?'
He sniffed down the line like a snorting goat,
'You hear that, Dad?'

'I hear it.'

'Clean as a whistle.'

'Okay, Billy, just be good, okay?'

'You got it, Dad.' He hung up.

That night I checked the phone messages at the office. There was one call from some jerk in Billy's college in Lansing, asking if I could phone the Alumni bequests and donations office before the end of the week for an urgent message. I guessed it was some prick trying to put the hammer on me for more dough to let Billy pass the September re-sits in Bolivian hysteria. Fuck them. Billy was on his way to a post-Colombian PHD in success if everything panned out properly for him. I realized that since he'd flown home, I'd found myself relating to him in a completely different way than I had in the previous seventeen years. Billy had talent. Okay, maybe not in departments I'd heard of, but, hey, who knew what might happen? Perhaps he *would* be a rock star and make tons of bread and last a good few years at the top. Who was I to stop him in his chosen path and make him sidestep my own shortsightedness in order to grab onto his dream? Iska was finding her feet too, so that was another phase to be handled as a father. I didn't want to stand in their way and have silent feuds with them when they were thirty. I wanted to be a part of their lives and, if I could prevent them from overdosing or under-achieving; perhaps that's all a fucking parent can do. Maybe the key to hanging on to your kids is knowing when to let go.

'George, please call me. I'm in Carrington Street Precinct station. There's been a terrible mistake.' Gloria's panicky sobbing sounded strangely authentic when I checked my phone messages again later the same day. I was delighted that she'd run into some trouble after her brush with the Angel Temerity in letting some plumber turn her taps.

'Mr Henry, sorry to bother you, but we got a little problem here in Carrington. I wonder if you could call us as soon as you get this message. It's probably nothing, but we got a broad here on a credit card felony who says you promised to pay for a new Mazda even tho' her card was maxed out. Ask for Sergeant Hanwick.'

I phoned the nice policeman back almost immediately, well actually two days later. By then, Gloria's heels had probably cooled down. Judging by the cloying timbre of her vocal pops on the answering machine, she'd certainly learned a bit of a lesson by then.

'George, it's me, Gloria. I promise you I will *never* see that lousy plumber again. It was a one-off mistake, it meant nothing to me, nothing at all. Can you *please* phone some cop called Hanwick at this god-awful station and sort it all out?'

I knew that the longest they could hold her on credit-card fraud without charging her was seventy-two hours. Somewhere about seventy one and a half, I called the number.

'I wonder if I could speak to Sergeant Hanwick.'

'Sure, who can I say is calling?'

'George Henry. I got a message from him about a credit-card thing.'

'Oh yeah, sure, hang on. I'll get him right away.' There was a muffling on the line, but I heard him clearly enough, shouting across the station; 'Hey Barney, it's Gloria Dinerclub's sugar daddy.' There was the slowly un-muffled laugh of a couple of voices, male and female, then Sergeant Hanwick came on the line.

'Hanwick speaking.'

'Officer Hanwick? George Henry here. I got your message.'

'Hey, thanks for calling. We have a situation here, Mr Henry. A female Caucasian was apprehended trying to buy a Mazda, with a credit card limit of *fifty* bucks.'

'That sounds like a real bargain of a car, Sergeant Hanwick. Surely at that price the purchaser must have been suspicious that the car was damaged in some way?'

'No. Mr Henry, you don't understand. There was nothing wrong with the car.'

'Then why get lawyers involved? Can't they just be happy with the deal and get on with their lives? We'll only make the whole situation more expensive. You know what lawyers are like?'

'Mr Henry,' he shouted across the Atlantic. 'Can you just give your mind a nap for a moment and hear me out?'

'Sure,' I said, helpfully.

At the end of the conversation I pretended to finally understand that my involvement was as guarantor of the credit card.

'Oh, I see. *That* Gloria Dinerman. Yes, well, I actually used to have an extra-marital sexual relationship with her until quite recently.' There was a short silence, then Hanwick of the police force spoke again.

'You see, she's told us that it was you who suggested to her to buy the car. Can you tell us anything about that?'

'Well, let me see now. I don't specifically recall her and I having a conversation about any particular car. But I'm pretty sure that if she'd asked me for my professional opinion, I'd have told her that a price tag of fifty dollars seemed pretty good value. Mazdas are good cars you know, the Japanese sure know-'

'Okay, okay, thank you, Mr Henry. You've been a great help to us with this situation.'

'Have I? Well that's fantastic because that's just what I want to do, you know, just help everyone.'

'So long, Mr Henry.' The tone was now a canny blend of fatigue and understanding.

'So long, Detective Hanwick,' I replied, promoting him momentarily from my residence in France. I guessed they'd probably let old Gloria go without charge after that but, to be honest, I couldn't have fucking cared less. The two-timing cow. I'd get round to reducing her limit a bit more after I got back to Boston. I knew the guy she rented her offices from, and once he knew she was under investigation for credit card fraud he'd toss her off the roof of the building himself. She wouldn't be sitting in that apartment with her binoculars at the end of September watching out for plumbers in helicopters if I had my way. Had she no compassion, the heartless bitch? Women, sometimes you *can* live without them.

I'd pretty much gotten a handle on the boules thing after a couple of weeks. I could feel myself beginning to unwind and even after one phone call to Ivel, where he laid some bad news on me about some commercial deal we lost to a rival firm, I kinda felt like, hey, so what, that's life. This was the first holiday ever where I wasn't itching to get back to the paperwork. The heat of the sun and the whiff of dried tomatoes and barbequed pork fillets have a wonderful way of chilling you out. Even the pace of Muriel's bitching and sniping seemed to have relented a little as the holiday passed its mid-point, and we began to forget all about Boston and our lives there. When she *did* open her Oscar-nominated beak one Friday, it didn't provoke me the way it normally would have.

'The smell of olive oil must take you back to your childhood, George,' she quipped, as we ate outside the house on the patio near the pool. Her dig at my father's lowly calling didn't bother me in the least.

'It sure does, Muriel. Thanks for helping me make the trip back down mammary lane to my mother's milk.' Muriel had this thing about kids being fed draught rather than bottled milk from the get-go. She'd never really struck me as the mothering kind herself. In fact, I often wondered if she hadn't chosen Pearl as a name for her daughter to arrest any chances of being outshone by her offspring. (I have to say tho' that I like to think I turned out pretty normal, even if I wasn't breastfed until I was twenty-four years old!)

Pearl was going to say something, but drew back at the last moment. Instead, she stuck her nose in a guidebook and invited us to share something she'd found in it.

'There's this place here called the Fountaine dee Vacuum or something. I'd like to visit it. It says here it's one of the most powerful natural springs in the world. Any takers? Mom? George?'

'Pearl, maybe you could take George to see it sometime at night and have him wear lead shoes,' my mother-in-law sniped.

'It's a powerful natural spring, Muriel,' I said. 'Maybe, if you stood on it, it could resurrect your career.' I waited for a response, but none came. I looked over my shoulder at Muriel, but it was as though she hadn't heard me. Her face looked even uglier than usual as though crossed by some pain or discomfort. Pearl stood up and walked over to her.

'Mom, are you all right?'

'I'm fine, Pearl.'

'It's just that you look a little -'

'I said I'm fine, Pearl,' her mother rebuffed this advance of concern. She got to her feet and began to slowly walk towards the open patio doors.

'Mom?' Pearl called after her. 'Are you sure you don't need some help?'

'I'm okay, Pearl. I'm not one to complain.' Muriel's voice trailed into mock weakness as she entered the house.

'Not one to complain? She has a fucking degree in dissatisfaction,' I said, to her fast-disappearing back.

'Please, George,' Pearl asked. 'Leave her alone for a moment, will you?'

'Sure, Honey,' I replied. 'I was only kidding.'

'I'm worried about her, George. She's been off her food for the last couple of days.'

'It's probably wind or something,' I said, in a low voice that no one heard. Iska appeared in the gravel driveway, whistling merrily and with a contented look on her face. I watched Pearl to see if she had guessed the source of Iska's happiness, but I figured not.

Billy was due back in the middle of our fourth week and on that Tuesday, forty-eight hours before his return, I found myself hungry after a beer outside the hotel with Cezanne and De Gaulle. The scent of fresh bread and pastry wafted down the street at me as I made my way back up from the square towards the house. As I neared the bakery the door opened and a woman, carrying two enormous cakes, stumbled out into the sunlight. The bell on the door of the shop jangled behind her and a wave of aromas escaped into the street, cutting me off in my march home. Unable to resist the temptation of an apple and strawberry pastry in the window, I caught the door before it closed. I stepped into the shop.

The main counter was glass fronted and contained every imaginable variety of pastry and cake. The artistry and attention to detail were a credit to the mastery of culinary skill which had given them life. The shop itself seemed to close in around me, and there was every shape and size of éclair and bun and birthday cake I'd ever fucking seen, and then some. It was like that film about the kids who find the golden tickets. Apart from myself, the shop was empty of customers and even the counter was unattended. I had just scooped a fingerful of orange icing into my mouth when the door behind the counter opened and a lady wearing an apron and a paper hat – and of course all the rest of her clothes – emerged from what looked like a sitting room. I recognised her from the previous week, as the owner of the bicycle I'd seen near the war memorial. She beamed the cutest smile you ever saw and then spoke.

'Ah, Monsieur, you are the man from Montmirail, no?' (It reminded me of the man form U.N.C.L.E. but I didn't spoil the moment).

'Yes,' I replied, staring at her breasts heaving up and down behind her apron.

'I must to asking you something,' she said, taking up a newspaper which lay folded to fly-swat dimensions on the work surface behind her. She walked slowly around the edge of the counter and out into the body of the shop. She opened the paper somewhat and a small headline caught my eye.

"Les Cousins d'Elvis en vacances a Gigondas."

I remembered Herb Vissing, (he'd found the place for us), telling me that he'd had to play the Elvis card to get the booking ahead of some Greek yogurt magnate.

'Are you the couzan of Elvis?' (She pronounced it "Elveese"). I gulped as she advanced towards me (preceded by those fabulous tits).

'Yes, indeed. I sure am.' I thought of old Louie, in his grave or wherever, trying to explain to the King what the actual connection between them was.

'I love Elvis,' she intoned slowly.

'Oh, do you?' was the best reply I could think of.

'Yessss,' she said slowly and deliberately. 'I have the most amazing collection of albums, CDs, posters of heem.' She smiled.

'I bet you do.'

'Would you like to see my collection?' she asked, through red lipstick, in a voice you just couldn't refuse.

I nodded, "You bet," aware of the biggest hard-on ever trying to trespass its way out of my pants. She reached a hand out towards me but, as I extended my own to meet it, she bypassed me completely and stretched round me to flip the sign of the shop door from 'ouvert' to 'fermé'.

'This way,' she said in a whisper, turning to leave the shop and enter the rooms behind.

'I'm sorry,' I said. 'This is all wrong, I've got to go. I'm happily married. I'm not really his cousin at all.' I turned and left. In my fucking toenails I did! I followed her like a ham to the slaughter. We made our way in single file through her sitting room.

At the foot of the narrow stairway, near the kitchen, was a life-size plastic statue of Elvis-Himselvis with a guitar round his neck and his hips frozen for all time in mid-thrust. My guide put one arm around the King's neck and kissed him on the permanently-puckered lips. Then, with a sway of her own hips and the faint aroma of tarte-au-pomme, she began to climb the stairs. I followed; entranced by the movement up beyond and bursting to capacity with the movement below. A step creaked under my foot as we reached the top. It morphed into the beginning of a creak from the door which the bakery lady pushed into the room directly ahead. She walked in before me and, as I pursued her shadowy form into near complete darkness, I wondered what the fuck I was letting myself in for.

A rustle of material, then the rasp of drawing curtains and, in a trice, the whole goddamn room was lit up. I rubbed my eyes to make sure I wasn't daydreaming but, let me tell you, I sure as hell wasn't.

'Jesus Christ!' I exclaimed.

'To me, yes, Elvis is more important than Jesus Christ,' she imparted, with obvious sincerity and delight.

Talk about shrines! This room was the most shriney of shrines on the main street of Shrinesville. Elvis was abso-fucking-lutely everywhere. There were posters on every wall of the man in every imaginable jump suit: The Gypsy; the Blue Phoenix; The Aloha Eagle, even The Aztec 'sundial' outfit which he wore in that concert we'd seen in Indianapolis. A blown- up framed photograph of him in the barber's chair having his hair cut on entering the army adorned the back of the door. On the wardrobe a luminous 3D picture, about two feet tall, showed him laughing on a movie set in Hawaii. I turned around and saw that the dressing table had been turned into a model of Graceland. A figure of Elvis on a motorbike sat between the plaster of paris pillars of that great Memphis house. Something above caught my attention, and, as I looked up I saw that the entire ceiling was crowded with album covers. There was barely an inch to spare. The light bulb protruded through the, "50,000,000 Elvis Fans Can't be Wrong", record sleeve with him in the gold lamé suit. So centered was the wire from the fitting, that it looked like an enormous dick hanging out of the trousers of the suit with a bulb at the end. (C'mon baby light my wire).

On the wall around the window hung a series of t-shirts from Graceland. One announced a sold-out appearance in Rapid City, Dakota. From cradle to near-death the great man was depicted in photos, badges, t-shirts, posters, record sleeves and every kind of memorabilia. The room was entirely devoid of furniture, except for a closet and a stereo system sitting in one corner on a hi-fi rack under a stack of CDs as high as a fridge. Now, I'm a guy who's pretty tough to impress, but I was blown away by this room and all the paraphernalia of utter devotion to someone who was an icon at home in the States and a pretty distant relative of the mother-in-law I hated.

'You like?' she said, from behind me. I turned around to face her.

'Well, it's certainly Elvis Presley, isn't it?' I said, meaning nothing really.

'I-love-Elvis,' she said slowly.

'So I see,' I stuttered.

'And you, you are his couzan, you love him too?'

'Of course, sure, I mean Elvis is probably about the most famous of all my cousins.'

'And you, your name is?' She advanced towards me on tiptoes.

'Em, George,'

'George Presslee?'

'Well not exactly-'

'Your name is not Presleeee?' She retreated slightly.

'Well, yes, my mother's name *was* Presley but my father was, eh, in the oil business so he used his own name for legal reasons.' I was now telling lies at a rate that matched my heart. She, however, seemed entirely satisfied with my explanation.

'Will you excuse me for a moment?' she asked, backing towards the door.

'Of course, sure, I'll just, well, look at old cousin Elvis.'

I turned and pressed a button on a statuette of Elvis with a hound dog at his feet.

'You ain't, you ain't, you ain't,' it repeated, stuck in a groove from 1956. I imagined for a second that the thing might give me away and complete its sentence by saying, 'you ain't no cousin of mine,' so I wrapped it in a t-shirt of Elvis on a Harley.

'Meester Presslee?' Her voice disturbed my attempt to smother the King of Rock n' Roll. I swung around, guiltily. The baker lady was absolutely buck naked in the doorway. She had boobs that looked like a pair of Cosmonaut apples. Her waist was so slim it must have been under pressure supporting her torso. I felt my eyes drawn down the length of her body to her tiny white feet.

'You like me?' she whispered. I could barely breathe. I tried to force the words up from my knees and through my throat up over the tonsils to the front of my mouth.

'I.... I....Yesss,' I whispered back, more from a lack of oxygen than an attempt to reciprocate her sexy tones. She stepped up to me and placed her left hand on my crotch and got all the answers she needed. She flicked on the light, which glowed suede-shoe blue, and re-closed the curtains. I stood transfixed, watching a thousand Elvises watching me back. I knew I shouldn't be there and yet I had no intention of leaving; it was Catch 52.

She swung the door shut. Then she kissed me on the mouth. Her tongue hinted at the insufferable pleasure to follow. As I caught my breath she broke away from the contact, and this bare sexy desirable cute petite baker flicked the switch beside the closet. The doors eased open slowly, revealing a double bed which fell silently from the wall into the centre of the room. A massive pink satin bedcover bore the painted face of her hero from the Jailhouse Rock publicity poster. Her hand took mine and led me to the silk county prison where the warden was throwing a party. She undressed me, with a skill I'd normally imagined only Broadway-show-extras to possess. Next thing I knew, I was on my back with the baker preparing to put me into her oven. Somewhere in the distance, away from the erection and its reward, the stereo system kicked in and the King invited someone to let him be their teddy bear. I closed my eyes and heard the distant sound of applause from the faithful patrons of the Las Vegas Hilton as the performance began.

Dear GBH,

Here's one you might like.

MÈRE DE MÉNAGE:

A favorite exhibition variety, by reason of its size and remarkably Fine Color

J. A. ×××

Wolf River Apple:
dual purpose

"one apple makes a pie"
Very large, dark red flushed
Soft juicy flesh.

Iskey

CHAPTER SEVEN

THE MEDIEVAL method of pulping rags into paper has been recreated here, and flowers are mixed into the process to allow the paper to be colourful.'

Our tour guide was an earnest English-speaking Frenchman who seemed genuinely pleased to see us. I hate those fucking types. They talk down to tourists and probably tell lies all the time. Who the hell is gonna crawl through the fucking mangle rollers to see if they use real flowers? Not G.B.H., I'm telling you. I just about managed to stay awake through the rest of the tour, with the patronizing tones of our guide resonating against the craggy rock surface of the fountain viewing-platform at the end.

'Have you any questions?' he said, as he smiled a sort of half-camembert grin while we prepared to escape at the end of the journey. One thick moo-cow stuck her hand in the air.

'Yes?' old cheese mouth responded.

'What temperature is the water inside the cliff before it reaches the fountain?' Can you believe it? Some people are just so dumb. This broad probably had a goddamn thermostat up her own ass and was just checking on the competition. I tuned out.

To be honest, I was exhausted; earlier that morning I'd had another workout in the Jungle Room with the baker. Her name was Carmen (like the song). An aunt had left her the bakery in her will and so Carmen moved to Gigondas from somewhere on the coast where she'd been working in hotels as a pastry chef. She told me she'd nearly been married once but broke off the engagement. 'Guillaume was unwilling to share me with The Keeeng!' I tell you, I had no such qualms. In fact, I coulda done with all the help available. She'd been a fan of the Memphis Melody Maker since she'd learned to tune her ears to anything outside herself. From what I could gather, her childhood had been a strict upbringing under the guidance of a father who was a control-freak. So Elvis took the place in her life of what should have been.

I found out all that during a break while we caught our breath, before going at it hammer and tongues again, I guess you'd say. That woman knew positions that would have impressed the crowd who wrote the Korma Sutra. It was a no-holds-barred, roller-coaster ride of bump and grind which took me back to my late teens and early twenties (tho' the journey seemed to take a lot longer than it used to). She sat every which way on me and made me feel like I was the best thing that had ever happened to her. She was incredible, inexhaustible, and exuded the kind of boundless enthusiasm people usually reserve for family feuds and lottery wins. Each time I left that room above the bakery I was in awe of my own equipment. It had moved from the "unremarkable" category into something like the, "surprisingly-able" box.

All through our bouts of lovemaking, Carmen made sure the stereo blasted out the King's hits. If I had to choose the high points of the roller-coaster ride, I'd say that two moments absolutely stand out. One was definitely taking her from behind to the strains of "Hound Dog." The other was probably watching her bob up and down on top of me during during the fadeout ending of "Suspicious Minds".

At other times, when I was slipping in and out of invigorating sexually-energized trances, I could hear in my head the soft incantations of some of the lesser-known film soundtrack songs like "Queenie Waheenie" or the gutsy blues riffs of "The Power of my Love." Hey, it was just like I'd sinned and still gone to heaven. And it wasn't just the main course she excelled at, no sireee, the starters and desserts were great too. Carmen could suck the air out of a bouncy castle and still come back for the tires on your four-wheel-drive. Talk about the Fontaine de Vacuum! It got so we had this routine each day. I'd finish the game of boules with the guys and then, 'round eleven thirty or so, we'd have drinks on the hotel terrace. I switched from beer to espresso's just to build myself up for the activities ahead and, you know, my boules-playing improved enormously over that time, too. Carmen shut the shop from midday to one thirty, anyway, and so those windows of opportunity became the parameters of our liaison. About five or six days into our 'connection,' Carmen introduced a new aspect to the proceedings. This was presumably to keep her own interest levels up because, to tell the truth, I had no difficulty keeping anything up including my interest level. Anything but.

'Eat this,' she said, climbing astride me with a pair of éclairs in her hands. She gave me one to eat while she nibbled on her own and when mine was gone (about six seconds later) she leaned teasingly over and lowered her face to mine, so that I could eat hers as well. Suffice to say that the symbolism of the cream exploding all over our faces wasn't lost on yours truly. One morning she even covered certain parts of herself with orange cream icing, the stuff I'd been sampling in the shop on that first day. Oh-my-God! is all I can say about that.

Billy got back when we had been exactly four weeks in the house. He looked great and, for the first time ever, seemed totally at ease with himself.

'Hi, Dad.' He smiled as he handed me a bottle of whiskey from the duty-free shop and an envelope displaying a crest with a stag on it.

'It's from Deerhunter Tours, open it, Dad,' he invited. I couldn't stand the suspense so I ripped it open.

'Dear Mr Henry,

Your luxury trip of a lifetime itinerary is enclosed.'

I rummaged through the papers stapled to it and read down through the catalogue of flights transfers and ten star accommodations. Jesus H. Christ. Memphis; The Bahamas and dinner in the Waldorf in New York on the last night, before a limo ride to see the Corgi's Reunion in Carnegie Hall.

'Billy,' I cried. 'I can't believe, I just can't.' I felt tears in my eyes and I let them fall. Most of them landed on Billy's shirt as I hugged him.

'Dad, forget it, it's a tiny, tiny thank you for sorting my head out and letting me sign the record deal.'

'We're so proud of you, Billy,' Pearl said, as she came into the room carrying a couple of plates of food that wouldn't fit onto Olivia's tray. Iska breezed into the room wearing a red Spanish-type dress Billy had bought for her, and she sashayed round the room doing twirls. It was the first time, I guess, I thought of Iska as a young lady about to take the elevator to adulthood. It was a moment for the whole family, and I just stood there looking at everyone; content in my position as head of an equally-contented household.

'Billy, I hope you've stopped taking drugs.' Muriel's voice invaded our momentary happy heaven. She strode into the room like a cat with a mouse stuck in its teeth and an anvil tied to its tail. The air was full of tension again, so I tried to pour oil on troubled waters.

'Muriel, do you ever shut up? Why don't you just leave Billy alone? Nothing's ever so good for you it can't be dis-improved with a little venom and bile.' I waited for Pearl to come to her mom's defense but she didn't. In fact, quite the opposite. She rallied to Billy's aid as well,

'Mom, can-you-please-butt-out? We have had a tough time in this family recently, and everybody except you is making an effort to help everybody else out. Why do you always have to be so negative? Why, Mom?'

I'd never heard Pearl talk to Muriel like that, and everyone, including Olivia, who didn't speak much English, seemed to grasp the feeling of the moment and get right behind Pearl and support her. Muriel looked dagger-eyed around the room in a display of last-ditch defense that had long since lost any of its steam. As the rest of the family stood in silence, Muriel's face began to show signs of realizing that she was in a minority of one and she finally backed off.

'What I meant, Pearl, about Billy, is that I'm glad he's moved on from that place and those things.' She sniffed a little self-pityingly and re-wrote her insult into a plaudit. Pretty fucking thin, if you were asking me.

About three days later, Iska brought her boyfriend home for supper. He was a nice quiet French kid called Michel. He turned out to be Olivia's nephew.

'Are you really the cousins of Elvis?' he asked, as I bit into a cheese and ham sandwich on garlic bread. I nearly choked on the Gruyere and looked up. Pearl was smiling and Iska had put her hand on her boy's arm as if to dissuade him from this line of questioning. Muriel said nothing, so I braved the waters.

'Yes, yes. We *are* related to Elvis,' I said with a smirk. 'In fact, Muriel is the closest relative here, *of* Elvis. Muriel is the very, very old lady over there. She's Iska's grandmother.'

I watched Muriel's face go red from the neck up, as she fought against her obvious instinct to pull a gun from nowhere and blow my head off. Her face became crossed with train-tracks of hatred, and she held both hands slightly above the table surface like they were hovering or something. We all waited for her to explode, yet she did not. There was some feral power inside her now, forcing her back from the brink of all-out war. It was impossible to say what that force was. I really felt that it was a bit late in the old bat's life for restraint to be making an appearance, but there it was. I recalled Pearl's concern, of a few days earlier, about her mom's health. But, to be honest, I really could not believe that anything as fortuitous as serious illness could be the case either.

'I wonder if you would all excuse me, I'm feeling a little tired,' she said, pushing away from the table and getting to her feet.

She left the gathering without saying another word and, you know, it was right then that it struck me that the battle between myself and my dragon of a mother-in-law might suddenly be over. It had first manifested itself on God's earth twenty-five years earlier, with her sneering laugh (about my father's method of earning a living) on the very day I met her for the first time at their home in Cambridge, Mass. I suppose it was inevitable, but I hadn't ever imagined that anything short of either Muriel's death (or even my own) would end the long-running war of attrition between us. In a way, I was kind of disappointed. I'd sort of been preparing for a showdown with her for years, and now it looked as if it was more high hopes than High Noon which would befit the cessation of hostilities. Oh well, you win some, you tie some.

'Let's go to Orange, Dad. Just you and me,' Billy suggested a day or two later after I'd returned from my daily pilgrimage to the bakery. I was getting fitter now, and could feel the walk up and down the village much less in the back of my legs than when we'd arrived almost five weeks earlier. Orange is a pretty big market town near Gigondas.

'Sure, Billy.'

I was glad of the opportunity to spend a bit of time alone with him. Now that I'd realized he was finally grown up, and was soon to depart the family nest altogether in search of fame and fortune. We rented a car from the small garage on the road to Seguret, and Billy drove.

'How'd you get on with Ivel, about the investment side of things,' I asked, as the wind messed our hair while we drove down from the mountains along the hot dusty roads.

'Awesome, Dad. He's told me about the new block of condos

being built near Fisherman's. Your firm is handling the leasing, right?'

'Yeah, they're a pretty good investment, from what I recall. What did Ivel say about them?'

'He says he can pull a few strings with the construction company and get me two of them for thirty or forty percent less than market value.' Billy swerved to avoid a chicken on the road. 'So, what you do you think?'

'I told him to buy them for me and to give the leasing to a local real-estate firm. Ivel says that they'll provide me with an income, even if the second album never gets made.'

I was proud of Billy and this display of common sense. I figured that it was important for our relationship that I be at arm's length from any decisions he made from here on out, but I knew that Ivel wouldn't give him a bad steer. We got to Orange and parked and wandered through the small market streets. We had a beer in a small bar on the Rue St. Florent and we talked about Billy's week in New York in the studio.

'It was amazing, Dad, you know. Like we'd been waiting for years for our chance and here it is. Hairy played the best fucking guitar riffs of his life and Joe sang his heart out. We're just, you know, so lucky that it's happened to us and we're not going to blow this shot at making it.'

'Tell me about the single.'

'The Pussy Farm?'

'Shhhsh,' I put a finger to my lips. 'Don't tell the whole world.'

'They're gonna find out soon enough, if I have anything to do with it.' Billy laughed. 'Wanna see the sleeve design?'

'Sure.'

Billy pulled a sheet of paper from his pocket and unfolded it. The design was certainly novel, I'll give them that. It depicted a stallion with an enormous erection. The horse was up on his hind legs and apparently about to get it on with some cat woman, near the edge of the page, who was looking back anxiously over her shoulder. The probable point of contact was obscured by the name of the band, 'East Pole'. Down at the foot of the activities, the name of the song brazened its way with the letters of the words pockmarked by tiny cats peeping out here and there.

'Whaddya think, Dad?' Billy was obviously very proud. I was loath to disappoint his expectations.

'I can see how it might attract attention, alright.'

'Great, Dad, I'm glad you like it. I'm gonna get it blown up and framed for you and one for Ivel.'

'That's fantastic,' I said, wondering secretly if this might be the catalyst for my sole ownership of the law firm. Ivel Schwartz was the kind of guy who got offended if you wore the wrong shoes. Fuck knows what this might do to his dicky ticker.

Later on, we made our way to the fifth-century Roman theater where they still hold concerts.

'I'd love to play a gig here, Dad,' Billy said.

'Maybe you will, Billy. Maybe you will.'

'It's ironic really, Dad, but we had to fly halfway round the world to find a building that's older than Grandma.' We both laughed. It was a gloriously hot sunny afternoon in Orange, and we walked round the place for a couple of hours until the day cooled down. As we drove back to Gigondas and the mountains came into view, like a giant set of fucking dentures or something, Billy slowed the car and pulled into the entrance driveway of an old factory.

'I gotta tell you something, Dad,' he said solemnly.

'What? Is it the fucking drugs thing again?' I snapped.

'No, no, Dad. I just wanted to stop everything for a moment and say thanks for punching my lights out and locking me in that room to get that shit out of my system. I want you to know that I realize how fucking close I was to ruining my whole life. Thanks for stopping me.' He hugged me and we both made brave efforts not to cry. As he started the engine up, I responded in kind.

'Think nothing of it, Billy. If you can't rely on your own father to punch you unconscious and throw you from a roof into a swimming pool, who the fuck *can* you rely on?' We laughed together and all was well with the world.

'I've got to find something else to replace all that junk in my life, Dad,' Billy continued. 'The band is great, but when I'm not playing music I'm not gonna be hanging round nightclubs or shooting light bulbs in the swimming pools like-'

'Like cousin Elvis?' I suggested.

'Abso-fucking-lutely not,' he said as he grinned.

I have to say that in the immediate aftermath of that bonding afternoon with my boy, I felt a twinge of guilt for the first time about Carmen. It was like I was cheating on my whole family in a way.

'Oh Elvis, Elvis, Elvissssssssssssssss.'

Carmen roared like an opera singer, as she climaxed to the strains of "Easy Come Easy Go,' and I just lay below and watched as the worshipping continued on top. She was amazing, this shy cake-baker. I'd never had so much sex in my entire life, yet I felt I was enjoying it more than I ever had before with anyone. I was fifty-one and felt thirty years younger. You're probably wondering how I was able to live with the deception and lies and infidelity but, let me tell you, Gloria Dinerman hadn't crossed my mind in weeks. I know it may seem a bit hypocritical to be banging the baker, when I was supposed to be atoning for my previous indiscretions and simultaneously rebuilding my marriage. Sure, there was an element of deception, but really I've never been one to dwell on things. The truth was that things really *were* improving between me and Pearl, and I knew that the icing sessions with Carmen weren't going to last forever. There's no point in having a conscience you can't live with!

'Billy's been on the internet and found some sports place near the coast,' Pearl said, near the end of our fifth week, as she and I had breakfast together in Gigondas for the first time.

'He told me he was looking for some interests outside of music to keep him sane,' I said, scooping raspberry jam out of a croissant where I'd mistakenly deposited it moments earlier.

'He's grown up a lot lately, George.' Pearl smiled and laid down her coffee cup near mine.

'He sure has.'

'And most of it is thanks to you.' She put her hand on my arm.

'No, not really, he's had to make all the choices himself, Pearl.'

'But you helped him make those choices, George.' Pearl's voice was kinder now than I'd recalled it being in years. She rubbed my arm gently, and I realized that the shadow of my tryst with old Gloria Diningroom had begun to lift from between us. Now, to be fair, it may well have been that the half of that shadow which lay closest to me had been blown away by the baker opening the curtains in that temple to His Presleyness just above the bakery; only a few hundred yards away from Montmiral, with its shimmering pool and candles stuck in wine bottles.

Pearl confirmed my suspicions, about the demise of the darkness between us, by opening the Pearly gates, so to speak, and renewing the physical commitment of our union that same night. As we lay side by side, after the best sex we'd ever had, she commented on my performance.

'All that walking and playing boules is really paying off, George. I'd forgotten what a tiger you were. That was fantastic.'

'Grrr,' I growled, and rolled over towards her with my claws in peak condition and ready to pounce again.

"Splat, splat."

The consistency of the soapy liquid, from the container in Carmen's bathroom, suggested the work ahead of me as I cleaned the grime of the boules game from my hands. This was the Saturday of our last week in Provence. The sun was splitting the rocks outside, and I knew that my own rocks would be receiving like treatment shortly from the pastry queen of Provence. I looked at myself in the mirror and thought that, even though I wasn't really the Casanova type, I was in receipt of more female attention now than I'd ever got in my whole time on this sun-kissed, bikini-mad earth.

Billy was in good shape too, and was even talking about visiting some adventure center in the Camargue (wherever that was) before we returned home at the end of the week. Old Gooch Silverspoon, or whatever, had been on the phone earlier that day, raving about the single. There was a good chance of the song being showcased on national TV at some music award ceremony in Madison Square Garden, the day before we were due home. It might mean Billy had to fly back a couple of days early, but it seemed to me like he had made a quantum leap in maturity in the last month and really was intent on grasping this opportunity with both hands. Iska was happy. Her latest notes on apples seemed to confirm her new found confidence. The note spoke of, 'Wolf River' apples and said that it had a dual purpose in the States. '"One apple makes a pie."' I was no closer to understanding the notes but I have to say that my view of Iska, as someone who needed looking after, had moved on considerably. Muriel had finally shut up and Pearl was back in the marital bed, so the doomsday scenario, of divorce and lonely old age, now seemed like the distant threats of fictional warriors.

The intro to the Madison Square Garden Concert of 1972 was blaring as I got back to the bedroom. Carmen turned down the music and handed me a wrapped gift which was about the size of a large cushion.

'What is it?' I asked.

'It's for you, George, I made these for you,' she said suggestively and, although I was anxious to open it, my eyes were mainly drawn to her black lace bra and panties which were emblazoned with the TCB logo of Elvis's with a lightning rod. Taking care of business? Was she what? I set the parcel on the floor and, as I unwrapped it, Carmen began to undress me with startling efficiency given my own state of activity. Her arms seemed to be all around me and under me and everywhere as I managed to unravel the package from about forty miles of scotch tape.

'Jesus H. Christ!' I exclaimed, as I unfolded the bundle to reveal a huge jumpsuit, complete with detachable cape showing an embroidered eagle on it.

'Do you like it?'

'I, I can't believe–'

'Please, try it on. I hope it is to be the fitting for you,' she said anxiously as she turned down the stereo.

I hesitated for about two seconds, then I slipped off my shoes and began to step into it.

'One moment,' she said, reaching out to stop me as I lifted my foot to try it on. She slid my boxer shorts off so that I would be naked under the suit.

'Well, I suppose it might be a little hot in there,' I agreed. Naked for a second, I pulled on the skin and cover of the King of Rock and Roll and it fitted as though it had been made for me. I mean, I know it had been made for me, but you get the picture.

It was snow-white with a royal blue pleat at the end of the trouser-legs and on the cuffs of the sleeves. It was studded all over with semi-precious stones, all sewn on individually with care and skill that to me was as mesmerizing as it was alien. A zip ran from the waist to the collar and the few hairs on my chest avoided mischief as Carmen zipped me up. The music re-emerged now with the drum snaps of 'Power of my Love' underpinning the slow rhythm of the guitar chords which pushed the song up and out into the room.

'Can I take your photograph?' Carmen asked.

'No, no, absolutely not, you know I just want to enjoy this with you, no photographs please.' I imagined the mayhem a snap of me in this costume might create. Carmen began to sing along with the lyrics. **'Crush it, kick it, you can never win. No Baby you can't lick it, I'll make you give in. Every minute, every hour....'** The stereo was back up to full blast.

Carmen began to dance around me now, rubbing up against me in a questioning manner which could only have one answer. As she wound her way up and around me, her hand strayed in the direction I'd hoped. I wondered how we'd manage anything, as the zip only went to the waist, but I soon found out. A small and un-resistant Velcro join opened my body to the air at just the right position. The high tones of the Sweet Inspirations and J.D. Sumner and the Stamp Quartet groaned at us from the 1970's.

The baker was on her knees now and I remembered Billy's promise (not to blow his opportunity) as Carmen began to do just that to mine. Didn't I think of Pearl and her honest attempts to revive our marriage, at that point? Didn't I worry about the example I was setting to my own children with this display of wanton infidelity? No way, José! When a pretty woman, twenty years younger than you, has your dick in her mouth by mutual consent, you don't bother your brains with complex moral dilemmas. No siree, you just lie back (or in my case lean slightly) and close your eyes and thank your fucking lucky stars. As far as the bakery-lady thing went, I guess you could say I wanted to have my cake and have it eat me. "Suspicious Minds" began on the sound system.

FLASH! Fuck. What was that? I opened my eyes but couldn't see for a couple of seconds. Two or three more flashes in succession lit up the room. Elvis was only halfway through the second chorus when the wires on the stereo were ripped out of the wall and thrown across the room like a whip. The stars cleared and I became aware of Carmen, unsuccessfully trying to stifle my member from arriving prematurely.

Muriel stood in the doorway with a camera. She raised the Nikon to her face to capture my rapture forever, as I came uncontrollably, in the most bizarre circumstances you wouldn't wish on your worst enemy. The music died, too. Carmen stayed on her knees and tried her best to look angry but, in fact, seemed on the edge of laughing. Muriel spoke menacingly.

'George Baxter Henry, what have you got to say for yourself now?'

I gulped.

'Would you say that, on balance, you prefer the version of "Suspicious Minds" with or without the backing vocals?'

I wouldn't have thought it possible for her to become more enraged, but she did. Her face lit up like a warning light on the Titanic, "holes-in-the-hull", meter. She was choking with rage, but not enough to actually choke. She spat out at me the very words of which I had had nightmares.

'Your marriage is over, George. And you're about to become bankrupt.'

She turned and left me in my rhinestone jumpsuit with nowhere to jump. Oh, my sweet fucking eagle cape!!

CHAPTER EIGHT

I GOT OUT OF THE SUIT as fast as I could. Even Elvis, at the change-around after the matinee show in the Las Vegas Hilton, could not have out-jump-suited me on that sunny but embarrassing afternoon in Provence. I pulled on my clothes.

'Where are you going?' Carmen hollered after me as I careered down the stairs and fell, landing on top of the King in mid-thrust.

'To try and save my law-firm,' I roared back, as I exited the cake shop.

Once I was out on the street there was no sign of Muriel. I reckoned she'd go back to the house using the conventional route, so I had to try and head her off. I opened the first garden gate I came to, and sprinted down the side of a house into a small yard. I vaulted the back wall like a chicken on springs and landed, feet first, in a swimming pool. I recognised the turreted house, at the other end of the garden, as being directly opposite our own. Like Burt-fucking-Lancaster, in that movie about swimming pools, I doggie-paddled to the other end and got out, soaking wet. Just then, an old man on a ride-on mower came out of a shed to my right. He motioned angrily at me. I'm not sure what happened next, but it ended up with me trying to out-run the mower up to the back of the house where a Doberman was tied by a chain to a concrete block. It was clear to me that if the old guy got to the dog before I got to the gate, then all of my problems would be over (except for only in that kind of awful way you never want). I got to the side of the house and a small green door lay between me and the outside, non-dog, world. It was locked. I overturned some antique-looking half-barrel that had angels carved on it. I stood on it to climb the wall. I heard the sound of angels grinding into the pavement, simultaneously with the scrape of nails and the woof of death behind me. I tell you, I could feel that mutt's breath on my fucking ankles as I scrambled over and out onto the street. I lost one of my shoes in the process and took the other one off and threw it back over the door at the barking dog. For once in my life, a direct hit! The Doberman yowled. I danced up the avenue on the hot gravel; fully expecting to see Pearl in tears at the door with her bags packed. No sign. Then, I remembered that she had been talking about going shopping with Billy. She wanted to get him new clothes for the publicity shots that the record company had phoned him about the day before. They were sending a photographer to take some photos of him in France for an article in their in-house publication. I met Olivia in the hall.

'Ah, Monsieur Henry,' she said, looking me up and down as I dripped all over the floor.

'The old lady?' I asked. She pointed upstairs and I could hear the sounds of clumping overhead.

'Madame Henry, Billy, Iska?' I asked.

'All to the shopping,' she replied. I could have hugged her.

I dashed upstairs and changed into dry clothes and began the hunt through my suitcase. I found what I wanted; a faded red ring-back binder with the words, 'Silent Scream Star', written on the cover. I combed my hair and put on a jacket and then rummaged for a tie in the drawers, and found one with the crest from the Law School of San José; my alma mater. A last look in the mirror, and I was as ready as I was ever going to be. I took a couple of deep breaths and went downstairs. From the fifth or sixth step from the bottom I could see the suitcases packed and piled up in the hall. The door of the living room was slightly ajar, and I pushed it open further and stepped into the dragon's lair. She was at the other end of the room in an armchair with her arms folded. On her head she sported the ridiculous hat I'd last seen her wear at Billy's christening.

'Muriel?' Silence. Then I spoke again. 'Muriel, I wonder if I could have a word with you, please?'

She ignored me and looked straight ahead out through the front window, waiting for her daughter. I walked into the middle of the room and blocked her view. I tried again, 'Muriel.' This time she beat me to the punch.

'George, you and I have nothing to discuss. I am waiting for my daughter and my grandchildren to return, and then we are leaving for the airport. There's a flight at seven.'

'Muriel, Muriel, listen to me. We have to talk. There are a couple of things I need to ask you.'

'*You* need to ask *me* something, George? How dare you? You're nothing but a two-timing gutless weasel of a failed lawyer from olive-oil-stock, George. There's nothing more to say.'

'Oh, but I think there is, Muriel,' I said, firmly, moving backwards towards the door. 'I have a couple of questions to ask you. It shouldn't take long.' I produced the bound file from under my arm.

'You little whippersnapper, don't you dare raise your voice to me.' She stood up and walked a couple of steps in my direction. I opened the file and flicked to the first page.

'Let's begin with Carole Lombard, shall we?' I said softly. Muriel stopped and looked at me and at the papers I held in my hands.

'Begin wherever and with whomsoever you wish, George. But I'm not going to answer any of your silly questions.'

'That's a pity, Muriel. Because everybody is entitled to a fair trial and-'

'A trial? What on earth do you mean by that, George? You haven't seen the inside of a courtroom for-'

'I know, I know, twenty years or more. But you know what,

Muriel, I'm still pretty good at putting a case together. Of course, if you'd prefer, I can simply hand over the information to Pearl and let her make up her own mind.'

'About what?' I clearly had her interest, at least momentarily.

'About you, Muriel, of course.' I stood aside to let her leave the room, but she wasn't leaving now.

'What *about* Carole Lombard?' she said, in an I-couldn't-care-less voice which said I-couldn't-care-more.

'Well,' I said, moving back into the center of the room. 'Why don't you take a seat and we can clear up these historical details before Pearl comes back.'

'You mean, before I show her the photographs of her husband having-'

'Oral sex?' I suggested. She didn't even dignify me with a 'thank you'.

'I'm going to tell Pearl all about you and your little pastry-puffer, George. There's absolutely nothing you can say or do to change that. Unless, of course, you're prepared to murder me, which I wouldn't think even *you* are capable of. Or, have you some hidden reserves of strength and purpose we've missed all these years?'

'You hold onto your Polaroids, Muriel, and do whatever you want with them. All I'm interested in is your own glittering career, and there are just a few things which need to be clarified for your biography.'

'A biography?' She was beside her original chair now and sat down again.

'Not that anyone's writing an official one, Muriel. Nothing as incredible as that. No, this is just, let's say, a family history. I've got some notes I've kept about things you've told us over the years. I just want to straighten them out in my own mind before I can do anything formal like write a book about your life and your career, et cetera, et cetera.' I could see the interest welling up now behind her eyes, and blending with her irrepressible ego at the thought of posterity being bothered by a biography of Muriel Hale.

'I'm happy to indulge you for a few minutes, George. This will probably be our last ever conversation together, although we'll almost certainly meet at the divorce hearing. Carole Lombard?'

'Yes, Carole Lombard. You've told us that you spent a vacation with her in Miami just before you started shooting the movie "Mr-"'.

'And Mrs. Smith?' she said, patronizingly.

'Correct. Now, from my research, that movie was shot at the RKO Studio in Burbank from April eleventh until May thirty-first, nineteen forty-one.'

'So what?'

'Bear with me. When did you return from Miami? Was it the day before shooting began? A week earlier? Two weeks? Now, if you can't remember just say so.'

'I remember all right, George. Lucile Watson hosted a party on the weekend before filming began, and we arrived that evening from Miami in Carole's car.'

'Who drove to the party?'

'Carole did. I don't recall the make or model or number of the car, George, but I hope you're satisfied with the details.'

'As a matter of fact, no, I'm not. You see, the information I have is that Carole Lombard had broken her leg in an auto accident four weeks before shooting began. In fact Harry Edington, the producer, insisted that she appear for the first three days on the set with her leg in a cast so that scenes other than full length could be shot. All of her action scenes were put off until the last ten days of the production.'

'I don't believe you, what you're saying is-'

'That you couldn't have been on vacation with her in Miami and she certainly couldn't have driven to the party with her leg in a cast.'

'Don't be ridiculous, George, I was there, you weren't even born. I know the facts,' she snapped, in an off-hand way that I did not find at all convincing.

'I thought you might react like this, Muriel. Are you saying she wasn't in a cast, or didn't have the accident, or you *were* on holidays with her or she *did* drive the car, or do you still stand over all of those, "facts", as you call them?'

'Absolutely, it's all true.' She folded her arms.

'Then perhaps you'd like to have a look at this, Muriel.' I handed her a sheet of paper.

'What is it?' she asked, before accepting possession of Exhibit 'A'.

'It's a copy of the hospital admission records. You'll see that it contains the date of the plaster-of-Paris cast being put on. That appears to be March third 1941, and it was removed on the nineteenth of May 1941.'

'You could have typed this yourself on an old typewriter, George. It's absolutely worthless.' She tossed the paper aside. I picked it up and replaced it in the file.

'I *could* have typed it, but I didn't, Muriel,' I said, taking out the next page from the folder and handing it to her.

'What's this?' she asked dismissively.

'A letter from the current head of administration at the hospital, certifying the records as authentic copies of the original.' I let her read it, then I snatched it back. 'But, of course, that could be another forgery couldn't it, Muriel? Well the lady has very kindly provided me with her phone number in case she can be of further help. I'm sure Pearl could phone her to check.'

'And I could simply say to Pearl that I remember it the way you've told me now, and that your 'records' simply confirm my own recollection.' She grinned in an evil manner.

'You could, but even that wouldn't explain why in the first place you said you were on vacation with her when it's quite clear you weren't.'

'You don't know that.'

'I don't, but I can find out. Can you provide me with the name of the hotel you stayed in, the airline you used to fly to Miami, times and dates of departure and arrival, Carole Lombard's home address?' Muriel looked angry but said nothing.

'Okay.' I smiled. 'Enough about Carole Lombard. Let's move on to some other people you claim to have known.' I began to flick through some pages and stopped at a black and white photograph of Marlene Dietrich.

'That's mine,' she snarled. 'Where did you get it?'

'Don't you remember? You gave it to Pearl on the day Marlene Dietrich died in 1992. I'd been out drinking with Herb Vissing. It was our wedding anniversary and I forgot all about it.'

'May sixth,' she said bitterly, as though she'd been married to me herself.

'Yep,' I said. 'I forgot the anniversary, so you gave her this; a lifelong treasure from your own career. It's signed, "*to Muriel, hugs and kismet. M.D. 1943*".'

'So?'

'Where did she sign it? Was it on a film set, or did someone get it for you second-hand?'

'How dare you? I met with Marlene at MGM during one of the breaks. I was at the studio meeting some people from publicity.'

'So you met her?'

'Met her? I *knew* her. We were great friends. We both had our hair permed by Sidney Guilleroff, *that's* how close we were.'

'It's a forgery,' I said.

'You bastard, how can you denigrate the name of Marlene Dietrich? She was a goddess, an angel, you know nothing of her, absolutely nothing.'

I ignored her ranting and produced a letter from a handwriting expert in the CIA who had been in law school with me.

'Here. Read it for yourself, Muriel, "99.7% certainty that it is not her handwriting". If you read on, you'll see that he has done about a dozen comparisons from signatures on contracts at MGM

and remarks that nowhere else does she ever sign herself, "M.D.".
It's a classic way to forge autographs; have a personal message and
just use the famous person's initials. Of course you never meant to
sell the thing, your purpose was much more personal. That's why
you reckoned it would never be tested. Giving it to Pearl on our
anniversary was the perfect way to use it to persuade her that-'

'That what, George? What was I trying to persuade her of?'

'That you are the person you pretend to be. An actress, a star
who rubbed shoulders with stars and who achieved greatness
herself.'

'I *was* a great actress, George, I was nominated for an Academy
Award.'

'I know, I know. We'll get to that later, Muriel. But I note you
don't deny that the signature is a forgery. Let's move on, shall we?'

'If you like, George. You can continue this farce of a cross-
examination but I'm a ninety-one year-old lady and I don't have to
take this kind of retrospective historical rewriting from anyone. I
bet Pearl will be shocked when she finds out-' she got up from the
chair and began to stride toward the door.

'I'm afraid she will, Muriel. I'm afraid she will. She's going to
be very shocked indeed when she reads what I've found out by
doing a little digging.'

I heard the footsteps stop (if you know what I mean) and then
I turned around slowly to see Muriel's face crossed with a pallor
which was right out of Funeral Weekly. She put one hand behind
her to feel for the door and pushed it closed. It clicked shut, and
then a glance passed between us that meant that we both understood the game now. That small noise of a door shutting in France,
at the tail end of August, was like a starter's gun for the confrontation which we had both always known to be inevitable. The rules
were clear; I had until Pearl returned, to continue my questioning,
and Muriel would ultimately be judge and jury as to the value of the
information presented or the admissions elicited. Twenty years of

my lack of experience in the courtroom would now face its sternest test.

I'd been collecting information about Muriel since even before our wedding day. Up until recently, though, the final pieces of my investigation had not really been complete. Allied to that, I must confess that I'd never really had either the opportunity or the guts to produce my folder and cut loose. Any such doubts were now cast aside as I had no other choice; it was do or divorce. The witness returned to the stand and the lawyer resumed the cross-examination.

'Charles Chaplin.' I announced.

'What about him?'

'You claim to have been asked by him to play the female lead instead of Virginia Cherrill, in, "City Lights", in 1931.'

'That's true.'

'Is it? You said that you were under contract at RKO and they wouldn't release you for the part.'

'Correct.'

'But RKO didn't renew your contract after "Brooklyn Bridge", a year earlier, did they?'

'I was under contract, and Wilfred Kaufmann refused to release me to make pictures for anyone else.'

'I'm not sure that's quite true, is it? My understanding is that you and Kaufmann parted company shortly after the Oscars in 1930, the previous year.'

'I don't know what you mean, George.' She had a haughty expression, but it was cracking. I reached for the evidence and showed her a whole quarter-page article in the LA Times of July 1930 which was headlined:

"RKO'ed, Hale falls from grace."'

The tears started to well up in her eyes now, but she somehow managed to kinda suck them back in.

'Can you explain this, Muriel?' I waved the headline at her and began to read. "Hollywood was shaken today after RKO announced the termination of the six-picture contract it signed in December last year with Oscar-nominated Muriel Hale. In a press statement-'"

'Alright, alright. So, I was let go. We had a disagreement, a row about-'

'Don't tell me, artistic differences, Muriel?'

'Yes, I wouldn't expect you to understand anything about Art, George.'

'But I do understand about times and dates and lies, Muriel. I'm afraid you've spun us quite a lot of tall stories over the years about your career. Let me continue. Clark Gable. You say you starred with him in, "The White Sister", in 1933. I'm afraid that despite my very best efforts to locate you in that movie, there's no sign of you. I rented the video recently and you don't even get a credit.'

'That's outrageous. I never told you that I was in that film. I said I *auditioned* for that film.'

'Funny you should change your story now, but it's actually recorded on our wedding day when Dick Grobbe taped the speeches. You warbled on for ten minutes and listed that as one of your film credits. I have a transcript of the tape here if you'd like to see it.' She didn't want to.

'Are you quite finished?' She looked at her nails in a show of apparent boredom.

'No, I'm not, Muriel. In fact, I'm only getting to the good parts now. What about your Oscar nomination?'

'My nomination? What the hell are you trying to insinuate about my nomination, George? You're a cruel, spiteful man.'

'Steady on with plaudits, Muriel, my girl. You're not too shy in the hate and cruelty department yourself, if I'm not mistaken.'

'What do you mean?'

'Well I did a little searching through some files and libraries in Los Angeles over the years, but I never could find anything to link you to the process of Oscar nominations until just a few months ago. I did some digging and I discovered a very interesting little thing.' I watched her now and she began to blush. Ever so slightly at first, but the color intensified as I whispered the magic name, "Christopher Power".'

'What? I don't know any directors of that name.' She was panicky.

'Who said he was a director, Muriel? Not me.'

'No, no, I didn't mean that I knew him, it's just that the name, the name is-' she was hyperventilating now.

'Yes, the name, "Christopher Power", is a business alias of Steven Hardone, who directed your fabulous picture. "Christopher Power Limited" was the company used to front the bribing and blackmail of the Academy, or at least enough of them to swing the nomination. I think I'm right in saying that, Muriel. I only made the connection when I read the newspaper reports from the time, about the whiff of scandal in relation to the nomination process. The trail stopped cold at a recently-formed company with a fictitious address. But I managed to find out, through a law-searcher firm in California, that there was an investigation by the DA's office in the same period into corporate fraud and tax evasion. It threw up some very interesting information and names and addresses.'

'You can't prove anything, this is all speculation.' She was defiant now, like the wasp on its back, which still thinks it has enough energy to fire the sting.

'The address used for the corporate tax return was your home address, Muriel. Incidentally, this was the same address given by Hardone when he was arrested the following year for drunk driving. You were being boned by him, weren't you, Muriel?'

'My private life is absolutely none of your concern. Who do you think you are, snooping into other people's pasts and making horrible and false allegations? '

'But they're not false, are they, Muriel? You were having an affair with this guy and he put you into his picture. Maybe you even got the screen test without having to give him a good time, but it's absolutely clear that RKO wanted nothing to do with either of you when they found out. You were a small-time actress who got a break and blew it; or found a director and blew him. You moved on to Louie then and he was your meal ticket right up until he died.'

'I loved Louie,' she sobbed.

'Maybe you did love Louie, Muriel. But it seems he wasn't enough for you either.'

'What do you mean?' The crying stopped like a faucet being turned off. She looked startled.

'Louie wasn't Pearl's father, was he?' I asked calmly.

Outside, the sound of the taxi bringing Pearl, Iska and Billy back crunched up the gravel driveway. Pearl would be in the house in moments. I pulled out another page from the book of evidence.

'What do you -?' she began, but I silenced her with my hand in the air and passed the information to her.

'Blood type,' I said. 'I had a look at Louie's autopsy report and it says: AB negative, he couldn't possibly be Pearl's father.'

'But when did you-?'

'I started looking, right after you advanced the money to Pearl so I could buy into the partnership. I found out that the Register of Bequests had you down for a load of dollars from the estate of this guy Hardone, a couple of years earlier. I reckoned no one would be so stupid as to leave money to a person fifty years later who wasn't family, unless he'd rattled his sabre at you sometime. The rest is-'

'The rest is guesswork, George,' she said, simply.

'You're right there, Muriel. But that's what intuition is; pure guesswork. You didn't have the guts to leave Louie, because Hardone was never going to leave his wife is my guess.'

'Pearl won't even listen to this, this bullshit. Once she knows about you and that cup-cake whore. She won't even-'

'Speaking of whores,' I said, as I played the final card of the hand it had taken two decades plus to build. It was a hazy enough photograph of a police raid on the Emerald "Entertainment" Club in February 1934; but the effect was instantaneous. The fox-like eyes of this insufferable nonagenarian narrowed in absolute fear. I could hear the children and Pearl in the kitchen with Olivia now. They'd be with us in seconds.

'What happens now, George?' The old dragon asked for terms.

'Here's the deal, Muriel. You keep your mouth shut from now until the coffin-makers arrive. Don't ever utter a single word about my marriage, my infidelities, my qualifications, my lack of trial experience. In fact, don't ever fucking criticize me again. In return, your grandchildren will never get to find out that you humped your way to a bogus Oscar nomination, made fewer personal appearances than Salman Rushdie, and Pearl will always believe that Louie was her father. So, it means she's not directly related to Elvis but, hey, you can't have everything. Oh, and speaking of Elvis, nobody need ever see my jumpsuited performance or your own Viva Los Angeles appearance at the Emerald Club. Perhaps it's time for you to go silent again, Muriel. The talkies never really suited you.'

'Mom? Where are you?' Pearl's voice sounded through the door like the end of a dream as I waited for Muriel to decide. The door swung open and Pearl was in the doorway, standing between forever and me.

'Why are these suitcases packed? Mom, what's going on?' Pearl's face was covered in worry. I coulda bitten my fucking wrist off with the tension. Muriel rose slowly from the witness box to deliver the verdict. ('Have you reached a verdict on which you are all agreed?").

'I've decided to take Iska to Avignon for a few days, Pearl. Billy's flying home early, so I really think that you and George should have some time together, alone. After all, that's what you came here for in the first place.'

Pearl turned around to call up the stairs for Iska. As Muriel came out of the room past me, she handed me an envelope with the Polaroids. I burned them that evening and, no, I didn't fucking keep one for posterior. I was free again. Good old Liberty, Equality, Paternity!

CHAPTER NINE

'YOU SEE THIS PLACE, Dad? It's amazing.'

I looked over Billy's shoulder, at the gleamy screen of his laptop filled with flashing photographs of expensive cars and helicopters.

'What is it, Billy?'

'It's this awesome place called *Au Fond du Monde*. It means like the edge of the universe, or something.' Billy clicked an icon with his mouse, and the screen changed to reveal the stilted image of someone falling from a plane without a parachute. 'It's just amazing, Dad. This place has got sports, adventures and the most incredible edge-of-this-fucking-world activities. And it's right here in France.'

'Are you thinking of paying a visit to it?'

'Am I what? Absolutely, Dad. I'm gonna scoot down there day after tomorrow and see what's cooking. I could really dig some of those activities.'

'Be careful, Billy,' I warned. 'Some of those things look pretty dangerous.'

'Lighten up, Dad. What could be more dangerous than trying to snort two tons of cocaine in between cramming for Bolivian history exams?'

'Oh,' I said. 'I got a message from the college at the office yesterday. Judy told me that they wanted to know if you're going back in the Fall for the repeat exams. I told her to call them and say you were quitting to become a rock star, so don't let me down now.'

'I won't, Dad. I talked to Hairy and Joe last night by e-mail and they said that the publicity's really heating up in New York. The single's out this week. You know, I still can't quite believe it's all happening, really happening.'

'Believe it, Billy, and savor every goddamn moment, because it won't last forever. The best things rarely do.'

'You've lasted a long time, Dad. What's your secret? You must be nearly what, seventy?' he joked.

'Get outta here, I'm closer to forty than I am to seventy.'

'I guess they keep moving it, huh?' Billy laughed loud and long and I was as proud as hell of him. What parent wouldn't be?

Pearl was even happier than I was about her mom taking a hike to Avignon for a few days.

'Oh, George, I'm so glad to have you all to myself for a change,' she said, as she arrested my dressing habits one morning and led me back to the bed for some unexpected connubial exertions.

'I don't think you've really had to share me with your mom,' I said, as I laughed.

'No, not Mom. The kids. Everything. Well, it's all beginning to work out so well, George. Don't you think so, too?'

To be fair, when you're getting more sex than you ever reckoned you could handle, and it's hot outside as well, and divorce is on the most recent train outta town; I gotta admit it's pretty close to the working-out-so-well stakes.

'I do, Pearl, I do,' I replied, feeling slightly out of breath. The sex had improved in quality as well as frequency. Those smart-assed young lawyers from downtown Boston, with their Rolex watches and racquetball coaches, woulda been hard pressed to process any more loveabilia than I did that summer. I had begun to ease out of the situation with Carmen, but with the action at home on the increase, the overall volume was down very little, if at all.

'You don't visit every day now,' Carmen complained later that week, as I snaffled some cream from the cakes in the shop. We began to trek upstairs, past the wounded figure of Elvis I had injured in my haste to race Muriel back to the house only days earlier.

'Well, Carmen, I have to be more careful now with -'

'Your wife?' she suggested, in a hurt voice like I was actually cheating on her or something by sleeping with Pearl. Can you believe these broads?

'Yes, I've got to be careful about things now. We're going back to Boston on Sunday.' Carmen looked a little surprised.

'Boston? I thought that you were to be the staying to be ze buying of the house?'

Oh Christ, I thought. Just what I need; another fucking sexual dependent.

'Yes, yes, of course, Carmen. But there are lots of things to sort out back in America. I have to think about my business, but, of course, there will be other holidays here in Gigondas.'

'Holidays? You said that you were going to live here for always, George Preslee.'

She looked mad now, and I understood why. I recalled that, in a particularly weak moment some weeks earlier, I had sort of imparted to Carmen a vague intention to move to Gigondas at some near point and to continue our liason. I might even have spoken of divorcing Pearl. Carmen also knew, through the local newspaper, of our option to purchase the place. To be honest, I was stunned that she'd really believed me. I began to see now the classic hallmark signs of infidelity going horribly wrong.

It's such a fucking mess when trust and expectation intrude on afternoon sex. It's like water seeping into a ship; the meaning of, "going down", changes completely. Suddenly it's all, "me," "me," "me," instead of the inherent selflessness of the liaison itself. How could I have been so blind and altruistic as to imagine that the calm, detached, warmth and honesty I'd brought to the baker's table would be ultimately thrown back in my face; marinaded in commitment and demand? Oh, the caring professions, where do we get our grace? I didn't want her calling round and ruining everything, though.

'Yes, Carmen, and I *will* be coming back. But there is so much to organize. I mean, we have to get back to our home in Boston and sell that house and sort out my divorce first. Then I'll be able to come back and you and I can make arrangements perhaps to be-'

'Married?' She whooped. 'I will be Mrs Preslee, Madame Preslee?'

'Maybe, yes,' I lied, putting my head in my hands. 'But first I must get a divorce and think of the children, and, of course, the business will have to be sold. I'm very tired, Carmen. I have so much to think about, so much to organize. I cannot let Pearl find out about you. The old lady almost told her everything. You must trust me to do this in my own way.'

'Yes, George, I understand, you have very much to do,' she agreed. 'Please let me help you relax,' she said, heading in the direction of the lower deck of the jumpsuit where only flapping Velcro stood between happiness and me.

'Oh, oh,' I groaned, encouraging her in her endeavors. I'd have to pack pretty soon.

I was definitely going to have to get rid of Carmen from my life A.S.A.P. But I had to be careful about how I did it. The last thing I wanted was some fucking scene down at the house, now that Muriel was out of the way and Pearl and I had reached a level of understanding which looked certain to be enough to save our marriage (oh yeah, and of course, my financial hide). I was pretty proud of myself, all right, the way things had turned out. Billy had grown up all of a sudden and Iska was well on her way to adulthood. I was surer than I'd ever been that she was anything but, 'a little slow'. Of all of us, she seemed the only one who hadn't had to undergo all manner of stress and strain to reach out and scoop a handful of water from the fountain of contentment.

I suppose I couldn't really believe the luck I'd had in facing down Muriel with the stuff from her past. I had spent a good many hours over the years, checking out this and that, and jotting down the snippets of "facts" she'd fed us for decades about how great an actress she was.

Actors. God. They gave me a royal pain in the ass even before I'd met Muriel. I knew this one prick from college in San José in the drama club, Jack Harvey. At least, I think that's what his name was. He was such a prick that if there were a shortage of pricks he'd make two. He was always walking around the campus, 'getting into character,' he called it, wandering about, talking aloud, and having these imaginary conversations on his own where he was always, like, taking offense or something;

"How dare you?" or, "I can't believe you're standing there telling me that."

He was such a pretentious moron. You'd see him in the cafeteria with his head stuck in some notebook, like he was writing the great American novel or something. The thing about this guy was it was all show; when you actually got to see him in action, he was awful. He was worse than awful, actually, because he was so bad playing other characters he was almost like, well, if you could imagine, he was like Hamlet playing Jack Harvey instead of the other way around. You know, what I always wondered was, if these guys were such great actors, then why don't they just find a part where the person is a decent soul instead of a prick and then, "get into", that character and fucking well stay there? All great ideas are simple, yeah?

'YEAA-YESSSSSSS-YES-YES' Billy's voice echoed through that old French house on the morning of the day he was leaving for the edge-of-your-seat theme-park place. His cry brought Pearl and myself together in the hall from opposite ends of the house.

'What is it, Billy?' I asked, as he put down the phone. His face was a mix of delirium and wonder.

'The single, the single,' he chanted, jumping up and down like a man with pogo sticks instead of feet.

'What about the single?' Pearl pitched in.

'We're in the Top Ten, the fucking Billboard Top Ten.'

'In the charts? Hey, Billy, that's fantastic.' I threw my arms around him.

'Number eight, number eight, number eight,' Billy sang to the unoriginal tune of, "Here We Go, etc". 'The new chart will be announced on Sunday, so we might get to Number One".

My son was in the charts and everything was right with the world.

'Oh, Billy, we're so proud of you,' Pearl sobbed, as the three of us hugged in the hall.

'And you know the best thing of all?' Billy came up for air.

'No,' we both answered.

'The video has been banned by ninety percent of the TV channels in the U.S. and here in Europe.'

'And that's good?' Pearl was uncomprehending.

'Sure, Mom, nothing sells quicker than something the government doesn't want you to have.'

'The government? What has it got to do with the single?' Pearl showed her age.

'It's a figure of speech, Mom,' Billy said, grinning.

'Yeah, just a figure of speech, Mom.' I echoed my son the rock star's coolness.

This was bliss; my family around me (well two of them anyway), and the scent of success in the air. I wasn't yet sure as to how I was going to extricate myself from the bakery without getting too much flour on my hands. But I'd work that out before we left, or just after we got home. Iska and Muriel were due back on Saturday, and we flew Sunday, so there were only a couple of days left really to tie things up. Billy had to be in New York on Friday night for the awards ceremony. They were the guest artists for the event and would perform their song live in front of an invited audience of stars, and a television viewership which was expected to top twenty million. I wondered how many people had seen the Aloha from Hawaii via Satellite Special in 1973. On the other hand, perhaps it was a bit premature for comparisons. The cat song had only just jumped out of the door-flap at the world. Now we would all just have to wait to see how big a splash it made on landing.

I played my final game of boules on Thursday morning, just after Billy had left in a rental car to go to the place in the Camargue. Old Pinochet, De Gaulle and Cézanne were off to the coast to play in some tournament over the weekend, and I told them I would not be in Gigondas when they returned the following week.

'Goodbye, Msieu,' they each said in turn, as they shook my hand when the game had ended. It was as though they'd rehearsed the words for days in advance. They presented me with a brand new glittery set of boules.

'Au revoir, mes grandes amis,' I read from a phonetically-spelled prompt card which Carmen had helped me to write. They seemed suitably impressed. We exchanged addresses. (Well, they gave me theirs and I handed them details of a place I'd lived in Los Angeles some thirty years earlier). I was very anxious to make sure Carmen would have no leads to follow if she began to sniff the trail after it dawned on her that old Georgie-boy wasn't coming back. The rental agent only had contact details for Herb Vissing, and I'd already closed off that avenue.

'Can you show me your passport, please?' I asked her during what was to be our last sexual encounter, although she couldn't possibly have known that.

'My passport? Why do you ask this, George?'

'Well,' I began shyly. 'It's because-'

'Yes?'

'Well, I suppose I should be honest and say that I need your passport number to apply for a marriage license in Memphis. You're not an American citizen.'

'Memphis?' her jaw dropped. 'We will be married in Memphis? It is incredible, no?' She was laughing now, and crying the first set of actual tears of joy I think I'd ever seen.

'Yes, Carmen. You see I had hoped it would be a surprise, but I am confident that the family will allow us to have the wedding reception in Graceland.'

'Grace-land,' she stuttered. It was though I'd got her a back-stage pass to heaven itself. 'Oh, George, George, I love you, I love you, I love you.' She threw her arms around my neck and kissed me all over my face. Once she'd calmed down, I noted her passport number and her family name (Morel) and tucked the information into my wallet for immediate future reference. I put a call through to Charlie Nagy in the CIA from the phone booth outside the hotel on my way back from the bakery.

'Hey, George, what's new? Need some more autographs tested? Who is it this time, Shirley Temple?'

I laughed. 'No, nothing like that, but in fact that information became very useful pretty recently.'

'Glad to hear it, George. I'm always happy to do a favor for an old University-of-San-José man.'

'So am I, Charlie, and in fact that's why I'm calling. I'm on vacation in France for a few weeks and I've got a little piece of information which may be of use to you guys.'

'Oh yeah? Tell me more, George, I'm interested.'

'Well, I don't know if it's anything, but I was in a bar here and I got talking to this couple and, over a few drinks, tongues loosened and you know the way people start maybe speaking a little too freely.'

'Yeah? Like how freely, George?'

'Well that's the thing, Charlie. This girl, all sweet, like cheese-cake wouldn't melt in her mouth, she produces her passport to prove who she is and then she asks me if I would be interested in helping them establish contacts in the States to raise funds for their campaign.'

'What campaign, George?' I had Charlie's interest now, alright.

'Something strange, let me think, oh yes, I remember; they're called the "Liberation Front for an Independent Provence with European Union Funding and Reduced Public-Transport delays."'

'Jesus-H, that sounds ominous. Did they mention any other organizations that they have connections with?'

'Hmm, she did mention something about some crew who separate baskets.'

'Baskets?'

'Yeah, from Italy or maybe Spain,'

'Oh fuck, George. You mean the Basque separatists in Spain?'

'That could be it, Charlie, any help to you?'

'Oh God, yes, George. The boys upstairs in Counter-Terrorism are going to be very interested in this. Anything else you can tell me?'

'Well nothing really, except for her name and passport number if that's any help?' I could barely stop myself from laughing out loud now. I gave him the details.

'Oh, George, you're absolutely amazing. This is great stuff. You better be careful yourself. I'd advise you to have no further contact with this person or her associates.'

'My thoughts exactly, Charlie. Tell me, what will happen to her? I mean she seemed to be planning on visiting the U.S. pretty soon, so, like, can you have her followed or something?'

'Let me put it to you this way, George. If this dame uses that passport or if that's her real name, and it may well be, then she won't get past Immigration. Even if she does, she'll be picked up by our operatives within twenty-four hours and shipped back to the Independent Railway Republic or wherever, faster than you can say Iraq oil. You know those bastards wouldn't let us use their airspace in -'

'Gotta go, Charlie,' I cut across him as the beeps began to get louder and faster and my money ran out. It would be the best value couple of coins I ever spent. I was pretty sure of that.

Iska phoned on Friday.

'Avignon is great, Dad. We've been all over the place. The food is wonderful and Michel has come down to join us for two days. We found this wonderful church. It's so tiny, and it's right in the middle of a bridge that only goes halfway. Oh, Dad, this has been our best holiday ever. Can we come back?'

'We'll see, Honey. We'll see.'

'Anyway, we're back to Gigondas tomorrow. Grandma has been a bit quiet but I think she's enjoying herself. She seems to be tired all the time. See you tomorrow, Dad.'

' See you tomorrow, Honey,' I said, handing the phone to her mother.

I bet old Muriel was down in the dumps for a bit after our set-to in the front room, but at least the air had been cleared and we both knew where we stood. I was so glad that I hadn't blown the whistle on her with Pearl or the kids. To be honest, I don't think I ever would have. That kind of threat is always much more potent when it's undelivered. Once the cat is out of the bag (or off the farm) the desired effect may quite often not be achieved, or it may be diluted. I was pretty sure I knew Pearl well enough to know that. Faced with the information about each of us, she would still have chosen Muriel over me. Maybe Pearl loved me, but she was scared of her mother and, in my experience, fear always wins out over love. No, that card was played at just the right time.

I still couldn't believe how lucky I'd been. I knew the old bat would crank up the volume again and it would be impossible for her to ever completely hold her tongue, but I think I knew that she would never risk my wrath by disclosing my affair with the, "pastry puffer". She wouldn't have been able to live with the fall-out of Pearl finding out that Louie wasn't her real father. If Pearl ever found out about Carmen I knew that even if I could prove that Muriel was the Boston Strangler, my marriage would still be over. In any event, Pearl and I were back on track now and in a couple of days we'd be home. Our marriage and my law firm would remain intact, untouched, and ready to roll into the future while G.B.H. reaped the rewards on both fronts.

I worried for a few moments on that Friday night, about Carmen gaining access to my real address in Boston through Michel's contact with Iska. What of it, I thought finally, as I drifted from semi-sleep into half-action as Pearl returned from the bathroom and slipped her nightdress off to reveal the Las Vegas lingerie ensemble. The CIA would clean up the doggie-doo long before it achieved its destination of my doorstep. Somewhere, early the next day in the midst of a bizarre dream, in which nubile bakers were covering themselves in different flavored cream while the marriage counsellor stood outside the window crying, the phone rang. I realized it was a real phone and I woke and picked up the bedside receiver.

'Yes hello?

'Allo? Is this Mr Henry?'

'Yes, yes. This is George Baxter Henry,' I replied, still halfway through licking one of the iced bakers.

'This is the *Centre Au Fond du Monde* in the Camargue.'

'Yes? Can I talk to Billy?' I said.

'No,' said the voice. 'You cannot speak to Billy. I am sorry, but there's been an accident'.

Fenouillet De La Chine:
false France; known 1883.

Iskar. A.

CHAPTER TEN

I DROVE LIKE A LUNATIC from Provence to the Camargue but, let me tell you, that's nothing in a country where everyone drives like a lunatic. There are more people killed on the French roads every year than died of TB in France in the whole of the last century. How about that for a statistic? Now, either they knew how to tackle TB ahead of the rest of the world, or they have an outrageous level of road carnage. Each way you slice it; it's pretty impressive. I remember seeing a survey somewhere that said most car accidents happen within six feet of the home, or was it six miles? I have to say that I found that statistic less than impressive. I mean, hey, you spend most of your time *at* home, so if there's an accident to be had, chances are you'll be around for it and available to take part. Anyway, I drove pretty hard in Olivia's husband's car. As we left Gigondas, I saw Carmen sitting outside the bakery on the steps thumbing through what looked like a bridal magazine. There was absolutely no way I was ever going to buy that house now. There was more chance of me getting Graceland through the mail in a ten acre envelope !

The guy on the phone hadn't said much about the circumstances of the accident or how Billy was, only that he was now in a hospital in a town called Aigues Mortes. Of course when he'd told me the name of the place, I'd panicked and thought he was describing Billy's condition. Olivia phoned them back to get the details of where the hospital was, and by 8.30am we were on the way to seeing if Billy was on the road to recovery. The hospital had given little enough information over the phone, so we were pretty much in the dark.

I was worried as hell. I thought that I would never forgive myself if anything happened to Billy. It would have all been my fault for signing that goddamn consent form and for getting him off the cocaine. It took us just under three hours to get there, and after a couple of wrong turns on roundabouts I found the, "hopital", (as they insist on spelling it). Pearl must have guessed what I was going through and laid no blame on me during the drive down.

'We're looking for our son, Billy,' I said to the receptionist.

'Where is he?' she replied with a question.

'How the hell do we know where he is? That's why I'm asking you,' I roared. Pearl put a hand on my arm to calm me.

'Msieu and Madame Henry?' a voice from behind cut across the misunderstanding.

'Yes?' we said, both turning round at the same time. A doctor in a white coat with a stethoscope around his neck, beckoned us with his hand like a traffic cop.

'How is he?' I spluttered.

'Is he okay?' Pearl enquired. The guy ignored our questions and simply turned and began to walk purposefully away.

'Please follow me,' he said, and so we did.

I gotta tell you that I had skedaddled through every emotion, from shit-scared to, "why me?" and back, in our drive down from Gigondas. Pearl was worried too, but she remained as calm as hell. Come to think of it, she's never been one to panic. I didn't know if Billy had survived the crash or whether he would be permanently disabled or brain-dead or whatever, or anything at all. That's parent-hood for you; you raise them to fend for themselves just so that you can continue to worry about them when they become adults. When they're small, you wipe their nose or put a band-aid on their knee and watch over them twenty-four seven. Every door-hinge is a potential guillotine. When they're even smaller than that and just babies, you watch over them at night in their cots and wake them up just to make sure they're still asleep. It's crazy. They grow up, and then it's worse because you don't see them most of the time, but you still worry. They never worry about *you*. They just get big enough to know that you still worry about *them*, and then they use that as leverage for, like, more fucking money or later nights out. Who am I, the goddamn tooth fairy? (Well I used to be). We followed the doctor until he stopped at the room marked with a sign saying, "Morgue", and my heart pressed the button for the basement of my stomach. Pearl took my hand and squeezed it. The doctor buzzed the door, and a nurse peered out of an office window and handed him a chart.

'This way,' he said. I closed my eyes and wished I were dead myself. I pushed the door.

'No, no, Msieu, not that way.'

I opened my eyes and saw that he'd begun up the short flight of stairs to another wing of the hospital altogether. I sighed with relief and felt an irresistible urge to fart, but was afraid under the conditions that I might follow through. So I sucked in my stomach and tried to reverse the traffic. A body in the first bed was covered from head to toe in plaster cast.

'Hi, Mom, Hi, Dad.' Billy called across the room from another bed. His arm was in a sling and he was sitting up enjoying a pretty healthy-looking lunch.

'Oh God, Billy, are you alright?' I said, rushing over to him. 'Your mother was worried half to fucking death.' Pearl got to him first and kissed him on the cheeks.

'Well, I'd like more orange juice, but, apart from that, I'm fine,' he said, grinning at me.

Billy let me catch my breath and then, as we sat beside him and ate dry bread and apples, he explained what had happened.

'The adventure place was incredible. I nearly lost my mind during the whole thing.'

'You nearly lost your life,' I reminded.

'Steady on, Dad. I'm here, aren't I?'

'Just-a-fucking-bout,' I said. 'What the hell went wrong?'

'I got there at lunchtime yesterday. They made me do this medical. They did all kinds of fitness tests, even a brain scan.'

'Don't tell me. They scanned but found nothing?'

'Hey, Dad, save it for the Oscars. They had this showroom with every car imaginable and I picked out a brand new Ferrari. Then they brought me to, like, a small cinema and showed me the options.'

'The options?'

'Yeah, Dad. There were dozens of wild things to do but I chose this adventure called, "Fly Dive".'

'I don't want to hear the details,' Pearl said as she stood up. 'You're not badly injured, and that's all I need to know. Tell your dad all about it if you want, but I'm going for a walk.'

'"Fly dive?"' I asked, as the door of the hospital ward creaked closed behind my wife.

'Oh, yeah. The kick about, "Fly Dive", is that I got to drive the car at a hundred and seventy miles an hour on a disused stretch of highway about thirty miles long. At the end, the road just stops in mid-air and I drove the car off it into a lake.'

'Into a real lake?' This was incredible.

'Oh no, Dad, not a *real* lake. An artificial lake but still with lots of water, just no fish.'

'And you drove the car into the lake? Are you fucking crazy? Wouldn't it have been cheaper to buy a sledgehammer and break your arm in the comfort of your own home?'

'Relax, Dad, it's all covered. The lake is only a couple of yards deep and they've got frogmen standing by to rescue you once you hit the water.'

'Why don't they just get you to stop the car before the road ends? That way you wouldn't run the risk of drowning.'

'You don't get it, do you, Dad?'

'Get what? What's to get? You're almost killed driving a fast car into a fucking pond; that's not so hard to understand.' I was furious now, as well as relieved.

'Cool it, Dad, it's okay. These guys are professionals; they hauled me out of there in less than two minutes. I was just a little bit wet that's all. I had nearly a whole minute to spare before the car exploded.'

'Exploded? Is that how you broke your arm? Some of the debris?'

'Oh this?' he said, wagging his sling. 'Nah, I fell, climbing up the steps to the office to pay my bill after the rescue.'

'You *paid* for this? Are you crazy? How much?'

'Fifteen, Dad.'

'Fifteen *hundred* bucks?' I couldn't believe it.

'No, Dad, fifteen thousand.' He grinned.

'Are you out of your fucking mind, Billy? Are you sure you're not mistaken?'

'"*We all got to cut loose sometime and make our own mistakes,*"' remember that, Dad?'

'Who said that?'

'You did.'

'When?'

'That day we made the deal.'

I'd remembered the phrase immediately he'd said it, but had hoped he'd forgotten where he'd heard it.

'I never said that, Billy,' I said, but, as I did, I knew that both of us knew I was lying. I took a couple of deep breaths and looked at my son and said.

'You scared the fuck out of me and your mom, Billy. I thought you were dead or paralyzed or something, this guy phoned in the middle of the night and -'

'I'm not dead, Dad,' he said with a smirk.

'I can fucking well see that,' I said. 'That's why I'm so mad at you.'

'Because I'm not dead?'

'Yes. No. I mean, yes, I'm mad but not because – damn it, Billy, don't ever scare me like this again. I let you out of my sight for an instant and this happens. Jesus, you could have been killed. Do these guys have permits to do this, training, licenses?'

'Absolutely, Dad. It's very very safe. The statistics show that you're safer here than you'd probably be in your own home'

'Bullshit, Billy.'

'No, Dad, really. You know what the chances are that something awful would happen, like say; being punched in the face and knocked off a roof into a swimming pool when you're out of your head on drugs?'

'Okay, okay,' I said. 'I get the picture. Let's phone Iska and tell her you're okay. We left a note for her in the house for when she gets back from Avignon.'

I already did that, Dad, first thing this morning. I talked to her and Grandma. They'd just arrived.'

'So when we were driving down here, worried sick about whether you'd even survived, everyone else knew you were okay, is that what you're telling me?'

'Uh huh.'

'For God sakes, Billy, what's wrong with you? You live two different lives at the same time. In one life, your poor fucking father, namely mutt-face, yours truly, and your long-suffering mother are driving, probably even faster than you did yesterday, thinking you might be dead and meanwhile, the rest of the family is packing to go home knowing you're safe and sound. Is that right?'

'That's right, Dad. But it's not deliberate. I couldn't reach you while you were driving.'

'And that makes it okay?'

'That makes it *human*, Dad. These things happen. It's not like I knowingly fed you and Mom different information so that you wouldn't know what was happening while I kept Iska and Grandma in the loop.'

'Billy, if you knowingly did that, I'd rip your head off. Would you even understand why?'

'Sure, Dad. I mean, that would be like having an affair behind someone's back and pretending all the time that you loved them. Right, Dad?'

'Exactly, Billy....' My voice slowed to silence. Who did I think I was, moralizing to my son in a hospital in France? I might as well just qualify as a surgeon and take the hypocrisy oath. Billy looked at me and smiled.

'I gotta get to the airport, Dad. The awards ceremony is in less than twelve hours.'

Pearl arrived with two big bunches of grapes, and Billy and I devoured every last one. One of the nurses had a pretty decent pair of peaches herself.

Billy had made his flight with very little time to spare, and Pearl and I checked in for the night to the Hotel Grand Aston in the centre of Nice. Iska and Muriel met us at the airport the following day. Olivia's husband had driven them, and all of our luggage, in a rental car and then picked up his own from me at the car park outside the departures lounge. I expected Iska to be heartbroken about having to leave her first real boyfriend behind.

'Hey, no way, Dad. It's cool. Michel is coming over to Boston for Christmas to stay with us. It was Grandma's idea.'

Over the previous twenty-four hours I'd had a bit of time to do some thinking. I gotta say that I'm not much usually for thinking, but, in a way, that period of time, between waving Billy goodbye and meeting Iska and the others before our own flight, was no bad thing. I had felt really close to Pearl on the trip down in the car. I mean we were right beside each other in the fucking car, but you know what I mean. On our last night in France, eating out at a restaurant where they served steak and French Fries, some piece of the jigsaw had slotted into place as I watched Pearl return from the rest-room and approach our table. I realized in that instant, as she side-stepped a waiter carrying a tray of wine glasses over his head, that this was my wife, this was my life, and I was better off than millions of other guys all over the world who still had their heads halfway up their asses.

'You look very pleased with yourself, George,' Pearl said, as she sat down opposite me.

'I *am* pleased,' I said. 'I'm pleased to be able to say that, even after all these years, you're still the best thing that's ever happened to me.' Pearl smiled, and in that smile I saw the girl who had captured my heart in the days before the Oil Crisis threw everything upside-down. It was great to be alive.

I suppose that, really, it was the drive down to the hospital, when we didn't know how Billy was, that had started the grey cells cavorting with each other. In that frame of existence, trapped in someone else's car in another country in the stifling heat, I had thought about death for the first time. Now, don't get me wrong, I've seen death before. I mean, as a lawyer you get to go to lots of funerals. But thinking about the end of the life of a child you've raised. Well, that's different.

With Iska's twin, there had been absolutely nothing we could have done to prevent her death; but I'd got Billy from kindergarten to Playboy without ever dreaming for a second that he wouldn't outlast me. Even when Billy was in the Olympic Snorting Team, I never thought he'd die. I figured the worst that would happen would be that maybe he'd never hold down a job, or he'd vote Democrat, or go fucking sterile or something. And then, before I knew he was okay, I imagined all kinds of horrible things that I'd never had to face before. It made me stop and think of my own life and of how I was spending it.

'Are you okay, George?' Pearl placed a hand on my arm as some twit in a uniform weighed the bags at the check-in desk the following day.

'Of course I'm okay, Pearl. I'm on my way home from my vacation to six weeks worth of paperwork. Why shouldn't I be okay?' 'Oh, nothing,' she replied. 'You just seem, well, I don't know. A bit subdued or something. Are you sure you're alright?' She kissed me on the cheek with the tenderness of a lover, which was a sensation I'd almost forgotten. 'Pearl, I'm gonna sit with my granddaughter on this flight,' Muriel said. 'She's going to let me read her manuscript about apples.' Muriel edged ahead of me in the line. She handed in her ticket and passport with one hand and held Iska's arm with the other.

I watched these three generations of women and, for the first time ever, saw a clear resemblance in the jaw lines and in the eyes. I thought about Carmen and her bridal magazine, thumbing her way into the future in a rush of choices between off-white and light blue. What the fuck was I doing with my life? How many lives was I trying to live? I wondered if the CIA was already circulating her passport number to all ports and airports. I suddenly thought, for no apparent reason, about my honeymoon with Pearl in 1976 and the Elvis concert we'd attended in Indianapolis the following year. I remembered Pearl screaming when he'd arrived on stage, to the 'Also Sprach Zarathustra' riffs. Somewhere back there, twenty-odd years ago, we'd had some great times and had each rebounded sufficiently strongly to form one fucking bouncy marriage together. I wondered what life would be like without her, but I didn't really want to think about that much, so I didn't.

'Hey, George, we'll miss the plane if you don't hurry,' Pearl shouted to me from one of the duty-free cashier desks, as she bought perfume while I idled in the whiskey section and chose nothing.

'I wonder how Billy got on at the awards ceremony,' Iska said, as I was caught in a traffic jam in the aisle of the plane behind some guy with an ass the size of New Jersey.

'I don't know how he expected to play the drums with his arm in a sling,' I muttered.

'He told me they were gonna set it up so he only had one drum and they'd make a big deal out of his accident,' she said back.

I imagined old Goose Silverspoon and the boys in the publicity department lapping that up.

'What song were they performing?' Pearl asked from behind me.

'Something about cats,' I said, turning slightly, to look at her over my shoulder.

'Oh,' she said, and blushed. Only the previous day, on the drive to the hospital, we'd discussed the gestures she'd made to me when I'd been up on the roof trying to stop Billy from committing suicide.

'I was trying to signal to you about that song they have, called, "Sheriff and the Posse",' she said. She'd been highly embarrassed when I'd explained.

The in-flight entertainment consisted of the usual fucking assortment of films, which I had either seen hundreds of times before or had deliberately avoided.

'It's always the same,' I complained, as Pearl settled down to listen to some classical music on the radio headset.

'What? Did you say something, George?' She lifted the earpiece closest to me for a second.

'I said it's always the same'

'What's always the same, George?'

'The goddamn movies they show on these goddamn flights. It's always some stupid cop story with clever dogs and a police chief who stands in his office with his sleeves rolled up shouting at the main character, "You better not screw up on this or you're finished," or, "You're off the case, just let the guys at Homicide do their job".'

A lady, passing by to go to the can, stopped and stared at us as I spoke the lines. She looked horrified.

'Oh, George. Why don't you just put the eyemask on and go to sleep.' Pearl resumed her enjoyment of Ludwig Van Mozart, or whoever.

I must have drifted off to sleep pretty shortly after that because

I don't even remember tuning out from the movie. In my exhausted fucking trancelike rest I had the strangest dream. In it, I flew over Graceland, wearing nothing but the eagle cape. Down below me, I could see someone driving a car toward the swimming pool. As I got closer, there was a crowd of people all wearing baker's hats and applauding as the car crept closer to the pool. I strained to see the driver and I think I expected it to be Billy. Only it wasn't; it was Pearl. I tried to call out to her as a group of frogmen filed out of the pool house one after another, thumbing through bridal magazines as they walked. Somewhere behind me, a voice was calling. At first it sounded like Gloria. She was hysterical.

'George, George. The plumber still hasn't come back to fix my boiler.' Her voice morphed into the muffled laugh of the cops in the station. "Hey, Barney, it's Gloria Dinerclub's sugar daddy." I was right over the pool now, and as I hovered about three or four feet from the water, it turned to glass and then the glass slid back to reveal Billy, in a nurse's uniform, handing me a clipboard. "This way Msieu, and Madame Henry," he said. "The doctor is waiting, the doctor is waiting, the doctor ....".

'Is there a doctor on board?' The announcement woke me, and I blinked as I lifted the eye-mask and saw that most people around me were awake and eating some plastic food. 'Please make yourself known to one of the cabin crew.'

'Mrs Henry?' A stewardess blocked the aisle and spoke to Pearl.

'Yes?' Pearl looked up from the in-flight magazine and an article about mineral water from the Rockies.

'Could you please come up to row seventeen; your mother has asked for you. Please hurry.'

Pearl immediately understood the urgency of the situation and jumped into action. As I let her out, I thought to myself, oh fuck, the old bat is about to kick the bucket and wants to make sure it's full of shit to pour over yours truly after she's gone.

We were half an hour from New York and no emergency

landing was possible. I watched helplessly, as a makeshift curtain was put up around my mother-in-law at forty thousand feet. Some off-duty doctor tried to haul her back from eternity with mouth-to-mouth. Iska came down the plane to sit with me.

'Is she going to be alright, Dad? She just suddenly went all funny and grabbed at her throat.'

'She just skipped the line,' is what I wanted to say but didn't. The paramedics were on the plane like lightning when we touched down. A couple of shakes of the head, like in the movies, and my wife was an orphan. We were the last off the plane and Pearl was distraught. I hugged her as tightly as I could.

'She's gone, George. She's gone,' she sobbed.

'I know, I know.'

Iska came to join us and she and Pearl held hands leaving the plane just as, six hours earlier, she'd sort of held hands with her grandmother at the check-in desk in Nice. As we walked down the short corridor to the electric walkway, I looked at Pearl to try to see if I could get an inkling of what had passed between her mother and herself before death had gate-crashed their conversation. I could learn nothing. As we entered the baggage-reclaim area, a guy wheeling a trolley past us unfolded the New York Times and took out the sports section, abandoning the rest on a counter where some lazy airline lady was biting her nails. My son, Billy, looked up at me from the front page in a photo, where he played a single drum with one hand and proudly displayed his other arm in a sling.

"Arm in a sling, head in the clouds, Number One in the charts," the headline read.

I was surrounded by my family in the fucking baggage reclaim area in JFK, with Iska and Pearl looking for our luggage somewhere behind me, and Billy on the front page in my hands. Somewhere, in between Billy's head being in the toilet over the Azores, and this discarded newspaper, in six weeks I'd found out something about myself. Nothing fancy or philosophical, or religious or profound.

But something so glaringly fucking simple that the only amazing thing about it was that it had taken fifty-one years for me to realize it; we're all gonna die someday, and in between being born and then, you only have one fucking life. If you spend more time being happy with what you've got, than you do being unhappy about things you don't have, then you've cracked the secret.

∽⟋∾⟋∾⟍∾

Billy's gonna be twenty next week. East Pole are in the middle of recording the difficult third album and Billy's dating some broad who's just made a movie and looks like being nominated for an Oscar next year. What is it about this family and Best Supporting actresses? Iska's still at school, but her book has been published and sold a couple of thousand copies. Now she's working on one about different varieties of beetroot. God only knows what she'll do when she gets to Q.

I heard from Charlie Nagy at a class reunion last November. Carmen tried to brazen her way into the country some time back, and got three weeks in Guantanamo Bay for her troubles. Some people never give up. The translation service upstairs from Schwartz, McNaghten, Stamp & Henry have moved and a male impotency clinic have taken their place. Their slogan is "If you can rise up to the ninth floor, anything is possible".

And me? Am I happy? Who's ever fucking happy? I'm a bit older and maybe not much wiser, but I'll tell you one thing, I'm probably less of a malcontent than I was, and that's something. The woman who had my children, and who's put up with me for over a quarter of a century, is the only woman for me and I think I've finally realized that. I've gone almost three years now without even thinking about being unfaithful (unless you count the internet chat-room thing with Angeline from Dallas who turned out to be a guy when I phoned her; in which case it's only two years, nine months). Business is booming and I'm healthy except for haemorrhoids, peeing more often than I want to, and finding it a bit hard to hear TV sometimes. We took that trip of a lifetime Billy had paid for with his advance, and there's a photograph on my bedside table of the four of us outside Graceland. We've got tickets to see the Corgi's second, "final reunion concert", on New Year's Eve next at the Boston Coliseum. I hope to stay around long enough to see their next, "final reunion concert", whenever that is.

I never did find out whether Muriel got to tell Pearl about my dough rising with the bakery lady, but in a way it just doesn't matter anymore. What has happened has happened and you can't change it, but you *can* change the future and that's what I'm trying to do. I'm crankier now than Henry Fonda was in the " On Golden Lake" film but at least it's contented cranky instead of demented cranky. Nobody really makes you do anything, it's all inside your own fucking head, the choices, the answers, hey, even the questions.

I think about Muriel every once in a while whenever I hear Elvis on the radio, and I imagine the two of them somewhere arguing the toss about the best version of Suspicious Minds. I guess I even miss her a little now she's gone, but, let me tell you, she was impossible to miss when she was here.

I don't think I'll ever go back to France, but who cares about that? Not me. We had a good time there and maybe that place can even take a little of the credit for straightening out old GBH and family. Yeah, I guess it can. But you gotta draw the line somewhere. As old Dubya Bush says,

"Those guys in France don't even have a word in their language for *entrepreneur*."

How could you trust a fucking country like that?

THE END

ᖇᖇᖇᖇᖇ

<u>Unless</u> the tree is exeptionly damaged and <u>very</u> <u>old</u>, it is rarely so depilitated that it cannot be Saved!!!!

Lots of Love

gska Henry.

THE LAST ESTATE

ACKNOWLEDGEMENTS:

I would like to express my gratitude and appreciation to the following people, who all helped me in some way in the writing of this book:

Mary Honan, Mary P. Guinness, Celine Sheridan, Karl Sweeney, John Murphy, Sylvie Archimbaud, Robert & Francoise Leterrier, Roger Sweetman, Dearbhla Ní Ghríofa, George Allen, Catherine Higgins, Annette Foley, Mark de Blacam, Siobhan Gallagher, Fabienne Pleyben, Colette Griffin, Colette Crus et sa famille a Gigondas, Pat & Ann O' Malley, Annie Leonard, Auntie Betty, Liz James, Florence Kponsou and Anthony Previté.

Joy Kleinstuber travelled to the village and the region to undertake invaluable and in-depth research. Mary Kelly was a huge help; she provided first-hand information about the art of winemaking and makes great wine herself at Domaine du Pech Rome. pechromevin@wanadoo.fr

A special word of thanks is due to Richard Quirke who is the driving force behind Clockwork Press. He is a man who believes in the inherent capacity of people to change and to make a difference for the better. Small ideas catch big fish!

The Last Estate

CONOR BOWMAN

CLOCKWORK
PRESS

Published in 2008 by
CLOCKWORK PRESS,
AT 8-10 COKE LANE, SMITHFIELD, DUBLIN 7

www.clockworkpress.com

ISBN: 978-0-9548403-1-0
(The Redemption of George Baxter Henry & The Last Estate)

10 9 8 7 6 5 4 3 2 1

TYPESET BY: Linden Publishing Services in 11.5 on 15 point Quadraat
DESIGNED BY: Susan Waine
CENTRE ILLUSTRATION BY: Celine Sheridan, 'Teeth of Dentelles' (Watercolour)
PRINTED IN IRELAND BY: Betaprint Limited, Dublin

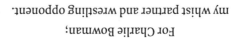

For Charlie Bowman;
my whist partner and wrestling opponent.

Chapter One

W HEN I WAS NINE YEARS OLD, a boy at school cut me on the left side of my face with a hunting knife, in a fight about nothing.

"You don't even own a dog," he said.

"Yes, I do," I replied, "Mangetout."

"He's not yours. He belongs to your brother."

"We *both* own him."

The air between us grew damp with argument and we crossed the divide and fought as if *we* were two mongrels. A crowd of our school comrades encircled us; each boy calling out the name of the warrior he supported. In the heart of the fight, my opponent pulled out a knife and I was injured. I think the wounding frightened him even more than it did me; the battle ended the instant blood had been drawn.

The scar was three and a half centimetres long and it lay diagonally across the top of my cheek, pointing simultaneously at my left eye and the bottom of my left earlobe. "Cicatrice" is the French word for a scar and for a while people called me that as a nickname. I didn't mind the nickname, it's not the worst. I suppose I don't even really mind the scar itself. When I was almost seventeen, and in my last year in the village lycée, the scar had grown slightly longer, but also more vague, as my skin tightened and stretched the cicatricial line to its thinnest. The boy who slashed me died from tuberculosis in 1914. He was eleven. His name was Yves

Couderc. Less than a month after they'd buried him the war began.

The last time I'd see him he was shopping in the village square with his mother. He'd been waiting for her outside the bakery and he stood beside a small grey poodle that was tied by its leash to the handle of one of the double doors. Yves was coughing into a handkerchief. Over his hand, in the bunch of the cotton (like an opened flower), small flecks of red mottled their way into the hem. It was the only time in two years that he hadn't pretended to secretly smile to himself about my scar when we'd met. It was the only time, in those two years too, that I hadn't tried to hide my left cheek from his view. There was something special about that shared moment in the village square which has remained with me to this day. Some strange, almost barely perceptible thought or emotion passed between us and it was as if we knew were saying goodbye. He nodded a greeting and I acknowledged it in return. I then discreetly allowed my attention to be drawn elsewhere in order to permit him continue his bloody coughing in peace. Even the small dog looked away. Nobody wants to catch a glimpse of death if they can avoid it.

To be legally classed, as 'Côtes De Rhône-Villages,' wine from this region has to be made from at least twenty-five percent of Syrah, Mourvédre and Cinsault grapes. It is less clear what the blood of a person must contain to be classed as local. What I do know is that my great-grandfather served under Napoleon at Waterloo and that made us locals of all France. Our family prided itself on its heritage and, I suppose, that was a start. Nothing comforts us in the present perhaps, so much as the knowledge that our forebears endured hardship and survived. We draw solace from the gene pool. It draws continuity from us. We live side-by-side in the here and now; confident that the march of progress and industry has fashioned a slightly more cushioned world. That is the theory at least.

In 218 Hannibal passed through Provence and then on to the Alps. In 1720 The Great Plague crept north from Marseille and

devastated the region. In 1918, on a Sunday in October, the Germans proposed an armistice and yet the war did not end for some weeks after that. This region, with its holm oaks and olives and cypress and almond trees, has always been holding its breath; just as the entire nation did that October. Good news usually seems too good to be true here. When the waiting is over, the confirmation of that news has usually been overtaken by some greater and darker realisation; that things are actually worse *because* of the news we'd waited for but never got to enjoy. Forest fires, when they occur, drive with the wind and the drought and often only stop at the coast. There are few mountains but here, in the department known as Vaucluse, the Dentelles provide a backdrop for the minute portion of this country which I really call home. You can smell the lavender all summer. In the winter, the small cloth bags of it usher the scent out the doors of every wardrobe. This is the place where I spent all of my time and my energies as a boy; trying to understand the entirety of the outside world through my small experiences in the village of Gigondas.

Our home is a chateau on the western approach road to the village. It was called 'Montmirail,' after the tallest peak in the mountain range that hugs the village to the east like a surprise embrace in a shop. It is not really a castle but it is the largest house in the village. It earned its title 'Chateau' more by default than anything else. It is a grand building, with a tree-lined avenue which sweeps rather impressively up from the main road to Sablet, a neighbouring village. The house was reputedly built on the site of the wedding-ring exchange, of Pierre of Provence and Princess Maguelone of Naples, in medieval times. Legend has it that the couple travelled to the Dentelles from Aigues-Mortes where Pierre had been restored to his health by the Princess. She had turned her hand to charitable works as a way to forget her previous unhappy love. True or not, we all believed it and it made Montmirail even more special than it already was.

9

It is a huge, grandly-built house with six bedrooms and an enormous dining room on the ground floor with south-facing windows which suck in the sunshine all year round. It is built of local stone and the outside walls are imbued with a sort of russet solidity which is typical of Provence. The roll-tiles on the roof are the colour of sunset and the house is clearly visible from the summit of its namesake in the Dentelles. From the air I imagine it resembles a red tortoise, sleeping at the entrance to the village.

Our village is like thousands of others. It has a café, a small hotel, a school, a bakery and a town hall. There, the mayor, Monsieur Gustave de Vay, kept a tiny office which allowed him refuge from a wife he'd never loved. Each year, under the mellow September heat, on the feast of St.Cosme and St Damien, all the inhabitants of the village gathered to hear the priest deliver his sermon, dressed in his ceremonial robes. Later on, in the evening, after the magnificent feast at the fountain, we would all stand and stare up into the benign Provencal sky and wait, while a member of the police (from the station at Carpentras) supervised the fireworks display. It was perfect and, in September 1919, it was no less so, in the first celebration of this feast day since the war.

"Christian," Miss Pleyben the geography teacher said, as she touched me on the shoulder at the display. "Some day that will be you. You'll be the one setting off the fireworks."

I turned around, and saw her gorgeous face illuminate, and become dark, as the Catherine Wheels and Fizz Rockets exploded and died away above us. She was slightly shorter than I was, with long hair the colour of sunlight. Her shapely body was gathered in at the waist, as a curtain might be by a drape holder, and her eyes sparkled all the time as if she knew something she wasn't yet prepared to share. Sometimes her face was sad, as if she were remembering when really she'd rather not. But the combination, of all of the elements comprising her, was a person whom it would be impossible not to notice in a crowd.

Everybody knew that her husband had left her because he was going to be conscripted. He was an evil man, who beat her so regularly that it was almost shocking to finally see her natural beauty when she no longer needed make-up to hide the bruises. On one occasion, years earlier, I'd seen them arguing in the square and he'd raised his hand to strike her. He'd noticed me standing there and had allowed his hand to make some mawkish false diversion to his own head, where he smoothed down his generous allocation of greasy hair. Most of the other teachers occasionally called me 'Cicatrice,' or mentioned my scar in some oblique nasty way, but not Miss Pleyben. I wanted to hurry up and grow into a man so that I could marry her. I would take care of her and love her and never ever treat her badly and she'd never have to spend another sou on mascara. I would lie with her and, well ,you know- And in the mornings I'd bring her breakfast in bed and make her coffee with fresh milk and black coffee beans from the market in Sablet.

"Yes, Miss," I answered. "Someday that will be me."

The lifeblood of the region is wine, and my family have been wine-makers for more than two centuries. In 1672, when the original (and smaller) house was built on the same site, it was a very similar terrain which bordered the foothills of the Dentelles. The soil is not much good for anything except vines and olives. As a result, the area has developed in the only direction open to it. The massive granite pudding-shaped stones, which give an impression of being unwelcome where cultivation is concerned, in reality are more than a factor in the successful production of wine in the area. These stones, in areas where the vine has been established, act as reflectors and direct the sun back onto the grapes. The end result is to produce big high-in-alcohol reds, and even some respectable rosés. The eleven and a half hectares attached to Montmirail produce deep red wine every year. The cellars are among the oldest in France and even pre-date the original house. I have to say, though, that this weight of tradition was not sufficient to convince

me of my role in its continuation. That belief is perhaps at the heart of my story and my life. I never believed that just because something is one particular way, that it must remain so forever. I cry out for the right of the individual, the self, the soul, to reach out past itself and into the heart of others, rather than to constantly look back over its own shoulder. I yearn for the freedom of spirit, the latitude, the opportunity in myself and in everyone else, to become what we want, and to refuse to continue to be who and what we are if those manifestations do not reflect our own desires. I believe, most of all, in the inherent capacity man and woman possess to change. In the countryside, where the village is the kingdom and the child is the peasant, the father is king. The son is like a granite rock on the edge of a vineyard; his job is to reflect and his destiny is to remain in that place forever. The only power higher than man is God, so that even in the kingdom the high priest is sometimes the real king for a time.

"The onset of puberty is a dangerous time, when the adolescent is beset with desires more importunate and more sudden than those which affected the young in the more guarded times of our forefathers. Holy Purity is called the Angelic Virtue because it makes man like the angels. It is the most beautiful of possessions. The very name 'Purity,' is, in itself, a shining and attractive word. We speak of the purity of the water in a stream high up in the hills."

Father Leterrier was a Jesuit. He came twice a month, from the monastery at Crillon-le-Brave on the other side of the Dentelles, to lecture us in religious instruction. Despite the separation of Church and State (common to most areas in France by that time) the power of the landowner-class was still very much in evidence. The Jesuits owned the school; and their trade-off for nominal rent, was to insist on at least a modicum of religious instruction by one of their number to every class. As I progressed through the lycée the classes became smaller and smaller; people drifted out of the education system and back into their farms, having mastered the ability to

count and read road-signs and medication labels. He was a tall, almost elegant-looking priest with an air of great confidence and self-importance. He also possessed a religious fervour which he was unable to impart to his students. As I grew tired, in my early teens, of attending his classes at all, Fr. Leterrier seemed to grow commensurately more and more interested in his students' moral welfare so that, in my last two years at the lycée, the lessons he taught us dealt solely with the moral state of near-perfection which he called "Holy Purity". This man, who had begun our religious instruction years earlier with lively stories about Noah and the Ark and the struggles of Daniel and David, began to transform before our eyes, on a twice-monthly basis, into an obsessive fanatic. His every waking moment seemed dedicated to the care of a warped ideal he had planted years earlier in some earthenware pot deep in his churning heart. For the girls, he was twice-monthly menstrual pain.

"I say particularly to you young girls, you good and innocent girls. Beware of temptation. Why do I say this to good and inno-cent girls? Because temptation is sure to come: you cannot main-tain that priceless pearl without a struggle; the enemies of your soul will try to steal it. Oh the bright and happy glance of the eyes which are pure. The pure of heart are folded in the Divine arms, they are fit company for angels. No one is so happy. On the other hand; the impure of heart have fallen into an appalling shadow. Laughter may be forced from their lips, but it does not come from the heart. It is a mockery, a mockery! The soul of the impure is no longer in harmony with God's infinitely holy designs; the beauty of the baptismal robe has been sullied, and this soul is no longer fit company for Heaven. To die in this state would be a calamity beyond words."

I wondered if Yves Couderc had died in such a state. Had his actions, in scarring me, marked his own soul out as unfit for Heaven? I was terrified that because we'd never made up the argu-

ment, never spoken of forgiveness, I might have unwittingly condemned him to eternity in a furnace. Perhaps I should have gone to him and said, "It's alright, I don't mind the scar, it's not the worst." Would this have wiped his slate clean? Did God send him sickness because of his sin? I just didn't know and, yet, I harboured a residual hope, in the corner of my mind, that, somehow, the last time I'd seen him, the glance, which passed between us, might have meant more than goodbye.

When I was fifteen-and-a-half I went one July evening to the Chapel of Saint Cosme, on the small hill on the Vacqueyras Road. I pushed open the warm wooden door and made my way inside. As usual, the place was empty. It was just myself, and God, and the chipped statue of Saint Cosme, with its flickering wax candles on the brass stand in front of the side-altar. I knelt in the front row on an embroidered kneeler which was old and red. In a way, I suppose, I thought that the further up the church I went; the closer to Him I'd be. I told Him that I didn't mind the scar at all and that I wished Couderc well, wherever he was.

"You know, God, if you cast your mind back to that day I saw him for the last time, outside the bakery; I'm sure you probably thought that I was only saying goodbye to him, or something like that, when we looked at each other and nodded. It may have looked that way but what I was actually thinking, in my mind, and my heart, was that I forgave him. I didn't realise it at the time, but later on, looking back, I'm pretty sure too that he was saying sorry. I know he *was* sorry, although he never *actually* said the words. Anyway, I just thought I'd let you know in case you watched that day and weren't sure that the whole scar thing had been settled for good before he died. I know you're pretty busy; what with looking after all the people who are dying in the war and everything. My mother used to say before the war, that when the winter comes you get really busy. But you probably haven't had a moment to draw your breath for a long time. I have to go now, but, just one last

thing; if you get a chance, say hello to Mangetout for me and tell Eugene that I hope he doesn't mind that I got his room."

I heard a noise behind me, as though there was someone watching, but when I looked around there was no one there. I had to get home for supper so I left, but the door was ajar and I'd been fairly sure I had closed it when I'd entered the chapel. Maybe God was saying "I hear you". Maybe He actually does listen sometimes.

My life, for the most part, up until the time Couderc died, had been happy. I suppose that the people who complain by saying, 'Oh I can't complain', or, 'I'm keeping the best side out', are really only happy when they *are* complaining, but I have to say that my own life *was* happy. I draw a line across my life at Couderc's death but if I am truthful, or if a mental doctor of psychowhatever-they-are were to examine my head and grope around my thoughts for a bit, then my childhood probably ended a little bit later. On the twenty-fifth of February 1916 my brother Eugene was killed in action near Verdun; at the battle which led to the falling of Fort Douaumont. It was then that my life, as I now have it, really began. I looked up in geography class that day, at a quarter-past-two in the cold afternoon, think-ing I'd heard a scream. I saw that everyone else was still writing silently and attentively, having apparently heard nothing. Miss Pleyben glanced around for a moment from the blackboard and smiled when she saw me. I smiled too. It was our moment, like that time with Couderc, only better. I've always wondered since whether I heard my brother scream as he died. If it *was* his voice I heard, then Miss Pleyben was with me when Eugene died and this has only served to reinforce my affection for her.

My mother was an enigmatic woman in many ways because she never told us what she really thought. It was her post in our house to tread the thin line between her loyalty to my father and her affec-tion for Eugene. She stayed at that post until it was no longer neces-sary to make the choice she'd always really stopped short of making anyway. She was a beautiful woman; untouchable in that eternal

way which actresses often have about them. She had the face of an angel and, yet, her eyes were always sad. She was not from Provence; she was a Breton, from Plougerneau, in the northwest of Brittany. She always said that she missed the rain. I remember how once, when I was God-knows-how-small and in her arms -or perhaps in a cradle and her leaning over me- that she cried the most perfect tear and it absconded down her cheek. It lingered before it dropped down onto my face and I tasted salt for the first time. Even now, I recall that experience and I think again, as always, that I have tasted the sea on the rain from the place where my mother was born. Those delightful people, with their own language and their binds to Celtic mysticism and the sea, lay then and lie now in the background like a chorus line at the end of the performance; too happy for words, too unhappy for silence. My mother held the line and, when she no longer had to do that, she retreated to her room at the back of Montmirail; to wait for death and the intermissions of cold love my father rationed, even after the war had ended.

On Christmas Morning 1916, I came downstairs at the exact time when my parents were in the dining room exchanging presents. Maman had made him a jacket, from light grey material she had scavenged from somewhere. He wore it as if he were a peacock; twisting this way and that to see himself in the mirror. My mother stood by, meekly, admiring him and sharing in his happiness.

"Your gift is in the box on the table,' he said.

Maman unwrapped the ribbon from around the package. Inside, a long red dress lay folded in on itself. As she held it to her shoulders it was clear, even to me, that it was far too small to fit her. She stood there, bathed in uncertainty, not wishing to seem ungrateful and, perhaps, frightened that he might ask her to try it on. She need not have concerned herself in that regard.

"There's a war on, you know, Helene. Try to eat a little less. For France." My mother began to sob quietly.

"You cruel bastard," I shouted from the doorway. He spun

round; clearly embarrassed at having been observed in this act of malice. He said nothing, but simply walked out of the room past me. That afternoon, just as we sat down to dinner, he looked across the table at me and said, as he carved.

"Christian, the dog caught its paw in a trap. It was in too much pain.' I discovered later that he'd taken Mangetout's head off, with an axe, as an act of 'mercy.'

For my father, the only warmth lay in wine. Not in his consumption of it, but its consuming of him. The sole thing he lived for was himself. Anyone who could help to reflect glory back at him was welcome, in the cruellest of ways, to catch the light and turn it back upon him day or night until they dimmed from the effort and he glowed from their sacrifice. For Robert Aragon, the world narrowed into a point which almost touched his feet. He was the king of a dynasty, which stretched out behind him like a cape in the wind. Almost all of his expectations had been fulfilled. His two final quests were to prepare his heir for the throne (by any means necessary) and to die clutching that most elusive of all viticultural plaudits; the Medaille d'Or from the Concours National, which was held in Paris each July.

He was a man capable of enforcing his world-view with violence, and I often found myself to be the *beneficiary* of this method of education. On the day of Couderc's funeral my father came into my room in the afternoon. I was sitting on the edge of the bed and it was clear that I had been crying.

"I suppose you've been whingeing about that boy they buried. The one who gave you the scar." I looked up, but said nothing. "You know he probably already had the disease when you fought with him, so you shouldn't blame yourself. Anyway, he's gone now and you're still alive." I dried my eyes and began to stand up, but a punch in the face from him laid me flat on my back. "You selfish little pup. You didn't even have the courtesy to go to his funeral. What do you think people will say about our family *now*?"

"But, Papa, I –" I tried to explain myself to him, but it was no use. He never listened to any voice other than his own. Next day at school, people asked me about my black eye. I told them I'd walked into a door. Everybody has some kind of scar, and I have already intimated how I came to have my own. Lines drawn across my face or under my life or dividing horizon marks behind me, marking the end of my childhood and the beginning of another phase, all blur into each other if I am honest now. In fact, the only true line, which meant anything to me, was the one drawn across my life, on the day I finally realised that I was in love with my geography teacher; Vivienne Pleyben.

Chapter two

"I'M NOT A BIG FAN OF ALGERIANS." My father spoke as he lifted a forkful of pork to his fat mouth at dinnertime in early May 1920. He'd put on weight since the war had ended.

"Why not?" I asked innocently, knowing the answer before I'd even formed the question.

"They're not French," he stated bluntly and patronisingly, as though there could be no other rational answer.

"Neither are the Americans and they helped us win the war."

"Don't be facetious, you know what I mean," he snapped.

"Oh," I said, with a facial expression that accused.

"Your father doesn't like to talk about the war," my mother said gently. "Robert, would you like some more meat?"

My father held out his plate like a child might and my mother scurried off to the kitchen to replenish it. When she had gone we sat in silence, averting our eyes from each other or from any commonage on the table where they might meet. We truly had nothing in common beyond our name. Eugene had been my father's firstborn and, consequently, all the dreams and hopes, which leaned out of my father, had been heaped upon him. He had only been eighteen when he was killed and would remain eighteen forever. I, on the other hand, was nearly seventeen then and had a lifetime of disappointing my father ahead of me. We both knew it.

When my mother said that he did not like to talk about the war, what she really meant was that he did not like *others* to talk about the war. He mentioned it himself at every opportunity, but that was permissible because in my father's mind only three Frenchmen had actually taken full part in the war; Eugene, Marshall Petain and, of course, my father himself. It was risible really, but he almost certainly believed it, although, of course, he was never foolish enough to express it in those terms. From his conversation and demeanour it was clear that somewhere back along the way they must all have met up, perhaps in a café somewhere, and drawn lots to decide their plan of action. As it happened, Petain was chosen to survive the war, Eugene to be killed in it and Robert Aragon to stay at home and contemplate, alternately, the enormity of both death and survival. The suffering of war was justified by a young corporal in 1915 who wrote home, *'I suffer, yes I suffer but so be it. I offer up my life in expiation of my sins and those of France.'* The Church, and my father, joined hands in inducting Eugene into immortality. The countless others whose names they did not know would have to rely on their families for their own dose of salvation.

"Algerians are the scum of the earth," my father said, when my mother returned with a second helping. We all knew that the learned commentary on Algerians had been prompted by the arrival in the village of a family from Algiers. The father was going to work on one of the other local vineyards; Domaine De La Mavette. It seemed incredible to me then, in 1920, a mere two years after the war had ended, that the differences between races would still excite hatred in this small-minded way. What exactly had Eugene been fighting for? So that we could defeat the Germans and be free once again to hate in our own language people who were different? People of other races were rare in Gigondas. But why should they not be instantly liked because of their difference, rather than reviled? It hinted at something in my father's make-up which was awry, but I was too young to be able to catch and describe it that summer.

"When does school finish, Christian?" My mother brokered a peace at the table with a smile and an innocuous question.

"July the twenty-sixth, " I answered.

"You'll be able to begin working then," my father stated. It was not a question. It was, in his mind at any rate, a fact. Eugene was gone and I would have to do as an heir to the business. I didn't answer him directly,

"May I be excused, Maman? I have other things to do."

"Of course, Cheri." My mother smiled in her shy frightened way. We all knew that the subject would come up for discussion again sooner or later. I walked outside around by the seized-up grape-press in the courtyard at the heart of Montmirail. George Phavorin, my father's foreman, was loading barrels of wine onto a cart for the weekly trip to the railway station at Sablet. From there the wine would go to Orange and onwards to Paris or Marseille.

"You're not at school today?" he asked with a smile.

"Half-day Wednesday. Remember?"

He was an enormous man with hands like baker's shovels. For most of my life he'd lived in the gite on the road to the sulphur springs at Les Florets and came to work at Montmirail every single day. My father never gave him credit for his real worth; but there was nothing novel in that. Without George Phavorin, Montmirail would have come to a standstill. If he knew it himself he never said anything and, so, it was impossible to discern, even if he did know, whether he was resentful.

"Want to come to Sablet?" he asked, heaving the last barrel on top of two more at the back of the cart where they made a pyramid. I thought of my school project in geography on which I had yet to make a start. It was warm and I was in no mood for burying my head in books for the rest of the afternoon. As an answer to his question I climbed into the driver's seat and began to untie the long reins.

"Move over, Cowboy," he said with a laugh, as he swung effort-

lessly onto the seat beside me. He clicked his tongue and the two horses stopped sleeping and began to amble toward the archway at the back of the property. As we edged out onto the track, behind the large barn, the house came sharply into view and we could see my mother at an upstairs window, pretending to close the shutters.

"How are things with you and your father?" George asked.

"The same," I replied. "Always the same."

Behind us, the giant teeth of the mountain range soaked up the heat and I turned my head to see whether I could catch a glimpse of Miss Pleyben's house, way above the church and the cemetery. It was like a buffer, halfway from the village to the foothills; a border of sorts between man and nature. I loved her with all my heart and she didn't know a thing. My project would have to be the best ever. I might even win the prize of an outing to Avignon if I worked hard enough. I'd make her proud. So proud. I knew she'd never love me back, but, in a way, that was half of the challenge. It pained me to think of my future, because the little of it I could see looked fairly bleak. The innuendo of the table talk that lunchtime was only a sniff of the battle yet to come. I did not know whether I would even be strong enough to take part in that struggle. Winning it certainly was not an option. If only Eugene hadn't been killed. Things would have been so much better. I remembered sitting with Eugene, years earlier, on the wall near the fever hospice, during the school holidays.

"You're the one he loves," I said. "He can't stand me."

"It's because you remind him of himself." I never understood Eugene's response.

"Want to know a secret?" George said, with a grin, as we passed the grangeons on the Sablet road. Tired ploughs and carts hid in these half-houses waiting to be useful again.

"Sure," I replied.

"You're going to be someone great when you grow up."

"What's the secret, George?"

"That is the secret," he said, laughingly.

"I think you're very greatly mistaken."

"No, no I mean it. You'll be another Napoleon, a Petain, or maybe a great writer, like Victor Hugo."

"You got me all figured out wrong, George." I smiled. "I'm not going to be anybody at all when I grow up."

"You mark my words." He wagged his finger in my face. I felt the scar on my cheek and thought of Couderc. He'd not really had the chance to grow up. Would he have been someone great if his lungs had been luckier? Who knows?

Ahead of us on the road we saw the 'diligence,' owned by Monsieur Vaton, carrying its passengers to Sablet to catch the train to Orange. From the back it looked like a large funeral carriage and I wondered about Eugene and remembered his funeral. Without a body, the ceremony had seemed to me to be a farce, with his summer uniform and a handful of letters in a warm box made of cedar wood. A half-hour crammed with prayers and tears. I tried to imagine now, as I had then, his real self, the body (which had contained his laugh and his voice) buried in a mass grave near Fort Douaumont. It would be lifeless of course, but warm perhaps, surrounded by comrades who had died quickly, or slowly, depending. How had Eugene died? For me, as for the younger brothers of every other soldier who had been killed, I suppose the only solace was that he might have died instantly and without pain. I envisioned some carpenter's son from a village in Bavaria; lining my brother up in his sights and then, 'Snap,' as death and sleep arrived on a bullet. It was too horrible to imagine any other scenario. Sometimes, you know, I even believed that he was still alive and that he would come walking up the avenue at Montmirail on leave, with his gun over his shoulder and some unusual confectionery in his pockets from a shop in the north. The last time he'd been home had been in October 1915. He'd arrived out of the blue and only stayed four days before being summoned back to the Front.

"Tell me about the Germans," I'd asked, excitedly. He was sitting on the bed in my room overlooking the courtyard.

"I don't know much about them, really. They have enormous cannon that fire shells bigger than wine casks." If only everyone had been drenched in red wine instead of blood.

"What are you daydreaming about?" George thumped me playfully on the back and I returned to May 1920.

"Nothing, George. Nothing."

"I don't believe you," he said. "You've got so many brains. Probably planning for your exams, eh?"

"Maybe."

George smiled and encouraged the horses to increase their pace as we caught sight of the mill on the edge of Sablet. In the distance, way off, over to our left, lay the simple solid form of the railway bridge over the Ouveze between Sablet and Violes. Rivers and railways were an integral part of geography, but nowhere near as important as the woman who imparted their whereabouts to us. She'd been with me when Eugene died. Father Leterrier, with all his claptrap about morality and his talk of, 'desires more importunate and more sudden,' knew absolutely nothing about love. How could he, hidden away in that monastery at Crillon-le-Brave, emerging twice a month to preach morals to unsuspecting adolescents? What did he know about anything, besides loneliness and the myth of miracles? How did he even know if there was a God?

Outside the railway station was a small square and, each Wednesday, the market there drew large numbers. When we arrived it was nearly over. The stalls were mostly empty. One of the vendors, still going strong, was shouting.

"Chanoux coffee; one-franc-fifty a quarter."

He was a small man with a moustache which bisected his face and headed for his ears. Behind him the butcher was shutting up shop, and only a couple of dead pigeons hung from the stand over the bloodstained marble counter. Pretty much everyone else was

finished and the cauliflower leaves, rotting at their edges in the gutter, had long since said goodbye to their heads. At the entrance to the railway station the front page from the previous week's edition of *Le Ventoux* announced;

"Hernia cured by the Leroy method. Hotel Du Commerce, Vaison, on the eighth of June next. All Welcome."

George and I unloaded the barrels and rolled them through the narrow archway past the ticket office and onto the platform. While George spoke to the loading officer and obtained a receipt, the train lay panting on the tracks, with steam escaping in bursts from the dull-green engine funnel. Two of the five carriages were about half-filled with passengers and the other three were at near-capacity with goods. Four men in light blue overalls were working full-tilt, loading and unloading. Sacks of flour and bales of wool were taken from the train and laid side by side on the platform, while barrels of wine and bales of silk got ready to take their place. As the train pulled out of the station, George and I stood together and watched it chug slowly past the signal box and on towards Orange. The sun seemed warmer now than it had at midday.

"It's tough work," said George. "How about a beer?"

"Okay."

I wanted to do anything which would delay the trip back home. The remaining stalls in the market were now closed. We left the horses tied outside the station. We walked into the village to a bar where there was only one customer apart from ourselves; a tiny grey-haired man with a goatee beard. He'd obviously come from the market, as his overalls were stained with grease. Beside him, knife handles protruded from a wrapping of cloth. Outside, I'd noticed his grindstone mounted on a wooden barrow. He nodded in greeting.

"Two beers." George ordered from the pretty girl behind the counter.

The knife-grinder saw me looking at the bundle beside him.

"Want a look?"

"Not really, " I said, but my face said 'Yes please.' He lifted the packet and rolled it on the counter. A grim collection of knives and skewers rattled open.

"Don't scratch my bar," said the barmaid. George and I looked at the knives.

"Try one if you like," said the man. I instinctively ran a finger along my scar and then picked up a large pocket-knife which was open. I coaxed my thumb over and back on the blade and felt it tease my skin with the double allures of danger and protection. The knife-man grinned, "Nice isn't it?"

"Not bad," I said.

"How much?" asked George.

"Fifty francs."

"I'll give you thirty-five." George took the money out of his breast pocket. The man wanted to say no, to bargain hard, but something in his eyes, perhaps a bad day at the market, changed his mind.

"You're robbing me, you know. But, all right, thirty-five."

"He probably got it to sharpen from someone who forgot to collect it," George remarked on the way home, as I held the knife open and tried to make it glint in the sunlight. I thought about bayonets, and wondered, if I had a rifle, could I fix the knife to the end of it, with wire or something. Outside Sablet, on the roadside, was a billboard, which advertised a cleaning tool.

"*Liquid Veneer Mop. World Champion.*"

"More rubbish," George said, as we passed it.

As we neared Gigondas, I fully appreciated, perhaps for the first time, its uniqueness; rising up into the hills and cocooning around the church at the top of the village. The Dentelles were grey-white like the stones they sell you for the bath. The towers at the back of Montmirail guided us in a direct line with the village square; Place Gabriel Andeol. The late afternoon sun bathed the whole place in

a yellow half-light, where sprinkles of dust floated to us on the wonderful scent of cypress. The soil was the colour of the inside of mushrooms and, somewhere up in the village, other school-children laughed towards the end of the half-day holiday.

"What next?" George asked, as I jumped down from the cart in the courtyard.

"My geography project," I said, solemnly. "I'm a bit late with it already."

"And she, the teacher, how is she? Good?" he asked.

"The best," I said.

"She'll kill you if you don't get it finished!" He laughed.

"I wouldn't mind. Dying like that wouldn't be too bad."

Chapter Three

"WE MUST BEWARE of certain books. I refer, of course, to books or pamphlets of impure suggestion." Fr. Leterrier droned on and on, but we only really paid attention when he seemed about to deliver some valuable advice. "And where would young people find such books?"

We held our breath. I saw Elise Morel blush, but also hold her pen at the ready to transcribe the directions when given. Joseph Hillion was nudging Abel Beaumet and they giggled like old geese. Fr. Leterrier must have had a diploma in disappointment.

"They are everywhere to be found that the Devil frequents."

"In the Convent of Prebayon, Father?" Everyone laughed.

Fr. Leterrier became angry and glanced up suddenly from his notes.

"Who said that?"

Charles Ferrier raised his hand and there was silence. The priest looked as if he were going to explode, and began to advance down the room to where Ferrier sat.

"That's just an old woman's story, a myth. It's not true, do you hear me? It's not true." He stared madly at Charles, but the pupil stood his ground and stared back. Just as he reached the boy's desk the priest seemed to realise that he was too old, and the boy too big, to be able to impose any physical rule on the moment. At the

crucial time in the scene the priest simply leaned over the desk at the student and hissed ,

"It's not true, I'm telling you it's not true."

Some well-behaved child, in the class below us, rang the hand-bell in the corridor and the confrontation ended. It was the first time that we'd seen the priest blow up like that. The Convent, and the story of the Devil building a bridge overnight for the nuns in return for their pledge of allegiance to him, was a local legend, but it was very interesting to witness the priest's reaction to it. Something in the hint of it had clearly unsettled him, or shaken his beliefs. It might be useful to us to remember the moment for future reference. At any rate, I was bitterly disappointed not to get more information about where to find books or pamphlets full of impure suggestions. Perhaps they were to be found in my dreams.

I have nearly always been able to fly in my dreams. Since I can remember, the deepest of sleep has brought with it travel unimag-ined and impossible in daylight. I find myself running along the corridor outside my parents' room, and then taking off like an aero-plane out of the front upstairs window over the entrance hall to Montmirail. During the war I'd seen an aeroplane once; at the airfield at Devil's Plain near Gigondas. I don't know if I dreamed I was an aeroplane before I saw one, but, when I dream, then I soar. I fly out of the domaine and over the village, the school and the square. I swoop low to the hotel to watch the birds picking for food behind it, in the courtyard where the scraps are thrown from the kitchen. The birds scatter as I shout. They abandon their meal and lift in all directions and surround me for a moment in the air like thieves around a gold watch. I fly for hours, over places I've only seen from the roadside. Below me, at the spa of Les Florets, all kinds of deformed and sick people bathe their problems away. Sometimes the waters are empty and I fly low and feel the heat on my face and smell the sulphur. One time, I flew over George as he was bringing barrels to Sablet in the cart. I'm almost sure he looked

up and waved. For years, school had always left me tired in the evenings but, that summer, I found myself full of energy in the afternoons and wishing sometimes that the school day wouldn't end. Even Fr. Leterrier's visits began to interest me on some level. I wasn't sure at first, because, until Easter that year I had resented his lectures and had been bored by him. As the summer approached, I felt my attitude changing slowly. At first I felt sympathy for him; an old man among a crowd of people who did not want him or his advice. Gradually, this gave way to my finding the classes humorous. I began to relish the thought that here, in front of us, a celibate wreck was salivating, while warning us about the acts he himself most wanted to engage in but could not. It was a pathetic scene; where the fat man who loved cakes was destined to meet bakers and cream-makers, but could not indulge his addiction. Yes, that was it. The addiction was feeding itself bit by bit to the drug, but could not take anything in return. I'm sure he got some perverse pleasure from talking to us in high tones about morality and purity, but even that precluded him from touching the words he, clearly, wanted. I do not know the precise moment when the transformation occurred, but, midway through my last term at the lycée, the same thought I had seemed to dawn on others in the class. The girls were the first ones to link in to this revolution. Mathilde Bremond began to wear shorter skirts, Julie Saurel's blouse was unbuttoned more than it should have been. Even Elise Morel, whom I had always thought to be saint-material, began to walk into religion class in a way which could only send a boy's mind in one direction. The boys, too, played their part and, like actors who have been in the same play for years with each other, drifted effortlessly in and out of the drama which was unfolding.

"Father Leterrier, what will happen to people who stray from the path of Holy Purity?" Abel Beaumet asked one afternoon.

"They will rot in the fires of Hell. Their flesh will melt and all of the impurities in their blood will be filtered onto the floor like a

carpet of evil dust." The priest's eyes were wide with rage and envy.

"Why are priests not allowed to marry?" Leopold Palon ventured, one hot Thursday in early June. The priest's face lodged in regret and he shook his head before answering.

"The Church teaches that Jesus was a man and that his disciples were men. As priests, we must keep ourselves pure in every way, so that we can do God's work, without the distractions, and the sins, of the flesh."

"My father says that the total eclipse of the moon, on May second, was God's way of telling us we're not doing enough to please Him," said one of the girls.

"We can never, ever do enough to please Him. We must continually strive to be better people." The priest sounded tired.

The classroom that day was like a cauldron. Even with one of the windows open, the heat shimmered into the room and bathed the group in perspiration. The girls' blouses were damp in patches, and, here and there, the day revealed the outline of a breast or the shadow of a nipple. The room heaved and the humidity made all of the chalk damp and useless. Through the opened windows the outside world supplied us with sunshine which seemed almost edible. The priest faced us on his chair, but we had become the captors now. The boys and girls, who were about to storm into adulthood, and the huge world beyond this little school, made a statement with their bodies and their minds. We were at the point in our journey when our bodies would cross the divide between guilt and pleasure.

Miss Pleyben's class had always been my favourite. I suppose it must have become my favourite at one particular point in time, after I'd experienced all of the other subjects, and their teachers, and made a choice of some sort. You probably have to taste all of the available fruits before settling on the one you like most. Yes, of course, that was logical. I had made that choice some years earlier, around the time Eugene had been killed, and I remained unshaken

in my selection. I knew, in the summer of 1920, that my decision to love her had been made much earlier, but I had not recognised that decision and its significance until then. At first, I was drawn to her by her kindness, by her refusal to comment on my scar and by her own sadness. Perhaps it was also because of my need to fill a gap in my horizon, which my parents had occupied until I was about twelve. Children need adults; they are like fence-posts on the edge of the field that is your life. They serve the dual purpose of keeping you from straying onto the road unsupervised and, at the same time, keep the world at large from trespassing into the field. The need to focus my attention on someone bigger was always there and, just at the precise moment when Eugene might have relieved my parents at their posts, that change of guard was rendered impossible by a German bullet. When I could no longer accept my parents' boundaries, or their rules, I switched my attention to someone else. She would become as constant in my life, and on my horizon, as they had been and, as Eugene should have been, but now could not be. My brother formed part of the soil in Northern France and was well beyond anything I could see out ahead.

Vivienne Pleyben was much more than just my geography teacher. She had nursed me through four or five years with encouraging smiles and precious eye contact. She had stood at the front of my universe; facing me and feeding me information and hope from tatty geography books written by dreamers in Paris. She had led me all around the world, from Venezuela to the Carpathians and to America, and back. We were like honeymooners each week, taking trips together. The rest of the class came with us, but they idled in museums while we ate in expensive restaurants and stole moments together at fountains in secluded squares in Lisbon and Cairo. We visited the Pyramids and Australia and were always back by four in the afternoon. I owed her so much, so very much.

"Aragon move your arse," Charles Ferrier said, as he edged me over on the wooden bench outside the science laboratory, one day

at breaktime. The sun poured into the schoolyard, through a gap created by the spire of the church and the slant of an escarpment halfway into the Dentelles. I eased myself over a little, and he ripped an apple in two with his inky hands and offered me one portion. I accepted it.

"I thought the priest was going to hit me last week, when I said that about the nuns at Prebayon."

"So did everyone else."

"Well, he wouldn't have done it twice."

"What would you have done? Would have you hit him back?"

The bigger boy thought for a few seconds and then bit into the apple and spoke with his mouth full.

"I don't know, Aragon, I really don't."

I was heartened by his answer. I would have been disappointed if he'd told me that he'd been hoping for the opportunity to take a swipe at the priest. That was not the spirit of the silent revolution taking place in the graduating class in the lycée that summer. A fly hummed around the fragment of apple, which had been sprayed from Ferrier's mouth as he spoke. The white, crushy, pulp lay on the lath of wood between us. Suddenly, Ferrier's massive right hand swooped on the scene and caught the fly as it attempted to leave its treasure-trove. Ferrier kept his fist closed for an instant and then opened it slowly and deliberately. The fly was thoroughly intact and alive. It delayed for a moment in the opened hand before flying away. Perhaps it was dazed by the event, or maybe it knew Ferrier meant it no harm. Both Ferrier and the fly went up in my estimation. Miss Pleyben walked by, inside one of the windows in the L-shape of the school. I felt warm inside, and the beginnings of an erection stirred in my grey flannel trousers. It didn't take much nowadays. I wondered had Ferrier noticed. I was almost certain he hadn't. I imagined that the fly would not have survived long if he'd remained on the palm of Ferrier's hand overnight. It was hot in every way imaginable that June and I knew that things were changing. I

thought of Yves Couderc and wondered if he were watching me.

"The geography projects have to be submitted by the seventeenth of July, Ladies and Gentlemen. There will be no exceptions, because the examiners' meeting takes place three days later. This is the final chance that the members of this class have to win the geography prize." Miss Pleyben took the last class on Friday afternoons. Outside the classroom window, the trees in the schoolyard were as still as monuments in the relentless heat. The geography project prize referred to an annual competition. The winner was chosen from among all of the pupils in the school. Two teachers accompanied the victor to Avignon and the prize was, in effect, a short holiday there. The money to pay for the trip was provided by a gift made to the school two or three decades earlier. I hadn't a hope of winning really, but we were all entitled to dream.

Out, over the school wall, I saw the top of someone's head walking in the direction of the village square. I was almost certain it was my father. We had barely spoken in the previous two weeks and the uncomfortable calm of argument lay between us since the day he'd denounced Algerians at the lunch-table. We'd passed in the corridor outside our rooms from time to time, and shared the table at mealtimes. I had perfected the art of arriving late, or excusing myself early, so that the long silences, which usually preceded his outbursts, had simply not materialised of late. I knew that a confrontation with him could end in violence and I feared that. The current state of affairs suited me, although I was unsure as to how long I could keep the tactic going. At any rate, it bridged the time between now and the end of the school year to a certain extent. That could only be good. I dreaded the looming vacation, as it would be my last, and also because of the inevitable life-choice which lay within its confines. August would be the final month of whatever bit of my childhood I still had to live out. I did not know what I should or could do next and, in a way, the fear of that unknown was a kind of comfort, as it postponed the decision even further. George

had suggested to me recently that I should become a doctor.

"I don't think I'd be able to help people when they get sick."

"Why not?" George washed his massive hands in the stone trough outside the woodshed at Montmirail.

"I don't know. I think you have to be able to face sickness and death and not get worried by it."

George laughed.

"I'm sure everybody thinks that before they study medicine at university. That's what they teach you, that's why they have to study for so long."

"I don't know, George. Maybe. It depends how I get on in the exams at the end of July."

"You'll be fine, Christian. You'll be just fine."

I did not want to be a doctor. The truth was, that the only people I'd ever have wanted to cure, Couderc and Eugene, were so far beyond the reach of any doctor now that I felt no real purpose could be served by me becoming one. Allied to this, of course, was the reality that no matter what I wanted to study, or where I wanted to go, my father stood in my way, insisting that I should take over the vineyard. That meant beginning as soon as I graduated from school. Eugene had always represented a barrier between my father and myself, soaking up my father's goodwill, and my own misgivings, and being everything to both of us. If Eugene were still alive, my relationship with my father might not have been much better; but it would certainly have been much less obvious. Of necessity, Eugene's death had drawn our family in on itself in a way which would other-wise have been avoided. My mother lived in her Breton imagination for the most part and only emerged to referee from time to time. Whether it was losing sight of the bobbing head, or hearing my name called, which revived me first from my thoughts, I am unsure.

"Christian Aragon, are you with us today?" I looked up and Miss Pleyben's voice surrounded me like a breeze.

"Yes.Yes, Miss?"

"Welcome back, Christian. I was saying that you're the only one who has not yet told me the subject matter of your project."

"Well, Miss I–"

"I know you've probably begun it already, but I need to submit the title with your name in order to get your exam number. See me after class please."

"Yes, Miss."

I was being chosen to speak to her on my own. I couldn't believe it. It was like in my dreams when I could fly; I could go anywhere I wanted. And now, although my excuse for being where I wanted was perfunctory and practical, the sensations it provoked in my head and my heart were ethereal and magical. I drifted out of the classroom window until the bell rang in the corridor and the sharp mayhem of exiting classmates had left us alone. Miss Pleyben and I.

Her crimson blouse reminded me of the colour of knights' blood in storybooks. Her hair was tied back, in a plait which became visible whenever she moved, and it shadowed behind her like a glimpse of someone else. I traced the outline of her body with my eyes and half-hoped she would notice. If only she would take offence, then she could at least know some of my feelings; however inappropriately the information might convey itself. I thought of Pierre of Provence and Princess Maguelone of Naples. They had exchanged wedding rings in this small village, but I had nothing to offer in an exchange. I felt at once wounded and breathless, waiting for her voice to begin again. She finished marking the roll-book, while I sat alone in the fourth row of the geography class-room, surrounded by maps of the world and charts outlining the decline of ore production in the Alsace-Lorraine region.

"Christian. Thank you for remaining behind." Miss Pleyben closed the roll-book gently and set it to one side on her desk.

"Yes, Miss," I answered, in a voice which did not seem familiar to me.

"You haven't selected a project yet, have you?" She smiled and

her eyes were at once both accusing and forgiving.

"No, Miss," I answered. "You see, I was–" She raised an index finger to stop me before I reached untruths.

"There is no need to explain. I have been thinking about you for a while now, Christian." I could feel myself blushing.

"This is a subject you can excel at if you put your mind to it." I did not speak because there was no need. I nodded my head.

"I have no doubt but that you have what it takes to win this trip to Avignon." Again I nodded. "Are you prepared to sacrifice some spare time to provide this project with the effort required?" She spoke quietly while averting her eyes from mine. Then she picked up an orange pencil from the desk with her right hand and, whether as a gesture of patience or something more, slid it between her lips and waited for my response. I felt like I was going to explode inside and I took some short breaths before replying.

"Yes, Miss. I'm prepared to sacrifice–" I couldn't think of a suitable noun to tag onto the verb so my voice trailed away. Miss Pleyben got up from her chair and came around to the other side of the desk. She motioned for me to come forward from where I sat, and she handed me some pages folded in on each other. One of her legs dangled in the air while the other foot was on the floor. From between her legs, the corner of the desk pointed out at me like an accusation and a taunt. It was where I wanted to be. I noticed that my hands were shaking as I took the material from her.

"These are just a few suggestions for the project, but you really need to begin working on this immediately," she said. I became aware of my own body almost as something alien, and I sought out her eyes for a sign of approval or rejection.

"Yes, Miss. Thank you, Miss," I murmured, as I made my way to the door. I glanced down the list and decided to choose Reafforestation in the Alps. On my way home I noticed my grey trousers were stained with adulthood.

Chapter Four

THERE IS A LEGEND about the origin of the name 'Montmirail'; the 'mountain of the mirror.' I have heard this story a thousand times but I will only tell it to you once, so that you may know it forever. A viper lived in a well in Gigondas hundreds of years ago. This snake was evil and constituted a danger to the entire village. Anybody who looked directly at the serpent, died immediately. As a result, many of the beautiful girls in the village, who came to admire their reflection in the water, met with a hastier end than they might otherwise have expected. It is surprising that some of the girls did not have a similar effect on the viper, as, of course, in any large group there will undoubtedly be some swine as well as pearls! Anyway, one day, a knight, wearing a suit of armour, came along and had the idea of holding a mirror up to the viper. The viper died and the mountain was named.

I never know whether or not to believe in those things. As with the story of the wedding-ring exchange, the legend of the Mirror Mountain lodged in my head early on in my life and stayed there. It was an old story, from nearby, and that, too, is probably how I stored it in my internal archive. When I became old enough to have a family of my own, I suppose that would be the time to hand on these stories. Whether I believed them shouldn't matter much. But it was something deeper than old stories, and future children, which stirred me, as the summer approached in 1920, to find my

own story, my own page in whatever novel God writes. I hadn't held a rifle in my hands in Verdun in the shadow of Fort Douaumont. I hadn't died for France. Nor was I festering inside; with dreams of the Medaille d'Or. I was just a boy trying to become a man. I was sixteen-and-a-half-years old, with a bundle of hormones, and a geography project which was almost finished.

Miss Pleyben lived in a small house on the edge of the village, just below the mountains. Night-time, on the day of the next market, found me making my way past the fever hospice to the stubborn track which led to her isolated home. I was not myself that evening. Please do not misunderstand me when I say that. I do not mean that I am distancing myself from my actions in shame or guilt. Quite the contrary. In fact, I am in awe of the soul which uses my body to chase dreams and ghosts from time to time. I merely give credit where due rather than dare to believe that I, Christian Aragon, could be the architect of these soulful chases.

In 1890 or 1891, the last of the wolves around Gigondas disappeared. I remember my grandfather telling me about hunting for them in the early spring. In the trees above her house, at the raw edge of the hills, these creatures had hidden and made dawn raids from there on the grangeons and chicken-runs in the village, snatching food for themselves and their young. I myself was only a cub on that evening, but I knew what I wanted to capture; an unguarded glimpse of the woman I loved. I left the village behind me as I climbed the track, keeping out of the line of sight of the windows at the front of the house. Was I a wolf? Did I come to take something which did not belong to me? I like to think not, but who can be sure what drives the heart to propel the body into certain situations? What fluid drips slowly from the brain to the feet and makes you walk one way and not another? There is an irresponsibility in youth which is at once restrictive and liberating. It enchants and disappoints all in a moment and leaves you in breathless hope of more. A cypress grove to the rear of the house invited me to sit and stare.

Miss Pleyben lived alone, and I wondered if she ever missed her husband. Stephane Pleyben was an awkward, awful man, who had barged his way into her life and then out of it again. It was widely accepted that he'd left to avoid fighting the Germans. He'd sniffed the gunsmoke from the newspapers and fled. By the time Eugene had volunteered to fight, that coward had been gone six months. The only trace of his absence had been the gradual emergence of Vivienne into our world with smiles and laughs; instead of the make-up she'd used before, to hide her marriage from the rest of mankind. In deference to the horror of her union, she was always called 'Miss,' instead of 'Madame.' A gas-lamp flickered on for a moment and then moved to another room. The evening was reeling in the night and soon it would be time for the cicadas to begin their song. I sat on a tuft of grass behind an old tree and, from time to time, saw her through the window, going about her chores. She washed a single plate and dried it with a patterned cloth, then sat at the kitchen table with a small glass of something in her right hand. She sipped from it from time to time. The mountains behind us grew dark and somehow more precise in outline, until at last the sun sank behind Orange and the day was over. I could see lights in the village below and, from down there too, the sound of a cart on the Carpentras Road floated up and into the leaves above me.

When it was totally dark I moved forward, and the wolf in me used the advantage of night to advance on my quarry. Where there was light within the house, I knew I could get closer and closer and still not be seen. So I crept, on my hands and knees, until I came to the final portion of my cover; where the edge of the light from within met the grass. At this point, the width of a fingernail separated invisibility from detection. Through the glass I could see her bedroom. There was a vivid red blanket on the bed, which seemed to gather the room around itself like a clown or a corpse might. On a stand in the farthest corner, a ewer and a china basin cast an odd combined shadow on the wallpaper whose design I could not make

out. The lamp must have been to the right of the window, on a chair or table, judging from the direction of the light. I had not seen Miss Pleyben for a while now and assumed she must be in the front room, reading or correcting assignments. But since she'd lit a lamp in the bedroom, I suspected that she intended to enter and use that room soon.

All of a sudden, the back door opened and a torrent of light spilled onto the grass. I heard a noise in the kitchen and knew that if she emerged holding a lamp then I would certainly be seen. (Perhaps I already had been). I felt myself redden. I contemplated making a run for it, but eventually decided to wait and let the light determine whether I was still safe. Vivienne Pleyben stepped out of the backdoor and onto a narrow patch of gravel. I heard the rustle of her clothes and then she sighed audibly and came right out and stood for a moment. The light had been ushered out in one direction and that was probably because the door was half-open. For an instant she looked to her right, and I felt so sure that she must see me that I almost spoke. She turned away and walked into the darkness. I heard another door and then I knew; she'd emerged to use the outhouse. I took three steps backwards and lay down on the grass on my stomach. I waited.

Sometime later I was conscious of waking, although I had no recollection whatsoever of nodding off. It was strange and dry under my stomach, and the grass pushed against my skin in the gap between my trousers and shirt, which exposed my tummy. The door was closed now and there was light only in the bedroom. Just as I was about to step forward, and dare the lamplight, Miss Pleyben moved into the space between the window and the bed. It was like a newsreel we'd seen once in the village hall; all light and shade, and movement which seemed unnatural in its speed. She was almost naked, wearing only a blue, striped, unbuttoned, chemise. I could feel my heart quicken. I know you will probably imagine that other parts of me were stirred too, and that desire or lust was my

41

primary reaction but, I must tell you, that you are wrong. My immediate feeling was a sense of overwhelming privilege that my time and hers had collided there, at that place and in that way. I cannot tell you how much my heart was bursting with pride and happiness at seeing her. Clothed or naked, day or night, for one minute or for a century, it was all the same to me. It mattered not a wisp of smoke or a dead leaf what the circumstances were that brought us to any shared time. I only cared that we were there, each alone and, yet, somehow together. Sure, I wanted her in other ways. Of course, I thought the thoughts of teenage boys at the sight of beautiful women. But, if I could not have seen her ever again, apart from that moment through her window, my disappointment could not have dented my joy. I loved her unconditionally. That kind of love is well used to making do with morsels and night-time glimpses, when breakfast and daylight are not yet possible.

What did you expect of me, there, in the darkness, with my heart's desire only paces away and almost entirely bared to me? Do you think that I will tell you that some sad eventuality of self-pleasure, and peeping, combined to complete my hunt? Do you attend on notice of youth and desire and await my confession? I can confess only this to you; that when pure skin and untainted lips and unfractured beauty stood at the window oblivious to my presence, then I stood still and watched and felt my heart seep out onto the space between us and prayed for the moment to last forever. I wanted to be pure too, and, I wanted to be able to say that, if a passer-by had seen me, he or she would have thought me proper and full of happiness; a little unusually situated perhaps, but courteous and mannered in the unknowing sight of the object of all of my love. I must tell you, that although I wanted my geography teacher, in the way that most men inevitably want women, I was beyond contented with my glimpse into her life. Had she been fully clothed, I would not have found her any less desirable. I ached and I wanted her, but I did not cheapen my chase, nor could I have

prized my quarry any more. If you have ever truly loved, you will know that I am honest about all of these matters. When the lamp had been dimmed, and the curtains drawn against the night, I watched her shadow slow to sleep and made my way back down the hill to my own bed.

The head teacher in the school, Monsieur Arsac, interrupted our class when we were in the middle of trying to solve some awful maths problem.

"Pardon me, but may I have your attention please?" He tapped his spectacles on the blackboard. We were delighted by this distraction from algebra. "The winner of the geography project prize for 1920 is—" He paused, and we all imagined it might be us in the seconds before the announcement would shatter those pretensions. —"Christian Aragon!" Monsieur Arsac spoke my name with as much surprise as I felt and everyone else must have been feeling. There was a short burst of applause and then some cheers from Beaumet and Ferrier.

"Avignon?" my father sneered, in the courtyard some days later. "What do you need to go there for? To see the Pope? I don't know what use geography or history can be to a boy like you. This place and the future are what should concern you, not anything else."

"It's a wonderful achievement, it really is," my mother said, with a frightened smile. "It's great that you've won this prize."

"What use is a stupid bloody prize?" he shouted. I immediately thought about the Medaille d'Or.

"It's only for two nights, Robert. It will be good for him," she said.

"He's not going," my father announced as he left the room, slamming the door behind him like a spoiled child.

"What could you have learned in Avignon which would have helped you make good wine here for the next thirty years?" my father asked, a couple of days later, as we stood in the courtyard. I didn't reply but, although it was a rhetorical question, I knew that

some response was demanded. Expected. An acknowledgement that he was right was probably his preferred reaction, but I sensed too that his tone sought to provoke. If my father could coax an argument out of me, it might be the drip before the deluge to allow the war about loyalty, family business, inheritance and the obsolescence of dreams to begin even before the school term ended. I have learned from experience that predictability is one of the great weaknesses; I ignored the remark, and pretended I had not even heard, by shouting at George who emerged from the cellar.

"Are you going to Sablet?" (I knew he wasn't)

"Are you listening to me?" my father snapped.

"Yes," I said, lazily.

"Then what did I say to you a moment ago?" His eyes cranked up the furnace in his face and he stood straight and moved closer to maximise the confrontation.

"You asked if I was listening to you, Papa." I could see his rage beginning. He spoke slowly and deliberately through his teeth. "Before that–".

"I have no idea. I thought you were talking to yourself so I blocked it out to give you some privacy." I smiled as I spoke.

BANG. My father's fist connected with the side of my face. I expected my immediate instinct to be to cry, but something stopped me. I managed to stay on my feet and keep my hands at my side.

"No wonder we won the war," I said. "Imagine how much sooner the Germans would have given up if you'd gone to the front instead of Eugene."

For an instant I thought he was going to hit me again, but, just then, we both sensed George's proximity to the courtyard, and the creak of a door gave away my mother's presence in the scullery at the rear of the house. My father made to speak, but I did not want to give him the opportunity to explain himself. I turned my back on him and walked towards the house. I listened out for footsteps, or the shouts that would be the signs of an attempt by him to re-

take the initiative, but none came. My hands were shaking and my left leg was shivering when I reached the safety of my own room. I lay on the floor rather than the bed, thinking that to relax now would mean being off-guard before time. My father had not struck me for some years now, and this was the first time I could have retaliated as a young man and perhaps even done some damage. I couldn't believe that I'd resisted. I would store up the event until I needed strength against him. I felt that the war had begun, but I was at a loss to understand how exactly it would be fought. Realizing that until that moment I had never believed I could win, somehow I knew then – as the raised voices of my parents, replaying the episode in the kitchen, reverberated in my ears through the floorboards – that I must not allow myself to lose. I did not want this inheritance. I wanted to make my own mistakes and my own life. Families are conspiracies of convenience, where abnormal behaviour sometimes steals the show. I had begun, years earlier, to question the validity of the inheritance of duty and obligation. What is it about families which blinds us to the behaviour of certain members, when we would counsel friends or strangers to leave their families if they told us of a similar experience? It cannot be love, because, when that dies out, we would be free again. Perhaps it is obligation, but you would think that criticism of the behaviour would negate any feelings approximating to loyalty. The only other possibility is fear. I was frightened, but I wanted to fight back. I felt for my scar and, for the first time ever, could not put my finger on it immediately. Had it healed? No. But to me at that time it was certainly less noticeable.

"It will often happen that vile influences insinuate themselves into the life of the young adolescent. These may come in the guise of comradeship, or shared stories of a lewd or reprehensible type. Peddling theories about freedom or adulthood, these influences, if unchecked, will inevitably lead that young person into secret acts of self-abuse." Father Leterrier was tired, but still he preached on

about Holy Purity. "It cannot be over-stressed that this is the point in one's life where choices may have eternal and irreparable consequences. The young mind must be fortified against such influences, and learn to recognise and ignore them as soon as they present themselves."

Although it was warm outside, the classroom was not particularly hot that afternoon. But Fr. Leterrier's classes were now overheating in an entirely different way. The good priest wiped his brow with a handkerchief and made his way to the window. He opened it out as far as it would go. Someone outside will hear him now, I thought, and, as if struck by a similar concern, he went back and closed it to half its open value. Ferrier sat to my left, picking his nose, using an open copybook as cover for this feast. The class seemed fragmented that afternoon and, despite the explicit nature of the teaching matter, no one seemed to be interested in upsetting the priest or provoking him into an argument. I cannot say how it came about, but it coincided with the warning that,

"Mankind expects a higher degree of delicacy and refinement from a woman than a man, and nowhere is this more evident than in matters of purity."

While those words were being spoken, there was a sense of disapproval at the sentiment, although I assure you no sound came from the class. No human sound, that is. It began behind everyone's horizon of hearing, but, gradually, was forced forward as all other sounds fell silent except for it and the excited tones of Fr. Leterrier. It was a creak.

"Now, once a girl begins to lose her self-respect, to make herself cheap, to lower the standard of maidenly refinement, her influence for good vanishes."

Creak. Creak. Creak-creak-creak-creak-creak.......

The voice stopped and suddenly the sound was all alone. I heard Abel Beaumet giggle, then Michel Darlan, who was sitting in front of me, turned and looked past me. I then looked to see. *Creak, creak.*

In the single desk at the rear of the class, Elise Morel sat with her eyes closed and her head tilted forward. *Creak, creak,* her desk squealed, as it rocked gently back and forth. The close concentration on her face was almost divine. Her arms pointed away down at the floor. Somewhere, in between, her hands were out of view and she rocked back and forth in ecstasy; her face framed in passionable pleasure. A mixture of shock and delight descended over the entire class, as we all seemed to turn our eyes to Fr. Leterrier, waiting for his reaction. His eyes were like saucers; a strange mixture of blue bloodshot fury and frustration. He put down his pen on the desk beside him and walked three paces into the centre of the middle aisle. *Creak.* Like a timid man faced with violence, he breathed heavily and rapidly until he forced his words out in a hoarse whisper and launched them at the back wall. *Creak creak.*

"Mmmiss Morel?" He hissed hesitantly. The creaks increased in frequency and then stopped abruptly. Elise's eyes flicked open, as if awakened from only a moment's closure,

"Yes, Father?" she said, in a tone which was neither embarrassed nor brazen.

"What are you *doing,* Miss Morel?" I could see that he instantly regretted asking the question and wished he'd simply asked her to stop or leave. Anything, except invite an explanation.

"Doing, Father? Surely you know only too well what I'm doing?"

"I do not, Miss Morel. I do not." His voice got stronger and louder but he retreated like an exorcist who has taken on too big a task.

Slowly and deliberately, Elise Morel licked her lips provocatively, and began to raise her arms. As she breathed in, her breasts swelled in her blouse. The class and the priest were transfixed and no one knew what to expect. Her wrists, then her hands, came into view and she exhaled. Elise Morel raised them the last couple of inches and then opened her cupped hands to the world like a

conjurer. In her palms, a set of rosary beads coiled in repose like a sleeping viper.

"Praying to Our Lady for maidenly refinement, Father," she announced.

The bell rang for the end of the class and our innocence.

Chapter Five

"DO YOU KNOW HOW Petrarch described this city?" Miss Pleyben asked, as we arrived through the gate in the wall onto Cours Jean-Jaurês, and my feet met Avignon.

"No, Miss."

"'A sewer where all the filth of the universe has gathered,'" Christian. That's what Petrarch made of it." She raised her hands and, in a gesture, presented the city to me.

"Why did he say that, Miss?"

"Because it was true, I suppose." She smiled as she spoke. "Do you know when Petrach made that remark?" I was being tested on the short history of Avignon she'd given me one afternoon the week before our trip. I had studied it minutely.

"After the Black Death in 1348?"

She smiled again but this time I felt that the smile was for me.

"Absolutely right, Christian. When criminals and heretics gathered here to hide in the shadow of the Papacy. When plague followed famine, and the scent of death was the first thing a newborn baby knew."

"But that was hundreds of years ago, Miss. Avignon is not like that now. Is it?"

"I hope not, Christian. But we shall find out."

It was another world, this blue and grey town; rising up like a

brick menace over the river Rhône. As we walked side by side in the street, people sometimes looked at us. I wondered what they thought about. Outside the Palais du Roure we stopped for a few minutes to catch our breath. A tiny fountain played into the afternoon air like a juggler. To the right, on the edge of a pillar with iron gates, a small drinking spout in the shape of a lion watered us until we were full. I felt the water splash onto my shirt and trousers, and then I gulped and gulped; water and air, air and water, until my stomach hurt and I knew to stop. All this time, Miss Pleyben watched me and I felt her eyes on my shirt, my head, and on the splashes of water which jumped past me onto the pavement. I drank longer than was prudent, but that was because I loved the attention. I craved the sensation of being watched but being apparently unaware of it. It reminded me of my night outside her house weeks earlier.

"That's enough, leave some for me." Her voice revived me. I lifted my head and let the water slow, as my hand released the head of the lion. I felt her behind me as I turned and I wished we were naked and beside running water. When I'd finished with the water, I was back in that afternoon, and my rotation ended with us standing toe-to-toe. She looked as though she were going to scold me, but then she shrugged her shoulders and ruffled my hair with her hands. For an instant I almost tried to kiss her, but held myself back. It was as though a part of me knew more about all of this than I did, and I bided my time without really knowing why.

We walked on together into the crowds of people going the other way. As we did so, I felt the sun on my shoulders; pushing me up the street. The dark corners of bright shops seemed to come alive and taunt the day through vitrines, as though our passing by had disturbed them into life. Here, a new dress leaned out to see, and, over there, the gorgeous smells of baking deliberately drew us nearer to one side of the street.

"Are you alright, Christian?" Miss Pleyben asked, as we took

the left turn just before the Place du Palais and entered the Rue de la Balance.

"Yes, Miss," I replied, without really considering her question. We had arrived at our lodgings; the tiny Hotel St. Sauveur. As we stood together on the front step, she turned to me and spoke to me for the first time as if we might have been the same age.

"Please call me Vivienne. 'Miss' is too formal I think. We only have two days here and then we'll be back to the school again but, while we're here, let's address each other as friends. Okay?"

"Okay." This time I'd heard the question and hoped I was beginning to understand.

The concierge was a small crooked man with an enormous straight nose. His eyebrows almost met in the centre of his forehead but some inscrutable reticence kept them apart. He looked at our two small bags with derision and then asked, slyly.

"Will your luggage be arriving later?"

Miss Pleyben, Vivienne, cut him in two with a swish of her hand and replied.

"We were advised to travel as lightly as possible because of the reputation of Avignon for thieves." She winked at me. The little man was put in his place and took our bags in his old rigid hands and led the way to our rooms at the top of the house. Miss Pleyben had told me earlier that Herve Duchen, who taught the fifth-years, and was supposed to accompany us on the trip, had travelled to Paris instead.

"He's gone to see his mistress in the Boulevard St. Jacques. If anyone asks, we're to say he was with us, alright?" I nodded and was delighted we were going to be alone.

She had made these remarks on the train from Orange to Avignon. Of course I was thrilled about having her all to myself, but there was something more. I think that it was at that point exactly that I began to entertain the faintest of possible hopes; namely, that she might have some sort of feelings for me. I smiled

in a sort of half-smile, which left it up to her to decide the extent or significance of what I might be thinking or desiring.

The room was simple; bed, chair, table and a tiny wardrobe that had a door which was glued shut so you couldn't use it anyway. I unpacked in less than half a minute and, over the back of the chair I put the clean pair of trousers my mother had packed. I went to the window and looked out onto the Rue de la Balance. The buzz of conversations drifted up from the street but fragmented into air and incomprehensibility by the time it reached me. I watched a boy with a hoop chase it down the street. I laughed to myself as it passed perfectly through the gap outside a clothes shop, between one customer entering and another leaving. It was late in the afternoon now and my stomach growled for food. I left the window open and sat on the bed. A small knock on the door announced her arrival.

"May I come in?" she asked, opening the door, but not enough to see into the room.

"Sure," I answered. My heart began to beat faster and we met in the mirror on the wardrobe before we met, if you know what I mean.

"I don't know about you, but I'm hungry," she said.

"Me too, Vivienne." There, I'd said it, used her name and now I moved closer to her world and it hadn't taken much courage, not much courage at all. She'd given me that key and I'd used it. Turned the lock and opened the door. I arrested my thoughts and followed her along the corridor and then down the stairs. The man with the huge nose barely looked up from the desk as we passed, and he said nothing. We were supposed to leave our room keys with him if we went out. So we didn't. It was a challenge to him which he was unable to accept. We stepped out into Avignon.

"Let's go left," she suggested. I nodded, and we marched with purpose back towards the Place de L'Horloge. I brushed past people who all seemed to be somehow smaller and lighter than myself.

We side-stepped a large pile of boxes outside a hat shop. As we rejoined on the other side (I cannot say at whose instigation it occurred), we were holding hands and saying nothing and looking for a restaurant. It is difficult for me to remember now what we ate or where we sat. I can only really say that I enjoyed the meal without noticing it, and noticed an erection in my pants without enjoying it. She drank a little wine, and I consumed glass after glass of water, hoping to distract my nether region into more ordinary use. She was beautiful. She wore a simple dress which revealed a mole on her right shoulder and hid most of her chest under a thin white-bordered collar. I did not know where to look most of the time and, whenever I did catch myself looking, it was at her warm face on my way back up from her breasts. She did not seem to mind and she spoke gently and kindly to me of how we would visit the Palace of the Popes on the following day, and the Porte St. Dominique and the ramparts near Porte Magnanen. She urged me to be vigilant.

"Christian, you have only two days to enjoy this city, so, keep your eyes open."

"I will," I promised. "I will."

She was calm, and measured, and kind, and open, and fresh and beautiful, and the words she spoke drifted over to me like butterflies crossing a meadow. I did not know whether I'd taken her hand or she mine. I was unsure if that was an accident or an indulgence. I was certainly in the dark as to whether what I should expect next was forgiveness for a mistake, or another tiny step on the road to intimacy. To be honest, I was completely confused. If I'd been out of line, she gave no indication of upset or reproach. I wanted to overturn the table and kiss her in front of the stuffy old men and women in the restaurant on that afternoon.

After dinner, we walked for hours around the streets of that great city. I took in the scenes and sounds and recall, in the most vivid of detail, the facade on the Hotel des Monnaies, with its spitting lions disgorging fruit and flowers in stone. The eagles and

dragons of the Borghese family were flattened by the rain in places, and scorched by the sun almost in their entirety. I was more acutely aware of Vivienne, however, and I walked beside her down the lucky streets of Avignon. We held hands, and I loosened my grip from time to time, inviting her to break away and tell me I'd been mistaken. She did not tell me that I had been mistaken. She pulled me closer to her as we walked and, as we did, our arms, too, were as close as our clothes would allow. The wrists of my shirtsleeves were damp with anticipation and I smiled at complete strangers, feeling for the first time ever that I belonged. I thought *about* her. I closed my eyes momentarily and I *saw* her inside my head then I opened them again and I was *with* her. We were with each other; together in Avignon. For all of those years I'd imagined myself in her company, taking trips to faraway places during class. In my mind; we'd soared over the Mediterranean and had visited Africa and Peru and Japan together, while the rest of the class stared blankly at their books, or looked half-heartedly out of the window. But now we really *were* travelling together, and Avignon was as exotic as heaven, or the moon.

We passed by cafés and heard laughter locked away. Then we were suddenly swept along by the people around us, and found ourselves at the west facade of the Church of St. Pierre. A statue of the Virgin Mary, in the west porch of that church, looked out at us and, for an instant, I knew that I was in some way still a child and also knew that I now wanted to advance beyond that point.

"I suppose *you're* a virgin too?" she said with a laugh, as we turned away and let our feet lead us towards the Pont St Bénézet. I thought I would blush, but I didn't. Instead, something in me recalled Fr. Leterrier, and I replied.

"I've become a little tired of Holy Purity lately."

Vivienne smiled and turned to face me and held me by both hands.

"So have I."

It only took the most slight of touches and we knew that the moment had arrived. A slip of hair fell thinly on the side of her face and I pushed it back and behind her ear. She whispered something, it may have been my name, and we kissed. Her kiss was so soft and reassuring and inviting and of wine and I kissed her back. She was the first girl I'd ever really kissed (if you don't count the lady from the Metal for Munitions Association who'd turned her lips to mine at the last moment as I kissed her goodbye on the cheek after Eugene's funeral). I felt a warm chill cover my body, and I put my arms around her neck and kissed my geography teacher as well as I thought I knew how. When we finished she kissed me on the eyes, and all over my face, and stroked my cheek and said.

"Oh, Christian, what has happened to our worlds that we are here?" I had no idea what she meant, but at least I figured she wasn't mad at me or anything. We began to walk again. "St. Bénézet was a shepherd who began to build this bridge in 1177 after divine inspiration even though–"

"Even though the people of Avignon mocked him."

I finished her sentence from the notes on Avignon which she'd given me. Vivienne smiled and, for an instant, we were teacher and pupil but then, our bodies hauled us back to the present where we were something altogether different.

In the middle of the bridge in Avignon lies the Chapel of St. Nicholas. It is an odd building, split into two levels. The stone was cold to the touch and, through the open windows, I heard the sound of the Rhône gushing south to the sea. An old lady carrying a basket of firewood passed us as we entered the chapel. She looked up as she went by and in her eyes I sensed a disapproval which reminded me of my father. For an instant I thought of my class-mates: Ferrier, Beaumet, Elise Morel, Mathilde Bremond, Julie Saudrel. I knew all of their names, and they knew mine, but I could not really describe them as close friends. When I thought about it, George was more of a friend to me than they were. Couderc, in a

way, had been the nearest I'd achieved to close contact with anyone, apart from Eugene. Eugene had been *my* hero long before he became one for France. A drop of water fell from the ceiling of the chapel onto my head and I stood where I was and looked up so as to try and catch the next one in my mouth. It struck me on the nose and I tasted it as it slid down my face. It was clear and pure and reminded me of the salt from my mother's tear I'd tasted in the cradle. I closed my eyes.

Vivienne must have been watching me, because I heard her laugh. I kept my eyes closed. I felt the warm comfort of her breath on my face. Her lips closed in on mine and her strong tongue explored my own mouth. I continued to keep my eyes shut and she kissed me deeply. I felt her hands release my shirt from inside my waistbelt and, suddenly, her flesh was against mine. She guided me, slowly backwards into a corner at the end of the chapel aisle. I put my arms around her neck, but she gently lifted my right hand and linked her fingers in mine and led my hand under the arm of her dress. I was unsure what to do but, as she placed my hand against her breast, I felt her nipple harden. I caressed it and it grew in my fingers and her whole body shook slightly as we manoeuvred ourselves against the cold wall.

Now I opened my eyes, and hers were closed, and we kissed and kissed and I felt that I was going to explode down below in my pants. A sound outside the chapel door startled both of us and, for an instant, I expected Father Leterrier, or the police, or the woman with the basket, to fling open the doors of the church and rebuke us. The moment passed as the sound faded, and Vivienne took me by the hand. We walked to the other side of the chapel. There, a confessional box guarded the right-hand aisle from the light through the stained-glass window of St. Bénézet and his sheep. She put a finger to her lips and opened the door in the centre with a tiny squeak. I saw the small seat with its velvet cover, and Vivienne pushed me ahead of her and I sat down and faced her. Quickly

and effortlessly, she leaned and undid my belt and button and released my excitement from the confines of my mother's laundry. I wanted to speak, to ask what to do next, to say "Is it alright? Am I big enough? Are you okay?" But I could not.

Vivienne closed the door behind her and we were in complete darkness. For a long moment we were silent, and I could hear the sound of my own breathing. I felt her hands about my face and then we kissed and, as our kiss ended, I felt her ease a finger into my mouth and we both licked it and each other. There was a small noise as she moved forward, and I felt her lever herself onto the seat with a knee either side of me. Before I could really assimilate and wonder what to do next, I felt her legs around me and in the dark she eased herself down onto me and her wet, snug, other lips were all around me too. Her weight was nothing to me and she lifted herself up and down ever so slightly, while simultaneously edging her finger in and out of my mouth. My hands were under her now and I felt the smooth silkiness of the body I'd spied on only weeks earlier. We kissed again and she blew on my face and cooled me. I was dying to come inside her but was afraid. I asked her in a breathless voice which seemed alien to me.

"Is it okay? What about babies?"

She shushed me and whispered,

"It's fine, Christian. Don't worry about that, it's all fine, just come, come inside me."

I moved her up and down more quickly now, pleasuring myself and losing all concerns in a feeling which welled up around me and consumed me inside-out. I could feel the tide rising within me now, and I thought for a split-second about how this time I wouldn't come inside one of the clean towels from the airing cupboard, and wouldn't have to think about pillowcases or sheets. Vivienne squeezed me with muscles inside her, and it was as though she had an extra hand and it was bringing me to a climax. I'm in a confessional box and I haven't any sins to tell, I thought, as I exploded up

inside her and a wave of wetness enveloped me deep inside my geography teacher in a cold stone chapel on a bridge. Criminals and heretics gathered here, and I hadn't thought about my scar all day. I was no longer a virgin; I'd been deflowered sur le Pont D'Avignon.

Chapter Six

"Tell me about your husband."

"Stephane?"

"That was his name, wasn't it?"

Vivienne poked me in the ribs with her elbow as we lay in her bed that night, while a clock, somewhere below us in the hotel, chimed half-past one. The sound of unexpected rain through the balcony window was like a barrier between us and the world.

"You're a smart one, aren't you, Christian Aragon?"

"I don't really remember him, except that sometimes when you came to school he would wait outside the gate until you'd gone inside."

"You saw that? You noticed it?"

"Sure. I was watching you once and you turned to look at him and you waved, but he didn't wave back."

Her eyes narrowed and I saw a tear form in the corners, just above the line of her cheek.

"He never waved back, Christian. Not once, not one single time. He walked me to the school all right, he wanted to know where I was every minute of the day. He was the same when I got home in the afternoon; always wanting to know where I'd been after school, who I'd talked to, what we'd spoken about."

"Why?"

"So that he had control of my life, Christian. So that he knew where I was at every moment of the day."

"But why? Surely he had things to do himself, work, going out, hunting?"

She shook her head.

"I'm afraid not. I was his obsession. He did nothing that didn't contribute to that control over me. He became angry if anyone spoke to me in the street and later, when we got home, he'd quiz me over and over again. 'Why did that person stop to talk? Are you having an affair with him?' Sometimes, he'd even wake me up in the middle of the night and turn on the lamp and begin his questions all over again. 'Why this? Why that?'"

I lay on my side, with an arm propping my chin, and watched the contours of her face as she spoke. I traced the line of her mouth with my free hand and she pretended to snarl and try and bite it. Outside, someone screamed 'Salud,' from a window high enough to drift on up to us un-fractured. A small candle flickered from the nightstand on her side of the bed, and its shadows giddied their way up and down the wall. I was sleepy and yet I dared not sleep, because the night held the promise of more love and learning. I hated to think of her husband and the way he had treated her. I hated to imagine her being touched, taken, violated by him.

"You wore a lot of make up back then," I said, broaching the subject in a way which allowed her to reveal a little more of herself if she wanted.

"Yes, Christian," she said, petting my face with a hand. "I certainly did." As she finished speaking, she held my shoulder and pulled me towards her. In a short time I was on top of her and she was guiding me inside herself for the third time that night. It was slow and uncomplicated, and fulfilled every dream I'd ever had about her and about how I wanted her.

In between, we talked and laughed and ate chocolates we'd bought on our way back to the hotel. We balanced the chocolates on

each other's bare bodies and allowed those hor d'oeurvres lead us on to other tastes of forbidden flesh and hidden fruit. I was sixteen, but soon I'd be seventeen and, now, and forever after, I'd no longer be a boy or a child. She taught me the language of passion over the course of our stay in Avignon. I experienced the awesome heights of desire, expectation, appreciation and fulfilment; which only wonderful, slow, unhurried, illicit love can bring when you're not quite seventeen. Love? Yes, that was there too, in huge un-quantifiable chunks, as I pleasured, and was pleasured by, the only woman I'd ever loved or could imagine loving. I worshipped her body with mine and tasted every single part of her with the wild satisfaction of a gourmand in a chocolaterie. She encouraged me and praised me and, when my eagerness brought closure too early, she welcomed it and transformed my errors into heroics with the kindest of words and touches. She moulded me, through those two nights, into someone who could finally feel loved in return. We fused in the most intimate way imaginable, and each touch and whisper hauled us closer and closer, until I felt that I could slip into her life, unnoticed by the world, and remain there forever, as enthusiastic and as passionate and as adoring as if I was still only an admirer from afar.

"Why me?" I'd asked, in the course of our first night together.

"What do you mean?" Her face was close to mine. The scent of her made me dizzy.

"I mean, how come you're here with me and not, say, Ferrier or Beaumet? I mean, if they'd not finished their project, would you be with one of them in Avignon instead?"

I knew from the silence that I'd hurt her. I didn't mean to, but I had. For a few seconds I thought she might get out of bed and leave me, but instead she spoke and explained and reassured me.

"I've been alone for some years now, Christian. But I've been lonely for much longer. You see me as what, a teacher in control? An adult with freedom to do as I please, go where I choose? I'm just

another person, Christian. A little older than you perhaps, but a person nonetheless. I've been aching for so long to reach out to someone else, to have them reach out to me too. I need more in my life than I have, or I'll die of a broken heart. I'd have died long ago if I hadn't met you. I've watched you from a distance and seen your struggle and your heartache. I know I should have waited until you'd left school, but I honestly didn't know whether anything would happen between us here in Avignon. Sure, I hoped it would, I can't deny that, but I don't know what I can say or do to make you know that you are the person I desire and need. Nobody else would have done, if that's what you're asking."

She held her hand out to me and we linked fingers and grew closer in every possible way. She answered my questions with an intimacy and a vulnerability which left me in no doubt as to the truth of the words she spoke. Later, she told me how repeated assaults by her husband had left her incapable of bearing children.

" You saved me from a beating by him once," she said, looking up at the ceiling as we lay side-by-side later that night.

"That time in the square?"

"You remember? You were such a child then, so young, so small. How could you recall such an event? How old were you? It must have been before the war."

" I don't know, nine or ten maybe. I'll never forget the look on his face."

"We had been arguing," she said.

"About what?"

"About nothing, everything, oh I don't know, but I do remember how he was about to hit me and then he saw you standing nearby in short trousers, watching with your fists clenched."

"I don't know about that."

"Yes, yes, they were, tiny clenched hands. Do you remember what you said to him?"

" I didn't speak to him. I think I just looked at him, that's all."

"No, no." She turned her face to mine and kissed me. "You told him that you would fight him if he found you a box to stand on."

"I don't remember that."

"I remember it, Christian. I think it was from that moment on that I began to care about you. You were the only person who ever stood up to Stephane and I will never forget that."

"Where is he now?" I asked, as we began to drift off to sleep.

"I don't know," she answered. "Wherever he is, I hope he's dead."

"I have a confession to make," I said, as we ate breakfast in a café on the Rue Boisserin on our final morning in Avignon.

"Oh yes?" Vivienne looked up from her coffee and smirked. "Are you happy enough to make your confession here or would you feel more comfortable in the chapel of St. Nicholas?" I felt myself blush, but only for a moment, and for a different reason than she thought.

"No, I mean it, there's something I should tell you." I didn't want there to be any secrets between us and I did not want to keep this one at all.

"So tell me," she invited, smiling in a warm way which complemented the day around us, which was shrouded in the scent of coffee.

"I–" It was hard to begin. "I went one evening to–"

"To where, Christian? Tell me." She put down her cup.

"To your house, I went to your house and –"

"Was I there? Did you knock? Why didn't I hear you?"

"Yes, yes, you *were* there," I stammered. She reached across the table and took my hand. "Tell me," she said. "It's alright."

"I watched. I saw you clean a single plate. I monitored the shadows and lay in the grass. I saw you in a blue chemise and I devoured every single moment of that evening while you went about your chores and then undressed and went to sleep."

"Did you want me? Did you desire the person you saw that night? " She asked the questions softly.

"Yes, yes I did. I wanted you, but also I knew then that I–"

"Yes?" she whispered.

"That I loved you." I told her straight out.

"Oh, Christian," she said, kissing my fingers. "How wild and kind and honest you are." She was laughing now and we linked fingers across the table.

"You're not angry?"

"Angry? Oh God, no, Christian. I'm not angry. I'm flattered, I'm pleasantly surprised, I'm as wet as a waterfall and I'd love to have you, here and now, in this café, before I finish my coffee. I'm a lot of things because of what you've told me, but angry is definitely not one of them." She was gorgeous and I could not believe that I was with her.

"Who was it you saw, for the last time ever, outside the bakery in Gigondas?"

Her question came out of the blue as we looked at the murals later that morning in the Chambre de Cerf in the Palace of the Popes. I was engrossed in the fishing scene and was trying to make notes. I looked up and answered without thinking.

"Yves Couderc."

"Oh," she said. "The boy who died of TB?"

"Yes."

"The boy who–"

I reached for my scar. "Who gave me this? Yes"

Together we walked backwards from the mural in silence, seeking a different view of the scene.

"How did you know I'd seen someone for the last time outside the bakery?"

"I too, have a confession to make."

"What confession?"

"I heard you once in the Chapel of St Cosme, talking to God."

"You were there? Why?"

"I was just passing by when I saw that the door was open. I

hadn't been in a church for years and, so, I thought I'd visit when there was no one around. But there *was* someone there."

"You know, I thought I heard someone. But when I looked around, the place was empty."

"I hadn't been in a church since, not until..." We both smiled and remembered.

"That's the first time I've been in a confession box in ages," I said, with a grin.

"I hope your soul is clean now," she said.

There was an easy happiness between us and it was as though we'd been friends and lovers for years. I didn't want it to end. A newspaper boy stood on the street outside the Palace of the Popes. He sold copies of Le Quotidien du Midi with an arrogance that could only have been earned. I saw an advertisement on the back of a folded copy: "*Végétaline*"; "*Cheaper than butter, lighter on your stomach. Keeps better and can be used for all kinds of cooking.*"

I remembered that my mother had bought this product earlier in the year, just after Easter. She'd been trying to save money, after George had told my father that the foreman at Domaine Grapillon d'Or predicted a poor crop for that year. My father always knew better than everyone else, though.

"What's this?" he'd asked aggressively, holding up the glass dish with the yellow, oily substitute.

"It's Végétaline," my mother answered. "You'd hardly know, and, anyway, Paulette Canchier says it's much cheaper." CRASH! My father dropped the dish onto the stone floor. It shattered and yet the centre of the dish stuck to the Végétaline in a stupid pattern, and my mother went down on her knees to pick up the pieces. A shard of glass cut the thumb of her left hand and it bled onto the floor.

"It's much more expensive than butter, Cherie," my father corrected; intoning deliberately, while my mother crawled about the room. "You see, we'll have to get a new dish now, and I suppose you'll be off to the doctor about that tiny cut as soon as you get the chance."

"Hey, Christian." I felt a pull on my arm whisk me back to Avignon. Vivienne dragged me playfully by the sleeve, across the street, to a shop which sold candles and chocolate. It was a shop made for us. I looked at her from behind as she paid for the chocolates. I imagined being a ghost or spirit, and just gliding forward to envelop her like a stencil captures the outline of a figure on a page, and doesn't lift its head until the design is completed. For the first time since we'd made love and kissed and been together in Avignon, I began to think about the future. Not years ahead, but even the following day. How would it be back in Gigondas? Would we still be lovers? Would it be possible to carry on our relationship at all, under the watchful eye of its inhabitants? Everyone presented a possible obstacle to us, from the Mayor, Gustave Le Vay, to the children in the first class at the school. I was glad that Vivienne had been the one who observed me at the chapel, when I'd tried to resolve the whole thing about Couderc with God. I told her so.

"I'm glad too, Christian. I'm happy that for one moment I was allowed inside your heart. It made me realise how far I've drifted from God in my own life."

"You've been in my heart for a very long time," I said.

"Thank you, Christian."

Around us, the air was heavy with people and summer. The clatter of commerce, and the grinding turn of cartwheels on the stone streets, had no appeal for me. I had begun to miss the sound of the cicadas in the afternoon, and the high rustle of different shades of green leaves in the Mistral. The pitch and rush of that great wind in the trees, sometimes sounded so loud in the grounds of Montmirail, that it drowned out my thoughts and tossed George's shouts of 'hello' to the Dentelles, instead of over in my direction. Yes, these were the sounds of my village, but my father's wish, that I should never hear any other sounds, made me even more sure that I was unlikely to stay in Gigondas after I left school. I split an apple in two with my pocket knife and we ate without

speaking, crunching our way to the train station. The nasty man with the big nose was nowhere to be seen as we left the Hotel St. Sauveur. I was sorry to leave the hotel behind because I knew that I was leaving a part of myself there too. Some awkward, inopportune portion of my childhood was trapped forever; between the glued wardrobe door and a window over the Rue de la Balance. I was out now, away from some shadow that had held me back.

"What will we do when we get to Gigondas?" Her question surprised me, as I had expected to be the one to ask.

"I don't know, Vivienne."

"You'll have to call me 'Miss Pleyben' again." She smiled. "That's certain at least."

"It's going to be strange, sitting in class and watching you and knowing that...."

"I know, Christian. It's going to be difficult for me too. But we will have to be careful."

"I know. I don't want you to get into any trouble at the school. I don't think they'd like it if–"

"No, they wouldn't. It's going to be difficult. People will be watching us anyway because we've been away. Make sure you say that Monsieur Duchen was with us."

"My father will be back from Paris tomorrow."

I shuddered to think of what would happen if *he* ever suspected anything. In a way, I almost hoped that he might find out. It would be another skirmish in the mountains before the confrontation on the battlefield proper. My mother had consented to my making this trip; only because he'd be away either side of it. I think that, in a sense, her defiance of his wishes in this manner accorded her a degree of independence. Perhaps too it was even a little retribution for things like the Végétaline incident, or the gulf of emotion between them, which was only ever bridged physically in the most base and thoughtless way. In the same expanse of Provencal landscape in which some people cultivated Mulberrry leaves to nourish

67

silk worms, the Aragon household stood its ground and maintained its place in the village, through a mixture of tradition and obduracy. I was on my way back there now, with some extra knowledge, and, maybe even the strength to break away from what was expected.

"We must be careful, Christian."

Vivienne spoke in a whisper as we stood on the platform of the station at Avignon, waiting for the train to Orange. I knew that she was right, but part of me wanted to take her hand and hold it up to the sun and the world and scream, "I love this woman." I knew that whatever lay ahead of us would not be easy or kind. We needed each other, that was clear to me at any rate. She; the abandoned wife alone in a village of parents and pupils , and me; the ungrateful son of the oldest wine cellars in the Rhône valley. We'd made plans. I spooled recollections through my mind's eye, while we waited and watched the heat rise off the iron tracks which petered off to a point in the distance. I remembered our voices in the dark as we'd made plans in the cosy warmth of the hotel.

"Will you wait for me to grow up and be with you always?"

"Yes, yes I will, Christian. But when you're older you won't want an old lady like me."

"How old are you now?"

"Twenty-four."

"That's not old."

"Not even when you're only sixteen? Doesn't it seem very old?"

"No, you're young, you're like me; looking for someone to share your dreams with."

"Will you wait for me, Christian?"

"Forever, if I have to."

"I hope it won't be that long."

"I hope so too."

The train made itself known to our ears before we sensed it in any other way. A mellow hum and buzz on the iron tracks was like

a bee trapped in a demi-john. As it approached, we glanced at each other and Vivienne began to cry. She looked away from me when she knew that I was watching her.

"What is it, Vivienne?" I put my hand on her shoulder and turned her so that we faced each other.

"Nothing, it's nothing. Really."

"I don't believe you."

"I'm crying because I'm happy, Christian. You've made me so happy."

"School finishes in three weeks," I said. "Then our lives can really begin."

I made myself a promise, there and then on the platform, that we *would* be together forever. I knew that there would be obstacles, no matter what I did or where I went. I remembered the fireworks the previous year on the feast of St Cosme and St Damien. I recalled her features in minute detail, lined up against the colours of the September sky. I'd buy coffee beans at the market in Seguret one day soon and bring her breakfast in bed. No one and nothing, not my father, or society manners in Gigondas, or anyone or anything else, was going to stop the inexorable march of Christian Aragon towards his chosen destiny. I would be strong and tall, and alone sometimes if I had to. But I would take every single step on that path, even if it meant forsaking the plans of men, gods or devils, to be with the woman I loved. I touched my scar with a pride for the first time ever. I wished for the heat of battle and the sting and mark of steel to cross and cover my body, if necessary, in the burned insignia of passion and love. As the train came to a halt, I pulled her to me and kissed Vivienne for the last time before she became Miss Pleyben again for a while. A figure in the carriage behind her back, returned my gaze over her shoulder. I opened my eyes and took up my small bag from the railway station floor.

"Oh, God," I said quietly. "It's Father Leterrier."

Chapter Seven

"TAKE OFF THAT UNIFORM, you're not fit to polish the buttons on it," my father roared. It was the day after the telegram had arrived, telling our family of Eugene's death. I undid the tunic and took it off, folding it awkwardly before laying it on top of the trunk in which I'd found it. My father stood in the doorway of the bedroom.

"And the rest of it," he ordered. I stepped out of the trousers, with their blue stripes down each leg. As I turned to place them on top of the tunic, I heard the slap of his leather belt being whipped from around his waist. I raised my arm, instinctively, to protect my face, but was a fraction too late. The double force of the leather struck me before my hand could shield my cheek, and the clout knocked me to the ground. The blows began to rain down on my bare torso, my arms, my legs and on the back of my head, as I sat in a huddle trying to stop the belt accessing my face. I do not know how long the beating continued for, but it seemed that no part of my flesh escaped my father's grief and wrath in that room on that February afternoon in Gigondas. I began to lose consciousness at one stage and felt my head spin as my skin burned in weals and welts. The musty smell of my brother's uniform reminded me that I was now an only child.

"Robert," my mother screamed, from the same spot in the doorway from which he had ordered me to undress. "Stop it. Stop it."

It was the last beating I received from him, apart from that punch in the face in the courtyard in Montmirail, during my last days there, when I'd deliberately misunderstood what he'd said. I recalled frequently how he'd not uttered a single word during my beating over the uniform, and how neither of us had spoken of it afterwards.

"Your father is very sad about Eugene." My mother made a half-hearted excuse for him, as she treated my injuries with ointment.

"So am I," I whispered, beneath my crying. "So am I."

The Algerian man who'd come to work at Domaine De La Mavette had a kind face. He saluted me in the Place de la Fontaine on the Wednesday after I'd returned from Avignon. This act of kindness and courtesy was in contrast to the reception which had greeted his own arrival in certain parts of the village. I understood, from local gossip, that someone had taken a swing at him when they'd met him on the road to Les Florets. By all accounts he'd been more than well-able to look after himself, and the assailant had wound up in the ditch. I couldn't understand this type of antipathy towards a man because of the colour of his skin. My father had no such difficulties;

"Parasites, that's what they are. God-fearing Frenchmen work their hands off to the wrist and these half-breeds come to take their jobs and their land. What next, I wonder? Mixed marriages?"

I'd saluted the Algerian in return at the fountain. To me, he was a better man than my father would ever be.

"I suppose they just have different traditions," I posited in response, across the dinner table.

"Traditions? What traditions?" My father sneered. "They breed camels, eat sand, and sit out in the sun all day, dreaming. Of what, I wonder?"

"Hardly the Medaille d'Or," I said, remembering that my father's trip to Paris had been to lobby support for his latest bid to capture the prize. He began to go red at the junction of his chin and his collar. His rage rose like water in a basin when you put your foot right down into it. He held in his anger, in a rather uncharacteristic display of reserve and, instead, opened his defence on another front.

"I hope you enjoyed Avignon, Christian?"

"Yes. I did."

"Good. It's no harm for you to have travelled as far as that this early in your life. From now on, though, there will be no more trips anywhere, except Paris at the end of the month, until you've begun to earn your keep around here."

I looked at my mother. She looked away and I saw, in that instant, that they had argued about her having allowed me to go. I suspected that whatever meagre portion of affection he had left to give her, would be withheld until he satisfied himself of her support in the battle to keep me at Montmirail after my schooling finished. I knew that she'd sworn allegiance to him years ago but, I suppose, every now and then I hoped she might reconsider the wisdom of that blind faith. I guessed that her sanctioning, of the trip to Avignon, marked the very end of her thin supply of independence. I heard George pottering around outside in the yard. I excused myself from the table and went to join him.

"There's a wild boar in the wood behind my house," he said, as I approached. He held a rifle in his hands. He was clearing the barrel, and the grey-white dirt on the cloth sparkled as it fell to the ground.

"There's a wild boar in Montmirail too," I said. "If you're quick, you'll get a clean shot at him as he grazes unsuspectingly on his cheese."

"You're funny, Christian. I know you're not serious about these things, but you make great jokes." He clapped me on the back with one of his huge hands.

"Want to come and help me kill it?" he asked.

"Only if you return the favour."

We left the courtyard and went through the arch, to the edge of the estate, and set our sights on wild meat. The gun made me think of Eugene and, somehow, George sensed it from me.

"You miss him, don't you?"

"Very much, George. I just wish he were here or that he'd never gone to war. Sometimes I even wish I'd gone in his place. Maybe I'd have survived."

"I'm sure you would," George said, gently. "I'm sure you would."

I wondered whether Eugene had killed anyone during the war. Had he wandered that landscape of death, patrolling or prowling for some victim to come along? Had he marched with his comrades and tried to dislodge the Germans from some hill or plateau? Had he inflicted some damage, himself, before his own life ended? I found it hard to imagine his lining someone up and pulling the trigger. Even harder still, was to countenance that he'd taken a life at close quarters; bayonet to heart, revolver to face, hands to throat. Why couldn't I just be reassured that he'd walked in some grand way, shoulder to shoulder with other heroes, and fallen? What is it about death, that demands explanation? What mystifies or terrifies us into corners, where the minute details are required to bring closure? Perhaps that's just it; we need to know everything about the moment of death because we really know so little about death itself, or what lies beyond it.

I read out my project to my schoolmates in the next-to-last geography class of my life. I tried to avoid her eyes, but couldn't. Even the casual timbre of her voice swept me back to Avignon.

"Thank you, Christian. I'm glad you won the prize and I hope you enjoyed the trip."

"Yes, Miss," I replied. "It was great."

My fear that someone in the school would find out had been

revived a couple of days earlier. Ferrier had leaned over to me when I was having a pee in the school toilets.

"Hey, Aragon. Did you give her the treatment when you were in Avignon?"

"Did I give what, to who, in Avignon?"

"Miss Ore-Production-in-the-Ruhr, who do you think? The teacher and the pupil, you know?"

"Oh, yes, I forgot," I said. "We ate chocolates off each other's naked bodies and finally made it in a confessional box in a chapel on the Pont St Bénézet."

"Rubbish," he leered. "I knew nothing would happen; you're not her type, you're too ugly."

I was glad of the dismissive view of Charles Ferrier. I *was* worried however, about the priest. He'd certainly seen us, although he might not have been sure who we were, as the train was still moving at the time. It was a thin hope. I encountered him in the corridor of the school on the day I'd presented my project to the class.

"Ah, young Aragon. I've been meaning to talk to you. Do you have a moment?"

"Not right now, Father, I've got some preparatory work to finish for maths. See you later perhaps?" I didn't mean a word of it and I somehow felt that if I could just avoid him until the end of the term, then I'd be fine. It was not meant to be.

"Christian, isn't it?" The voice surprised me as I drank lemonade on the terrace outside the hotel, delaying my return home after school on the same day. I looked up. The wide brim of the priest's hat hid the sun from most of my face, but I shielded my eyes anyway, and pretended to be surprised to see him.

"Yes, Father. It *is* Christian."

"Good," he said, as he sat down in a chair opposite me across the cheap, clean table. "I suppose you know what I want to discuss with you?" He smiled in a mock benign way.

"Actually, Father, I don't. It's all a mystery to me," I said, in as cool a tone as I could muster. I sipped more than I'd intended from my cold glass.

"Is it a mystery, Christian? You *really* don't know what I wish to discuss with you?" I didn't reply further. "Let me help you then," he said. "Because, make no mistake about it, Christian. You *do* need help. You need protection and guidance and advice. You are the real victim here. *She* is the instrument of evil."

"I don't know what—" He stopped me, by slamming his open hand on the table between us.

"Please, don't compound this situation by lying. I need to know everything so that I can help you. When were you last at confession?"

I could feel the laughter beginning right down in my toes. It crept up through the veins in my legs, until it lodged in my throat and tried to scorch out over my tongue. I managed to turn it into a cough. I almost wanted to tell him the details he sought, but I knew that to do so would have very serious consequences for Vivienne.

"There's nothing to laugh about. This is most serious and I intend to get to the root of it, one way or another. You are a white flower in a meadow, and she is a sow who has defiled you and taken advantage of your soul. And your body."

He leaned at me over the table. I got the faint smell of alcohol from him, as he began to whisper in a hoarse, strangled voice which frightened me a little.

"If you think that nobody will find out what is going on, then you are very much mistaken. I will make it my primary concern to find out. Your mortal soul is in peril. I cannot tell you how much God wants to bathe you in salvation, but, even now, your foolish decision to engage in wrong acts against honesty, is driving you further from Him. I cannot allow it. I *will* not allow it. Do you wish me to speak to your parents about this?"

"Do what you like, Father. Speak to whoever you wish, but I

have to repeat that I do not know what you are talking about. I really most sincerely do not. "

To be honest, I was frightened more by his demeanour, as he spoke, than by what he said. I knew that if he approached my parents, and made these allegations, my father might as easily lose his temper, and beat the priest to a pulp, as believe every word and seek me out to punish me. The priest's eyes were set deeply into his face, as though straggling behind his other features, in hesitation or fatigue. It seemed to me that, even taking into account his sighting of us kissing on the platform at Avignon, he was still not completely sure of his ground. Even if he'd been standing right beside us, and had photographed the moment, he could not know anything more than that, unless someone told him. The only people who could betray us now; were ourselves. I sensed too, that each denial by me, or any expression of ignorance as to what he was talking about, forced him backwards a couple of steps. What did concern me were his tone, his malice, and his clear determination to act on his suspicions. Perhaps the sexual rebellion in the classroom was now driving him; to take revenge where he saw weakness in the ranks of the adolescents who had mocked and frustrated him. I did not know for sure, but, I was worried. Vivienne was the other key to his suspicions and I realised that we would have to meet, sooner rather than later, to plan a united defence to this threat. I was not concerned as to what might happen to me, but I feared the priest's accusations. They pointed in the direction of exacting some retribution from Vivienne if the scene unfolded and revealed the truth. I knew that I loved her, there was no doubt about that, but I began to feel afraid that I would lose her. Two nights of lovemaking in Avignon may not seem much to others, in terms of forging an enduring relationship, but, for me, it was the physical realization of a previously inchoate love. We had discussed the priest on the train journey back to Orange, but came to the conclusion that he could not have been sure about what he'd seen; given the crowds on the platform and the motion of the train.

His entreaty to me, to confess my liaison to him, led me to the conclusion that if we told him nothing then he could *do* nothing and find out no more than he already knew. What would the consequences be for Vivienne, if it were openly known that she'd become involved with one of her pupils? I could only guess that she would lose her job at the school. Herve Duchen would have to support the position we had adopted if he were questioned. I wondered if the sad old priest might be curious enough to make enquiries at the Hotel St. Sauveur. I knew too, that Fr. Leterrier had an influence at the school and that he would, most likely, be able to persuade the Board of Governors to get rid of her if he wanted. In my opinion, it was nobody else's business who I fell in love with or who Vivienne chose to allow eat pralines from her nipples.

"This is our last class together."

Miss Pleyben spoke in a slow matter-of-fact tone. The rest of the class seemed bored, but I was not. I watched as she walked over and back between the blackboard and the table, pointing at maps and making notes on the board about the upgrading of canal connections near Bordeaux. Each movement of her hips reminded me of our lovemaking, and I longed to stand up and say, 'Myself and Miss Pleyben are getting married and you're all invited.' Imagine what would have happened. The girls would have begun to cry perhaps and the boys might have applauded. I do not know. In any event, I said nothing.

As the class came to an end with the bell in the corridor, I glanced up at her and tried to make contact. She avoided my eyes and handed out our end-of-year cards which contained the seat numbers for the exams the following week. As I took mine from her, I noted a look in her eyes which seemed to direct me to linger. I went out and then came back, past Elise Morel, who was the last to leave the room. Vivienne was gathering her books from the table and the last chunk of chalk lay on the edge, like a mouse about to jump. I went to the back of the room and searched fruitlessly for a

pencil I had not lost. When I prepared to leave the room, I saw Vivienne at the blackboard, writing. She wrote "Lime, Saturday, 3" and wiped it when she saw I'd seen it. We had not discussed how we might communicate, but this was clear at least. I knew that in a few days I'd no longer be a schoolboy, but I could not wait to be alone with her again and to lie with her.

"The Concours National is only five days away, now," my mother said, that evening at supper. My father lifted his head. He was dipping bread in a bowl of olive oil and he looked diagonally across the table at me.

"You're coming to Paris, Christian, I assume?"

"No, Papa. I have an exam on the twenty-sixth, so I'll have to stay in Gigondas." I didn't look up as I spoke.

"Exams! What bloody use are they to you? You don't need–"

My mother made a rare intervention.

"Robert. I thought we agreed that Christian would finish all of the exams."

My father snorted and then smirked.

"Alright. That's fine. But the very next day you'll be working on the estate. When I return from Paris on the twenty-eighth, you and I will sit down with George and plan a set of works to take us through the next year. It's about time you started to accept responsibility, Boy. This work is hard and physical, but, if you're going to own Montmirail some day, then your investment of time and work cannot begin soon enough."

"And if I don't want to own Montmirail some day?" I asked, in a soft voice.

My father's sweeping arm knocked a bottle of wine and the bowl of oil, as he rose and pushed back his chair and stood to dominate the room and his family. The wine rushed to the edge of the table and began to drip onto the floor like thin blood. The oil seemed content to restrict itself to the table top.

"I have worked for thirty-five years with this red soil and heavy

sun. I have sweated, so that you and your mother can have food, a roof, comfort. Don't you dare defy me in this now, Christian. Your brother would have done anything to be alive himself today and working in those fields. He understood that family, loyalty, inheritance, pride and blood is what we are about. He died so that runts like you could live in a free country. You will take your place in this family, even if I have to beat these values and this obligation into you. Do you hear me?"

I didn't reply. I rose from the table, and walked out of the room to the salon at the front of the house, where the good china cups were kept in a cupboard. An empty fireplace lay cold in the summer, near the good chairs and the small bookshelf of books nobody read. My temper was provoked, but I knew that I could not do anything yet. I felt the heat of his words on my face and I saw my scar in the mirror near the door. I sat down on the expensive seat by the window, and looked out at the front garden of Montmirail, to where the sunshine had driven a cat in under a stone trough for shade. I wanted to close my eyes and fly away, but knew that I could not. The battle was coming closer now, and very soon I would have to fight or run. I needed her and I needed to speak with her.

My head was a mess. It pounded, with my father's words echoing inside it. 'Loyalty, inheritance, pride.' What was that all about? How could I feel loyalty to a world bordered only by obligation and fear? I wasn't a willing participant in all of this. I wanted to do something else, to travel, to love, to be free. Okay, so there was no great plan ahead of me but, within that void lay the possibilities of my own life-choices and errors. Even that vague future was preferable to having inheritance cast upon me like a yoke. What about Vivienne? Surely she had the right to determine her own destiny, and to choose who to be with? I could not begin to imagine what would happen in my family if I simply declared my love for her, and refused to be a part of Montmirail and its duties. What was increasingly clear now, was that we would have to leave Gigondas if we were to have a life together.

The priest, and the rest of the village, or my father's wrath and my mother's indifference, could not provide a sound basis for our future here. They guaranteed its failure. I knew that I would have to go elsewhere and start a life on my own. If I stayed; I would crumble like the soil in the sun, and eventually be trampled into becoming part of the cycle, whether I liked it or not. I would be cut back in April and harvested in September, year-in, year-out, while my father stood watch over me, waiting, until I succumbed enough to the past to be trusted with the future. Could I be a doctor, as George had suggested, or a soldier, like Eugene? Any bloody thing was possible as long as I made the choice myself. I was nearly my own person now, and a couple of exams, and hard days and nights alone, stood between me and forever. I knew that Vivienne and I could be together and that, if we were, then I would be happy. Even picking stones, out of the gardens of rich widows in Marseille, would be better than the comfort offered by remaining here and succumbing to the fantasy of gold medals each July!

The lime tree lay on the right-hand side of the rough path, which cut up into the Dentelles above the village. The needle-like points of the mountains arched, like so many spires, over the top of the pine forest below, and reached up into the Saturday afternoon sky. I was there almost an hour before the appointed time, and sat out of view from the path on a slope up into the pines. Huddled there in the shade, the absolute silence cocooned me from the universe. The uneven scraping, of wooden wheels on stones, roused me from my trance. Monsieur Alombert lived alone in the village and collected firewood from the forests and sold it door-to-door. Most people could have collected it themselves for free, but gave him a couple of francs to keep him alive. He walked ahead of the cart. The tired mule between the shafts of the vehicle followed him, at a pace which suited both of them because of their age. I watched them disappear down over the crest of the hill and, as soon as they vanished from view, Vivienne came walking slowly up towards the lime tree. I whistled softly

and she stepped off the track and looked over her shoulder cautiously, before ascending the slope to join me. I had been afraid that she mightn't love me any longer, because of the time we'd been apart. I need not have worried. We kissed before we spoke, and an urgency held us both, as we lowered ourselves to the ground and embraced as tightly as I could ever remember us having done.

"Vivienne," I began. "I've missed you so much. I need to talk to you about Fr. Leterrier." She silenced me with a kiss and then took my hand.

"It's dangerous here," she said. "Someone might hear us, we've got to go up into the forest. No-one must see us." We stood and she brushed some pine needles from my shirt and held both of my hands and looked at me the way a mother might. We walked over the dry undergrowth, with the cracking of twigs and the rustle of dry grass as an accompaniment to our thoughts. When we were deep among the trees, we found a clearing and sat side by side and spoke of the future and the present and the fear surrounding both.

"Fr. Leterrier has been to see me, Christian. He knows about us, or at least thinks he knows. He's spoken to Duchen. Herve told him that he was with us and that nothing happened, Leterrier is still unshaken in his suspicions. Of course, Herve is curious now too. The priest says that he will go to the school authorities and have me dismissed. He says he can prevent my ever working as a teacher again in France. He's obsessed with us. He says I've stolen your soul. He wants me to leave Gigondas."

"I know. He's spoken to me too."

"Where? When? What did you tell him?"

"Nothing." I laughed. "Not even when he asked me when I'd last made my confession."

"Christian, this is serious." Her eyes widened in concern. "If they, if the school authorities find out, I'll lose my job and I'll never teach anywhere again. The school is rented from the priests; so they have an enormous power. We must be careful. I'm sorry now that I –"

"Sorry that you and I?"

"No." She shook her head. "I'm not sorry about any of that. But I'm afraid that if the priest pursues this, he may involve the police, the school, the education ministry."

"You're afraid that something will happen? What can happen?"

"Oh, Christian." She wiped a single tear from her cheek with the back of her hand. "You're only a boy, not yet seventeen. I'm your teacher and I'm responsible for–"

"My mortal soul?"

"Yes. Yes. I suppose so," she said. "It's such a mess, all of this now."

I told her about Fr. Leterrier's outburst outside the hotel. I told her how I'd made a decision to leave the village if I had to, in order to be free; in order to be with her.

"And what will we live on? Fresh-Air Pie?"

"You can teach and I'll find some kind of work. I'll even pick stones from the gardens of rich widows in Marseille if I have to. We'll be fine and we'll be together."

"And what about your family? Your inheritance?"

"My inheritance?" I laughed. "My *family* is my inheritance, and I want no part of it now. I don't care if I never see them again. It's not them I want. I want you. I love you, Vivienne."

She stopped talking and she stared at me for an age. Then she leaned in, to whisper into my ear, (although no-one but me would have heard even if she'd shouted).

"And I love you too, Christian. I love you."

She began to unbutton her blouse and, under the shade of two huge pine trees, I laid out the blanket I'd taken from the airing cupboard. The sunlight infiltrated the cones on the branches and eased its way deep into the forest, where it spread its warmth around us like an angel.

Chapter Eight

I F SOMEONE crept up on me in the middle of the night, and nailed my hands to the bedposts, and told me not to see her again; I would gnaw my hands off at the elbow and run to her, with my limbs trailing blood through this tiny village. I might have been a bird down at the sea, or up over the Dentelles, or a boy who was able to fly. I flew like mad up, up, up over the village and swooped down and landed on a window ledge and saw myself in through the window, huddled around a math paper I did not understand. Eugene was in some faraway place, as were the millions and millions of other souls who had absconded in death at the Somme or the Marne or Verdun. There was a famous recruitment poster designed by Faive and it was everywhere during the war. The picture showed a man in civilian headdress with an army greatcoat and a rifle, rushing forward and urging France to follow, with the slogan; 'We have them.' I remembered thinking, at one time, that he was beckoning the dead to follow and giving them heart with the cry of; **"We have them,"** meaning something dead people needed; like blocks of ice in hell, or white shirts to wear in heaven. I saw Eugene's face in the math paper, where the numbers gathered in the centre of the page and rearranged themselves back up at me in his features. My lover was beneath me, on a bed of pinecones and math papers. I was aching to see her again.

"Five minutes," Herve Duchen said, signalling the final

moments of my education. I wondered what position his mistress on the Boulevard St. Jacques liked best when he was hard and ready for her. Perhaps she preferred it from behind, and waited on all fours for him, on silk sheets, in a rented room, until he announced his arrival and the anticipated duration of the act; 'Five minutes.' I was angry with the world, and he was an easy target. I remembered that he had helped us thwart the priest, and I regretted my anger.

My father had tried to re-establish the ground-rules for the future when he arrived, unannounced, into my bedroom on the previous morning.

"We're going to Paris."

"I know," I commented. I struggled to adjust my eyes against the light as he opened the shutters on the window.

"When I return, I expect to see the four hectares above the church cleared of rabbits. George will show you what to do when that's finished."

"I –"

"Please don't waste your breath, Christian. I'm tired of your stories and excuses. I've waited long enough for you to finish at that damned school. You will now do the things your brother would have undertaken gladly. That's the end of it."

"I'm not Eugene," I shouted, as he turned and left the room.

He hesitated and, then, glanced back bitterly over his shoulder.

"That has been all too apparent for a considerable time, Christian. But, I'm afraid, Montmirail will just have to make the best of it. There's no alternative."

I wanted to run after him, and beat him on the face with my fists, and shout into his ears about how I missed my brother, and how this mess was not of my making. But I did not do so. I was beginning to make my own plans about cutting this place from my life, like a petrified twig pruned from the vine between December and March. I was not destined to crush grapes.

After the maths exam, we exited into the voracious sunshine.

The noon heat cradled the class, as a unit, for the last time on the front steps of our lycée. Some began to shake hands, and embrace, and mark the moment with a sort of uncertain affection. I felt my hand pressed, and my cheek kissed, but I could not tell you now, nor could I have identified then, who the kissers or the shakers were. Couderc's mother was standing outside the gates of the school as I left. Her son should have been graduating with us, but his lungs had exercised first refusal on his life. She stared at me. I nodded, and instinctively reached for my scar with a finger.

"You can hardly see it now, Christian." She smiled and spoke as I touched my cheek. I was unsure as to the appropriate response, so I moved my finger to my forehead and flicked my hair back, like I wasn't even looking for the scar. In her eyes I saw the loss of her son. Without warning, she was enveloped by a cascade of children who rushed by with skipping ropes and hoops. Down in the village, the mayor was dressed in his full ceremonial robes. He had invited the parents of the graduating class to drink wine at the Mairie, while their offspring tackled mathematics. Elise Morel's mother was a big lady, with cheeks as red as roof tiles. She walked up and down the village square, looking anxiously in the direction of the school for a sign of her daughter. I could make out some of the other parents, but I knew my mother would not have been there even if she hadn't gone to Paris to attend the annual embarrassment of the Concours National.

Twenty minutes later, I had doubled back behind the hotel and made my way, past Domaine de la Mavette, to the Vacqueyras Road. My shoes hurt and I took them off and walked barefoot on the warm dust. The Chapel of St. Cosme was like a permanent sentinel at the edge of my world. I eyed it with relief, it grew in size as I neared, and I recalled how small I'd felt beside it when I was a child. My temperature soared, and my heart stalled and re-started as I contemplated my future. My head pounded and shadowed my foot-fall in tempo, as something beyond my control caused the choice,

and my feelings about it, to oscillate over and back in a small space directly in front of my eyes, which would have fit easily inside a pair of racing goggles. I wanted to run and hide and then to stay and confront and, all at once, I was gripped by a palpable sense of despair, as I wondered what damage I would cause in her life with my emotions for her. She was older, yes. But perhaps I was stronger than I imagined, bolder than I deserved to be. Was I hunter-gatherer racing, stalking, following, watching, kissing, coveting, loving her? Or *was* it part of some grand design that God hatched for me; to compensate me for the loss of my brother? Could it be that I was powerless to resist, or to vary the course of the thing? Was I the driving force behind this pattern of action we'd embarked upon? Perhaps it was my *fault* rather than our *fortune* or destiny. The thing we share; do we create it, or is it already there and waiting to be eaten? I would contest the prize with my father. I would challenge his myopia and lay my own desire before him. I couldn't run away like a child or a coward, no, I'd have to be open and honest about it and choose my life in the confident glare of the sun; not pilfer it, in the cowardly hue of darkness.

"Father, I have something to say." I rehearsed out loud as I climbed the incline to the rear of the church. "I am in love with someone and I want to be with her. I cannot be who you imagine me to be, I am nearly seventeen, and I will not be moulded by you to chaperone these eleven hectares into a harvest of my own blood."

"That sounded good."

I started. Vivienne was in the archway of the sacristy door. She'd clearly enjoyed my monologue. Her smile lit up the alcove and she stepped forward to take my hand. We kissed.

"How was math?" she asked.

"I was rehearsing what I'd say to my father when he returns from Paris," I said. Answering a question she'd never asked.

"Are you sure you want to go through with his?" she asked gently.

"More sure than ever," I replied.

The chapel was locked, as it often was during the week. This stone house of worship leaned out over the village into the day like a nosy neighbour. I used my knife to lift the latch on the shutters of the sacristy and, as it flipped back with a tiny noise, the wind suddenly blew up and caught the inside of the shutters. They opened out towards me and knocked me off balance. I almost fell to the ground. The noise of the shutters slamming in the wind seemed to me to be loud enough to echo across the village, or at least down onto the Vacqueyras Road. But I need not have concerned myself. The rest of the world was somewhere else and we had the place to ourselves.

Inside, the chapel was cold but it was not damp or musty. The air was chilled and refreshing. The empty pews awaited us as we opened the door fully from the ante-room to the altar. A pair of brass candelabras stood on the marble table of worship and, further down the church, over the baptismal font, the room edged upwards and out at the sky through two narrow windows above the main door. I remembered Avignon. Vivienne touched her lips with a finger and hushed me to listen to the sounds of the moment. A bird twittered in the rafters and the Mistral insinuated itself into the little chapel and surrounded us in a swish. Tiny details of the place remain with me in lighted prominence, protruding out of the scene like embossed letters on expensive paper. I recall a purple sash, draped possessively over a velvet-upholstered chair to the side, where a priest might have sat. On the warm mosaic tiles, depicting the flight from Egypt, my bare, dusty feet left tracks. A drizzle of dust danced in a shard of sunshine and sparkled to its death on the floor of the aisle. We sat on the edge of the raised level of the altar and held hands and talked and talked. Fr. Leterrier had confronted her again.

"I saw something in his expression this time which frightened me," she said.

"Maybe the same thing on the terrace I saw at the hotel."

"Something I can't quite describe worried me about his voice and his threats this time, Christian. I thought that he would grow weaker in his accusations and that I would–"

"Prosper in your defence?" I offered.

"Exactly. But it was as if he had gained the actual knowledge by my denial or rebuke. I can't explain it but–"

"There's no need, Vivienne. It's like me and my imaginary conversations with my father. It's only rehearsal, not real, until I stand toe to toe with him and face him down with my dream, my choice, my–"

"Life?"

"Yes. Yes," I said, with a nervous laugh. "That's it. I'm just marking time until I tell him who I am, and what I am going to do."

"And what you've done?" She smiled. I thought about it for a moment.

"Well, maybe not everything. Not yet. It would be too much for him." I smiled inwardly, thinking of how my father might react if I told him all of the details of our trip to Avignon. In time, perhaps very soon, he would come to imagine and reckon these things for himself. To be honest, I simply wanted to discharge my bare duty as a son and tell him I was leaving, and why. After that, his impressions, or suspicions or concerns, were entirely a matter for himself.

"I'm going to leave the school," she said. I watched her lips release the words, and anticipated that they would leave a fine trace of regret, or uncertainty, after them on her mouth. I saw none.

"Are you sure?"

"Yes. I've thought about it and, I see now, that we must leave Gigondas if we're to have any real chance of happiness."

"And what about your house?"

"Monsieur Vaton has often asked me to sell it to him. I'm sure he would revive his offer at a moment's notice. The Notaire will transfer it into my name, to allow a sale."

You should know now, that at that exact time, an uncertainty had bumped off my soul and receded a little. But still it spun like a top, at the edge of my line of sight, and threatened to return. I was strong one moment and crippled the next, vacillating between love and desire on the one hand, and fear on the other. I was out now in the thick of my own life and this passionately beautiful woman, seven years my senior, was throwing away her life this far in order to begin again with me. As the bride abandons her father's arm at the door of the church, the symbolism of that leap from past to future was now all about us. Here, in a tiny church overlooking a tiny village at the feet of a mountain range, I was about to jump into my future with the comfort of this woman, and the discomfort of the damage I might do to her life by joining it with mine. Montmirail was just a house and, to be frank, all that lived in it was just the dust of a family long-since disintegrated. Eugene had been the soul of that place. It was he, and no one else, who had brought Christmas alive there, and made the harvesting of the grapes seem worthwhile and good. He had supplied life from his own store of it to that place. The war and the rain, and the trenched damp that plucked him out of our lives, had not been of his making. His death had not been his own choice, and his absence from our lives now was no-one's fault. He had lived as long as he could and that was all there was to it. I slept in his bedroom, and perhaps he slept there still, and infused my sleep with a dead corporal's strength. It was not my house anyway. I knew that. The rooms were a committee of spaces and divisions; the entire was only the sum of the parts, and the plaster barriers and creaking presence of stairs and doors, only hummed along with each other. For me, they provided no sense of belonging anymore. The trees in the avenue, and the sunshine through the dining room windows, were all I counted as precious in Montmirail. What happiness I'd eaten there was a distant memory, and the calculated and vitriolic silence of my parents' union was not a thing I cared to live beneath for a moment longer than necessary. If I continued to live with my father,

it would only be a matter of time before he battered me into the type of son he really wanted. Only George drew me to the place now, with his big hands and enormous heart. I would miss him, and maybe he would miss me, but he had settled a life for himself there and, to be fair, it did not depend on me in any way for its survival.

We held hands and stood up on the step below the altar. Vivienne took a ring from one of the tiny pockets of her dress. I had made a ring for her from one of the hinges of the chest in which we kept Eugene's things. The hinge was broken and made from light metal. I'd hammered it and heated it and then wrapped it around a piece of cork and fired it in embers before cooling it in water. I hoped it would fit her. You probably think that it sounds dirty and clumsy, but it was all that I could think to do, besides stealing from my mother. That would have been an awful lapse of independence. We placed the rings on each other's fingers and promised to take each other, and to hold them in our hearts, and to worship each other with our bodies, and our minds, until the unwelcome shadow of death cut us off from the sun. It was a simple exchange; made hundreds of years after Pierre of Provence and Princess Maguelone had done the same on the site where Montmirail now stood. I had thought of trying to replicate the exchange, in the kitchen, or even the bedroom of the house in my parents' absence, but I decided against it. I felt it might, in some tacit way, represent an honouring of the house by me, and I did not want that. Also, I felt that it would require a revisiting of the house at some time, and I did not intend coming back. The Chapel of St Cosme was quiet, private, and, above all, symbolised for me the making of a commitment before God. We would someday, I hoped, be married in a proper ceremony by a priest who neither knew us nor disapproved of our union. Every place, from a hamlet to Paris, had a church, so that, no matter where we ended up, there would be a place to go when we needed a touchstone or a renewal of our vows.

"So I'm Madame Aragon now. Am I?"

"Oh, no. I didn't think of that. Perhaps I'll be Monsieur Pleyben instead." We stood silently for a short time; regarding each other in an altogether different way. I thought about the essential ingredient for a valid marriage. So did she.

"I'd like you to come and spend the night at my house. Our house." She invited me with a trace of nervousness I had not detected before. It would be the perfect way to say goodbye to the place in which she had lived.

It was agreed. I would return to the village and make an appearance at the festivities before going to Montmirail to pack a small bag. We would leave in a day or two, after my parents returned and I had delivered the news to my father. I couldn't run away, elope, whatever. That would be cowardly and easy and ultimately, I suspected, it would destroy me from the inside out. Facing my father would be the most difficult thing I'd ever chosen to do, but it had to be done to complete the circle of the decision-making process. I would say goodbye to George. Perhaps even help him clear the rabbits, as the last act of the pair of us together at the work I was choosing to abandon. He deserved the courtesy of an explanation, and I could easily imagine maintaining a correspondence with him in the future. How else would I learn of my parents' death? We left the church and returned to the village separately. I thought about the sacrifice she was making, in leaving her position in the school. She would surely find another job somewhere. She was a marvellous teacher. I wondered what would happen if my father tried to physically stop me from leaving Gigondas with her. Surely he would not be able to restrain me? Would he even try? I tried not to think too much about it. I would deal with it when it happened, *if* it happened.

The festivities were in full swing. A man from Seguret, with an accordion, played polkas and the village danced. I eased through the crowd and smiled and nodded without saying a word. Strong fingers gripped my arm.

"Eh, Aragon. Why aren't you drinking?" Ferrier held onto me, waiting for a reply. When I said nothing, he simply pushed me aside and returned to the long table at the edge of the gathering, where the wine was being poured and spilled. I saw Elise Morel and her mother dancing together. Abel Beaumet was swinging a tiny girl, in a display of dancing which was comical but, also, tinged with a sexual energy. It was a force that I doubted he would have been possessed of, without the mix of graduating and alcohol. The Mayor had abandoned his ceremonial robes and I think I saw his wife somewhere, watching him enjoying himself. It was close to the spot from where I'd watched the Fizz Rockets and Catherine Wheels explode above us that night. Vivienne had stood beside me at the display on the Saints' day. This was my goodbye; my passage from graduation to adulthood. I took in the sight of the people, I drank it up like a memory to be stored for later, when I needed to remember where I'd come from, and who I was, or might have been. I turned from the crowd and ambled into the Place de la Fontaine. I'd gone to Montmirail first and packed a bag and left it beside the fountain. I splashed my face from the fountain, and leaned backwards over the stone basin to drink from the loop of cold water sauntering out of the mouth of a small lion.

When I could drink no more, I picked up my bag and made my way past the graveyard, and the fever hospice, to the track which led to the mountains. I looked over the wall of the cemetery and tried to find Couderc's headstone. Instead, the first grave I rested my eyes upon was Eugene's. I never came to see him there. I always spoke with him like he was a ghost or a cloud or something like smoke; all around, but moving, and still alive in some curious comforting way. The headstone and the plot were too cold for me. They called it his resting place, but he wasn't even in the grave. His uniform, lying there crumpled in a box in the ground, was not him. In fact, it was almost a perfect acknowledgement of his absence. He was somewhere else, so I could not even begin to imagine him

here in the cemetery. I think I would have found it almost impossible to leave Gigondas if he really had been buried there.

The track grew steep and I saw the Dentelles in their white splendour. About halfway from the village to Vivienne's small house, I stopped and took a pee in the bushes. As I emerged out onto the track, a figure came down the hill towards me. It was the priest. We kept walking until we were face-to-face and I saw a cruel laugh begin to invade his face.

"Ah, Mr Aragon. Isn't it?"

"Yes?"

I saw him look at my bag, held at my side like a piece of game. I knew now that he knew all about us. If I'd ever doubted it. Vivienne had been correct.

"Off on holidays, I suppose?" he said, with a sneer. I said nothing. He nodded back in the direction of the house. "You'll be going alone. I think she's changed her mind."

I immediately thought that he'd damaged her, and I was torn between demanding reassurance from him, and seeking it myself.

"Priest, if you've harmed her, I'll kill you," I said, calmly. I began to run up the hill in my bare feet as he continued on his way. What the hell has he been doing visiting her, I wondered. I was short of breath when I reached the house and I went around to the rear. I could hear raised voices, but the words were utterly indistinct. I pushed open the door. Vivienne was cowering in the corner of the kitchen. A man stood over her with a pine branch in his hand.

"Don't touch her," I warned. He turned around. It was her husband, Stephane. He smiled through his rage.

"So, it's the little bastard who's been fucking my wife. Is it?"

He advanced in my direction and threw the branch to the ground. He reached into his belt where I saw a knife in a sheath.

"Run, Christian, run!" Vivienne screamed. He turned back to her and kicked out at her face with his boot. I could not see if he made contact, but I did see that her forearm was already bleeding.

I reached into my pocket and found my own knife. In a flash it was open. I charged forward at him, and knocked him into the wall, where he stumbled and lost his balance. When he got to his feet, I saw that the knife from his belt was in his hand. He was taller than me, and a good bit heavier. I weighed up my chances. His knife was a hunting one and had a polished wooden handle. I remember thinking, for a second, about throwing mine at him and hoping for the best. But we were too close. There was a small saucepan on the table and it seemed full of liquid. I tried to put my free hand out to grab it as we circled the table like prizefighters; both unsure of what to do next.

"You thought you'd move into my house did you?"

He snarled as he looked down at my bag. I swung it up and across the table and into his face, and tried to push the table at him as well. It collapsed, from weak legs or something. Suddenly, we were at each other on the broken table; grappling, struggling, kicking, biting and roaring like wild animals. There was a clatter as he lost his knife, and I remember his face in mine. I became conscious of the smell of soup, coming up at us from the floor, where the saucepan had overturned. I head-butted him, hoping to break his nose, and he fell backwards. The last movement of the oak table beneath us favoured me, and I finished falling by rolling across him. He landed heavily, striking his head and, as he collapsed, his eyes spoke of the horror to come if he lived. My knife was at his throat. Seconds later, he was between two worlds; spluttering blood up at me out of his neck. He was dead in a matter of moments: lying on the floor of the house he'd fled from to avoid conscription in the Great War.

Chapter Nine

THE TRIAL WAS HELD in August 1921, in the Palais
de Justice in Carpentras, in the Cour d'Assises. It was
the same courtroom where five soldiers from Eugene's
battalion had been tried for desertion and treason, two weeks after
the war had ended. My father had gone to Carpentras for that trial,
and had bathed in the horror of their execution less than twenty
minutes after the verdict had been brought in. They had been lined
up against the rear wall of the Cathedrale St. Siffrein. For my father,
it was a real opportunity to revel in the memory of his heroic son,
and to watch France blood-let in honour of the brave.

From the date of my arrest, in July of the previous year, until the
beginning of the trial, on August eleventh, I had been held in the
fourteenth-century prison on the Rue du Chateau. My cell was
small and damp, and the barred window some eight feet above the
floor gave a singular if un-enchanting view of the Porte D'Orange.
I would dearly like, in dramatic terms to infuse my account now
with tales of wild mistreatment, and the daily challenge of battles
with rats and disease, but I cannot, because that is not how it was.
The fact that I was awaiting trial, and not serving a sentence upon
conviction, meant that I was a guest of the prison, in the legal sense
at least. I was housed in the most benign of its accommodations.
The aroma of the plane and lotus trees from the Place D'Inguimbert
entertained me for both summers and, on countless evenings

during all of my incarceration awaiting trial, somebody, a child perhaps, threw black olives at my window with varying degrees of accuracy. My eyes were, in one way, my greatest hindrance. When they were open I saw only stone and straw. When they were closed, however, I was transported back to the pine forest at the foot of the Dentelles where we'd made love, or to the gushing water from the fountain on the little street off the main square in Gigondas. Vivienne was a constant source of calm and reassurance, and her monthly visits punctuated my stay. Each time she came to the prison we were closely supervised by warders. We made particular efforts to convey our feelings across the cold stone table, where intimacy was impossible. On her final visit before the trial, we talked for the first time about what it would be like.

"Are you afraid, Christian?"

"Not really. A little though, I suppose." She took my hands across the table and, although one warder seemed about to rebuke us and make us disengage, a look from the other seemed to satisfy him that there was no security threat posed by the contact.

"Don't worry, Christian. Everything will work out."

"I know. I know."

"What does Monsieur Jourdic say?"

"He's hopeful, but it's hard to read him, you know. He talks a lot, but doesn't really say much that I can hold onto."

Leopold Jourdic was my lawyer. He was the Public Defender for the Vaucluse region. My family was not going to pay for a lawyer from Paris or Marseille so the defence of my case was in his hands, and paid for by the taxes of everybody in the region. I think that even had my family offered to pay for my defence, I could not have accepted it. It would have been a renouncing of my life-choice to seek, or accept their assistance now. The predicament in which I found myself was pretty much all of my own making. Monsieur Jourdic was originally from the Ardeche. He had a reputation for being a hard-nosed lawyer who never gave up on any of his clients,

until they were acquitted, or, 'La Veuve' (the widow) had cut off their heads. Neither Vivienne nor myself knew anything about the law and, so, we placed our complete trust in Leopold Jourdic and hoped for the best. My pre-trial consultations with him had been long and to the point in a roundabout way. He lectured me on the law, the guillotine, and sometimes recounted stories of past triumphs and, it should be said, some failures too.

"I had one particular client, Henriette Gontier. She was accused of poisoning her husband with salt. I knew in my soul that she was not guilty; she had no trace of malice, no hint of evil about her. The trial lasted three weeks and the defence hinged on the evidence of an apothecary from Rouen, who was an expert on salt. He was exposed on his own testimony and eventually the jury disbelieved him too. Henriette lost her life because of the incompetence of someone else. We might even have won if we hadn't called him at all to the stand." He shook his head sadly.

Between anecdotes from his brilliant career, Monsieur Jourdic and I discussed tactics. We debated whether I should give evidence at the trial.

"Much of it depends on the prosecution case. We may not know until it ends, whether or not you should take the oath, Christian."

"Won't it seem strange to the jury if I don't give evidence?"

"They are not allowed draw an adverse inference from your refusal. The Judges will instruct them about that point."

"But all the same, surely it's to my advantage?"

"The things which are to your advantage in my view, are your age and your relationship with this lady; the wife of the Deceased."

"Vivienne."

"Yes, Madame Pleyben. Now, if the jury sees you as the impressionable young schoolboy, induced into the bed of this older woman, and then provoked into killing her estranged husband in a fit of anger and—"

"Passion?"

97

"Yes, that's it, passion, Christian. Passion. This is the emotion at the heart of our being. As Frenchmen, Christian, we are driven to achievement and to anger because of our passion. Our hearts are the charioteers of our destiny."

He looked down momentarily and then up again, to gauge my reaction. I could feel him beginning to formulate his closing remarks to the jury. With the addition, perhaps, of some tinkering later on, for effect, I felt I'd been treated to the bones of his final submissions to the court.

"No," I said

"No?"

"No. I won't let her be dragged into this."

"She's already in this, Christian. If she gives evidence in your defence then you may be acquitted. I know that she wasn't in the house when the fight occurred. She was–"

"In the out-house and then went to the well near the trees." I finished the sentence for him.

"Yes. I have read her statement, and she would seem to be of no use to the prosecution as a witness. However, she is central to any attempt by us to paint the full picture for the jury."

"Of what use is it to call her, when she can say nothing about the fight and the death of her husband?"

"The jury will want to know what passed between her and the Deceased after the priest left. The mood of the husband seems to have been very aggressive, but I need the jury to hear it from her own mouth, and to listen to her tell of how he said he would 'kill the boy,' as she says in her statement, and how he treated her in the past."

"Vivienne will only be used by the Prosecutor to discredit me and to blacken her own name. They will try to have the jury believe that she and I planned to kill him or something like that."

"And did you?"

"Of course not." I was getting angry now.

"Then, why are you afraid of calling her?"

"I don't want her to give evidence because they'll ask her about her relationship with me. She will have to admit certain things and then– "

"If she admits to having sexual relations with one of her underage pupils, then she'll most certainly be prosecuted yes. But if she does not give evidence on your behalf, then you will probably be convicted of murder and sentenced to death. In any event, she can be called by the Prosecution. It is only if you were married that she would not be a compellable witness."

"Perhaps they won't be able to prove the charge," I suggested.

"I wish you were right. But I'm afraid that they have substantial evidence against you. I have read the charge, and the Prosecutor seems definite about the circumstances. It was your knife?"

"Yes."

"And you were holding it when the doctor and the gendarme arrived?"

"Yes."

"You had blood on your clothes and your hands?" I nodded.

"Then we shall just have to do our best with what we have," he said, with a sigh. "See you on Tuesday."

My ability to fly in my dreams, deserted me sometime during the course of that year. I could still imagine myself elsewhere, and dream of being with Vivienne and of making love in the most awkward and strange places; olive groves; behind barrels of wine at Montmirail; churches; or the baths at Les Florets. I even saw us once, under my parents' bed, coupling, while they slept at the extremes of the mattress above. My father had his own room. The frequency of the creaking visits he made to my mother's, decreased enormously after Eugene's death. But my own power to fly inside of those dreams, to determine the direction of the dream itself, and to hover above the snippets of life occurring beneath my flight, that vanished. It vanished and I was a prisoner twice.

Apart from Vivienne's visits, and the meetings with Monsieur Jourdic; nobody came to see me. My mother wrote to me once to tell me how proud she was of me and how she believed I was innocent. My father wrote to me twice, once to tell me how ashamed he was of me and how he knew I was guilty. The other time he wrote to say how ashamed he was of my mother, for having written to me, and how he'd forbidden her to write again. To be honest, I nearly expected her to write a second time expressing her own shame at having written the first time, but that really would have been too much !

"You will hear, Gentlemen, of how this murder was planned down to the last detail. How the Accused secured the purchase of the knife weeks earlier, in anticipation of the return of Stephane Pleyben. You will learn of the sordid details of the love affair which the Accused had with Madame Pleyben. You will also hear about how it drove him to murder her husband, when Monsieur and Madame Pleyben were on the precipice of a reconciliation. All possibility of that reconciliation was ended by a young boy with a knife of steel and a heart of stone."

The Prosecutor, Monsieur Icard, was the master of dramatics and overstatement. His track record, as a prosecutor of murder charges, had the sort of statistics between success, failure and re-trial, which would have worried me as a healthy and fit boxer if he were my opponent. Monsieur Jourdic was a marked contrast in presentation and force and it seemed, to me at least, that the case might very well hinge on which of them the jury preferred. The first witness was the doctor.

"I attended at the house of Monsieur and Madame Pleyben at a minute or two past three o'clock in the afternoon. Madame Pleyben had called to my house in quite a state of shock. I was tending to the ingrown toenail of a patient when she arrived. I left immediately, and met Sergeant Bezart, just behind the main entrance to the fever hospice. He also was on his way to the house."

"What did you find on arriving there?" Icard looked at the jury

when he spoke, giving the impression that he was *their* instrument; asking the questions they themselves wanted to.

"I found the Deceased in a prone position on the floor of the kitchen. He was lying on his back and his left arm was bent around the leg of a heavy table, which was broken, and partially covered his lower body. The leg of the table and the immediate area of the Deceased's head and torso were almost entirely covered with blood. From the back of the shoulders, which lay on the floor, for a distance perhaps two feet outwards, the entire stone paving was splattered with congealed blood in a semi-circular pattern. I examined the body and confirmed that the Deceased had died from a single stab wound to the neck. This incision had simultaneously served a major artery and punctured the windpipe. I concluded that the probable cause of death was a brain haemorrhage from lack of oxygen and partial blood asphyxiation."

"He choked on his own blood?"

"Yes, at least in part. You see –"

"He choked on his own blood. Thank you, Doctor. Now, did you find anyone else at the scene?"

"Yes."

"Who?"

"A young man from the village; Christian Aragon. I know his family for many–"

"The Accused. You mean the Accused, there?" He pointed at me. The Prosecutor was not going to allow me to be described in personal terms. That might humanise me to the jury.

"Yes, the Accused. He was sitting on a chair beside the sink area and he had, I don't know if I can say this..." the doctor looked to Icard for guidance.

"If you saw something then you *must* say it. If it is true, it must form part of your testimony. You saw the Accused. He was sitting on a chair and he had..?"

"A knife. He had a large pocket-knife in his hands." The Doctor

looked over at me, apologetically. I smiled at him to show I bore him no ill-will.

"Was it the same knife which caused the wound which led to the death of Stephane Pleyben?" The Prosecutor paused, and then looked from the jury to the witness and back again, conveying the question and the expectation from the twelve to the doctor.

"Yes. In my opinion it was."

"Did you examine the knife?"

"Not there and then."

"When?"

"Afterwards, in the police station at Carpentras. I was invited by the Investigating Magistrate (he bowed to the middle Judge) to view the knife and to compare the blade, and its dimensions, with my notes on the nature and extent of the wound."

"And your conclusion?"

"It was the same knife."

"Thank you, Doctor."

Monsieur Jourdic asked a series of questions about the measurements of the wound, and the work on bloodstains being pioneered in the United States at that time. He was polite and gentle in his cross-examination and, to be honest, he made no real impression of challenging the doctor, or his findings. It was almost as if he were simply giving the witness a second opportunity to repeat his quite damning evidence. Including the part about finding me with the knife. All of that was true, of course, and we were not going to challenge the doctor on his account of the truth. Sergeant Bezart was brief and enthusiastic in the witness box.

"I was invited to the graduation celebration by the Mayor, Monsieur de Vay, to supervise the fireworks display later that evening."

"I believe the display was cancelled?"

"Yes."

"Why?" Monsieur Icard feigned ignorance.

"Because of the death of Monsieur Pleyben."

"The *murder* of Monsieur Pleyben. No?"

Jourdic was on his feet in an instant, before the policeman could reply,

"That is a matter for the jury, My Lords. Not for this witness, surely?"

The Judges nodded and the trial continued. The three Judges were all men in their late middle age. Of the two on the wings; one was silent for the entire trial. The presiding Judge was a man of few words also, and only spoke when it was absolutely necessary to do so. All evidential or procedural disputes were resolved by a conference of nods or shakes of the head. Decisions were made known, by the presiding Judge pointing his crooked right index finger at the advocate in whose favour they had decided the issue. It was like appearing in front of three mute, or very shy ghosts.

"Did the Accused say anything to you at the scene?"

"Yes, as I escorted him from the house, and indicated that we would have to meet his parents and inform them of the situation, he said, 'I didn't want to lose her.'"

"He said he didn't want to lose her, is that correct?"

"Yes."

"And who did you understand him to mean, by, 'her'?"

"Why, Madame Pleyben of course."

"Thank you." The Prosecutor sat down.

The jury all turned as one to look at Vivienne, where she sat impassively, about four rows of chairs behind the Prosecutor's table. I sat side-on to the Court on the opposite side of the room to the jury and had a clear view of everyone.

"And what did you understand by the phrase, 'didn't want to lose her,' Sergeant?" Jourdic eyeballed him.

"I don't know. Maybe that he loved her, and the husband had come back, and now that was an obstacle to him being with her. Perhaps he meant that it was as if he could now lose her, but did not

want to allow that to happen. I don't know exactly."

"Correct. You don't know *at all*. Do you?" The tone of the questioning was, for the first time, accusatory rather than probing.

"Well I –"

"Do you know from your own knowledge that this is the case, your theory?"

"No. No. Not from my own knowledge, but from what I've ...." he hesitated and stopped.

"Continue, Sergeant Bezart. From what you've *heard* perhaps. Is that it? Rumour and speculation among the curious and interested citizens of Gigondas and Carpentras and Seguret and Sablet?"

"Well, what I can say about that, is that everyone has a, a.."

"A theory? Like yourself, Sergeant. Couldn't Christian Aragon have meant something different from what you thought, as easily as he may have meant what you speculate he intended?"

"Perhaps." The Sergeant looked quite demoralised now and considerably less enthusiastic.

"Could he have meant that Madame Pleyben's life was in danger from her husband, and that he feared he might lose her as a consequence of *that* threat?"

"I don't think he meant that." The Sergeant's tone was a shade more confident now that he was expressing an opinion about an opinion, and not a theory about a fact he was unsure of.

"You found another knife at the scene?"

"Yes."

"Belonging to whom?"

"It may have belonged to the Deceased."

"*May*? It *may* have belonged to the Deceased?"

"I do not know for sure."

"Did he have a sheath on his belt?"

"Yes."

"Did the knife fit that sheath?" No reply. "I will repeat my question, Sergeant. Did the knife fit the sheath?"

"Yes." The policeman spoke through his teeth.

"So it *was* his?"

"Possibly."

"Probably?"

"Yes. Probably. But –"

"But what?"

"But it was a long way from the body, and the Accused himself was completely unscathed. All of the blood on his hands and clothes came from the Deceased." The policeman looked at the jury, as if trying to coax them back to the side of the prosecution.

"So it may have been self-defence?" Jourdic introduced the notion for the first time.

"Yes," said the policeman. Jourdic smiled and turned to face the jury as he repeated the question. He was now employing the device used by the Prosecutor.

"It may have been self-defence?" The jury leaned out at Jourdic ever so slightly, and waited for the confirmation from Sergeant Bezart of the Carpentras Gendarmerie.

"Yes. Monsieur Pleyben may have drawn his knife in self-defence, but it obviously did not save him from having his throat cut and choking on his own blood." The jury recoiled as one with this new theory to digest. Monsieur Jourdic sat down.

The Prosecution called two more witnesses on the first day of the trial. Vernon Pesiere was the crooked concierge at the Hotel St. Saveur. His nose was even longer than I had remembered. He clearly savoured the opportunity to give evidence, and his discernible salivation during his testimony, was a mark of the low calibre of moral mix which drove him through life. He gave evidence of renting out two rooms, but only having to change the bedclothes in one of them. He heaped his own concern about my welfare onto his sworn information, but it appeared as insincere as it undoubtedly was.

The other witness was the man who had sold George the knife

in the bar at Sablet. The man identified George; by pointing at him in the body of the courtroom where he sat. It was August and baking hot. George was perspiring heavily, and it was impossible to say whether it was the season or the situation that caused him to sweat. Perhaps it was a combination of the two. The witness identified the knife, and then agreed that George had been accompanied by a young man. He nodded in my direction when asked whether that person was present in Court. The Prosecutor indicated that he had one more witness, and would call them when the Court re-convened on the following morning. I was taken back to the Rue du Chateau, and Monsieur Jourdic came to see me later that evening.

"How do you think it's going?" I asked.

"Not as well as I'd hoped," he replied. "I had expected them to make more of your relationship with Madame Pleyben. At least that might have allowed us not to call her, and to use their own conclusions to drive the jury into the area of passion crimes. Their decision, not to call her character into question in any concerted way, has left the focus of the trial on *you*. I had hoped that the jury might begin to believe that you had been driven by *her* to commit this act of violence. That impression, of pressure exerted on your young mind by the older woman, might have combined with the self-defence argument to make them unsure as to what exactly happened. In the case of the jury being divided; I think they would acquit you. Our problem now is that we have to make all of those pieces appear ourselves. Both Madame Pleyben and yourself will have to give evidence."

"No, no. We cannot go down that road, Monsieur Jourdic. I do not want her to give evidence. I will not ruin her life as well."

"Then–" he shook his old head in a resigned gesture, "-then I am afraid, Christian, you *will* be convicted. You could only have killed this man for a small number of reasons. The jury will be left with a view of only one of those possibilities. You can make the self-

defence argument, but I think it is unlikely to succeed. His knife had fallen from his hand before you killed him, yes?"

"Yes. It was already on the floor and out of his reach, but he had held it in his hand–"

"*Before* you drew your own?"

I hesitated and thought for a moment.

"No, Monsieur. I know that he reached for his knife before I drew my own, but it would be untruthful to tell the Court that he had drawn it first."

"Then they will believe Sergeant Bezart's theory; that he drew it to defend himself against you, and not the other way round. Icard will tease out the point and the jury will be left with no choice."

"What should we do then?"

Leopold Jourdic stood up and began to walk up and down the cell talking to himself in a low voice. As he quickened his step, so too did his voice speed up and his words were now so rushed that I could not decipher them. After a long period of time, he turned and came and stood over me with his eyes closed for what seemed an eternity. With his eyes still shut he asked me one more question.

"Are you certain that you do not wish me to call Madame Pleyben to give evidence in your defence?"

"Yes, Monsieur Jourdic. Absolutely certain."

"Then there is only one thing left to do, Christian."

"Yes, Monsieur?"

"You must take the witness-stand and plead self-defence. I shall do my very best to save you from the guillotine!"

Chapter Ten

TELLING THE POLICE that Vivienne was not in the house to witness the death of her husband, was a deliberate attempt by me to shield her from the trial as much as possible. As she had been the one who went to get the doctor, the prosecution had no real interest in her as a witness. They knew that if they called her to give evidence, she could muddy the water by disclosing the facts of her violent marriage. This might sway the jury against the Deceased and therefore encourage them to acquit. On the other hand, the prosecution knew that there was a risk that Monsieur Jourdic could put her into evidence for the defence, and the information about her violent treatment at the hands of the Deceased would come out anyway. The difference was that then they would be able to cross-examine her on her relationship with me, and discredit her in that fashion. It was a calculated risk but, for the Prosecutor, it made more sense to leave her out of it rather than to have a hostile witness who might sabotage their case.

Vivienne and I had discussed the matter before she went for the doctor. We agreed that the further she was from the scene at the time of the fatal wounding; the better. Her statement to the police spoke only of hearing a commotion in the house. She said that she believed Stephane was venting his anger on her house and her things, instead of on her, and thus she only returned to the house

after it fell silent. In the kitchen she found her husband dead, and her geography pupil bloodstained and in shock. She finished her statement by saying that she imagined I'd had to defend myself; because she knew only too well of her husband's propensity for violence. Again it seemed to Monsieur Jourdic that, although she had absolutely no basis in fact for saying that she believed her husband to be at fault, (because she'd seen nothing of the row), the prosecution would be anxious to avoid this statement getting into the mix of evidence. If *they* called her, they would be stuck with her statement, whatever its genuine value. In hindsight, perhaps I should have been more careful in my statement, because it seemed that my intimation, that the knife was out of his hand at the time Stephane died, might now completely undermine the self-defence argument. My response to the threat posed by him had to be commensurate with that threat. *Was* my life in danger at that moment in time? That is what the jury would have to ask themselves. If I had said *his* knife was at *my* throat first, they would only have had that evidence to test. As it was, I had described the fight in some detail and omitted only that Vivienne was there. I thought that the closer to the truth the statement was, in every other respect, the easier I would find it to be consistent in my evidence if I took the stand.

On the morning of the twelfth of August, I awoke at first light and heard the chattering of finches on the window ledge. I saw, beside my bed, two olives which must have been thrown in during the night. My dreams had hurried in and out of my sleep and I could remember nothing of them. It was warm in the cell and the straw on the floor was thin and wispy, like little hair on an almost-bald man. My clothes were neatly folded on a chair and I realised that these were clean fresh garments for the second day of my trial. I had supposed that the clean clothes I'd been given the day before would have to be worn throughout the trial. It was a small point, but one which elevated the whole process to a level of humanness I had not expected

to encounter. I thought about the village, and the Dentelles, and, for some reason, of Montmirail itself. It was the house in which I had been born and, although I'd chosen to reject it, along with its inhabitants, I wondered with some fear whether I would ever see it again. In truth I know that at that point I wondered if I would ever see the outside world again. Perhaps it was at that moment too, that my heart became suffused with fear and regret. Before then, I had never really imagined that I would be convicted and sentenced to death. Now, I imagined "la Veuve" sliding its metal smile down on the nape of my neck. People say it's over in an instant but then I suppose they're not really speaking from experience! Before I realised it, I was crying, in a strange little way which was a mixture of sobs and breathlessness. I heard the sound of keys in the door down the passageway. I quickly finished dressing and dried my tears. I touched my scar and blessed myself and, for some reason, imagined Couderc would turn up in Court to speak up for me, and tell the world that every experience I'd had with knives had ended badly.

In the courtroom, in the Palais de Justice, the jury box was empty and the public gallery now bristled with even more faces I did not recognise. I spotted my mother, in a corner at the back of the Court talking to the lady who owned the bakery in Gigondas; Elise Morel's aunt. I was surprised that Maman had come at all, as I supposed that my father would have forbidden it. My feelings, upon seeing her, were unclear to me, they were neither warm nor cold, and beyond my surprise I could not really describe cogent thoughts or emotions concerning her one way or another. I pictured myself standing on the road to Les Florets, looking at Montmirail down two rows of vines; where earthy clods of russet soil and stones led like an avenue to my childhood. I had been so eager to grow up, and put it all behind me. Now that this had been achieved, I was unsure about what to do next. In the most obvious of ways this choice had been taken out of my hands. Perhaps the last choice I would ever freely make had been made in the kitchen

of my geography teacher's home over a year before.

As we had expected, the last witness for the prosecution was Father Leterrier. He had gained weight in the thirteen months since I'd seen him on the path into the Dentelles below Vivienne's house. His face was more lined than I remembered, and his hands shook slightly, from time to time, like someone shell-shocked from the war. All in all, he seemed older and more tired. The flare of confidence, which had marked his conversation with me in those last weeks at school, seemed to have all but disappeared. It was impossible to know what had passed through his thoughts as a result of all of this. I hoped he might feel responsibility for some of it.

"You are a member of the Community of Jesuits at the Monastery of Crillon-le-Brave?" Monsieur Icard began.

"That is correct." There was a false humility about the way he held his eyes as he replied.

"I think that you teach religion at the lyceé where the Accused was a pupil until the end of July of last year?"

"That is correct. I have been in sole charge of religious instruction at the lyceé in Gigondas for six years. I began work there properly in 1915, after the death of Monsignor Chapus. Before that, I had given occasional talks at the school when the Monsignor was away, or ill, or when he invited me to speak to a class on a specific topic. At first, I taught in both the boys' and the girls' schools. They have been amalgamated since 1917 because of a shortage of teachers."

"Are you the only provider of religious instruction for the lyceé?"

"Yes."

"And can you tell the Court, and the jury, what is the nature or form of your instruction?"

The priest cleared his throat and I almost expected him to whisper 'Holy Purity' hoarsely at the Prosecutor but, of course, he did not.

"I teach each class according to their age and understanding, Monsieur. In the lower years we discuss bible stories, the Commandments, the life of Our Lord, the festivals of Easter, Communion and Confirmation and preparation for–"

"And with the older classes, the children who are preparing to leave the lyceé?"

"I teach a range of material dealing with theology and the Apologetics and, of course, I hope for vocations from those older children, to perhaps join the priesthood or the convent."

I thought of his anger at the mention of the story about the Convent of Prebayon and the Devil's Bridge.

"Do you provide any instruction in the area of personal and public morality?"

The Prosecutor looked directly across at me for the first time during the trial. The priest looked up at the jury and addressed his answer to them.

"It is quite difficult when you are dealing with adolescents, both boys and girls together, to strike the right balance when instructing them in the subject of morality. One has to be careful, but also, one must not shy away from the responsibility of providing a moral framework for their young lives."

It struck me that in his dealings with my class, Fr. Leterrier had appeared neither careful, nor shy, in bombarding us with his theories about 'Holy Purity.' Still, I was sure that all of this evidence would have been rehearsed with the Prosecutor a number of times before. Perhaps the zeal and enthusiasm, with which he had imbued his lessons on the subject of sexual morality, had been rehearsed out of him.

"But you do instruct them about issues of morality?" the Prosecutor insisted.

"Yes. Yes, I do. I feel that the short time during which these young people are under my guidance, should be used to steel them against the pressures of early adulthood and the temptations of the

outside world." The jury were clearly interested in what the priest had to say.

"Do you know the Accused?"

"I knew him by sight as one of my pupils, yes."

"Did you know his name?"

"No. I did not know his name until I made it my business to find it out."

"When and why was that, Father?"

Now the jury were drawn in to the prosecution case more fully than they could have been on the previous day. The earlier witnesses (apart from the hotelier) dealt with the mechanics of the death. Now they were being presented with the evidence which could nail down a motive; if the Prosecutor controlled the priest properly as a witness.

"I saw them on the platform at Avignon."

The information escaped quickly but hung in the air like an arrow in mid-flight. It was clearly an arrow, but it was not yet apparent whether it had a sharp or blunt edge. I suspected the former.

"Now, Father Leterrier, please take your time. What did you see on the platform at Avignon? Perhaps you should tell us first what platform you mean. There are many different platforms, as the jury will know from their own knowledge. There are platforms in market squares, where politicians make speeches, or, in theatres where actors play out parts. Also, in an execution there is a platform upon which the execution takes place, the convicted person kneeling with their ..." His voice trailed off.

"The railway station!" Fr. Leterrier exclaimed, like a man who had just solved a riddle in a treasure hunt.

"Ah, the railway station. At Avignon?"

"Yes, at Avignon. I saw the boy, Aragon, and the widow of Monsieur Pleyben."

"Of course she was not a widow at that time?" The smile on Monsieur Icard's face indicated to me a belief that things were now

going as well as they could for his side of the case.

"You saw the Accused, and Madame Pleyben. Is that right?"

"Yes."

"On the railway platform at Avignon Station?"

"Yes."

"But, surely, there is nothing unusual about that, Father? They were there as teacher and pupil, on a trip awarded as a prize for a geography project?"

"The only geography I can imagine them learning is that of each other's body." The priest was now getting angry in his tone. His eyes began to exhibit the fury and frustration he'd displayed when Elise Morel had creaked her desk a year earlier.

"I don't understand what you mean by that, Father. I am sure My Lords and the jury are similarly at a loss." Icard invited the explanation, although it was clear he already knew the answer.

"They were kissing on the platform, Monsieur."

"Kissing?"

"Yes."

"A display of affection and respect perhaps? A small dusting of the lips on the cheek to say, 'thank you for your assistance in arranging this educational trip.' Could it not have been that?"

"No. Absolutely not, Monsieur le Prosecutor. They kissed as man and wife, or lovers; passionately on the mouth and in public. A shameless display of lust and sexual gratification."

"Perhaps you were mistaken, Father?"

"I was not mistaken, Monsieur Icard. The train in which I was travelling came to a rest exactly behind them. As the embrace ended, the boy's face came into view and he observed me in the carriage of the train."

"And what did he do when he saw you?"

"He turned the colour of a setting sun. His face was a clear mixture of shock and embarrassment at being caught in the act of adultery and fornication."

"Are you sure you are not mistaken, Father? I must repeat that possibility to you."

"I have never been more sure of anything. I know what I saw." The priest shook his head for effect and the jury looked over at me. He continued, "I learned, later, that the other teacher who should have been with them also, Monsieur Duchen, he had gone to Paris on, ... business." He spat out the last word. I could begin to feel my face going red. I looked at Vivienne and she was crying.

"You began before lunch to tell us of your contact with Stephane Pleyben; the Deceased. I think you were about to indicate when you first learned of his whereabouts after the war."

"Yes. That is what I was talking about before lunch. I think I had told the Court that Stephane had written to me sometime in early 1919. February perhaps."

"And why did he write to you, Father?"

"It's hard to say. I suppose we knew each other from meeting occasionally in the village before the war. I had come to the school at the invitation of Monsignor Chapus. This was before the schools amalgamated and used the Order's premises exclusively. Once or twice, I'd met Monsieur Pleyben when the school held a celebration dinner at the hotel for the retirement of a teacher, or at graduation ceremonies."

"Did you know him well?"

"No, I hardly knew him at all. But one of the priests at Crillon-le-Brave met him in Bordeaux at a church mission kitchen during the war, and they discussed Gigondas and the school and, of course, he asked about his wife. He would have known then that I was now chaplain to the lyceé."

"So, what was the purpose of his writing to you?"

"To enquire about his wife, in general terms. He also furnished me with an address where he could be reached if something befell her, or if she needed anything."

"Did the letter speak of anything else?"

"Yes it did. The letter included details about how he regretted leaving Gigondas, and his wife, shortly after the war had commenced. He said he longed to return, but knew that the military authorities might want to talk to him about having missed out on conscription."

"Do you have the letter still?"

"Yes. I have it here." The priest rummaged in a small cloth bag tied to the rope around his waist. The letter was shown to the Judges and to Monsieur Jourdic and then to the jury.

"When did you next have a communication with Monsieur Pleyben?"

"After confronting the boy, and Madame Pleyben, and receiving no satisfactory response from either of them, I wrote to him. Despite being given the chance to be truthful about the affair and to end it, neither of them appeared prepared to take the necessary steps."

"So you wrote to Monsieur Pleyben?"

"I did."

"And when you wrote, what did you tell him?"

"I informed him of his wife's infidelity. I urged him to return to Gigondas to save his marriage, her soul and the entire life and future of an innocent young boy."

Monsieur Icard allowed the import of the last phrase to sink into the subconscious of the jury. One man looked over at me with a degree of sympathy I had not detected before. The priest continued his evidence about meeting Monsieur Pleyben at the train station in Violes, and bringing him to Gigondas where they confronted Vivienne together.

"Can you tell the jury what the mood of that meeting was, Father?"

"Yes, I can truthfully say, that although it was a great surprise for Madame Pleyben, I detected a willingness in her voice and demeanour to consider the long-term benefit of a reconciliation. I

had already spoken on Monsieur Pleyben's behalf to the military authorities in Orange. I hoped he might simply be reprimanded, or fined, or perhaps engaged by the army for some period performing manual work, as a sanction for not having obeyed his conscription requisition. The mood had softened somewhat I think, and there has been great debate about the manner in which the war was conducted; so that perhaps leniency was a real possibility."

"In any event, Monsieur Pleyben was prepared to face those consequences, be they harsh or lenient, in order to save his marriage?"

"Undoubtedly, Monsieur. Undoubtedly."

"You left Monsieur and Madame Pleyben alone?"

"Yes. I had warned Stephane to be patient with her, and not to expect too much too soon. I knew it might be difficult for both of them, but I was greatly optimistic as a result of their reaction to each other after the understandable initial surprise."

I looked down at Vivienne. She was shaking her head silently.

"You left?"

"As soon as the introductions had been completed, I left."

"Did you detect anger in the attitude of Monsieur Pleyben?"

"Certainly not. He was worried, of course, about having been away for so long. He was concerned about the Military, what people in the village would think. But this was, in my opinion, a natural reaction to the situation."

"In her statement to the police, Madame Pleyben spoke of difficulties they had had in their time together before he left Gigondas. Did anyone ever speak to you about this? Did you ever observe anything which evidenced this?"

"No, I cannot say that I did, but all marriages have problems, Monsieur Icard. The plan of God is that people work together to overcome those, 'difficulties', as you call them. Our Lord expects us to face temptations resolutely and that is how we defeat them."

Sensing a morality lecture, Monsieur Icard steered the priest back

on track. I wondered why he had mentioned the problems Vivienne had in her marriage to Stephane. I concluded that it was a pre-emptive strike in case Vivienne was called for the Defence. Icard would have no witnesses to contradict her evidence. He was trying to counter that possibility, by using the priest's testimony in a subtle way, which could be used in the closing speech to rebut any of her evidence about maltreatment by Stephane. If Vivienne was not called; then the issue was not properly opened to the jury and posed no threat to Icard's case. He was a very clever lawyer despite his apparently casual approach to the examination of his witnesses.

"Did you meet anyone on your way back to the village?"

"Yes, I met young Aragon."

"The Accused?"

"Yes."

"Where?"

"On the pathway down to the village, just above the hospice and the graveyard."

"Did you speak?"

"Yes, we did have a brief conversation, yes."

"What did you speak about?"

"I told him to turn back from his journey. I meant, Monsieur, both in the physical and moral sense."

"Yes. Continue. Did he respond? Did the Accused say anything?"

"I'm afraid he did, Monsieur."

"Can you recall, Father, what it was he said?"

Father Leterrier shook his finger in the general direction of the people present, as though warning them in advance never to say whatever it was he was about to recount.

"He threatened that he would kill me if I continued to interfere in their lives."

A silence descended over the entire room. Everybody, except me, looked shocked. I looked at the priest and shouted.

"This is not true. That's not what I said."

I stood up, but was restrained by a prison warder who forced me to sit down. Monsieur Icard turned slowly to face me front-on, his back to the jury, as if he were their commander and they a small band of soldiers on a march.

"You will have ample opportunity to tell everybody your side of the story. If you choose to."

Monsieur Jourdic was incensed and made an immediate objection to the remark. He spoke of the adverse inference that the Prosecutor was trying to insinuate if I did not give evidence. The Judges were not on our side; the Presiding Judge made that clear.

"If the Accused chooses not to give evidence then, of course, no adverse inference can be drawn, Monsieur Jourdic. But neither will we permit un-sworn evidence to be shouted from the benches."

I knew I shouldn't have spoken out but it's bloody hard to shut up when your neck is at stake.

"You are sure about what he said?" Icard spoke in an offhand manner to emphasise my transgression.

"I am sure of it, and what is more, Monsieur, I must confess that from his words and his eyes, I believed him."

"Did you believe that Madame and Monsieur Pleyben would be reconciled?"

"I did, and I can say that nothing has happened to move me from that view."

"The death of Monsieur Pleyben was the event which prevented that reconciliation?"

"Obviously," the priest said, in a tired tone. Most people in the room smiled at this rare moment of levity.

Jourdic was brief in his cross-examination.

"You were outraged by what you perceived as the affair between Christian Aragon and Madame Pleyben?"

"I was concerned and worried about the welfare of both parties." The priest looked smug.

"You were *concerned* enough to confront both of them separately, and threaten them."

"I warned them, yes. I felt that I had an obligation to intervene and to deflect them from the path of –"

"Evil?"

"If you like. Their relationship was an affront to God and to the community."

"So, you took matters into your own hands and contacted the conscription-avoiding husband who had deserted his country, *and* his wife, at a time when at least his country wanted him?"

Icard rose to his feet.

"I presume, that if a slur is going to be cast on the character of the Deceased as regards his treatment of Madame Pleyben, then Madame Pleyben will be called to give evidence of this?" The Presiding Judge looked down at Jourdic and raised his eyebrows.

"I will not be calling any evidence in that regard, My Lords."

I saw the clear shadow of a smile pass over the visage of Monsieur Icard. He sat down and looked over at the jury as he did; undoubtedly conveying to them his assessment of the significance of the Public Defender's statement.

"Could you have misheard Christian Aragon, Father Leterrier? Could he have perhaps indicated that if *you* had harmed Madame Pleyben, then he would make you accountable?"

"No, Monsieur. There is no reason why he should have believed that I might harm her. I am certain that it was in the context of his seeing me as interfering in their relationship."

"You were simply trying to help?" Jourdic smirked.

"Yes."

"By bringing back her husband, after six years, to effect a reconciliation?"

"Yes. I have already said that."

"But your aim was to disrupt the liaison, that of Madame Pleyben and Christian Aragon. No?"

"My aim was, and let me be very clear about this, my aim was to effect a reconciliation. To restore the marital unit so that it could continue and prosper. That was my principal purpose, Monsieur!" The priest was ebullient now.

"Then, please tell the Court and the jury, Father, why you did not take any steps for the seventeen months, between February 1919 and July 1920, to bring about this reconciliation, your *principal* purpose?"

The priest was silent.

"Two further questions, Father. You brought Monsieur Pleyben to Gigondas by yourself. No one else knew of his arrival, in Gigondas, in July 1920?"

"That is correct."

"So, when Monsieur Icard said, in his opening speech, that the murder was planned 'down to the last detail', he cannot be correct can he? Christian Aragon could *not* have known about the return of Monsieur Pleyben, until he reached the house and found it out for himself?"

"I suppose not." The priest finally looked defeated.

"No more questions, My Lords," said Monsieur Jourdic.

"The prosecution case has finished," said Monsieur Icard, with a little less confidence in his tone.

Chapter Eleven

I WAS OVERWHELMED with gratitude and surprise when George Phavorin was called as the first witness in my defence. Monsieur Jourdic had told me nothing in advance about it, and I suppose his instinct in that regard had been right. Had I known, I would have urged George, with all of my heart, to stay away from my trial. The taint of loyalty to me might damage his standing at Montmirail, where his future livelihood and lodgings were at the mercy of my father. I could not bring that down upon him. However, he was a good witness, and he lent to my defence a fresh sprinkling of humanity and honesty, that I could see appealed to the jury.

"Have you ever known Christian Aragon to be violent?" Jourdic asked.

"Never."

"Are you quite sure about that?"

"Yes, Monsieur. I am. I have known Christian for a long time, since he was a young boy of four or five, and in all that time I have never seen him raise his hand to anyone."

"You bought this for him?" Jourdic held up the knife and I could see him closing the blade deliberately slowly into the handle; trying to convey an image of an implement capable of indolence as well as activity.

"Yes. We were at the market at Sablet and I offered to buy it for him."

"Had you gone to the market for the specific purpose of buying the knife?"

"No, not at all. I was delivering wine to the train and we went into the bar for a drink. The man who sold it to me was also there in the bar. I think he'd been in the market all morning."

"Did Christian Aragon ask you to buy the knife for him?"

"No, Monsieur. He did not. I offered to buy it as a gift for him."

"Thank you, Monsieur Phavorin. I have no further questions?"

Monsieur Icard rose from his seat, with an air of someone who was weary and anxious for a boring conversation at a party to end. He looked at me and then at George.

"You are fond of Christian Aragon?" This was the first time he'd used my name.

"He is a great friend. Yes."

"And the son of your employer?"

"Yes."

"You feel affection and respect for Christian?"

"Yes."

"And loyalty?"

"Naturally."

"You bought him the knife?"

"Yes. I have agreed already with Monsieur Jourdic on that point. You see—"

"You did not know what he was going to do with the knife?"

"How do you mean?"

"I mean that, when you purchased the knife, you had no sinister motive for doing so?"

"Of course not."

"And you imagined that it would be used for—" He paused. "To skin rabbits perhaps or to carve wood with?"

"Perhaps some of those things. Yes."

"But you never imagined it might be used to kill a man? To puncture his throat? To make a spray of blood reach into the air

over his face, and to splatter on the stone floor of his own home?"

"What do you mean, Monsieur?"

"I mean, Monsieur Phavorin, that you never imagined that your gift would be put to that use. Did you?"

"Of course I didn't. I never for a moment believed that it would play any part in, in any of the things you said!" George was quite shaken by the questioning, and it was hard to say whether it was the topic of discussion, or the manner of delivery of the questions, that disturbed him most. Icard paused.

"But it did play such a part, did it not?"

"I don't know whether it did or not." George's tone was defensive now.

"Oh surely, Monsieur Phavorin, you have heard the evidence of the prosecution witnesses; Sergeant Bezart and the doctor?"

"No, Monsieur. I did not hear their evidence. I was not here."

"I apologise, Monsieur Phavorin. It was unfair of me to assume that you had been here for their evidence. Of course you could have no idea, of what either of them said, if you were not here when they *gave* that evidence. Please accept my apology for that presumption."

"Of course, Monsieur." George straightened up a little in the witness chair and began to look more assured.

"And, on the twenty-sixth of July of last year, in the afternoon, at about three o'clock, where were you?"

"Working in the four hectares belonging to my employer, above the church. I was clearing them of rabbits."

"How long were you working there?" Icard looked at his fingertips, as if bored with his own questions.

"All day, Monsieur. I had lunch at Montmirail at midday, and returned to my work until sunset."

"Presumably then, if you were not there, you can have absolutely no idea what transpired, at the house of Madame Pleyben, on that same afternoon?"

Icard looked up from his nails and I saw a sneer creep over his

face, as he glared at George. It was a look of arrogant triumph and it was the first time it appeared to me that the prosecutor had a personal interest in the outcome of my trial. I feared for George, and felt that he was about to be discredited in his efforts just when I needed his assistance most. I need not have been afraid.

"Were you there, Monsieur Icard? Was the doctor there during the altercation? Was Sergeant Bezart there?"

The jury sat up as one and leaned out into the room, engaged by this small act of defiance. The prosecutor moved to quell the challenge.

"How dare you address me like that, Monsieur? I am asking the questions here. You are a witness for the Defence, and your function at this time is to answer my questions. Not to ask your own."

Icard sought the support of the judges to trample down this insubordination, but it was not forthcoming. The tension between the two men began to rise, as the prosecutor sought to retake the advantage in their exchange.

"I shall repeat my question, Monsieur. How can you have any information to offer the Court, about what happened on that afternoon, in that house, when you were not there yourself?"

George paused, but only for an instant.

"Let me say this in answer to your question, Monsieur Icard. Do we have to be outside to know that it is raining? We can hear the sound of the drops on the roof when we are half-asleep. We may hear nothing at all, and wake the following day to find the countryside wet and the water barrels full, we–"

"Answer the question." The prosecutor's voice became raised now, and his hands fumbled aimlessly through papers on the table in front of him.

"If you will allow me the opportunity, Monsieur. I may not have your education, or your eloquence, but–"

"ANSWER THE QUESTION!" Icard roared at George. I thought for a moment that he was going to climb over the table

into the witness stand and shake the life out of him.

"Please control yourself, Monsieur Icard," the presiding Judge's voice cut across the argument, like a bucket of cold water on two frisky dogs. Icard glowered at George, who smiled at him, then Jourdic rode to the rescue like one of the musketeers; raising himself halfway between sitting and standing.

"My Lords, can the witness be permitted to answer *without* being bullied by Monsieur Icard?" The tone of suggestion was just right and it had the effect of widening the crack in the proceedings to a size that would allow George to continue.

"I am sure that Monsieur Icard has regained his customary composure now," said the Judge to the left of the presiding one. "Please continue, Monsieur Phavorin." No further interruption could have been countenanced; this solitary intervention from a new voice was final in its authority. George glanced at me and then at the jury, he took a sip of water from a glass offered to him by the court clerk. He began again and we all listened, even Monsieur Icard, until he had finished.

"I do not have to be everywhere to know anything. I want you to imagine your own lives, and the things that you believe, but which you have not witnessed with your own eyes. Every single day we accept the word of others who have borne witness to things which are mundane or exciting or frightening. We know people who fought at Verdun and the Marne; we accept their accounts of the horror from which they protected us. We *know* from our history." He laughed. "What do we *know*? A man comes home with one arm, and says that while fighting the Germans a shell blew it off in a trench filled with water and rats and rotting corpses. Do we challenge him on his story? No. We allow him to be believed, because he said that he was there, and that this is how it happened. Do we say to him; 'you must be lying' or, 'are you sure?' Perhaps he was running away from the front line, or helping the enemy, and maybe something like an accident happened. If we *know* that man, if he is our friend or our brother or

our son, we know whether he is lying. We are so quick to judge, to say it must have been this way or that way, when we have not seen it ourselves. Monsieur le Prosecutor, I can tell you that I know this man, this boy, the Accused. I have known him for most of his life and for a large part of my own. I know that if he had sought out the Deceased, Monsieur Pleyben, to kill him deliberately, then you would have no need for this trial, because Christian Aragon would have pleaded guilty. Whatever happened on that afternoon in that house at that precise time, you are correct, I did *not* witness it myself. Nevertheless, I *can* tell you something of what happened, because I *do* know one of the two men who were there; Christian Aragon. He may have a knife, he may have blood on his hands, but he is not a murderer. I do not think that he has murder in his heart. If Christian Aragon killed this man, then it was not because he murdered him in cold blood. Self-defence, provocation, I do not know what words you lawyers use to convey this absence of intent to kill for its own sake. I do not care about theories and assumptions and the trail of blood-stained clothes. I know the boy and he is not a murderer. I do not have to be everywhere to know anything, and I most certainly do not need to have been there, in that house at that time, to know this."

My eyes were streaming with tears as the room fell silent. I felt the weight of attention that warns you people are looking at you, when you cannot see them. Nothing in my life had ever prepared me, for a moment within which I could feel such tidal-waves of admiration and inadequacy, at the receipt of such a gesture of support and love from a fellow human being. The jury was still quiet, but some of them were scribbling notes on the papers before them, that until then had remained blank. It was the most extraordinary moment in my entire life and, for a minute or two, everything was silent and at one with my spirit. All I could hear was the beating of my own heart. I saw Monsieur Icard lean across the desk towards Jourdic. They spoke for a moment in whispers. Jourdic then got to his feet and addressed the Court.

"I wonder if My Lords would be so obliged as to allow us a short period of time for consultation?" The judges nodded and rose and the room rose with them. They left the court, walking slowly behind the clerk, to the curtain which covered the door to their chambers.

"Let me explain to you what's happened here." Leopold Jourdic gripped my arms to emphasise how serious things had become. We were alone in a small room with the door ajar.

"I'm listening, Monsieur."

"This is extraordinary, Christian. I've never seen anything like it before."

His eyes were like that of a child seeing snow for the very first time; all bright and wide and excited.

"Like what before? Never seen anything like what?" I was still completely in the dark.

"Icard is worried about the jury. He thinks that after your friend George's performance, there is a very real chance that they might acquit you."

"That's good, isn't it?" I could see a prison guard outside the door.

"Yes. Yes, of course it is. But it may not be good for very long."

"I don't understand this, Monsieur."

"All right. Here is how the cards stand at the moment. Icard is concerned that you might be acquitted on the charge of murder, so he is prepared to offer another, lesser charge, if you will plead guilty."

"Why should I plead guilty at this stage? We're only beginning my defence now. Isn't that correct?"

"Yes, that's true. But you are going to give evidence next. You will be asked about the knife, the one the Deceased had. Your statement says it was out of his hand before you struck with your own."

"That is correct."

Jourdic was beginning to sweat now. The room itself was warm,

and only one tiny barred window gave any natural light to the situation. He continued.

"If you give evidence, you will be asked about the knife and where it was when you killed him. If you say it was away from him and, therefore, no threat to you, then you will not be believed when we maintain that it was self-defence."

"And if I say something different?"

"For example?"

"If I say I don't remember, or I'm not sure now where it was."

"Then you will be lying. You cannot do that. Unless of course you were lying when you made your statement and you're telling the truth about it now. Either way, the statement will be before the jury. I am sure that Icard will convince them in his closing that it was not self-defence."

"But why does he fear an acquittal if you are so certain that I will be convicted, Monsieur?" It made no sense to me that they could be so divided in their views.

"Because–" he smiled a wide grin, "–because of George Phavorin and his dramatic speech. Icard now feels under threat from the Defence and is thinking, not logically, but emotionally. For the moment at least he is seeing the jury, and not the evidence, as the most important piece in this puzzle. I think that our case, such as it is, is at its highest point now."

"What will happen if I plead guilty to a lesser charge? What is the charge?"

"Unlawful killing. The benefit for you is that it does not automatically carry the death penalty. That is up to the Judges. If you plead guilty it is almost impossible to imagine them sending you to the guillotine. Given your age, and a guilty plea, I think you will only get a prison sentence."

"How long would that be?" I thought of my cell on the Rue du Chateau. Could I imagine it as my home?"

"The maximum is life imprisonment, but I think somewhere

between ten and twenty years is probably what you'd get."

Twenty years? I was only seventeen years old now!

"The Court is about to resume, Gentlemen." A clerk with a black gown spoke in at us through the open door. I felt the weight of my whole life, bearing down on my head like a wood press. A whole rhapsody of mistakes and choices had conspired to bring me to that point, and I was in no real condition to properly evaluate the options now being presented. I thought of Vivienne, of my brother Eugene, of Couderc and, for some reason, of the woman with the basket on the bridge in Avignon. My soul leaped about in that tiny room and I felt the walls close in to try and catch it. I could hardly think straight, let alone speak.

"We must give them an answer, Christian." Jouridic's voice quavered in the heat and the situation.

"What should I do, Monsieur?" I held my hands out, like a beggar, and hoped that somehow I would not have to make the decision myself.

Monsieur Jourdic stood back from me and eyed me, as if I were his own flesh and he were haemorrhaging lifeblood with me, in this crisis, at an equal rate.

"The rest of your life is outside this room, waiting for you. Try to make the distance between now and the end of it as great as possible."

The door behind my lawyer opened fully and we were beckoned back to the court, with prison warders and policemen staggering in the heat in their heavy flannel uniforms.

"Alright, then." I gasped in the August air from the space between us and took my destiny into my own hands. "Guilty it is."

Chapter twelve

M Y INCARCERATION ended on the twenty-fourth day of October 1936. It was a hard and cruel time. I was lucky, in some respects, to have managed to survive without gaining some more serious injuries, both visible and unseen, than I had accumulated during that time. A trail of years behind me led from the Palais de Justice in Carpentras, to the nearby prison and eventually, in 1922, on a cold February night, to the notorious confines of the small but inhospitable Prison Caisserie in the shadow of the remains of the Eglise Des Accoules in Marseille. It was never explained to me why I was moved from Carpentras, but I guessed it may have been to put some considerable distance between Vivienne and myself, so as to make visiting more difficult for her. If someone was hoping to sever the bonds between us, by this crass act of bureaucracy; they failed utterly.

Prison is like an animal, a wolf perhaps, which creeps into your garden at night and demands attention. You have to decide, from the earliest time possible, how you are going to treat it. Will you let it stalk you and lie in wait for you and advance at you out of each evening? If you do that, or try to do that, you will find that no matter how much you believe you have placated it, it always returns and each time it is bigger and stronger and even more difficult to face. Eventually it will kill you or, more likely perhaps, it will drive you to perform that task yourself.

"Is this your first time inside?" an inmate called Lautrec in Prison Caisserie asked, as he approached me with his cup held out in front of him for my rations of thin watery soup. It was two days after my transfer to Marseille. All around us, prisoners huddled in the pairs and threes they had worn themselves into from desperation and fear. This was my test. I had heard, from one of the jailors in Carpentras, that life in Marseille would be very different indeed. He addressed his remarks to a location below my waist.

"They'll like you down there, in Marseille." He smirked at his double meaning. "You'll have to find out very quickly who does what; to make sure you stay alive."

I felt myself begin to shake as Lautrec's cup clanked against mine. There was a hue of excitement around us, and some men began to nudge each other. Others sniggered. I thought about George and of his courage in defending me in court. I had to keep my mind on being free again some day and, to do that, I had to stay alive. The animal was in my garden and I was being forced to make a choice. The cups clanged again.

"You are very kind, Monsieur. To offer to share your soup with me," I said. Lautrec stopped short and looked around at the others with a cackle.

"I'm offering him am I?"

There was a loyal laugh from the huddle around us. He turned his face to mine and rattled the cups again, this time tipping his own towards me so that I could see that it was empty. Now, he grew in confidence and turned his enamel receptacle upside down; so the watching world too would know that it was empty. Our eyes met and I saw that, in behind his green pupils, the slightest hesitation was hopping about, amongst vast reserves of violence.

"This must be your first time inside, Friend. Because you don't understand the rules. You are the one who is going to show the kindness by giving me your ration." The audience shuffled a little more easily now, now that their leader was re-asserting his control on them

through me. I smiled and bowed my head in submission.

"Of course, Monsieur. The error is mine." I reached out my left hand and took his empty cup from him. As slowly and as carefully as I could, I poured my ration. Not a drop was spilled and when the transfer was complete I handed his cup back to him. Lautrec raised his second-hand soup in a toast to his subjects. As they cheered, he began to drink.

"AArgGhaCHAG."

Lautrec half-gargled and yelled as I slammed my right palm against the base of the cup as he gorged. The brittle edge, of the tired pocked-white enamel, cut into his mouth and forced his face back up into the light, which fell weakly into the dining area through two narrow slits halfway up the wall. He screamed and bled, and shook like a stuck boar. Everyone else in the room seemed to be at once drawn in to us and, yet, stopped short, as though an invisible fence surrounded that moment and the man and this boy. As the jailors flailed their way through that manacled mass, I knew that this animal called 'prison' was still in my garden and needed more attention. I wrenched the cup from Lautrec's red pumping face and held it aloft in a fresh toast to these people I had only recently met. As the jailors rained blows on me through the crowd, I lifted the cup to my own lips and drained the horror-draught of blood and soup. The animal might return to my garden each evening; but it would have to wait sometimes until I was ready to feed it.

Even now, at this remove, I do not know what possessed me to respond as I did. My early childhood had been the scene of repeated beatings by my father and yet I had never struck him. I had not hesitated to come to the assistance of Vivienne; when I came upon the situation in which she was being attacked by her husband. In that struggle, I had defended my own life from threat also. But this was the first time I'd ever pre-empted violence with aggression of my own. I can only imagine that at that one moment, all of my fears and experiences fused in an understanding. It was a recognition, that the

certain consequence of appeasement, in prison, was to be cowed by the threat of others to the point where my own life would have been worth nothing. I knew, at that point, that I had to face the fear or else drown in it.

I was devoured from the inside out by my passion and love for Vivienne Pleyben. Those feelings carried me out of myself, and my pain and horror, whenever salvation was required during that time. Much like my dream-flights, as a child and a young man, it was an external force capable of lifting me to a place of calm in times of peril. The combination of the 'Enamel Episode,' and my love for Vivienne, gave me the protection I needed in order to endure the heat and the cold of prison. For the most part, I was left alone.

My heart had not known when I was sixteen what lay out ahead of it. My designs for life were, I admit, fashioned from negativity; from a desire not to inherit Montmirail, not to replace Eugene in my father's future, not to be shackled by the smallness of Gigondas itself. All of those aims had disappeared, in the short time between the trip to Avignon and my being sentenced to thirty years for unlawful killing (with a recommendation that I serve at least fifteen). Any chance of returning into the service, so to speak, of the expectation of others, was destroyed in that small house at the foot of the Dentelles on the day I graduated from school. The view of those peaks down over the village, with its red roofs and chapel bell-tower and fever hospice and mayor's residence, was changed forever on that afternoon. I became the focus of the village and its people for a time; 'What about the teacher? Where were his parents during the trial? Did you hear of how they boasted about eating chocolates in Avignon?' All of these unanswered questions, and the thousands of insinuations those questions were midwives for, kept that little place in Provence going for a decade. It was like petrol for people. The scenes of our story, the locations of its constituent elements, became like a series of shrines for locals and inquisitive visitors alike. I could not have cared less. My part in the drama had afforded me a purpose in life, and I

had been allowed move off-stage to catch my breath. Now, a decade and a half later, I had truly caught it.

Vivienne had left the village a couple of weeks after the trial and lodged in Orange for eighteen months or so in a *pension* on the Rue Lacourt. She sold her house to Vaton for a fair price and used the money to be close by me, and to survive. It might have rained apples and pears on alternating days, for all I knew of the outside world. But her visits to me in prison kept me sane and gave me something to live for. When I was moved to Marseille, Vivienne made her own arrangements to be near me. She ultimately found work in a small school on the Rue Sylvabelle; where the pay was poor, but the past was not an issue. My days and nights were filled to capacity with longing and desire for her. No amount of discouragement, concealed in the ardour of prison life, deflected me from the belief that we would eventually be re-united and have a life together. For her part, I must say that she spoke, without fail, in positive and encouraging terms during her visits and in her letters. I could not have been surprised, at any time, if she had ceased to visit, stopped writing, or simply announced that she could not wait for me until France was ready to disgorge me from its prison system. None of these things happened. Our feelings for each other remained strong, and grew, in an intensity which sought to compensate for the lack of physical intimacy, by committing each day and hour and moment to the other. The hardship of prison life, and the unwanted attentions of the system itself, did nothing to approach breaking me or weakening my resolve or my heart.

"How are things in the school?" I would always ask first when she visited.

"Fine, fine," she would answer. "And how are you?" Vivienne would enquire even when my face bore bruises and gashes. Sometimes our words were accurate, and valid, and our exchanges carried real news across the table. Mostly though, our hearts spoke and our tongues prattled to give our hearts some privacy. There were no

words adequate to say what we needed to.

In the summer of 1936 I was informed, by Monsieur Jourdic's office, that the Board of the Southern Prison Authority had considered my case and recommended my release. Taking into account the period of imprisonment before trial, it added up to a total of slightly more than sixteen years. I had spent almost exactly half of my life behind bars. In the weeks and days before my sentence ended, Vivienne was allowed more liberal visiting opportunities, and we spoke of where we would go and what we were likely to do. I must say that all of those conversations had about them a hue of unreality, as we both feared that the recommendation for release might be withdrawn, or overturned, by some appeal mechanism open to the State. Vivienne had applied for a job in Biarritz and had been successful. Our plan was to go there if I was released before the end of October. The teaching position was only to come free on November first, when the current incumbent finished working their required period of notice. The post was as a private tutor, to the daughter of a family that had made their fortune in government bonds during the war. It carried modest enough remuneration but also a small home, free of rent, on the Rue Verlaine. The harsh buffeting of the coast, and the infectious laughter of rain on the roof, serenaded our reunion and they are sounds I shall love forever. Vivienne was forty when I left prison and, yet, we were like teenagers together; making love with a mix of passion and gratitude which left us both, at once, tired, satisfied and eager to recommence.

I do not mean to trivialise the years that interrupted our lovemaking. Of course, they had ripped us apart in an instant, and had left any hopefulness to ourselves to create. They weakened our bodies in the way that age must, but they did not dent our resolve or our affection. You may not believe me, because we are all products of our own experiences, but there is nothing in this world as forceful or unrelenting as the love of two people who are prepared to wait for each other. When I was sixteen my life was a torrent of fog and mist

and no clear way lay out anywhere that I could see. In that same period beyond sixteen, my whole existence and life and purpose became as clear as crystal. Doctors, lawyers, politicians, soldiers, undertakers and bakers; they are all necessary and noble professions. But, no vocation approaches the vitality and importance of that most exalted of callings; to love and to be loved in return. If my entire time in prison had served only the purpose of ensuring the opportunity to spend another five minutes with Vivienne; then it would have been infinitely worthwhile. My philosophy had become one of love and sacrifice, each completely justifying the other. The rest is just idle talk and overdone croissants.

Of course, there were parts of my life in prison I could never share with Vivienne. I think everybody carries small boxes within them, which they alone may open to view the contents. The barbarian in me could never be with her and be accepted. I am pretty sure of that. She would never understand, or would she? In any event, there are pieces of all of us which we cannot expect others to become comfortable with. Life, though, is sometimes kind enough to allow the boy, who carried the box in which the barbarian lives, to be loved.

My mother died in 1929. I was never clear what had caused her death (I suspected suicide) but I understood from George that her last years had been lonely and black.

"Your mother did not leave the house after your trial," he told me, on one of his visits to see me in prison in Marseille.

"And my father?"

"He has withdrawn into himself, now. He rarely speaks at all, except to order me around or to complain about the harvest."

"He was always an expert when it came to complaining," I said, with a smile.

George's visits were rare, although he wrote regularly and I wrote back. I addressed the letters to him at the Notaire's office. I did not want to make life for him at Montmirail any more difficult than it must have been after he had appeared at the trial. He made the long

trip to see me to tell me of my mother's death, and to save me from hearing of it in some other way. I have no doubt, and there can objectively be none; he saved my life and that is the short answer to all of that. Sometimes in July, when my father continued to travel to Paris in search of the Medaille d'Or, George would use that time to visit me. He continued to live in the gate-lodge on the road to Les Florets, and he was almost seventy when I was released. I wrote to him every month, and he gave us his blessing when I told him that Vivienne and I were to be married in Biarritz. I asked him to come and visit us there, but he said that he doubted whether he could travel that far, given his age. He wrote letters in a hand which continued to fail steadily.

Robert Aragon pursued his dream of the great prize in Paris, even after my mother died. I discovered later, from George, that my father did not shed a single tear at her funeral. How she had continued to live with him and follow his steps around that house, with food and love, is hard to understand. Perhaps I, of all people, should have been able to comprehend that kind of indefatigable devotion, but I must confess that it was utterly beyond me. That house died when Eugene was killed and, in a way, my father became soulless on that date too. I was a poor substitute for Eugene and the promise of greatness he held out in my father's eyes.

George was one reason perhaps why I should have returned to Gigondas upon my release. Maybe, if I had searched my heart, there would have been other, more obvious draws back to the village of my birth. It was the only other place I had ever lived apart from prison. Why did I not hanker to pay my respects at my mother's resting place in the village cemetery? Or long to feel the dust on my feet from the track above the fever hospital which had led me to my destiny? I cannot really say. But, it was as though the greater part of me had said goodbye to all of that, years earlier, when I knew that I was going to leave anyway. That is what I told myself, at any rate. And my father, what about him? I know that you may well look at my life and think this and that about my choices, but, perhaps even I too accept that in

one respect my business in Gigondas was unfinished. My grand plan, to declare to him my love for Vivienne upon his return from Paris in July 1920, was still unexecuted. My great hope of being open and adult about my feelings for her, or my expectation of hearing the rebukes or sneers, which would have been my father's response, never came to be played out. I wanted so much to break free decisively from his control and, yet, that planned moment of confrontation had never transpired. Perhaps that was for the best. Maybe all breaking of chains should be quiet.

I was lifted out of that place by romance, by blood and death and criminality and justice and revenge. The game had progressed from the original rules to a plateau way above all of us, which we could only stretch to and feel about in without our hands, seeking to make some sense of the things we touched. *'Why did you not attend the trial? What is it about you which drew loyalty from my mother? Did you know that I could never even try to fill the void Eugene left in everyone's life, including my own?'* These were questions which might have been asked had I returned to Montmirail upon leaving prison. It was not the case that I had never formulated those questions in my mind (because I *had*, almost every hour of every day). No, I think that the lure of the past had lessened in its gloss and I wanted to look ahead, instead of behind. That house could have been mine if I had stayed and never got involved in matters of the heart. Families are the great market place, where all members barter and trade on an ongoing basis, sometimes for great loss and little gain. From the moment we kick our way into them, families demand all sorts of bargains from us, and we from them. No argument or silence or caress or compliment comes free of charge. There is always a price to pay and, sooner or later, the debt is called in or the credit note encashed. No one counts their change quite like a blood relative. The price I would have had to pay to inherit Montmirail would have been enormous. It would have required me to paint my feet in a colour chosen by my father, and to walk so closely behind him that I would have had to become part-

shadow in order to survive. Of necessity, I could not have even contemplated a relationship with Vivienne if I had stayed; I would have been nudged in the direction of some local girl with the background and outlook which most closely coincided with my father's. The vines in that estate were rooted to the spot and bore the only kind of fruit my father ever liked. Likewise, I would have had to behave in the same, predictable, safe way in order to earn either his respect or my inheritance. It was, in my view, too high a price to pay for one's own destruction. Eugene was the only one who could have filled the shoes that he himself had left behind; my feet were either too small or too cold. That entire place, with its granite pudding rocks and ancient cellars and tired wine presses, and expensive delft, was now not mine by choice. After the death of Stephane Pleyben there was no way back for me. The history within Montmirail's walls and windows owed me nothing, nor I it. Even if I were wrong in my assumptions, I would never know now.

"I love you," I whispered, and shouted, and called, and mimed to Vivienne a thousand times a day after my release. She echoed those words so frequently it was impossible to keep count of who spoke them or how often, in any given period of time. It mattered little, because we were together, and each moment spent in each other's company was a gift.

"Did you ever think of giving up hope?" she would ask.

"Never," I would reply.

"Not once?"

"Not even once. And you, did you ever consider for a moment that you would be unable to wait, or that I might never be released?"

"Never," she would reply. "Not once".

I have to live with the consequences of my actions. My hands never did anything I had not asked them to. I am shocked by the brutality of which people are capable. Yes, I do mean that. I do mean that my own moments of madness shock me on some level. To avoid solitary confinement in the Prison Caisserie, during one particularly

harsh winter, I held lighted cigarettes against the palm of my hand for ten minutes, while my captors made wagers on the time I would last. The winner had predicted four minutes! The solitary cell was bordered on three sides by narrow iron bars, leaving it open to the weather at all times. I would not have lasted a week there. My replacement lasted ten days.

How can I explain this to you, in language which does not appear either too weak or too forceful, what it means to love and to be separated and to reunite? It is to have in your hand a piece of sunshine. That sunshine is snatched away and you are left with black ashes in your palm. One day, in the most unexpected fashion, you bathe your skin in apparently filthy water and, when you draw out your arm, angels appear on each one of your fingers and remain there forever. This is what it is exactly like.

The one place which I had resolved to visit, was the location where Eugene met his death. I made the trip to the ghostly quiet ruin of Fort Douaumont some short months after my release. The story of its ultimate collapse, and of how easily it occurred, made me sad for Eugene. A Lieutenant Radtke, and Captain Haupt, virtually stole the Fort from the French forces with a handful of men. Eugene was one of the many soldiers who died in that manoeuvre and, I must say, that I often question the sanity of his fighting for France when it seems that France was so ill-equipped to protect him during that struggle. Wars are the public display of private uncertainty; that now seems clear. I met veterans of the Great War in prison, and many of them regretted ever getting involved. They were the rabbits in the lantern light, while the men who made the light shine stayed in the shadows. I do not know how close I may have walked, on that excursion, to where my brother fell, but what mattered to me was that I had physically got as close to him as I humanly could, given my limited knowledge and the regeneration of the ground beneath my feet.

We married in January 1937. The Popular Front Government

had come to power, months earlier, and it really seemed as if, politically, France had turned the corner from 1914-1918. My visit, to the battlefield where Eugene was buried, occurred only a week before our wedding. The ceremony was held in the onion-domed church of St. Alexandre-Nevsky. Vivienne's employers, Madame and Monsieur Allegre, attended. I had sent an invitation to George, but I did not expect him to come. As the ceremony began however, I heard the creak of the massive door at the other end of the aisle. Somehow I knew it had to be him. He had travelled for four days to reach Biarritz and he stayed with us for a week, before returning to the foothills of the Dentelles. He was older of course than when he'd last visited me in prison, but he seemed as bright in his eyes as he'd ever and always been, although his clothes were much shabbier than I remembered from his visits.

"He's still there, you know, Christian. Waiting."

"Waiting for what?" I replied. We walked along the esplanade du Port-Vieux.

"For you perhaps, Christian. And for Death. He is not well. He only has a short time left on this earth." George stopped and turned to face me. The perfect Atlantic roared at his back as he whispered these words into my face.

"He abandoned me a long time ago, George. I just stayed in the same house with him for a while beyond that, that's all".

"Even if you don't go back for his sake, go back for yours. He's getting old."

"We all are, George. Even me. I'm more than twice the age I was when we last went to Sablet on the cart."

I knew, as soon as I'd said the words, that I was condemning George to an immediate recollection of the moments in that small bar when we'd ordered two beers, and bought a knife while we waited.

"I...I-." he began. I stopped him with a wave of my hand, and tried to make amends.

"George, let's have this out in the open for once and for all," I said.

"Christian, I need to–" he protested.

"You need to listen, George." I smiled. "You had absolutely nothing to do with what happened to Stephane Pleyben."

"But, I bought the knife for you."

"Yes, but if you hadn't, I would probably be dead now instead of him. You saved my life, George. You saved it twice; once by buying me that knife and the second time by insisting on giving evidence for me in Carpentras."

"I wish I could believe you, Christian." There was a quiver in his voice and the lightest spray of tears in his eyes. It might have been the sea but was probably not.

"You *can* believe me, George. There's nothing in my life that I regret. I have *lived*, because of Vivienne, and I have survived death twice because of you. That's an end to it. Alright?" I held my hand out, to seal the version of history I wanted to convey to this ageing foreman whom I loved as if he, and not Robert Aragon, had been my father. He took my hand and the rain on the sea wind encased our handshake.

"Eugene would be very proud of you," he said, as we sought shelter.

"And of you, George," I replied, as we ducked our heads into the squall.

He boarded the train east some days later. I realised that I had probably seen my great friend for the last time. He was the oldest person I knew and yet, in a way, he had retained his youthful freshness and loyalty as an antidote to a changing world, where the value placed on life was a poor stock-market risk. He last wrote to me in May 1937 and properly predicted that his time on earth was almost done.

'Elise Morel knows of my correspondence with you, Christian. She is instructed to convey to you the details of my final resting-place if you should ever return to Gigondas. Pay me a visit there, and tell me of your life and your dreams.

It has been a pleasure and a privilege to know you and to count you among my friends. I enjoyed your wedding as if you were my own son and I hope that, if nothing else, our friendship has imbued you with the knowledge that time and age mean little, and acquaintance and affection mean almost everything there is to know. Live long, be happy, and never take the love of your wife for granted; but greet it anew every day, as fresh as the first moment you met.'

A letter from Elise Morel carried sad news; George Phavorin died on the sixteenth of August 1937. My heart was shattered. My last real link with the village of Gigondas was gone!

It was almost exactly a year to the day later that Vivienne and I decided to leave France. We would travel across the sea to a new world, where opportunity and anonymity awaited in America. If the mood of the newspapers that summer were to be believed, then the corner France had turned two years previously had doubled back on itself to a new Europe; where the horror of war loitered again.

"It was like this before 1914," Vivienne said one day as I read the headlines. They spoke of dark clouds in Germany. Monsieur Allegre had made his fortune in the war. He confidently predicted that the scent of innocent blood hung in the air over all of us, in view of what was happening in Berlin and London and elsewhere. I think that if I had believed that Eugene's death had not been in vain, then, perhaps, in the summer of 1938, I might have been tempted to stay and play my part. To be frank, I felt that I owed France very little at that point. The intimations from Vivienne's employers, that they intended to leave the country before any hostilities began, made our decision all the more simple.

I had worked at odds and ends since arriving in Biarritz. Mostly I earned money on an irregular basis, by gardening for old people, or well-to-do folk; who loved flowers but hated weeding. It was ironic that I chose outdoor work, cultivating flowers and vegetables, when that was essentially the life I'd run away from. The difference was that now it was entirely my own choice; to toil in the sun or the rain, pitting myself against the seasons and the sea. There was no obliga-

tion to conform to any plan or path, or to lose sleep over whether I was a disappointment or a credit to anyone other than myself. There were questions which were still unanswered. But I thought that the further away I got from Montmirail; then the closer I was likely to get to their resolution. At least that is what I told myself. We booked passage in August 1938 to sail out from Lisbon for Liverpool in November. From there, we would board a liner for America.

In the autumn of that year I began to feel ill. It was nothing definite at first; more of an uneasy feeling in the cellar of my stomach. I ran a temperature, but had no vomiting. I was seized with irregular headaches and although different doctors came to see me, they could find nothing wrong. Nothing physical, that is. The latest physician to see me called in October. He turned to me just as he was about to leave.

"It's really none of my business, Monsieur. But I must ask you something."

Doctor Crus was an elderly and honourable gentleman. " My attitude towards illness is, at times, unconventional. I believe in the twin remedies of true love and easy sleep." I did not know what he was driving at. "How have you been sleeping?"

"Not well," I answered.

"Since when?"

"A couple of months now, Doctor." The kindly physician lit a cigarette and blew the smoke up at the ceiling of the room.

"Since you decided to leave for America?"

I cast my mind back to the day of the decision, and the visit to the shipping office to reserve our tickets.

"Almost to the day, Doctor."

He took another long drag of his cigarette and spoke as he exhaled.

"That which is left undone can always be finished. For a time."

I knew what I had to do, and where I had to go.

Chapter Thirteen

THE WALLS on either side of the gate had begun to crumble. Weeds and ivy did what they liked between the plaster and the old stones. I assumed that, after my father had died, Montmirail would have been bought by someone who would care for it. Perhaps no one had wanted it. The gates were open but one of them had clearly been in that position for years, because it was bound to the ground by grass and earth creepers which were undisturbed. The house itself was virtually unrecognisable from the place I had left on the day of my graduation. The reddish quality of the stonework was compromised in patches; where some growth or weakness had allowed decay to set in. The shutters were all closed and the front door was unwelcoming and isolated, behind a stone trough which may once have had flowers growing in it; but now was a clutch of spindly dry brown grass, flopping over the edges where it could.

In the courtyard to the rear I was greeted by the sight of the old wine press; overgrown with moss. Discarded tools and implements were welded to the press by rust and time. The massive doors of the cellar were nailed shut by boards in an 'X'. Through a gap in the buildings I saw some of the vineyard itself. It was bare of vines. At least a portion of it seemed viable. However, large tracts of it were overgrown and, anyway, as it was winter it was difficult to judge. Somewhere, far away, dogs barked at the evening but,

beyond that intrusion, I heard only a sad awful silence. I walked to the back door of the house and tried to look in at one of the kitchen windows, but it was caked with dirt and neglect and I could see nothing. I thought I saw lamplight in the middle-distance inside, but was unsure. It was more likely to be the setting sun, refracting through the bones of this deceased house. I knew that the evening was drawing to a close, and I remembered that I'd promised myself to see the graves. Elise Morel ran the bakery. She would tell me where George was buried; although I presumed he would be laid to rest in the village cemetery. I turned away from the window. Something prompted me to try the handle of the door as I passed. It opened easily. I did not know who owned the property now and, although I was a trespasser, I could not resist stepping into the house in which I had been born.

"Who's there?" a voice shouted, from a room further in.

"Who's there?" The voice was a little nearer now.

I hesitated, and made to turn and leave before I frightened this new occupant. The glare of a lamp being carried slowly entered the kitchen. I think I had known when I heard the voice first, I cannot say, but there was no doubt when the figure stepped to the side of the lamp which now reposed on the table.

"Papa," I said. "Don't be afraid, it's only me, Christian." I stepped towards him and allowed him to see my face in the glow of the lamp.

"Christian is dead. He died in prison," he snapped.

"No, no. He didn't die. I'm alive, Papa. So much has happened. But I am alive."

"Eugene, you look so well. I have kept some of your clothes upstairs in your room. You must be very tired." He came closer to me now and put his hand to my face. I tried to remember all of the things I had once wanted to say to him. The touch of his hand reminded me of the time he had slapped me out in the yard.

"It's the light, Father. You mustn't be able to see property by it.

You don't realise who it is," I said sharply, in a reprimand to him. He pulled a chair out from the table and, as he sat down into it, with a wave he invited me to do likewise.

"We thought you had died at Fort Douaumont. They sent a telegram and I was out in the yard cleaning demi-johns when it arrived. No one, except me really, believed you were still alive you see-"

"Please, Papa, you must listen. I'm not Eugene, I'm Christian; your youngest son. Don't you see the scar on my face?" I pointed at my left cheek.

"You were one of the lucky ones, Eugene. So many men, and some of them only boys like you, went to their deaths in trenches filled with the stench of the rotting corpses of the ones who went before. How did you escape?" His eyes lit up like a child who needs to hear the end of the bedtime story. I looked at him now, this sick old man. He had longer hair than I had ever seen him wearing. His eyes were sunken into his head like marbles pushed into soft soil, and he had not shaved in some days at least. Here and there, his facial whiskers were longer than at most other locations and I sensed that even when he did shave he did not use a mirror. I could not tell whether he was really mistaken as to who I was, or if this were an elaborate game; devised to isolate and confuse me. I suppose that it might have been appropriate for me at that moment to deliver an ultimatum to him to recognise me. Perhaps I should have threatened to leave, but I did not do so. The light of the lamp was like a star, plucked from the heavens and balanced between us.

"I survived prison and I've made a life for myself," I said, brushing my shirt with one hand.

"You were lucky. They can do great things with medicine, now." He smiled. "When your great-grandfather fought at Napoleon's side, all they had to treat the wounded with were cauterising irons and cognac." He sighed and then looked proudly across the table at me. There were tears of joy in his eyes.

"I've got something to show you," he said. "Wait here."

He compressed his fists and pushed them down onto the wooden table to lever himself out of the chair. He stood and pointed at me, as if telling a dog not to move an inch, and then he left the room, leaving the lamp behind him. I glanced around the kitchen and saw that there were plates and cups piled high on the work-surface beside the cold-press, where cheese and milk were kept. There was a faintly stale smell about the place; which hinted at a combination of neglect and forgetfulness. I could not believe that he was still alive. Since George had told me he was ill, I had presumed him dead shortly thereafter. He had outlived us all, in a way, because even I was not the person I had been when I'd left to face prison. I heard him shuffling back in the darkness.

"Look," he said, as he held a small box in his hand. He opened it and I could see that it was a medal.

"The Medaille d'Or?" I asked. He shook his head and laughed.

"No, no, My Son, not the Medaille d'Or. But the token of your country's gratitude for what you did at Fort Douaumont." He took it from its case and handed it to me. I turned it over in my hand and then placed it on the table.

"It's not mine," I said. "It's Eugene's." My father reached out and took the medal in his hand again.

"No, Eugene, it's not just yours; it's ours."

I searched his expression for a hint that he was engaged on a course of deliberate deception, designed to un-nerve me and to put me at a disadvantage; I could find none. I decided to play along, for a while at least, and to see what I could learn from the situation, whatever the reason for his delusion was.

"And Maman. Where is she?"

He lifted his eyes to stare at me and shook his head.

"She is in the ground, Eugene. Right beside the grave where we buried your summer uniform in a wooden box."

"How did-"I began.

"She died of a broken heart. Her soul was battered with disappointment and destroyed. Your brother murdered her, Eugene. As coldly and as surely as he killed Stephane Pleyben, his actions led directly to her death."

I could not let this accusation go unanswered.

"No, no, you must be mistaken," I said, raising my voice slightly. "Surely there was some medical explanation? Had she been ill for long before she died?"

"Your poor mother had been ill for a very long time, Eugene. She suffered from that most common of ailments; weakness of spirit."

"You mean she was ill for some time?"

"Since before I married her, Eugene. The Bretons are a simple people, who do not possess the essential ingredients for correct living."

"*Ingredients*. What ingredients?" I asked. A smile lit up his face and he held the medal between his two thumbs and forefingers and raised it up like the priest would a host,

"Duty, patriotism and obedience." He announced the formula with an air of enthusiasm I did not recall his ever displaying when I was growing up. The mantra, too, was new. I suspected that this was a retrospective analysis of his life; expressed in terms he now wished to ascribe to his own actions and their underlying motivation. I recalled George's account of my mother's funeral, and of how my father had not shed a single tear for her.

"Really?" I spoke with a degree of defiance which would have been impossible in my youth.

"You disagree, Eugene?" He was clearly stung by my scepticism.

"They all sound the same to me," I said.

"The same?"

"Yes, Papa. They are all really just euphemisms for doing what other people expect of you."

" You are very wrong, Eugene. These are the only true virtues,

and they should be innate, rather than acquired, if the breeding is correct."

I allowed myself a moment to take this in. I considered now that he really *did* believe that I was my older brother, returned years later from the war. But what did his theory, now expressed, mean? Was it that he believed my mother to have been below him in social standing? I already knew this, from the way he treated her. What more, then, did it mean?

"Have we all disappointed you so much?"

"Not you, Eugene. You have done everything you can, to be true to the family tradition and name. You have fought for your country and now you have returned to Montmirail, to continue the work of making wine and honouring our ancestors. I have not been able to work for a few days now and things have been allowed to get behind, but, together, we will soon retrieve the situation."

"And Christian. What of him? How has it happened that he was put into prison? Did he fail to honour some debt?"

My father's expression bore the marks of a genuine desire to cause me as little distress as possible, in imparting the news of my own transgressions to me, so that I now believed, in that moment at least; in his eyes I *was* Eugene. He rose from the table again and lit a second lamp, and we were as clear as day to each other. As he fumbled for two glass tumblers in a cupboard, he directed me to open a bottle of wine from a dusty group lying in a heap on the stone floor. As he poured, he began the sorry task of telling Eugene about my crime.

"Christian was a murderer, Eugene. We could not have known in advance, but his heart was cold and his head was soft. He murdered Stephane Pleyben. He had come back to face his own people, and to make amends for his refusal to fight in the war with you, and with the sons of Gigondas, in the Somme, in Belgium and in God-knows-how-many other fields of battle. Do you remember him? Pleyben?"

"I think he was married to a schoolteacher," I said.

"Yes, yesss," he hissed. "That's the one. He married a whore, but did not know it either."

"And Christian killed him?"

"Yes. In cold blood, as he slept in his own bed after journeying for days from the Atlantic. Your brother coveted his wife and was not afraid to kill him for that purpose."

"I heard in the village that Pleyben beat her so badly that she could not have children. Are you sure Christian didn't defend Vivienne against her husband? Could it have happened like that?"

The use of her name provoked my father's rage.

"Vivienne –" he said slowly, "was that the whore's name? She should have had the decency to stay away from your brother while he was still her pupil. But no. Lust and irresponsibility drove her to seduction, and drove him to murder. He was a disgrace to this family even before then but, that, that was the end for me and for your poor mother. He killed that man in cold blood while he slept. In the same way in which he killed your dog in a fit of rage with an axe. He was a coward too. The animal had not been ensnared, that was a lie. Your brother was afraid to take his place in this family, and a cheap slut convinced him that his cowardice was admirable." He drank the full glass of wine and began to refill it. "I do not wish to talk of him any more," he said, coldly.

"And what of George? Does he still load the barrels onto the cart and drive to the station in Sablet?"

My father's eyes narrowed.

"Monsieur Phavorin too betrayed Montmirail, My Son. He was bribed by someone, I do not know whom, to give evidence at the trial in Carpentras. I assume that your brother promised him some share in our home and lands if he were acquitted. Doubtless feeling guilty for having bought the murder weapon, the poor fool gave evidence. But it was to no avail; a conviction ensued and the murderer went to prison.

"And George?"

"That man was given another chance, by me, to redeem himself. I continued to provide a home for him on our property and he worked well enough under my guidance for some more years, but he could not leave the past alone."

"How do you mean?"

My father drank some more and then looked pityingly into the air over my head.

"I had suspected him of continuing to maintain contact with the murderer, and I discovered some letters in his lodgings which confirmed the fact. I could not have that. I could not allow that treachery to occur under my own roof, at my expense." He was livid now and the colour of his complexion became crimson with the rage these recollections carried with them. "I did not allow it to continue."

I became afraid now of what I was about to hear, concerning my oldest and dearest friend and ally.

"What happened, Papa?"

"I told Monsieur Phavorin that he was no longer welcome in my home, or on our land. I dismissed him and he went to the workhouse in Orange. He did not last too long without my charity." He laughed as he said this, and I was gripped with a desire to physically hurt him in retaliation for the cruelty he had heaped on George. Yet I wanted to know more, about myself, and the past, and so I held myself to a degree of calm and drank some of my wine; almost biting through the glass as I did. I now knew why George had told me to contact Elise Morel in order to find where his final resting-place was. He would be in a pauper's grave, somewhere in Orange. George had concealed his own banishment from me, in the hope, perhaps, that I would be reconciled with my father.

"You have had quite a portion of disappointment, then," I said, with sarcasm. "It might have been so different if I had not gone to war."

"No. No. No," he shouted. "Please do not say those things to me. You are a shining example of what this family could, and should, have been. You understand the meaning of blood, of sacrifice, of tradition. No, My Son, it would never have been any different; these people were weak, small-minded, too intent on the selfish fulfilment of warped ideals. No, Eugene, you cannot blame yourself, we cannot blame ourselves. They lacked, the, the–"

"The ingredients," I offered.

"Yes," he said, decisively." The ingredients."

There was a silence between us for a moment as we drank. I could see, through the door behind him, that the rest of the house was getting darker. I thought about Vivienne, waiting for me in Biarritz, and I reminded myself of the other places I had wanted to see on my visit. It was extraordinary that I found myself in the kitchen of Montmirail drinking with my father, and pretending to be my own deceased brother. This was stranger than anything I had ever experienced because it was so utterly unexpected. Did he really not recognise me? That too was extraordinary. But perhaps it was absolutely necessary in my task to find answers, to questions I had asked myself for decades.

"What would have happened if he had not committed a murder or gone to prison?"

Now, for the first time in our conversation, I suspected a flicker of recognition in my father's eyes. Even if his mind was failing, it must have had some lucid intervals during which everything appeared to him as it really was. He took one or two deep breaths and then began to answer me.

"If he had never become involved with that tramp, then, when he had finished his schooling, for whatever it was worth, he would have been able to take his place in this family, in Montmirail. It would have been difficult to teach him the value of family and tradition, but some years of tutoring would finally have taught him what it is to be of Aragon blood. To understand tradition, Eugene, some-

times it is necessary for the tower of the spirit to be broken down and rebuilt with the bricks in the correct order. He would have married someone worthy of Montmirail, and his son would have carried the hopes of this family on into the next century."

He closed his eyes at the last portion of this speech, as though conjuring this vision of continuity in his mind. Then, suddenly, he looked into my eyes and I felt myself being drawn back through the years to when I was a child and we had argued about the value of education and my reluctance to become his heir.

I stared across the table at him and held my breath. Was he aware who I was, all of this time? Did he have, in him, the guile and arrogance necessary to address me through the employment of this elaborate device of apparent confusion? I sensed, for an instant, that he was laughing at me, in behind his pronouncements about "ingredients," and the rebuilding of towers of the spirit. Was this the ultimate display of contempt for me; to refuse to even acknowledge my existence? I did not know, and yet on one level, I felt sure that such a deception was impossible for him. He had always been so direct, so horribly blunt and obvious in showing his prejudices. Often wrong, but never in doubt; was how I remembered my father and his opinions. Like a goat on a mountain, always sure of where to put its hoof next, Robert Aragon had ruled over our family with a confidence which could allow no counter-view or alternative vision. However, was there any reason why he could not have changed over the intervening years, as I too had undoubtedly changed? I supposed not.

"I love her and she loves me," I said, with anger in my voice and in my heart.

His withered face refused to acknowledge my declaration by changing a single muscle or nerve. He stood up and walked to the window and began to wipe clear a patch of dust on it, so that he could look out into the yard.

"My hands are not as strong as they were long ago, but I know

that, between us, we can clear the weeds and be ready for next year. I think that next summer, or perhaps the summer after that, the name of our family will be inscribed on that gold medal in Paris. 'Aragon et Fils'. Will you imagine it? Can you travel with me, Eugene, to the Concours National des Vins and claim our rightful place?"

"She saved me from myself," I said to his back. "She took me away from this place and she has made me happy."

He turned and smiled into the light.

"And how did you find the Germans? Friendly and amenable, or difficult and sour?"

"Compared to some they *were* friendly and amenable," I replied. "At least they did not expect me to be something or someone I am not." I wanted to provoke him, and yet I knew that somehow my words could not succeed in that regard. He shuffled around the room, as though searching for something, but then turned to the door and opened it. Some mosquitoes, attracted by the light, came into the house with a faint whine of their wings.

"Let's have a look at the cellars," he suggested. " You haven't seen them for years."

He took one of the lamps in his hand and I followed him out into the evening. Behind us, the house groaned. I noticed the slow pace of his feet even more now that we were outside. He coughed as we moved and I felt that the night air would not allow him to last the winter when it came.

"1923 was the best year for decades, but we have had a few great years since then, Eugene. We have to make the most of what we have kept, because there are new markets now. I think our strength has always been that our wine is consistent, year after year."

When we reached the entrance, my father placed the lamp on a stone to the left of the doors and began to pull at the boards. He worked with the apparent power of a man half his age but, as the boards came away, I could see that they had rotted through. I stood

and watched as, one by one, the pieces of that once-great door crumbled in his hands. He talked as he toiled.

" We can sell what we have kept. The money will buy that new strain of vine. The one that Algerian bastard, at La Mavette, won the regional award with last year. Or was it the year before?"

His pace quickened now and he flailed away at the remaining boards. As he did, a stench rushed out at us. The opening became fully exposed and the deluge of smell putrefied out at us. I lifted the lamp and held it in front of me fearing, what I was about to see, revealed in its light. Hundreds, perhaps thousands of bottles, lay smashed on the floor of the cellars as far in as the eye could see. The rancid odour was like the scent of Hell itself, and it enveloped us in the frightening grip of dead wine; this vile adulterated smell of a decaying family. A carpet of green and blue mould sat on the surface of the scene, but through this coat of slime and age, thousands of pieces of broken glass peered up at us. Their jagged cuts combined in the reflected light of my lamp, to resemble a gargantuan display of horrible diamonds in a jeweller's store. It might have been a decade in this condition, I could not tell. But I did know, in an instant, that this scene was not the product of either accident or neglect. I lifted the lamp higher and saw a little further into the throat of the cellars. The two huge barrels, built to the right of the first hallway clearing, had been smashed beyond use, so that their contents too had joined the carnage and flooded the remainder of the oldest cellars in Provence.

"It's true what they say. Wine definitely improves with age." He began to laugh maniacally.

It was as though this was the punch line, in a terrible story or joke which he had been enjoying all my life. I had been astounded to learn that he was still alive. But perhaps even more disturbing, was this apparent charade he had engaged in since my chance arrival at Montmirail less than an hour before. He could not have anticipated ever meeting me again and, yet, he seemed to be

rehearsed in his behaviour and attitude. Was it part madness, part lucidity, and part history which had lain in wait for my return? He had disowned me before the trial. He never contacted me after my conviction. He had punished George for showing me the type of love and support he himself seemed incapable of. Now, upon my return, he had vilified my mother, denigrated my wife and had flatly refused to even directly recognise me; preferring instead to mock me as my own brother.

And my response? I had indulged him in his macabre fantasy and been whisked back into short trousers, and the ebb and flow of childhood, to be reprimanded like a boy and laughed at like a fool. I wanted to hurt him. Part of me even thought of killing him with my bare hands, to wring out of his old body some of the retribution I sought for the ineffectiveness of my mother, the loss of my brother and the humiliation heaped on a loyal foreman simply because he had written to me in prison. He had beaten me on many occasions, and I knew that he had enjoyed doing so. I realized that for the first time in my life I was not afraid of him. If we came to blows now I knew that I would not be defeated by him. How dare he try, in the twist of a few sentences, to dismiss the love that I had shared with Vivienne for almost two decades despite the adversity we had faced? Who was Robert Aragon to drag me back to sixteen years of age and condemn my entire life, just because of his own disappointments? I wanted to do something that would shake the bitterness out of him, or at least convey to him the final truth of life; Death stalks us all and each of us is only the sum of our own failures and successes. Nothing more or less than that.

"George Phavorin was more of a father to me than you could ever have been in a thousand years."

Those words formed in my stomach, and prepared to be loosed, but something stopped me from speaking them. From somewhere else, either inside me or beyond me, some rippling of change wooed my soul and made me think again. Perhaps it was the hint

of the future I was now going to enjoy, I have no idea. Maybe it was my past; finally allowing me to let it go. Perhaps it was nothing as remote or distant as either of those things, but maybe just something inside of me, which had changed or grown up. Or forgiven itself.

"There's a push on at the Front starting tomorrow, Papa. I'm due back with my unit in the next day or two, so I'm afraid I can't stay."

He looked at me in the lamplight and placed a hand on my shoulder.

"I think there are things which are more important to you than even the Medaille d'Or?" His voice suddenly seemed to lose its former trace of bitterness.

"I suppose that's the truth of it, really," I said, handing him the lamp.

I looked at my father for the last time and began to turn away. I could hear him humming to himself, and methodically kicking the rotten boards and door pieces into a heap in rhythm with his own tune. I walked across the yard past the rusted wine-press. I saw the light of the other lamp in the kitchen, although it was beginning to dim as the oil ran low. Around at the front of the house, I made my way slowly down the tree-lined avenue to the open gates. On my way into the village, I stepped off the road at one point and cut a small shoot from a vine to take with me on my journey. The earth was slightly hard beneath my feet, and I felt compassion for those varieties of crops or people which cannot flourish here in the heat and the poor soil. I saw the faint outline of those large pudding-shaped rocks which do their best to reflect the efforts of their masters back at them. I felt the chill of November swirl around me, but it left me no less warm inside. I continued up through the village and saw a light over a low wall.

In the main street, as I stood in front of the bakery, I saw the faint ghostly impression as Couderc and his dog both smiled and

then retreated. I knocked on the door. Elise Morel came out from the kitchen, wiping flour from her hands. As she undid the lock I watched her with peace in my soul, and prepared myself to tell her who I really was and what had happened to me since that hot July in 1920 had baked us all and turned children into men and women.

Epilogue

AYBE OTHERS would have acted differently had they been in my shoes. But then, that is probably always so. That house, and the village which insulates it from the Dentelles, are part of a way of life that I have declined. The day Eugene died changed my life forever, although I did not realise it at the time. I wonder if he is up there somewhere, making judgements about my actions and choices. It is impossible to know whether there is another life beyond this earthly one. In a way that does not matter really, because I know that I would not have lived my own life any differently even if I knew one way or another for certain. My life has been to follow my heart and not to allow others to dictate where my feet should fall.

When I think of Gigondas and the summer of 1920, I cannot be sad. As the propellers of this huge ship churn beneath the surface of the black Atlantic, and my wife sleeps in our tiny cabin on the lowest of six decks, I feel that the best of my living lies ahead. I am glad that I returned to Gigondas to make my peace with the past. There are portions of my life there which I will carry with me forever. Over the sound of the sea I can hear the gurgle of the water in the Place de la Fontaine; the tired sighs of the Mayor avoiding his wife by overworking; the rasp of the chairs on the terrace outside the Hotel and the chatter of children on a half-day from school.

In my dreams I can fly once more.

I am reminded of the day I'd been released from prison. We had made our way through the morning streets of Marseille. I tasted freedom and breathed in fresh air and heard the chatter of people who meant me no harm. We held hands like teenage lovers, linking fingers and knowing that the symbolism of that gesture led the way to something much more passionate and intimate. It began to rain just as we reached her abode, on the Rue Haxo. Vivienne unlocked the door. I was shocked by her action of making her way ahead of me into the rooms. In prison I was always forced to walk first through the unlocked door or gate, because the person with the key would have to lock it behind me.

In the bedroom, a razor and shaving soap had been laid out for my use beside the ewer of water. I shaved with the aid of a small mirror. As I lifted the razor I saw Vivienne standing behind me as I looked in the mirror. She wore an expression I could not decipher.

"Does my appearance frighten you?" I asked.

"No." She laughed. "It's just that there's someone handsome in there behind all of that hair, and I'm anxious to see him again." I continued my soapy task.

"Thank you," she said, putting her arms around my waist from behind as I shaved.

"For what?"

"For risking your life to save mine. For pleading guilty to a crime you did not commit, just to save me from the guillotine."

"It was nothing," I said, and I meant it. I would have done the same thing again that very day if I had had to.

"You know sometimes I'm sorry, Christian, that I did not insist on giving evidence. I could have—"

"You could have ruined everything, Cherie. You could have stood up there and told the truth, and then where would we have been? You would have been dead and, without you, I would be as good as dead."

Vivienne began to cry softly. I held her, then I finished shaving.

The symbolism of the razor was not lost on us. When she'd taken the knife from my hands and ended Stephane's days, she had given new life to both of us. We had watched her horrible husband die, and our complicity in that act of watching would bind us forever. We had had little enough time to decide what to do next and, strange as it may seem, it was I who had taken the initiative.

"Change your clothes and bury them in the woods. You will have to go and find the doctor and bring him here."

"And what will you do, Christian? Surely it would be better to pack our things and try to get as far away from here as we can?" Vivienne's blouse was stained with blood and one particular portion of the stain resembled the outline of a face. That was the moment for me to grow up and I did my best to.

"No. No. If we run, they'll follow us and we'll both be sent to the guillotine. We must stay and see this through. Leterrier knows we were here with your husband. He will make sure we are tracked down and killed if we try to escape, I will take the blame. Say you saw nothing."

"But, Christian," she screamed. "I've killed him, we must–"

"We must stay. You fetch the doctor. Tell him your husband is dead. We must decide on what to say and not waver from that version of events. Do you understand me?"

"But why should I say I did not witness the struggle? Surely it would be better if I said you killed him to save my life?" I shook my head,

"No. No. If you say you were here, then we will both be charged. If you are found guilty, you will certainly be executed. You must say you were somewhere else, outside at the well, anywhere, just not here. I am little more than a child to the law. Whatever chance we have of being together; it is if I take the blame. Do you understand?"

I took her hands in mine and wiped the blood from them onto my face. Time would be of the essence if the priest had spoken to anyone since arriving back in the village. Of all people, he could

not be relied upon to keep his mouth shut. Vivienne took a deep breath and began to undress. When she had changed she looked at the corpse, with its glazed eyes and blood-spattered surrounds. She took her stained clothes with her and hesitated at the door as she opened it. She was about to protest again but I spoke first.

"You were outside and came back and found me here, and Stephane dead. That is your story. Do not deviate from it. Leave the rest to me. Alright?"

When I was nine years old, a boy at school cut me on the left side of my face with a hunting knife in a fight about nothing. When I was almost seventeen, a pocket- knife cut me free in a fight about absolutely everything. I carry all of my scars with pride and hope. This is who I am.

"I love you, Christian," she mouthed silently, as she opened the door. She stepped out into the future. The rest you know.

THE END